"You're loyal..."

...he said, his voice a low rasp. "I like that. You're just loyal to the wrong guy."

Ryker's head bent, and I knew what was coming, but there was nowhere to go. He had me pinned to the door, and if I was honest with myself, I probably wouldn't have moved away even if I had the opportunity.

His lips met mine in a kiss that made my toes curl. Thoughts of Parker and everything else disintegrated, Ryker overwhelming them all.

The scent of his cologne and the leather of his jacket curled around me. His hand lifted to cradle my jaw, the soft brush of his l̶i̶p̶s̶ ... of his tongue as he deepen...

He tasted ... the soft notes of red wine, a... felt the door give way at ... turned the knob. Backing ... never left mine. Dimly, I heard the door close.

ALSO BY TIFFANY SNOW

Tangled Ivy Trilogy

In His Shadow
Shadow of a Doubt

The Kathleen Turner Series

No Turning Back
Turn to Me
Turning Point
Out of Turn
Point of No Return
Blane's Turn—Companion to
The Kathleen Turner Series
Kade's Turn—Companion to
The Kathleen Turner Series

Blank Slate

POWER PLAY

TIFFANY SNOW

FOREVER

NEW YORK   BOSTON

Copyright © 2015 by Tiffany Allshouse
Excerpt from *Playing Dirty* copyright © 2015 by Tiffany Allshouse

Forever
Hachette Book Group
1290 Avenue of the Americas
New York, NY 10104

www.HachetteBookGroup.com

Printed in the United States of America

First Edition: June 2015
10 9 8 7 6 5 4 3 2 1

OPM

Forever is an imprint of Grand Central Publishing.
The Forever name and logo are trademarks of Hachette Book Group, Inc.

The Hachette Speakers Bureau provides a wide range of authors for speaking events. To find out more, go to www.hachettespeakersbureau.com or call (866) 376-6591.

The publisher is not responsible for websites (or their content) that are not owned by the publisher.

For Jennifer, with much love and thanks.
Without you, this wouldn't have happened.

ACKNOWLEDGMENTS

Thank you to my amazing agent, Kevan Lyon, without whom this dream would not have come to fruition. Thank you for your unwavering support and for being my voice.

Thank you to my wonderful family, who've had it rougher than usual the past several months as I've had a lot of deadlines. Your patience and love helped get me through.

Thank you as always to Leslie and Nicole, my stalwart cheerleaders. I don't know what I'd do without you.

Thank you to Nicole, for knowing my voice so very well. Your input was invaluable.

Thank you to my editor, Leah Hultenschmidt, for her enthusiasm for this series (and the many brainstorming sessions to find just the right titles).

POWER PLAY

CHAPTER ONE

Y ou're dumping me?"

I couldn't believe it—not that it was completely out of the blue—but I hadn't even had a chance to order dessert.

"Listen, Sage, I just don't think it's working out," Brandon said. "I mean I like you, I really do, but it just doesn't seem as though you have time for a relationship—"

The buzzing of my cell phone cut him off. I didn't have to look to know who it was. Fighting my instinct to pick it up, I said, "I have plenty of time for a relationship!"

"Sage, we've been dating for three months and we've yet to have a dinner that wasn't interrupted by your cell."

"That is not true," I protested, frantically trying to remember a time when I'd had *any* meal without my phone ringing. My phone buzzed again, and I swear my eye twitched with the need to answer it.

But Brandon was shaking his head, a resigned look on his

face. "I'm sorry. I really am." He took some money out of his wallet and placed it on the table.

More insistent buzzing, as if the person on the other end knew I was there and not picking up. I clenched my hands into fists in my lap.

"Brandon," I tried again as he stood. He nodded toward my phone.

"Sage, you may not want to admit it, but you're already in a committed relationship. And he doesn't share."

I stared in dismay at Brandon's retreating back as he left the restaurant. The phone buzzed. Glaring at it, I reached out and snatched it up, knowing it could only be one person.

"What?" I snapped, allowing the hovering waiter to remove my plate. I grabbed the wine bottle and emptied the rest into my glass.

There was a long pause on the other end of the line. "Excuse me?"

I held in a sigh and rubbed my forehead. I felt a headache coming on. "I'm sorry, I thought it was someone else," I lied, modulating my voice into the usual pleasant tone I used for work. "What can I do for you, sir?"

Sir was Parker Anderson, and Parker Anderson was my boss.

"I need the margin projections on the Layne acquisition. Where are they?"

"Lyle brought them by this afternoon," I said. "I put them on your desk."

"I'm looking and I don't see them."

"They're underneath the stack of quarterlies that I printed off this morning," I guessed.

There was a shuffling of paper. "Okay. Found it. Thanks." He ended the call.

"You're welcome," I muttered, tossing down my phone.

Parker never apologized for calling me after official work hours. I thought it was because he worked so much. He never considered any hour as being free from work, for either himself or those who worked for him. Usually, I didn't mind because... well, it was complicated.

The wind had picked up and I pulled my wrap tighter around my bare arms as I gazed out at Lake Michigan. Brandon had picked one of the nicest restaurants in Chicago to break up with me, a place with outdoor seating and a great view. I guessed that was something.

I watched as the last bit of twilight faded into evening and sipped my wine. Brandon had already paid for it so no sense letting it go to waste. We'd met on Valentine's Day of all things and over the next three months I'd become more and more convinced that maybe he could be Mr. Right.

Apparently, I was Ms. Wrong.

On that depressing thought, I got drunk. Well at least I *think* I got drunk. I was vaguely aware of the valet calling me a cab and me stumbling into my apartment. I may or may not have taken a bubble bath—a weird predilection that came out when I was very drunk, no matter the time of night— since I had little memory of anything up to my head hitting the pillow. Some might say I passed out, but I'm a lady and ladies don't *pass out*. I just...slept very deeply.

The alarm woke me at the usual time and I groaned, slamming my hand on the button to silence it. My head ached from too much wine and I stood too long in the shower. By the time I was rummaging through my closet trying to find the match to the shoes I wanted to wear, I was already going to be late.

"Damn it!" I yelled in frustration, then heard my mom in my head.

Ladies don't use vulgar language.

"Ladies probably never have to take the bus to work either," I groused to no one.

The bus was just closing its doors when I ran up, out of breath and carrying my shoes. I rapped on the door and the driver opened it for me.

"Running late today?" he asked with a grin.

I was too out of breath to reply so I just smiled. He was a nice guy and knew all the regulars on this route.

Work was just under five miles away and I was one of the first off the bus, shoes now on my feet. It was a cool spring morning and probably too early in the season for the peep-toe sunny yellow heels, but I'd worn them anyway. I'd added a matching yellow scarf around my neck to go with the navy skirt and white blouse I wore. The yellow added a touch of whimsy to the otherwise staid clothes. I didn't mind. It was expected attire for the assistant to the Director of Investment Analytics at KLP Capital, which was *the* investment bank in Chicago.

Robin worked the morning shift at Starbucks and had my standing order ready when I walked in.

"Thank you!" I said, blowing an air-kiss in her direction as I grabbed the two cups and paper bag. A second later I was out the door and scurrying across the street. The wind whipped at my hair, but I always kept it pulled back tight. My hair was dark, thick, and long, and I never wore it down to work. A French braid tucked up into a bun kept it from getting in my way.

Used to juggling coffee, Parker's breakfast, and my purse, I showed my pass to Security, who let me by to the elevators. Thirty-five floors later, I stepped out.

It was still early enough for me to get things set the way Parker liked. I hurried to drop off my purse and coffee before getting a plate and silverware from the kitchen. After placing the scone on the plate and setting the coffee in precisely the right spot, I hurried back to my desk to listen to his voice mails, taking notes as I scrolled through them. Finally setting down the telephone, I let out a sigh. All set for Parker's arrival in—I looked at my watch—three minutes.

At eight o'clock on the dot, Parker Anderson stepped off the elevators and headed my way.

It was secretly my favorite part of the day.

Parker Anderson wore five-thousand-dollar suits and walked like he owned half the city. There was no one he couldn't intimidate, and he knew it. Some called him arrogant; he said it was confidence.

This morning he'd worn his usual kind of power suit, this one a dark gray pinstripe with a light gray shirt and what I recognized as a Burberry tie. His dark hair was long on top, parted on the side, and lay in a smooth wave back off his high forehead. It made a nice contrast to the clear blue of his eyes. His face was perfect symmetry, an oval with a straight nose that conjured adjectives like *aristocratic*. A strong jaw and chin were the perfect complement, while his lips—his lips were in the sweet spot between too-thin and too-feminine, not that I spent much time staring at his lips. At least, I tried not to stare. He was thirty-five, incredibly handsome, successful, wealthy—and as unobtainable as the moon.

But that didn't mean I couldn't enjoy the view.

"Good morning, Sage," he said, the deep baritone of his voice as smooth as a shot of twenty-year-old scotch. He took the stack of messages I handed him and glanced through them. This was our morning routine, too.

"Good morning," I replied with a smile. I caught a whiff of his cologne mixed with his aftershave. I'd become so accustomed to the slightly spicy scent that I didn't think I'd ever be able to smell it and not think of Parker.

Usually he'd give me a polite smile, then disappear into his office, but today he hesitated.

"I, um, I didn't get you at a bad time last night, did I?" he asked, still looking through his messages.

My eyes widened. He had never asked me that before and there had been plenty of times that had been "bad." I was gonna have to mark this one down on my calendar.

I was so surprised, I blurted out the truth. "I'd just gotten dumped."

Parker looked up at that. If my candor had shocked him, I couldn't tell. His blue eyes were steady on mine for a long moment in which I may have stopped breathing. He rarely ever focused that intently on me and I found myself wishing for the umpteenth time that Parker were a less attractive man. It would make concentrating at work a helluva lot easier.

"I'm sorry to hear that," he said at last.

My smile was as fake as the name-brand purse I'd bought off a street vendor on Michigan Avenue.

"It's fine," I said quickly with a nervous wave of my hand as I tried to figure out what to say. It wasn't like Parker and I often chatted about our personal lives. "He was bad in bed anyway."

Oh. My. God. Had I just said that? To *my boss*?

I gasped in dismay, both my hands flying to cover my mouth. Talk about too much information.

His lips twitched slightly and I swear his eyes crinkled at the corners, as though he were holding back a full-blown grin. He cleared his throat.

"Yes, well, um, that's . . . too bad. Guess you're better off then." With another fleeting smile, he headed into his office, the glass door swinging closed behind him.

If he couldn't see me through the glass wall, I would have

put my head down on my desk and moaned in sheer mortification. I'd mentioned sex to my boss. And that I'd been having *bad* sex. Maybe he thought it was me? What if he thought I was bad in bed?

"It doesn't matter!" I hissed to myself, grabbing my coffee and taking a steadying swig as though it were bourbon rather than a nonfat-grande-caramel-no-foam-latte (add whip). Who cared if Parker thought I was bad in bed? It wasn't like I'd ever get the opportunity to—

Nope. Not going there. I was not a secretary-with-the-hots-for-her-boss cliché. Any woman with eyes could appreciate the many wonderful attributes of Parker Anderson. I was just…normal.

Right.

It was business as usual after that and I made myself put aside my embarrassment and stop thinking inappropriate thoughts. Parker was as normal as ever as I transcribed from his voice memo recorder, edited a Power Point presentation he was giving in New York next week, coordinated the quarterly performance reviews, and all the usual things that made the day fly by. Mondays were busy so Parker always ate lunch at his desk. At noon, I ran out to get his usual from the restaurant four blocks down. He had their Monday special of Tuscan-style salmon with rosemary orzo.

I had a hot dog from a street vendor that I scarfed down while hurrying back from the restaurant. I always ate it plain because one time I'd dropped mustard on my blouse, which had sent me into a panicked tizzy and resulted in thirty minutes in the bathroom trying to unsuccessfully scrub it out. I'd tried to hide the stain, but Parker had seen when I'd had to take him some files.

"Problems at lunch?" he'd inquired with a pointed look at my stained blouse.

I hadn't eaten mustard, or anything else, on my hot dog since.

Parker was still in a meeting when I set the tray on his desk, arranging the plate and cutlery just so. The mouthwatering aroma of the salmon filled the air, making my stomach growl even after my hot dog.

I was just finishing folding the napkin into a bird of paradise when the door to Parker's office swung open. Surprised, I glanced up...and promptly forgot all about the napkin fold.

Holy shit.

Bradley Cooper all buff and badass in *The A-Team* immediately sprang to mind.

He was over six feet tall, his broad shoulders encased in a white T-shirt and leather jacket, with the outline of dog tags underneath the thin fabric stretched across his chest. Chestnut hair that had a hint of curl in it was slicked back from his face and begged for a woman's fingers to run through it. His jaw was grizzled with two days of whiskers while his eyes were obscured behind mirrored sunglasses.

The man slipped the sunglasses off and I swear my knees went weak. His eyes were a bright blue, the corners showing fine lines from either smiling or squinting. I chose to think it was from smiling because with looks like his, why would he *not* smile?

"Where's your boss, sweetheart?" he asked, hooking his sunglasses on the front of his shirt. He glanced curiously around the office.

I realized I was gaping and closed my mouth with a snap. The "sweetheart" set my teeth on edge. I wasn't his sweetheart—at least, not without dinner first.

My smile was like saccharine. "Who's asking, *sugar pie*?"

His eyebrows shot up and his gaze whipped around to

mine. Then he gave a low chuckle and took a few steps toward me until he stood right in front of the desk. He held up a badge.

"Detective Ryker, CPD."

Now it was my turn to be taken aback. The police? Here to see Parker?

"Oh, um, are you sure you're looking for Parker Anderson?" I asked.

The detective snorted in derision as he pocketed his ID. I glimpsed a gun and holster. "Oh yeah. I'm sure. Where is he?"

"He's in a meeting," I said, hurrying to finish folding the napkin. "He'll be back any minute for his lunch."

Detective Ryker glanced at the tray as I carefully set the bird of paradise napkin to the side. I frowned, nervously chewing my lip. If Parker didn't hurry, the salmon would be cold and I'd have to nuke it in the microwave. And if this cop was here to talk to him, chances were that might take a while so he wouldn't get the chance to eat until later. Maybe I should take the tray to the kitchen for now?

My thoughts were interrupted by the detective.

"You've got to be fucking kidding me."

Shocked, I glanced around to see what he was talking about; then I realized he was referring to the lunch, or me, or maybe both.

"What?" I asked. "What's wrong?"

But the detective just shook his head. I was starting to get a bad feeling about this.

"Listen," I said, rounding the desk to approach him. "Why don't you come with me for a few minutes? I can get you a cup of coffee or some tea perhaps, while you wait." Yeah, because this guy looked like he'd cool his heels in the lobby sipping hot tea, but whatever. I used the tone I always adopted when placating an irate or obstinate—usually at the same time—Parker, adding a soft smile. It nearly always worked on him.

However, it seemed the cop was a tougher nut to crack.

"Nice try, but I think I'll wait." Turning, he settled himself onto the black leather sofa in the corner.

I stared in dismay. He seemed wholly at ease, one ankle resting on the opposite knee while his arms were spread wide on the back of the couch. It was obvious he wasn't going anywhere until he was darn good and ready.

Parker was going to kill me.

"Please wait in the lobby," I urged, starting to panic. "It's really nice. There's a television, and magazines…"

He just looked at me.

I went for blunt honesty. "He'll get mad at me," I blurted. "Please wait in the lobby."

Honestly, I didn't know if Parker would be upset or not, though I did know he'd prefer some warning before finding a police officer waiting in his office. I'd rather err on the side of caution because nothing was as devastating as when Parker was angry with me.

"He'll get mad at you?" Detective Ryker asked in disbelief, his eyebrows climbing. "What a fucking prick," he added under his breath.

I winced at the name-calling and wondered what in the world the police thought Parker had done for this guy to say such things about a man he'd never met.

I didn't know if the detective would've done what I asked or not because that's when Parker walked through the door. If he was surprised to see a strange man sitting in his office, he didn't show it.

"Ryker," he said, barely glancing at the man as he passed me and rounded his desk. "Isn't there a murder to investigate

or somebody you should be arresting?" His voice was cold.
To anyone who didn't know him as well as I did, he appeared unfazed, but I could see the tension in his body.

"Aw, you've kept tabs. I'm touched," Ryker sneered.

Parker didn't even glance up from his plate. He spoke
around a bite of salmon. "Don't flatter yourself. Only a cop
could get in this building armed, and only homicide gets
away with dressing like shit."

I'd never heard Parker speak to someone like that. Ruth-
less and cutting? Yes. But deliberately insulting cops usually
wasn't high on his To Do list.

"I'd rather dress like shit than treat people like shit. You
make your secretary serve you lunch without even a thank
you? Color me surprised to see you're still a narcissistic
dick."

My face grew so hot my ears burned as Parker's eyes
flicked my way, as though he were just now noticing me in
the room.

"Was there something else, Sage?" he asked stiffly.

"O-of course not, sir," I stammered, hurriedly retreating.
"Excuse me." I couldn't get out of there quick enough.

My desk was a haven after the tension in Parker's office
and I eyed them covertly, pretending to work, though likely
neither would have noticed even if I'd pressed my nose to
the glass.

Parker seemed to be barely paying attention to Ryker,
though I'd seen him do that before and it was always a fake
out. Nothing slipped by him.

For his part, Ryker had abandoned his earlier relaxed
pose and was now bent forward, his elbows braced on his
knees as he talked.

Neither of them smiled.

They knew each other, and apparently hated each other—

or at least Ryker hated Parker. "Narcissistic dick" and "fucking prick" usually weren't terms reserved for a good buddy. It was an engrossing mystery and I did nothing but speculate, my imagination running rampant for the ten minutes Ryker was there.

Finally, he stood and walked to the door. He didn't appear to say good-bye and Parker was seemingly already absorbed in a file before Ryker even left his office.

I expected him to head straight for the elevators, but he caught sight of me watching him. A look I couldn't read flashed across his face and he changed direction, stopping in front of the raised counter that served as two walls of my "cubicle."

"So...Sage, was it?" he asked.

I eyed him suspiciously, tapping the nameplate that sat on the counter rather than answering him.

"Sage Reese," he read. "Executive Administrative Assistant."

"You can read," I said, raising an eyebrow. "I was worried you'd have trouble with the big words." If Parker didn't like Ryker, and it seemed pretty clear he didn't, chances were I wasn't going to like him either.

He grinned at me despite my sass and he had an honest-to-God dimple in his cheek. His teeth were perfectly straight and white, and his smile drastically altered the hard expression on his face to one of sexy mischief. I momentarily lost my train of thought.

Ryker leaned down like he was going to tell me a secret. The aroma of leather and something musky drifted in the air and I caught myself taking a deep whiff of it.

"I know what you're doing after work," he said.

I looked at him in confusion. "What?"

"You're having dinner with me."

That was the absolute last thing I expected him to say. I gaped at him.

Ryker reached toward me and my breath caught. His fingers brushed the fabric of the scarf tied around my throat. I was frozen in place, my eyes wide as I looked up at him and my pulse racing. I felt the softest touch of the back of his knuckles against my jaw; then he was reaching past me to snag a couple of peanut M&Ms from the little candy dish on my desk for when I absolutely had to have a bite of chocolate. Tossing them in his mouth, he grinned again, the knowing look in his eyes telling me he knew exactly how he was affecting me.

"Pick you up at six," he said with a wink, and then he was gone, striding toward the elevators, his jeans and leather jacket utterly out of place in the sea of suits and business attire. But you would have thought he was a model wearing the latest from Armani by the way he walked.

When he got to the elevator, it dinged as though it already knew he was coming. He'd slid his sunglasses back on and he turned before he stepped inside. I was still staring at him and he caught me at it, another knowing grin spreading across his face before he disappeared from my view.

"Wow. Who was that?"

I turned around to see Megan, my friend and fellow secretary. She worked for a group of analysts who reported to Parker.

Sliding her glasses up her nose, she turned to me. "Seriously. Please tell me he was interviewing and starts work tomorrow."

I laughed. Megan was an incongruous package. She was tiny, barely five feet tall, with curly blond hair and a heart-shaped face—a stereotypical sweet, shy type. She was sweet, that much was true, but she had a biting wit and an irreverent humor that made her a favorite with nearly everyone at KLP.

"Sorry," I said with an exaggerated sigh. "He already has a job."

"As a movie star, right?"

"He's a detective," I said with a grin. "And I think I have a date with him tonight."

"Get out!"

I shrugged. "He asked me out." I thought for a second. "Actually, he didn't ask. He just told me I was going to dinner with him." Which should have ticked me off, but instead I found it to be kind of . . . sexy.

"If I didn't like you so much, I'd hate you right now," Megan sighed. "As if it's not bad enough you work for the hottest guy in the building. Now you have a date with a sexy detective."

"There are some days I'd gladly trade you bosses," I said dryly. "You know that."

"I know Parker can be a total pain in the ass," she said. "But don't give me that. We both know you'd come to work even if you were miserable sick—and have—if Parker said he needed you. So don't play that 'I hate my job' card with me. I know you're full of crap."

"He's not that bad," I said.

Megan snorted. "You're the only one here who'd put up with him. Even I could only let that pretty face go so far before I'd have to slip something in his coffee."

I couldn't argue with her. There were some days *I* wanted to slip something in Parker's coffee.

"So I take it Brandon's no longer in the picture if you're going to dinner with a smokin' hot detective dude?" she asked.

"His name is Ryker and no. I got dumped last night."

"No shit," she said, looking completely unsurprised.

I held up a finger. "Don't say it."

"Say what?" she replied, all innocence.

"You know what."

"You mean that I've been telling you for months now how you're never going to have a decent relationship so long as you let Parker rule your every waking moment? That I keep reminding you that this is a job and not your life? That Parker doesn't appreciate you and that I can't for the life of me understand why you allow yourself to be at his beck and call to the point where you can't even date? Is that what you *don't* want me to say?"

I sighed. I couldn't be mad at Megan. Nothing she said was wrong. I knew she only said those things because she loved me and worried about me, but it was what it was. I needed this job. I liked this job, despite the demands it made on me. The pay was awesome, the benefits were great, and I liked living in Chicago. Though Megan would call me a masochist—and probably had at some point—because most of my waking hours were consumed by Parker and my job, I liked it that way.

At my silence, Megan looked contrite. "I'm sorry," she apologized. "I should just keep my mouth shut sometimes."

I shook my head. "No, it's okay." It was kind of depressing when I thought about Brandon dumping me—yet another short-lived relationship to add to my tally—so I pushed the thought aside.

"So I texted Brian this weekend," she said, and I was glad for the change of subject. Brian was a guy who worked in IT. He was really nice and very good-looking, but I thought he wasn't terribly bright when it came to women.

"And?" I asked. Megan had had a thing for Brian since the day she first met him a year ago. They'd had to work together on a project and had become good friends. "Did he text you back?"

"Yeah, a little," she said with a sigh. "I think I'm permanently friend-zoned, though. He doesn't seem to get it no matter how much I flirt."

"Of course he doesn't," I said. "He's in IT. You'd have to parade in front of him topless for him to get it."

She laughed. "I don't know what it is with him. Any other guy, I'd just ask them out. But him...I don't know." She sighed.

"It's because he's different from all the other guys you've dated," I said. "You're actually friends, which is awesome. They're supposed to make the best husbands."

Now it was Megan's turn to look slightly uncomfortable. "What was a detective doing here anyway?" she asked, changing the subject.

"No clue," I replied. "But I think they know each other, him and Parker. Their conversation was a bit...hostile." A massive understatement.

"Huh. Weird. Maybe he'll tell you?"

I shrugged. "No way to know. But I'll definitely give you the gossip if he does." I shot her a grin. Megan loved gossip.

"You'd better."

After I swore to tell her all the juicy details of my date with Ryker, Megan headed back to her desk and I went to retrieve the lunch tray from Parker's office.

He was deeply involved in something, judging by his frown and fierce look of concentration, so I didn't speak. His jacket had been discarded and flung onto the sofa. I picked it up and hung it on the valet in the corner closet so it wouldn't wrinkle. Parker always kept an extra suit and a couple of extra shirts at the office. Once I'd done that, I picked up the tray he'd pushed to the side of his desk.

"Thank you," he said.

I glanced at him, for a moment wondering if he was speaking to me, but he was still engrossed in the computer screen. Since there was no one else there and he wasn't on the phone, he must have been speaking to me. It was a little odd. He didn't usually say anything when I took away his tray or hung his jacket.

"You're welcome," I murmured, since it would have been weird to just ignore him. I couldn't help but wonder if Ryker's biting comment earlier was why I was getting a thank-you now, which kind of took the pleasure from it. Not that I did my job for thank-yous; I did it for a paycheck. But still.

"Could you get me the file on that new Russian firm we've been buying from?" Parker said. "Rogers has it, I believe."

I frowned, thinking. "You mean Bank ZNT?"

"That's the one."

"Of course." I headed for the door, then hesitated, glancing at Parker. He looked up.

"Yes?" he asked.

"I was just wondering, and it's probably none of my business, but about the detective who was here earlier. Um, is...everything okay? Do you need anything? Something I could do..." I was rambling now so I shut up.

Parker was looking at me in that intense way of his, which had me rethinking sticking my nose in something that was obviously private. I looked down at the tray I held, unable to meet his gaze, and uneasily shifted my weight from one foot to the other.

"Never mind. I shouldn't have pried," I blurted, balancing the tray on one arm so I could pull open the door.

"Sage," Parker called out, stopping me. I looked back at

him. "There's nothing you can do, but I...appreciate the offer."

That eased my embarrassment somewhat and I gave him a fleeting smile and short nod before hurrying out of the office.

I watched the clock much too closely that afternoon, the butterflies in my stomach getting more fluttery with each passing hour. By five forty-five, I gave up working at all and just started cleaning off my desk. I didn't know if the butterflies were from nerves, anticipation, or both.

What if he'd just been messing with me? The men I'd dated tended to be safe types, men who had solid white-collar jobs and worked in office buildings. I'd never in my life dated a man who knew how to shoot a gun, much less carried one on him. All my dates wore suits and ties, drove sensible cars, and didn't own leather jackets. And none of them embodied the guy-my-mom-warned-me-about cliché quite like Ryker did.

I must be out of my mind.

I went to the ladies' room to check my hair and touch up my makeup, looking myself over critically. I looked very...businesslike, I guessed. My pretty yellow heels and scarf at least dressed up the dreary white blouse and navy skirt. I had a decent body that should probably get to the gym more often, but my waist was narrow, my hips curved, and I filled out a C cup bra reasonably well.

Digging in my purse, I added some more blush to my cheeks and reapplied my pale rose lipstick. My skin was a warm peach and in the summer I tanned to a golden brown. My dark hair went well with my deep brown eyes, though I often wished I had light eyes, which was probably why I was always attracted to men with blue eyes.

After tucking some wayward strands of hair back into

my braid, I took a deep breath. I eyed my blouse. Should I maybe undo a button? It was done all the way up with only about an inch of skin showing between the bottom edge of my scarf and the top of my blouse. I hesitated, then undid a button, then one more. I had decent cleavage, might as well show it off. And now I looked a bit more like a woman who'd get asked on a date by a cop named Ryker.

Glancing at my watch had me scurrying out the door. It was six o'clock and I was going to be late, not that it was necessarily a bad thing. I'd rather he show up and wait than me stand downstairs waiting for a man who never arrived.

Parker seemed to be packing up, too, when I rapped lightly on his door and stepped inside his office.

"Anything else for today?" I asked, as was my custom to do before I left.

"No, I don't think—" Parker glanced up from where he'd been adding files to his briefcase. When he caught sight of me, he stopped talking. I waited, but he didn't continue, his gaze dropping to my chest.

Okay, maybe cleavage wasn't businesslike, but it wasn't like it was eight in the morning. Technically, business hours were over. I glanced at my watch again. Crap. Six oh-five. "Um, okay, well I'll see you tomorrow then," I blurted. I tossed a "Have a good night" behind me as I rushed out the door.

Grabbing my purse from my desk, I hurried to the elevator and punched the button, waiting impatiently for the car to arrive. What would I do if Ryker wasn't there? What would I do if he was?

I didn't race across the lobby. Instead, I took my time and walked at my normal speed, joining the dozen or so other people exiting the building. When I hit the sidewalk, I glanced around, trying not to be too obvious that I was searching. But within seconds, my eyes found him and I froze.

Ryker was waiting all right, his sunglasses on and arms crossed over his broad chest as he leaned against a massive black and chrome motorcycle parked at the curb. He saw me and his lips curved in a slow grin that made a warm tingle spread underneath my skin.

I got my feet moving again and Ryker pushed himself upright as I approached, waiting until I was near to speak.

"About time," he teased. "I almost thought you were blowing me off."

"Does any woman blow you off?" I asked.

His grin widened. "Nope."

I rolled my eyes, but I could admit it. Arrogance and cockiness turned me on, and Ryker had them both in spades.

Gesturing toward the motorcycle, I said, "I hope the restaurant is within walking distance because there's no way I'm getting on *that*."

"Ever ride a bike before?"

"A bike, yes," I said. "A death machine that can do ninety miles an hour with only a helmet for protection when my head hits the asphalt? No. I'm allergic to danger."

Ryker stepped closer, right into my personal space, and I tipped my head back to look him in the eyes. All I saw was my own reflection staring back at me. His proximity was electric, though, making my body hum as though a current ran from him into me.

"Sweetheart, I'm as dangerous as it gets."

The low thrum of his voice sent my heart into triple time. My gaze drifted down from Ryker's sunglasses to his lips, still curved in that shit-eating grin. What would it be like to be kissed by a man like him? To be swept off my feet?

"Whaddya say, Miss Prim and Proper? Wanna take a walk on the wild side?"

My eyes flew back up to his. "Did you just call me—" I began, indignant.

"Yep. Now let's get out of here. I'm starving." Grabbing a helmet from the back of his *bike*, he plopped it on my head. I would have protested, but was immediately flustered when he began fastening the strap beneath my chin. His fingers brushed my skin and suddenly it was harder to breathe.

"Well, don't you look as cute as can be," Ryker said once he'd finished.

I bet. Helmets were just oh so sexy.

He swung a leg over the bike and moved the kickstand back with his booted heel. A moment later, the engine fired up. At the noise, people nearby turned to look.

I stood, staring dubiously from the sidewalk. As if going to dinner with Ryker hadn't made me nervous before, the prospect of riding a motorcycle with him made me light-headed. My mother was so going to kill me.

"C'mon," Ryker said over the noise. "You know you want to. Don't be a scaredy-cat." He held out his hand to me.

My eyes narrowed. Schoolyard taunts were for children. And that's what I told myself as I reached out to take his hand. He tugged me forward, his mischievous smile changing to one of triumph.

I wouldn't have worn a skirt had I known I'd be climbing on the back of a motorcycle. For a girl whose mom had drilled into me the appropriate way a lady exits a car in a skirt, hiking my skirt up my thighs made me cringe.

Shoving aside thoughts of what my mother would say, I quickly got on behind Ryker, letting out a squeak when he reached back and pulled me tighter against him. At least the strap of my purse was long enough to hook over my chest so it rested against my back.

Grabbing his leather-clad shoulders, I steadied myself. I would've been showing the entire street the fabulous black satin and lace panties I wore if they weren't currently pressed against Ryker as I straddled the bike. His hand drifted down my thigh to hook around the back of my knee, his calloused palm warm against my skin. I gasped at the sensation, a flash of heat and want racing through me.

"You have to hold on like this," Ryker explained, turning his head to talk to me. He let go of my leg to reach up, moving my hands from his shoulders to circle his chest beneath his arms. "And hold on tight."

I was shaking now, fear—and, yes, a tinge of excitement—making adrenaline rush fast through my veins.

"Scared?" Ryker asked.

"Do I have reason to be?" I asked rather than admit to my fear.

I could feel him laugh, though I couldn't hear it over the noise.

"Trust me, sweetheart. I've got you." The motor revved and I tightened my grip around him.

Glancing at the sidewalk and people passing by, I suddenly saw Parker standing just outside the building entrance. He had an unreadable expression on his face, which wasn't unusual, but he was staring right at Ryker and me. There was something about the set of his jaw and tension in his body that made me uneasy.

Then the bike was moving and I lost sight of Parker as we shot down the street.

CHAPTER TWO

Riding on the back of a motorcycle was more exhilarating than I could have imagined. I tucked my head against Ryker's back to shield myself from the wind. The smell of his leather jacket hit me and I took a deep whiff. My arms were locked tight around his chest, which gave me the added bonus of a hands-on (ha-ha) assessment of just how muscled he was. And boy, was he ever.

Eventually the motorcycle slowed, the engine rumbled, and I felt Ryker's legs go down to steady the bike as we stopped and he turned off the engine. My body still seemed to be vibrating from the ride and I couldn't wipe the stupid grin off my face.

Turning over his shoulder to look at me, he said, "That wasn't so bad now, was it?"

The last thing Ryker needed was his ego fed, so I raised an eyebrow. "It could've been worse."

He laughed lightly, then held my arm to steady me as I

climbed off the back of the bike with as much grace as possible. Way too much thigh, and probably more that I didn't want to think about, showed before I yanked down my skirt. I unfastened the helmet and handed it back to him.

My hair hadn't fared so well scrunched inside the helmet, and I could feel that the braid and bun I'd fashioned this morning was now lopsided and falling out. Not really the look I was going for.

While Ryker took off his helmet and situated the bike, I hurriedly unpinned my hair and ran my fingers through it. The braid had given my usually straight hair a bit of a wave, which was nice. By the time Ryker turned around, I was standing there, hands clasped in front of me, waiting.

He stopped. Reaching up, he slowly slid his sunglasses down. Then he just stared at me, a slight look of surprise on his face.

After a moment, I grew very uncomfortable. Was there something on my face? Had another button on my blouse come undone and now I was dancing on the line between sexy and slutty? I patted my skirt as I shifted nervously underneath his scrutiny.

"What?" I finally asked.

Ryker shook his head, hooking his sunglasses on his shirt. "How the hell Parker got a bombshell like you to work for him, I'll never know."

I was torn on how to react to that. On one hand, I'd never been called a "bombshell" before and I inwardly preened at the compliment. On the other hand, it still seemed he was insulting Parker, which was not okay with me.

"Listen," I said, "I get that you and Parker don't like each other or something, but he's my boss and, well, you know, if you can't say something nice..." I let it go at that.

Ryker's lips twisted. "You're loyal to him," he said.

I shrugged. "He's my boss." In my opinion, I didn't need to elaborate. That pretty much said it all.

Ryker studied me a moment longer, then changed the subject. "Let's eat."

He took my elbow and steered me toward the door to the place I hadn't really noticed until now.

It looked like a dive, a bar I'd quickly pass by and make sure not to stare at for too long lest someone I'd rather not tangle with looked back at me. The sign above the door read BLUE STREAK.

"Is this really a place you want to bring a date?" I blurted, glancing up at him.

"What's wrong with it?" he asked with a frown as he propelled me inside.

My face grew warm and I realized I may have just made a huge faux pas. He was a cop. I knew they didn't make a lot of money. Maybe this was the kind of place he could afford and I was being all hoity-toity snotty about it.

"N-nothing," I stammered, quickly trying to backtrack. "It's fine." I gave him a weak smile.

The place wasn't as bad on the inside as the outside looked like it'd be. The tables were heavy, distressed wood and there wasn't a plastic chair in sight. There were lots of people here, with a higher ratio of men to women. Some were sitting at the bar drinking and watching the Cubs lose on television, while others shot pool at one of the two tables on the other side of the room.

"Hey, Ryker! How's it going?" A woman approached, smiling and holding two menus.

"Doing good, Rachel," Ryker said, his face creasing into a warm smile. "You?"

"Can't complain. Just you two tonight?"

At Ryker's affirmative, we followed her to a booth by the

windows. I slid in and he took the seat opposite me. Rachel handed us the menus.

"Christy will be right over to take your order," she said.

"You come here a lot?" I asked once Rachel had left.

He shrugged. "Often enough."

I frowned, a suspicion forming in my head. "Is this a cop bar?"

Ryker grinned. "Gorgeous *and* smart. That doesn't happen very often."

I shot him a look, but I was faking. I decided I could get used to his compliments. But that explained why he'd brought me here—it was obviously a place he felt at home—which made me feel kinda bad about prejudging it.

Christy came by to ask what we wanted to drink. I ordered a glass of white wine, then saw Ryker's lips twitch again.

"What?" I asked. He didn't answer, ordering a beer instead, and when Christy walked away, I asked again. "What's so funny?" I had the sinking sensation that I'd been right after all. Ryker's asking me out was one big joke to him for reasons I couldn't fathom.

"You know what? I should just go," I said, grabbing my purse. I began to slide out of the booth, anxious to get away.

"Don't leave," Ryker said, snagging my arm in a tight grip. "It's nothing, really. You're just…classier than I'm used to." He smiled a slow sexy grin that turned my bones to the consistency of warm butter. "I like it."

I cleared my throat, looking away from the intense blue of his eyes, and set my purse back down. "Well, okay then." *Classier than he was used to.* Hmm. I wondered how many women he'd dated to be able to use that phrase.

My attention was immediately diverted when Ryker shrugged out of his leather jacket. The T-shirt he wore fit him like a second skin, stretching tight across his chest and shoulders and leaving nothing to the imagination. His biceps and forearms were traced with veins from working out, leading to strong hands that were work-roughened, his fingers thick and long enough to make me imagine all sorts of inappropriate things. I said a silent prayer of thanks that a twist of fate in my otherwise dull life had afforded me this particular view tonight.

"So how long have you been a secretary, Sage?" he asked.

"Executive administrative assistant," I mumbled, correcting him automatically. I gave a little sigh and reluctantly lifted my gaze from below his neck. Our eyes met and his lips curved, as if he'd known exactly what I'd been thinking. Heck, he probably had been. No doubt he had women drooling over him constantly.

And he can add me to his list, I thought.

"My mistake. How long have you been an *executive administrative assistant*?"

"A little over a year," I replied. "Since I graduated college."

Ryker frowned. "Wait a minute. You have a degree and you're just—" He caught himself and stopped.

"I'm just a secretary, right?" I finished for him. I shrugged. "I had a hard time finding a job when I got out of school and didn't want to leave the area. There was a job opening, I needed to pay the bills, so I took it. Turns out I like doing what I do, so I stayed."

"What's your degree in?"

"Art History."

Ryker snorted a laugh just as Christy dropped off our drinks.

"What are you having tonight?" she asked, taking a pad and pen from the apron tied around her waist.

I glanced down at my menu again. "Um, I'll have the house salad with chicken and the low-fat Italian dressing on the side, please," I said. Christy wrote that down and turned expectantly to Ryker. "Wait," I said, and she turned back to me. "Are your tomatoes room temperature or refrigerated?"

She blinked once. "Um, I don't know. Room temperature, I guess?"

"Oh. Well, that's all right then. If it comes with croutons, could you leave those off, please? And no onions." Definitely didn't want garlic and onion breath tonight.

Christy wrote that down, too, repeating to herself, "No onions…"

I handed her my menu and glanced at Ryker, who was silently observing me again.

"What?" I asked, but he just shook his head.

"You want your usual, Ryker?" Christy asked.

"Yeah, thanks." He handed her his menu and she left.

"So what does an Art History major do, exactly?" he asked. "I can't imagine you got that degree just for kicks."

"No, I didn't. Ideally, I'd love to work in an art museum, which is why I like Chicago." And because it was near home. "But it's really hard to get a job like that. Openings don't come up very often."

Ryker considered this. "So a wannabe museum curator, but instead you're the executive administrative assistant to the great and powerful Parker Anderson."

"It's a living," I said, taking a tentative sip of my wine. It wasn't bad. It wasn't great either, but it wasn't bad. "What about you? Why were you at the office today? Did something happen?" I'd been worrying in the back of my mind all day and knew I'd rest a lot easier if I had some idea of what Ryker and Parker had talked about.

"Just a case I'm working on," Ryker said. "I thought maybe Parker might be able to . . . shed some light on it."

I noticed his entire demeanor changed when he spoke of Parker. His body grew tense and his jaw tightened, the lines of humor around his mouth and eyes fading.

"So you two know each other," I prompted when he didn't say anything more.

Ryker's smile was tight and didn't touch his eyes. "You could say that."

I was going to ask more questions, but he spoke again. "Since you're here with me, I'm assuming you're not seeing anyone."

Okay, I confess, my heart sped up a little at that. I felt like I was in high school again. Was the hot, popular guy in the cool crowd interested in me? I fought to keep my voice nonchalant when I replied. "No. Not at the moment. You?"

Ryker leaned forward, folding his arms on the table. "I wasn't, but I think I am now."

His eyes were fringed in dark lashes, the blue more intense with him this close, and for a moment I forgot how to breathe. Then I processed his words.

Had he just said what I thought he said? My eyes widened as a grin spread slowly on Ryker's face. My inner cynic was scoffing at how well he'd delivered that line, but my inner princess was preening at the compliment.

"Here you go," Christy said, setting two plates on the table and interrupting the moment.

I sucked in a breath, my lungs reminding me that air is generally required. I barely noticed my food as I automatically picked up my fork and took a bite of salad.

It turned out Ryker's "usual" was a double bacon cheeseburger with a side of fries. It smelled divine and I eyed the fries while I chewed a slice of cold cucumber.

"So tell me where you're from, Sage," Ryker said. "The life story. The works."

I liked hearing him say my name. "My life story won't get us to dessert," I replied dryly. Ryker laughed, which made me smile, too. "It sounds like your life would be way more interesting," I said. "How long have you been a cop?"

"Going on nine years now," he said, taking a swig of his beer.

"Your parents must be proud."

"I wouldn't know about my dad, but yeah, I guess my mom is."

I sensed more to the story there with his parents, but it also seemed like he didn't want to talk about it. "It must be exciting," I said instead.

He shrugged. "It can be. What about you? Parents still around?"

I nodded. "Yes. Mom and Dad don't live far, so I get to visit often." I didn't mention the town and hoped Ryker wouldn't ask.

"Where?" he asked, dashing my hopes.

"Um, Lake Forest." I took another big bite of salad.

Ryker's eyebrows went up, as I'd known they would. Everyone knew "rich people" lived in Lake Forest, which was why I hated telling people I was from there. It made them assume things about me, some of which were true and some of which weren't.

"Your dad retired, too?" Ryker asked.

"Um, kinda," I said, keeping my gaze fixed on my lettuce. "He owns some delivery companies for products in Chicago."

"So you're a poor little rich girl?" Ryker teased.

My gaze shot up to his. "I never said I was a poor little anything," I replied stiffly. "And I'm not wealthy; my parents are. I work to pay my bills like everyone else."

"Take it easy, sweetheart," Ryker said, the corner of his mouth tipping upward. "I didn't mean to ruffle your feathers." He paused before adding in a slightly roughened tone, "Though that sounds like a good plan for later." His gaze slid down to where I'd undone the buttons on my shirt and my skin burned as though he'd touched me.

Had he just implied we'd be having sex tonight? Was *ruffling feathers* a euphemism I'd just not heard before? I nearly choked on the cherry tomato I'd popped in my mouth.

Just then, my cell rang. Without even looking, I knew who it was going to be, and it didn't occur to me not to answer. I gulped down the pulpy tomato that was so *not* room temperature.

"Excuse me," I muttered, digging in my purse and finding my phone. "Hello?"

"Sage," Parker said, "the files for the Lawson account have arrived. They need to be stamped and logged."

"I know," I said. "I signed the boxes in earlier today." All six of them. "I was planning on doing them tomorrow."

"It can't wait," he said. "Tomorrow I'm meeting all day with GoTech and I'll need you in there with me. This has to be done tonight."

Shit. I glanced at my watch. It was after seven. Those boxes would take me at least an hour each, if not more.

"Um, okay. I'll be in as soon as I can."

"Good." He hung up.

I sighed as I slipped my phone back into my purse. So much for my date...or any other activity Ryker might've planned for later this evening. I wasn't sure how I felt about that. I didn't usually sleep around, but then again, I'd never before been propositioned by a man like Ryker. Speaking of which, when I looked up, he was watching me closely.

"I'm sorry," I apologized, "but I have to go back in to

work." I slipped my purse strap over my shoulder and took another hit of wine.

"Why?"

"There's some stuff that needs to get done and I won't have time to do it tomorrow," I explained, not bothering to go into detail. "But thanks so much for dinner." Half my mind was already on its way back to the office, where Parker would be waiting.

I was up and out of the booth when Ryker seemed to realize I was actually leaving, and he jumped up. Grabbing my arm to stop me, he said, "Wait, you're leaving? Just like that?"

"I'm really sorry," I said again.

"He really has you on some kind of leash," Ryker said.

My mouth dropped open in shock. "Excuse me?" I couldn't believe he'd just insulted me like that. "Did you just imply I was a *dog*?"

"No, I'm implying Parker's a fucking slave driver," he retorted. "Stay just a little longer."

"I can't," I said, shaking my head. I started tugging my arm, trying to free myself from his grip. Parker was waiting and so were those boxes.

"At least give me your number," Ryker said.

I rolled my eyes. I was done with this game. "Listen," I said, "despite what you might think, I'm not looking for a hit-it-and-quit-it kind of man. Dinner was nice. The ride on your bike was fun. And I'm sure you...ruffling my feathers...would be amazing." No doubt an understatement, that last part, but no need to dwell. "But I think we're done here. Nice meeting you, Ryker."

Finally freeing myself from his hold, I hurried away. The last glimpse of his face before I headed out the door showed surprise giving way to a blank, harder expression that reminded me a little of Parker, and not even the hint of a grin remained.

* * *

As I'd predicted, Parker was back in his office when I arrived. I guessed he must have stepped out earlier for dinner or something before returning. It didn't surprise me. He seemed to work twenty-four-seven.

The cab back from the bar hadn't been nearly as fun as the motorcycle ride there, and I hoped the smell of stale cigar didn't cling to me the way it had clung to the inside of the car. But by the time the ride was over, I'd rebraided my hair and tucked it up into a bun.

"Sorry to interrupt your evening," Parker said once I'd dropped off my purse at my desk and entered his office.

I was busy studying the boxes stacked in the corner, but his apology took me aback and my gaze swiveled to meet his.

"Um, it's fine," I said after a moment. This apologetic and polite Parker was new. Well, I guess that wasn't exactly true. He was always polite, professional—almost to the point of being cold and indifferent. But apologies were definitely new.

"I thought it might be easier for you to do these in here rather than at your desk," he offered.

That would be way easier, actually. Parker's office was huge and there was plenty of room for me to spread things out on the floor rather than try to put it all on my desk.

"Yeah, that'd be great, thanks."

I headed back to my desk to get my hand scanner, notebook, and tags. All files coming in were logged by hand and tagged with a bar code sticker. The bar codes were then scanned and uploaded to a database somewhere before being sent to another department that stored the actual documents into digital format. Cataloging was tedious and time-consuming, but essential.

"I'm heading upstairs to meet with Hinton," Parker said when I came back in, naming the vice president of the international division. He kept odd hours as well.

"Sure, okay," I replied, only half listening as I headed for the boxes and set my supplies on the table. Wow. It was going to be a long night. Should've put my wine in a to-go cup.

Parker left and I decided to kick off my shoes for crawling around the floor. I untied the scarf from around my neck and set it aside, the fabric now irritating me after having worn it for nearly fourteen hours. Kneeling on the floor next to the tower of boxes, I heaved a sigh and dug in.

* * *

Two hours later I paused for a break. I eased back onto my heels, trying to stretch out my back. It had been too quiet in the office, so I'd turned on the stereo Parker kept in the corner on one of the many bookshelves lining the back wall. Hidden speakers around the room now softly played jazz piano. I never changed the station from the satellite radio Parker had it tuned to and had grown to like the same music he did.

There were approximately twenty piles of paper, sorted by type of document, surrounding where I knelt on the floor. Closing my eyes, I rubbed the back of my neck and stretched, arching my spine and trying to ease out the kinks from hunching over for so long. I let out a groan as my muscles protested.

Someone clearing their throat made me jerk around in surprise, only to see Parker had returned. For a brief moment I could have sworn he was staring at my chest, but then he blinked and our eyes met and I thought I must have been mistaken. Like I said, Parker was always professional with a capital *P*.

"How's it going?" he asked, tossing a thick file folder onto his desk.

"Not too bad," I said, glancing at my stacks. "I'm halfway through the third box, so probably faster than I'd originally thought."

Parker discarded his jacket, tossing it onto the leather sofa before sinking down into its depths. He loosened his tie and undid the top button of his shirt, then rubbed a hand over his face in one of the few gestures of tiredness I'd ever seen him make.

Getting to my feet, I crossed to an antique highboy that used to belong to Parker's grandfather. It was where he kept his liquor. Opening the front panels, I took out a crystal old-fashioned and the decanter half-full of scotch. I poured an inch or so into the glass, replaced the decanter, and walked to the sofa.

Parker was watching me as I set the glass on the table at his elbow. It was a ritual we often had on evenings we both worked late. Personally, for as hard as he worked I thought Parker deserved a drink far earlier in the evening, but he never touched a drop until after nine o'clock. I wished I had half his discipline and self-control.

Leaning forward, he rested his elbows on his knees as he picked up the glass. His gaze dropped to my bare feet and I was absurdly glad I'd had a pedi recently. My toes were a sparkly *Cozu-Melted-in-the Sun* pink.

We didn't speak, but the silence was comfortable to me

as I resumed my spot on the floor. Parker and I had an understanding. At least, I understood him. He made me feel needed—necessary—and as an only child who'd never been really needed by anyone, I liked that. And I liked him.

My mom had been bugging me lately to "get a real job" that actually pertained to my degree, but I'd brushed her off, even when she'd intimated my father "knew people" who could help me. I wanted to get a job on my own merits. Besides, I had plenty of time to worry about my career in art history. For now, I was content being an executive administrative assistant to Parker, and times like this reminded me of why that was the case.

Dragging another box down from the now shorter stack, I began sorting through it, scooting between my piles as I labeled and made notes. The only sounds were that of the music, the quiet beep of my scanner, and the shuffle of paper. It was a companionable moment, just the two of us. Then he had to go and ruin it.

"I saw you and Ryker tonight," Parker said out of the blue.

I glanced around to see his gaze steady on me.

"Earlier," he continued. "You were leaving with him." His tone was difficult to read, his expression impossible.

Unsure how to respond, I opted for the truth and, considering their earlier hostility toward each other, vagueness. "He asked me to dinner," I said with a shrug. "So, I went."

Parker took a large drink of scotch before replying. I watched the exposed skin of his throat move as he swallowed.

"Ryker's not a bad guy," he said, his gaze focused on his drink. "Just perhaps not your type."

My eyebrows climbed at that. Not my type? A hot guy with abs of steel wasn't my type? "And you know what my type is?" Irritation tinged with exhaustion made me speak more sharply than was wise and Parker's eyes flashed to mine at my tone.

"I'm trying to give you a warning," he said, his voice flat. "I suggest you heed it." Tossing back the rest of his drink, he rose from the couch and went back behind his desk. With a few taps on the keyboard, I was dismissed, his attention now firmly fixed elsewhere.

Turning away from him, I resumed my task, now wishing I'd thought a little more before reacting to his words. I could've had a chance to ask him about this morning, about what Ryker had wanted, or even about how they knew each other, but it was pretty obvious Parker was done with talking, at least for now.

Focusing on my job—daydreaming and speculating wouldn't get this done any quicker—I kept at it. Crawling on all fours to the farthest piles for scanning, then restacking papers inside the boxes from which they'd come. I would've been a bit self-conscious about some of the positions I was in if I hadn't known that Parker had no interest in me in that way. In the year I'd worked for him, he'd never, not even once, said or so much as hinted at something inappropriate.

Which was a damn shame.

I sighed. Ryker must have ratcheted up my hormones. Normally I wouldn't let a thought like that even get put into words inside my head.

I glanced Parker's way a few times, trying to do so inconspicuously, just because I liked to look at him. With his tie discarded and his cuffs turned back, he sat back in his chair, an elbow braced on the arm, a frown of concentration on his face as he studied the computer monitor. A five o'clock shadow graced his jaw and a wave of his dark hair fell against his forehead, making me want to comb it back into place. With my fingers.

Yes, definitely tired. Usually I was able to keep thoughts of Parker at bay, but last night had been rough and today had been long. I was sure he was tired, too, and I knew from experience that he wouldn't leave until I was finished. That was always nice. I didn't know if he waited because he thought if I was working, he should be, too, or if he just did it unconsciously.

A sudden loud noise outside the office made me drop the scanner. My wide eyes flew to Parker's.

"What was that?" I asked. I glanced at the clock on his desk. It was after eleven and I'd thought Parker and I were the only ones left in the building, or at least on this floor.

Parker was up out of his chair before I'd finished asking my question. In seconds, he was hauling me none-too-gently to my feet and pulling me toward the closet.

"Get in," he said, not giving me a choice in the matter as he pushed me into the dark cupboard.

"What are you doing?" I squeaked, stunned even as I instinctively obeyed him and shrank back into the corner.

Parker reached above me to the top shelf and pulled something down that fit in his hand. In another moment, I saw it was a gun. He racked the slide on top and the sound made me jump.

"That was a gunshot," he said. "Something's going on and after what Ryker said this morning, I'm not taking any chances." He pointed at me. "Stay. Here. Don't come out until I come for you, understand?"

I jerked a quick nod, unable to speak. Without another word, Parker closed the door, shutting me firmly inside the closet.

CHAPTER THREE

I stood in the dark, my back pressed against the wall of the closet, Parker's shirts and suit jackets hanging on either side of me. It smelled overwhelmingly of him in here, which only sent my panic ratcheting higher.

A gunshot, he'd said. Why in the world would someone be shooting a gun in the building? At this hour? Certainly not for any good reason, obviously.

All these years I'd put things in this closet and I'd never known he kept a gun up there. It was too high for me to reach and I wouldn't have thought to pry anyway. Had it been there all this time?

All these questions and more swirled through my mind as I worried about what was going on outside the closet door. What if Parker got ambushed? What if they shot him? He could be lying somewhere even now, hurt and bleeding, while I was hiding in the closet waiting for him.

Another gunshot startled me. Then another. My breathing

sounded harsh in the tight closet, and I clenched my hands into fists as I fought the urge to leave my hiding place.

Parker had told me to wait, not to come out until he came for me, so as hard as it was, I waited. It felt like forever, each minute creeping by with agonizing slowness. With each moment that Parker didn't appear, my fear increased, until I was nearly hyperventilating. The closet didn't have enough air and tears stung my eyes as my imagination painted vivid pictures of an injured Parker. A sheet of cold sweat covered my skin as I strained my ears to catch any faint noise.

The door suddenly swung open, startling me. Parker stood there, and without even thinking, I threw myself into his arms.

"Thank God, you're okay," I mumbled against his chest, swallowing down a sob of relief. Adrenaline and fear made my knees feel weak and I clung to Parker, my arms holding tightly around his neck.

He'd instinctively wrapped an arm around my waist and I sensed his hesitation before sliding the other arm around me, too. I knew this was inappropriate, but I couldn't make myself let go. Not yet.

"It's all right," he murmured, the words rumbling in his chest. "I'm fine."

Embarrassment began to creep in now that the panic and fear were starting to fade and I became acutely aware that every inch of me was pressed against my boss. If I could've ignored that last part, maybe I could've enjoyed it, but common sense kicked in.

"I'm sorry," I sniffed, easing up the death grip I had on him. "It seemed you were gone a long time. I was worried. What happened?" My eyes were still watery so I stared straight ahead at the third button on his shirt.

"You're shaking," he said softly, as though he hadn't

heard a word I'd said. I'd expected him to let me go, but his arms remained solidly around my waist.

"I heard more gunshots," I explained. "I thought maybe something had happened to y—" My throat closed up and I couldn't finish.

Parker didn't respond. Gathering my courage, I finally lifted my eyes to his and my breath caught.

His blue eyes were closer than they'd ever been before, their soul-searching gaze locked on mine. Our faces were so near, our lips only inches apart. He was even more beautiful and perfect up close. My body seemed to melt into his, the pressure of his arms around me changing, from steadying and supportive to caressing.

Parker's eyes burned, making my breath hitch in my chest. His gaze dropped to my mouth and my lips parted in invitation.

Sirens screaming outside the building made us both look to the window.

"Police are here," Parker said, dropping his arms and stepping away from me. "Better put your shoes on."

Feeling suddenly bereft without him to support me, I hurried to slip on my heels.

"Did you call them?" I asked. "Did you see anyone? Anyone who might've fired that gun?"

By the time I'd put my shoes on and turned around, he'd straightened his tie. Glancing my way, he crooked his finger, beckoning me back to him.

I obeyed, waiting for his answers as I stepped in front of him.

"I called them," he said, reaching forward. His fingers caught at the button on my blouse that I'd undone earlier and he refastened it, then the next button as well, until only a scant few inches of my throat were exposed. "Hinton is dead."

I barely heard him, so taken aback was I by the intimacy
of him buttoning my blouse. It took longer than it should
have for the statement to penetrate.

"Hinton's dead?" I repeated. At Parker's nod, I said, "But
you were with him a few hours ago."

"I know."

The elevator dinged and we both turned toward it. Parker
moved to the closet, replacing the gun he'd taken back on
the shelf, then held the door for me as we left his office.
A bevy of uniformed policemen exited the elevator, but my
gaze didn't settle on them for long. It found the one person
I'd half-expected, half-dreaded would arrive when I'd heard
those sirens.

Ryker.

He was still wearing the same clothes he'd had on earlier,
though the flirtatious grin from dinner was gone. His expression was serious, turning hard when he spotted Parker.

"You were the one who called it in?" he asked Parker,
who nodded.

"He's on the floor above this one. Randolph Hinton, one
of our VPs."

Ryker turned to a couple of the uniformed cops and spoke
to them. A moment later, they were heading for the stairs,
weapons in hand.

"Did you see anyone? Hear anything?" he asked, taking out a small pad of paper and a pen from inside his
jacket.

Parker told them about hearing the gunshot. "I went to investigate and saw a man leaving the floor. When I called out
to him, he fired at me."

My blood felt like it turned to ice at this and I whipped
my head around to stare wide-eyed at Parker. He glanced
sideways at me, but his attention remained on Ryker.

"Looks like he missed," Ryker said, jotting notes on the paper. He glanced up. "Too bad." His smile was cold.

That set my blood pressure skyrocketing and I opened my mouth to let him know exactly how big an asshole he was, but Parker seemed to sense what I was going to do. His hand grasped my arm in a firm grip and squeezed. I shut my mouth, but I shot him a glare just to let him know that I didn't appreciate being silenced.

"What about you?" Ryker asked, turning his attention to me. "Did you see anyone?"

I shook my head. "I was in the closet."

Ryker's eyebrows flew upward. "Excuse me?"

Okay, well that hadn't made much sense. "I mean, after we heard the first shot, Parker—I mean Mr. Anderson—had me get inside the closet while he went to go see what had happened." I didn't mention the gun Parker had taken with him.

"So there's no one to corroborate the fact that you say someone else was in the building," Ryker said to Parker.

"Are you insinuating I had something to do with this?" Parker's body was stiff with tension, his voice cold.

"I'm just making an observation," Ryker said.

"Well, it's a ridiculous observation," I cut in. "I was with him when we heard the first shot."

"And your livelihood depends on your boss," Ryker said. "Not exactly a sterling recommendation of your truthfulness."

My eyes narrowed. "You're accusing me of lying? Why, you little swine—" I snarled, taking a step toward him, but Parker pulled me back.

Ryker's lips twitched, like he wanted to smile but knew he shouldn't. "Is that supposed to be a cop joke?" he asked, raising an eyebrow. "Because frankly, I've heard better."

By now I was so upset I wanted to claw his deliciously blue bedroom eyes right out of his perfect head.

The cops came back then and Ryker went to speak to them, leaving Parker and me standing by ourselves.

"I can't believe what an arrogant imbecile he is!" I seethed, staring at Ryker's leather-clad back. "Trying to say you had anything to do with it. What a jerk!"

"I appreciate your anger, but antagonizing the police isn't a good idea." Parker's mild reply had me glancing his way.

"I'm not going to just stand here and let him say those things," I said stiffly.

Parker's eyes gazed into mine and I was abruptly reminded of what had happened in his office before the police had arrived. My cheeks grew warm and I was suddenly acutely aware of his hand still wrapped around my arm.

"Forensics would like to swab your hands for gunshot residue." Ryker's voice intruded and I jerked around to see him standing behind us, his eyes calculating as he took in Parker and me.

"Of course," Parker agreed, letting go of me. A uniformed cop escorted him to where two other men in jackets with "CSI" stamped on the back were setting up their materials on a desk.

Ryker remained by me, but I crossed my arms over my chest and refused to look at him.

"I wish our dinner hadn't been interrupted," he said in an undertone.

My jaw fell open. "Are you kidding me right now? You practically accused my boss of murder!"

He shrugged. "I'm doing my job. It's nothing personal."

"You sure about that?" I retorted. "Because it sure *seems* personal."

"Parker and I have a history," he said.

"No kidding."

"Go out with me Saturday night and I'll tell you all about it." His eyes crinkled slightly at the corners as a slow grin lifted his lips.

Damn. It should be against the law for a man who could be that giant of an asshole to also look that good.

I snorted, glancing away from him to where the technicians were rubbing some kind of swab over Parker's hands.

"Trying to bribe me with gossip won't work," I lied. Who was I kidding? I wanted to know about him and Parker more than I wanted Reese's Peanut Butter Eggs at Easter, which was a whole helluva lot. I loved those things. And the hearts at Valentine's Day, and the pumpkins at Halloween, and the trees at Christmas…

"Sure it will," he said. "C'mon, it's just dinner."

"It's already Thursday," I stalled. "Maybe I have plans for Saturday."

"I'm worth breaking them," he said, which only confirmed that his arrogance knew no limit. He leaned down to whisper in my ear. "I can do things with my tongue that'll leave you begging for more."

Ho-ly shit.

That sent a hot flash through me, but I wasn't about to let him know. "Does that line actually work on anyone?" I sneered.

"You tell me."

Damn it all to hell. I had the spine of a jellyfish. I stepped into his personal space. "Fine," I said. "I will come to dinner with you. But that's *all*." I poked his chest for emphasis. Lord, but his muscles were lick-worthy. "No more…indecent insinuations or…or propositions." Though that line about his tongue would have a starring role in my fantasies tonight.

Ryker grinned outright. "I like how you talk," he said. "*Indecent proposition.* Sounds right up my alley."

"Don't you have a murder to investigate or something?" I reminded him. Not to mention that it felt a little uncouth to be flirting with someone when a man was dead. I hadn't known Mr. Hinton other than in passing, but still.

"Right after we get your hands swabbed, sweetheart."

I stared at him. "Tell me you're joking."

His grin just widened. "I never joke about my job. Let's go."

I allowed him to lead me to the CSI people, who did their job quickly and efficiently. When I was through, Ryker was occupied with more non-uniformed detectives who'd arrived. Since no one else seemed to want or need me for anything, I headed back to Parker's office. The boxes of files still left to catalogue stared accusingly at me.

"Not tonight, fellas," I said to them. "I'll just have to come in early tomorrow." Joy. I glanced at my watch. It was almost one o'clock. So early would be…in only a few hours. I sighed.

Crouching down on the floor, I started picking up my stacks. No way could I leave Parker's office like this and I was too tired to finish scanning the ones I'd already sorted.

"Don't worry about those tonight," Parker said. I turned to see him striding through the door. "It can wait."

"I was just picking these up," I said, reaching for another pile. "I'll finish in the morning."

"Leave it."

The order was curt and I knew that tone. Without another word, I set aside the pile and got to my feet. I grabbed my purse and scarf from the couch.

"I'll just see you in the morning then." I turned to go.

"Wait. It's late. I'll drive you home."

He was grabbing his suit jacket and shrugging it on, so he missed my jaw hitting the floor.

Parker had never driven me home. Ever. It didn't matter how late we worked. I'd grab a cab if I was too tired to wait for the bus.

"Um, okay. Thanks," I said once I'd recovered from my surprise.

By now, building security had called in more people and I saw the head of security talking with Ryker on our way out. I wondered if the person who'd shot Hinton had worked for KLP. The security for a company like this was heavy duty. It couldn't have been easy for someone to break in.

Ryker glanced at Parker and me as we walked by toward the elevators. He didn't smile and I decided I really didn't like Parker and Ryker in the same room together. Unnerved, I looked away as the elevator dinged and Parker's hand pressed lightly on my lower back to guide me inside.

I was slightly uncomfortable as we walked through the parking garage to Parker's BMW. This was a new situation for me, which made me nervous, so I started babbling.

"What an awful thing, right?" I asked rhetorically. My heels clacking on the concrete sounded really loud in the nearly deserted garage. "I guess they'll be watching the security footage and checking the card scans. Wouldn't it be awful if it was an employee? Did he fire anyone lately? Maybe it was an angry customer, though I don't know how they would've gotten in the building at that hour. *I've* had issues getting inside during off hours and I work here. I wonder if he was married—"

"He wasn't."

Parker's interruption cut off my nervous chatter and I waited while he opened the passenger door for me.

Parker owned a high-end BMW that wasn't quite a year

old. It was shiny, metallic black with a black leather interior, fully loaded with all the fun options, and had cost well into six figures. And the reason I knew all this was because I'd been the one to pay the invoice from Parker's bank account.

Most of his bills were set to auto-pay, but the rest I handled for him. A personal accountant would probably do the same thing, but it had been a duty that had begun gradually soon after I'd started and now was just something I did as part of my job.

So I was the only one who knew exactly how much his rent was, how much he spent on the suits that fit him so well, and when he was on the ins or outs with his current arm candy—depending on whether he was spending money at the florist…or the jeweler. The latter didn't happen very often because, frankly, none of the women Parker dated seemed to last very long. He worked so much, I assumed it precluded any kind of serious relationship.

Not that I was complaining.

I slid into the front passenger seat and Parker shut the door. I took a deep whiff while he rounded the car. Leather and expensive cologne. The stuff fantasies were made of.

Parker slid behind the wheel after depositing his briefcase and jacket in the backseat. The engine came to life with a gentle purr and soon we were exiting the garage.

"You should turn left up there," I said.

"I know," Parker replied, glancing at me, then back to the road. "I know where you live, Sage."

He did? Since when? I couldn't remember ever telling him where I lived or why he'd have cause to know it. This new information kept me quiet…for about a mile or two… then my nerves started acting up again. We were really close, like in proximity to each other, and it was nice. Too nice.

"So thanks a lot for taking me home," I said too brightly. "Usually, I'd just take the bus, but at this time of night, probably not a great idea. The driver in the mornings knows me, and he waits for me because I'm almost always running late. I gave him a Christmas gift last year—a box of fudge I'd made. I love fudge. I make a ton of it every year. I brought some in to the office, too, remember? Jane in HR asked me for my recipe."

Nerves were making me babble and although Parker didn't say anything, I saw the corner of his mouth lift slightly in the low light from the dash.

Deciding to get back to business rather than continue to discuss inanities such as my Christmas baking habits, I said, "I'll make sure to get those files done first thing tomorrow." Then I rethought that. "Though I guess it's already tomorrow, right? I mean, today is tomorrow, so I mean I'll get those done today..." My voice trailed off. God, I sounded like such an idiot. In my defense, I'd been up since six a.m. Okay, six-thirty.

"Tonight was rough," Parker said. "And it's late. If you want to take tomorrow off, you can."

I thought about that. He was offering me a day off? No, wait, not really. I was sure I'd have to take a sick day. This wasn't a freebie.

"Are *you* taking tomorrow off?" I asked instead, because I already knew the answer to that. Parker rarely took time off, which is why I wasn't surprised to see him shake his head.

"No."

"Then neither will I."

"Your loyalty is...appreciated," Parker said. "Thanks for not telling Ryker about the gun."

"Sure," I said. "I mean, it's none of my business why

you keep a gun in your closet." I waited, hoping he'd en-lighten me, but no such luck. "You said something about what Ryker told you earlier today...?" I prodded.

Parker glanced at me, then back to the road.

"He's investigating the murder of an informant, a pros-titute, who said she had information for him on a drug supplier. Unfortunately, she was dead when he arrived. And unfortunately for *me*, she was holding my business card when she died."

I gaped. "Your card? But why would—" And I stopped. I probably didn't want to go there.

He seemed to read my thoughts. "I wasn't a customer," he said dryly.

"I didn't think you were," I lied.

"Sure you did."

Now my face was so hot, I was glad the inside of the car was dark enough he couldn't see how red I had to be.

"I'm sorry—" I began.

"It's fine."

"No, it's just that your bills had been absent florists, jew-elers, or expensive dinners out lately so I'd just assumed." Yeah, I should really stop there. I covered my burning face with my hands, vowing not to say another word. Not that it mattered if he was dating anyone. Sex was freely available to a man like him and I knew he had his share of one-night stands.

"No, I'm not dating anyone," he said.

Confirmation that Parker Anderson was decidedly avail-able had me peeking through my fingers.

"Are you?" he asked.

I dropped my hands to my lap, my mouth suddenly dry. "I told you I got dumped," I reminded him.

"Yes, but then you had dinner with Ryker tonight."

And I was having dinner with him again tomorrow night, I thought, but didn't say.

"I don't think having dinner with someone necessarily says you're dating them," I said, evading his question.

"Then what does it say?"

I shrugged. "I don't know. It's just...dinner."

Parker glanced at me, but I looked away, afraid he might see too much in my eyes. I was too tired to be on my toes with him, and didn't want to argue about Ryker. It was quiet until we arrived at my apartment.

"Thanks for the ride," I said, my hand on the door handle, but he was already turning off the car.

"It's late. I'll walk you up."

Okay then.

My apartment was on the top floor of a building that included a doorman, though Harvey wasn't manning the door this late. My key let me in to the lobby and though we both knew it was unnecessary for Parker to take me farther, neither of us said anything as we stepped into the elevator.

"This is a nice place," he observed.

I stiffened, immediately self-conscious. Parker wasn't an idiot and he had to know that I couldn't afford a place like this on my own, even though a hefty chunk of my salary went to rent. My father had been adamant about me staying in a place he felt was nice enough and secure enough for his "baby girl." It had been easier to give in, especially when my mother got so upset when Dad and I argued.

"Do you have roommates?" Parker asked.

I shook my head. "No. It's just me."

He nodded and I could see the wheels turning inside his head.

Seven flights later, we exited the elevator and I walked to the end of the hall, Parker at my heels. This felt like déjà vu, only not with Parker. I'd taken this walk with dates too many times not to feel the similarity. Inviting a man to my apartment after a date really meant just one thing, and of course that was all I could think about as I tried to unlock my door. But my hands weren't cooperating, nerves and lack of sleep getting to me.

"Here, let me," Parker said, taking the keys from me and unlocking the door. I tried to ignore the brush of his fingers against mine.

He pushed it open and I stepped inside. I had absolutely no clue what to do. I mean, yes, if it had been a date, I'd have known exactly what to do next. Depending on how badly I wanted to jump his bones, it was either "Hey, want a drink?" or "Here, let me help you with that belt." Since I didn't want to be fired on the spot, I settled for Option A.

"Would you like something to drink?" I asked.

"It's late," Parker said. "I'm sure you're tired."

Parker Anderson was in my apartment. That alone would keep me awake and fantasizing for hours.

"No, it's fine," I said, flinching inwardly at the anxious-to-please note in my voice. *Hello, obvious.*

"Then…a drink would be nice," he said. "It's been a while since I've been shot at."

Oh yeah, let's bring *that* up again. I turned away with a shudder, wishing I hadn't known how close he'd come to getting hit tonight. Looked like I'd be having a drink, too.

"I have wine or bourbon," I offered. "Beer, too, if you'd rather."

"A shot of bourbon sounds good."

I set aside my purse and scarf and reached up to take two glasses from the cupboard. I briefly thought about undoing two buttons on my blouse again, but discarded the idea. That would be tacky and way too obvious. After adding some ice to the glasses, I poured a hefty shot in both, then handed one to Parker, who'd sat on my sofa. After a brief hesitation and deliberation, I sat there, too. Not too close as in right next to him, but not farthest away either. Something in the middle.

I was really glad I'd taken time to pick up my dirty clothes that had been strewn about this morning. I loved my apartment and kept it pretty picked up. My mother had wanted to send her cleaning lady out, but I'd drawn the line at that. I'd decorated in peach and earth tones. I liked natural wood, so a lot of it was handmade pieces I'd picked out myself, some bowls carved from tree roots, a few pieces of African art, and vases filled with branches.

Parker took a drink of the bourbon, his Adam's apple moving as he swallowed. Without his jacket and tie, the top button undone on his shirt, he looked less intimidating, though not by much.

He was a gorgeous man and when he dressed to the nines, he was more than enough to make a woman weak in the knees. Casual like this, his hair in slight disarray from pushing his fingers through it, a five o'clock shadow darkening his jaw, the muscles in this forearms flexing as he again raised the glass to his lips...the words *panty dropping* came to mind.

I sighed a little, realized I was staring, and quickly looked away. I took a steadying sip of the liquor, the cool liquid a contrast to the warmth it produced as it slid down my throat. I felt guilty and a bit embarrassed at the thoughts of Parker swirling in my head, but I blamed it on being tired...and the embrace we'd shared earlier. It had felt good, really good, to have his arms around me.

The thought made me frown. True, I'd always been attracted to Parker, but I needed to quit thinking like that. We had a professional relationship and that was all, no matter how sexy I found his controlling, power-wielding ways, which in itself felt like a reaction I shouldn't have to those particular traits. He was also incredibly smart, another weakness of mine when it came to men.

"You're probably wondering how Ryker and I know each other," Parker said.

I glanced up at him, my eyebrows lifting. I hadn't expected him to bring it up again, but he wasn't looking at me, at least, not at my face. His gaze seemed to be on my foot, dangling in midair from my crossed legs. The sunny yellow of my peep-toe pump cheered me a bit, as it always did. Parker's gaze slid up my leg, following my torso, until he met my eyes.

I cleared my throat delicately, trying to ignore that onceover. "The thought had crossed my mind."

His lips lifted slightly, giving me that pleased feeling I always got when I said something that amused him.

Parker leaned forward, bracing his elbows on his spread knees with the glass cradled in both hands, his gaze resting on the amber liquid in its depths.

"We grew up together, he and I," he began. "Met when we were just kids. We were thirteen, maybe fourteen. We lived in different parts of town, though. I was fortunate; my family was well-off and we lived in a good neighborhood. Ryker wasn't as lucky. He lived alone with his mom. His dad had run off and left them when he was five."

A pang of sympathy struck me. I'd been blessed with two parents who'd been happily married for over thirty years, but families like that weren't nearly as common anymore.

"How did you meet?" I asked. It sounded like Parker and Ryker had been on opposite sides of the proverbial tracks.

"He was one of those kids who lived in a bad part of town that they let attend a better school somewhere else. It was my school. He stood out, of course. The kids there were all wealthy and it was obvious he wasn't. I wanted to get to know him, somebody so different from anyone else I'd known, but he wasn't into making friends.

"Then one afternoon, I helped him out of a fight," he continued. "We were inseparable from then on, the poor little rich kid and the rebellious loner. Odd, looking back on it now, but we were kids. We fascinated each other."

I could picture it in my head, two scrawny teenage boys. One in worn clothes that were hand-me-downs, the other in pristine name brands, eyeing each other with suspicion and yet wanting to know more.

"So you're friends," I prompted when Parker didn't continue.

"We *were* friends," he corrected. "Past tense. Long story short, we joined the Marines together, even got assigned to the same platoon, but our friendship didn't last past our discharge."

Curiosity raged. Parker had been in the Marines? I'd had no idea. "Why not?"

"Life kind of got in the way," Parker mused, "and that's an even longer story." Lifting the glass to his lips, he drank the rest in one long swallow, set it on the coffee table, and stood. "I should be going," he said. "I just thought, after today, you had a right to know that while there's a past between Ryker and me, it didn't end happily. Be wary of him, if he comes around you anymore."

I nodded, wondering if I should confess about dinner Saturday, but Parker was already digging out his car keys and heading for the door. I hurriedly set down my glass and jumped up to see him out.

"Um, thanks for the ride home," I said as he opened the apartment door.

Parker turned to look at me. His gaze seemed to skate over

me before resting on my eyes. "You're welcome," he said. "You've worked for me for a while now, Sage. You're very… valuable to me."

Parker didn't do thank-yous or heap praise, so this comment sent a curl of pleasure through me. I smiled. "Thanks."

He gave a curt nod, then was gone, bypassing the elevator in favor of the stairs.

Closing and locking the door, I hurried to the window, pushing aside the curtains to look down at where he'd parked. A few moments later, I saw him emerge from the building and head to his car. Just before he opened the door to slip inside, he glanced up at the window.

I knew I was fully visible with the lights on behind me, but I didn't care. We stood locked in that tableau and I allowed myself to wish, however briefly, that there was more between us. But wishes were pointless and I couldn't change the truth. Parker needed me—I was "valuable" to him—and that would have to be enough. Because if it wasn't, if I ever acted on my feelings, then I'd have to leave him. And I couldn't handle losing Parker, so I'd take what he would give and be satisfied.

CHAPTER FOUR

Friday morning was merciless and pulling my ass out of bed with only four hours' sleep was an exercise in self-discipline, which I had very little of. If I had more, I'd have gotten myself to the gym, too. Megan was going to kill me for missing yet another workout.

Cheerful colors seemed inappropriate today—someone had died, after all—so I wore a black pencil skirt and a white blouse, somber and professional. Black slingback heels were also professional, but they had a scarlet red sole, which made me feel better. No one saw the bottom of my shoes anyway. I pinned up my hair like usual and tried to conceal the dark circles underneath my eyes with a pile of makeup. Scrutinizing myself in the mirror, I grimaced. I looked like I'd had a rough night out, and there was no amount of makeup that was going to fix that.

I had to run for the bus again, sending a smile to the driver who just grinned and shook his head at me. The coffee was ready to go when I got to Starbucks, as was Parker's Danish. He liked when I varied his breakfast, so I didn't get the same thing every day. He had a serious sweet tooth but was incredibly self-restrained about not giving in to it, so occasionally I gave him no choice but to indulge. I noticed he never complained.

I glanced longingly into the Dunkin' Donuts next to the Starbucks, but passed it by as I hurried in to the office. What I wouldn't have given for a jelly doughnut covered in sugar. Unfortunately, my luck would probably have had me wearing my breakfast on my blouse the rest of the day.

I'd just sat down at my desk when Parker stepped off the elevator. He was looking at his phone with one hand, while the other carried his briefcase. I wondered if what had happened last night would affect our relationship at all. I felt closer to him. His story about Ryker had given me a rare glimpse into his personal life.

To my disappointment, though, when he stopped in front of my desk it was business as usual.

"Good morning, Sage," he said, barely glancing up from his phone. "Any messages?"

I shook my head. "Nothing yet."

He nodded and headed into his office without so much as a glance at me. I tried not to be disappointed, but the lead in the pit of my stomach said otherwise. I didn't know what I had expected—maybe just a bit more warmth, a glance that was more personal, that showed I'd achieved something closer to friendship status than just merely being an assistant.

Shoving those thoughts away, I got to work. Due to the shooting and the fact that the police had cordoned off the upstairs, the all-day meeting Parker had scheduled was canceled and moved to the following week. That gave me some time before I had to finish cataloging the files.

I groaned. "Oh, shit," I muttered to myself. I'd forgotten about that. Now I was going to be crawling around on the floor in a pencil skirt, probably the least comfortable attire I could've worn. Stupid stupid. Well, I'd just wait until Parker left to go do something. No doubt I'd be scheduling three more meetings by noon for his suddenly open day.

"Tell me everything. And don't think I didn't notice you left me to sweat alone this morning."

I glanced up to see Megan leaning on the counter above my desk.

"I wondered how long it would be before you showed up," I teased.

"Rumor has it you were here last night when he got shot?" she asked. "Is that true?"

I nodded, sobering. "Yeah. It was scary. Parker and I were working when we heard a shot. He went to see what it was. Whoever killed Hinton shot at him, too, but missed."

Megan's eyes rounded. "Seriously? Wow."

"I know," I said.

"What did you do?"

"Parker stuffed me in his closet, told me to stay put." I shrugged. "So I did."

Her eyebrows lifted. "That was quick thinking of him," she said. "And chivalrous, too, protecting you like that." She grinned. "Real knight-in-shining-armor kind of stuff. Who'd have thought him capable?"

My eyes narrowed and I tried to keep cool. Lack of sleep had made me short-tempered. "I wasn't a bit surprised," I snapped.

Megan's eyebrows went even higher and her grin faded fast. "Hey, I'm sorry; that was rude to say. Don't be mad."

I sighed, my irritation melting away as quickly as it had risen. "It's fine. I only got like four hours' sleep, so I'm a total bitch today. Ignore me."

"Well, tell me how the date went," she said. "You know, with the cop who can come arrest me any day."

I laughed. "It was fine. Short. We had dinner, and then I came back here to work." I left out the part about Parker being the reason the date had been so short. I already knew what Megan would have to say to that.

She looked disappointed. "That's all? So, what, you didn't like him? Was he boring? All the really good-looking ones are. Or they're gay. He's not gay, right?"

I shook my head. "No, definitely not gay." The memory of riding behind him on the back of the motorcycle, my thighs rubbing against the denim of his jeans, sent a shiver through me. I wondered if he'd have his motorcycle tomorrow night. I lowered my voice, just in case Parker should come out of his office. "I have another date with him tomorrow night."

"No way! That's great!" Megan's face split in a wide smile.

"Wait," I said, suddenly frowning. "He didn't tell me where to meet him or a time." With everything going on last night, I hadn't thought to get details. "He just asked me out."

"He's a cop," Megan said with a shrug. "He can find out where you live. Maybe he'll call you today."

I shook my head. It didn't matter. Not really. If the date happened, great. If not, oh well. But I did have to tell her... "He has a motorcycle," I said, grinning. "We rode it to the restaurant."

"You rode a motorcycle?" she asked in disbelief.

"Miracles do happen," I said.

She laughed. "I guess so." Leaning over the counter, she asked, "So, if you go out with him tomorrow night, are you going to sleep with him?"

My face heated, as did my blood at the mere thought

of sleeping with Ryker, but I hesitated. "I don't know..." I
hedged. "It's a little soon—"

"Did you not see that body?" Megan asked. "*I've* been
fantasizing about it and I'm not the one having dinner with
him! You have to promise me that you'll at least think about
it, just for the sake of those who live vicariously through
you." She made a sad, pitiful face.

I rolled my eyes, but I was grinning. "Fine. But find your
own cop because even if I do sleep with him, don't think I'm
going to give you the details."

"Excuse me?"

I squeaked in surprise, jerking around to see Parker standing behind me, a file folder in his hand, his eyebrows up
nearly to his hairline. Oh God, had he just heard me talk
about sleeping with Ryker?

"Um, nothing," I managed, seeing Megan hurrying away
in my peripheral vision. "Just chatting for a minute."

He opened his mouth as if he was going to say something,
then shut it. "Can you have this messaged over to Hamlisch
& Thompson? As soon as possible, please." He handed me
the folder in his hand.

"Absolutely."

"I've spoken with Stan," he continued, naming our CEO,
Stan Wurley, "and he wants me to temporarily take over
Hinton's duties for the international division until he hires
someone."

Aw shit. That sucked. My work load had just doubled.

"To help out, Sawyer will be handling some of my stuff in
the interim as well," he said. Sawyer was one of Parker's un-
derlings. "Hinton was scheduled for a meeting in New York
next week, flying out Sunday night. Switch the travel plans
to myself."

I grabbed a pen and started scrawling notes while he talked.

"Meet with Hinton's assistant, see what I need to get up to speed on with that account, and have it on my desk by this afternoon. Book yourself for the trip, too. We should be back on Wednesday."

I glanced up. "Me too?" I hadn't ever gone to an out-of-town business meeting with Parker before, but he nodded.

"I'm not sure what I'll need on the fly so, yes, you're coming along, too."

Okay then.

He went over more things and I took notes rapid-fire before he left to meet a client for lunch.

I headed upstairs to find Hinton's assistant, combing my memory for her name. I'd met her a few times and she'd been really sweet. Sylvia. That was her name. In her early sixties, she'd worked for Hinton since he'd started at the firm.

Hinton's office had police tape across the door and heavy plastic had been hung across the glass walls, preventing anyone from seeing inside. Sylvia was digging through a drawer when I stepped up to the counter. In a style identical to my setup, a tall counter served as two walls to her cube.

"Hi, Sylvia," I said quietly. I wondered how she was doing, how she was taking the murder of her boss.

She glanced up and I got my answer. Not well. Her eyes were red-rimmed and swollen and she looked exhausted. When I'd caught glimpses of her before, she was always perfectly put together. But today her hair was slightly mussed and she wore no makeup.

"How are you doing?" I asked.

"Oh, honey, what an awful thing. I still—I just can't believe it," she said, shaking her head. Her eyes shone with tears.

"I'm so sorry," I said.

"They called last night, told me what happened, and of course I came right in," she said. "Mr. Hinton was a nice man, only two years from retiring. Why would anyone do such a thing?"

The question was rhetorical so I just rounded the counter into her cube, squeezing her shoulder sympathetically. "I have no idea," I said. "I hope the security and IT people will be able to figure out how the killer got in the building. Have you heard anything?"

She shook her head. "I'm just the secretary. They don't tell me anything." Reaching for a tissue, she blew her nose.

"I'm sorry to bother you," I said, "but I guess Mr. Wurley is having Parker take over Hinton's duties for now, until he...works things out. Can you give me the files on the client he was meeting in New York next week?"

Sylvia nodded, turning to a stack on her desk. "Sure. Here they are. They're new, Bank ZNT, out of Moscow."

I remembered Parker had wanted files on them yesterday afternoon, after Ryker had shown up. Taking the thick file from her, I flipped through it. "Haven't we already been buying from them?"

"Yes, but they're looking to expand the relationship. They have branches and ties to other banks in Ukraine, Belarus, Estonia..." She waved her hand. "All those countries over there, the old USSR."

I frowned. "I thought we weren't doing business with Russian countries."

The financial world knew to be on the lookout for any banks or firms that could have ties to the Russian mob. Of course, with the state-sponsored backing they had over there, it was hard to tell the good guys from the bad. Therefore it had become a policy of KLP Capital not to do business with them. The repercussions were too high should any transaction not be aboveboard, ranging from frozen assets to criminal prosecution.

"This one seems to be on the up-and-up," Sylvia said. "At least, Mr. Hinton thought so. He recommended to Mr. Wurley that we take them on. It's only been a couple of months since all the papers were signed."

"Okay, well, thanks," I said. "Can you have IT give us access to their account on the server?"

"Sure, honey."

I eyed her for a moment. "Is there anything you need?" I asked. "Anything I can get for you?" I couldn't imagine how I'd feel if something happened to Parker, and my heart went out to her.

"I'll be fine," she said. "I was planning on retiring when Mr. Hinton did. Maybe I'll just retire early, go visit my grandkids for a while. They're always wanting me to come stay with them."

"That sounds like a good idea," I said. "Let me know if there's anything I can do, okay? I imagine Parker will want more files than just this one."

"Sounds good to me," Sylvia said. Her smile was wan, but there nonetheless.

I impulsively gave her a quick hug before I headed back downstairs. I knew she was a widow with several children, some of whom obviously were old enough to have kids of their own. I hoped she'd retire and take that trip to see them. If nothing else, Mr. Hinton's murder was a reminder that life was finite and could end at any moment. Seize the day and not have any regrets.

That thought nagged at me as I returned to my desk. If something happened to me, would I have regrets? The answer was a big, fat yes, but I didn't want to dwell on it.

After leaving the file on Parker's desk, I grabbed Megan and we left for lunch. Since Parker was at a lunch meeting, that meant I could take some more time before he got back.

"So Parker's taking over Hinton's job for now," I said around a mouthful of apple-cranberry-chicken salad. "And we're going to New York next week."

"'We'?" Megan asked, spearing a lettuce leaf with her fork. "He's taking you?"

I nodded. "Cool, right?"

"Yes! I'm jealous. Of the trip, not that you'll be going with Parker," she added. "Do you think you'll get any downtime to shop?"

"I hope so," I said, nudging aside the mushy globs of croutons that were supposed to have been on the side but weren't. "Any more texting with Brian?"

She shrugged, immediately looking downcast. "Not really. I guess he's not much of a texter. He did e-mail me, though."

"Well, that's a good sign," I said, trying to encourage her. Megan was usually so cheery; it was almost painful to see her so depressed.

"He sent me a Bible verse."

I stared at her for a minute, sure I'd heard wrong; then I burst into laughter. I couldn't help it.

"I'm so sorry," I managed to say between giggles. "I don't mean to laugh."

"No, it's totally fine," she said with a wave of her empty fork. "I'd laugh, too, if it wasn't so incredibly pathetic. Is he trying to send me a message or something?"

I cleared my throat, swallowing down the laughter and dabbing at my tearing eyes. "Um, I don't know. What was the verse?"

"Some really long Psalm or something. I dunno." She

listlessly pushed the salad around her plate. "I think I should just give up, find someone else to obsess over."

"Don't give up yet," I said. "At least he was thinking about you, right?"

She brightened a bit at that. "Yeah, I guess so. I hadn't really thought of that."

"Well there you go." I unwrapped a cracker and ate it while she mulled that over. Maybe I should drop by Brian's desk sometime, drop him a hint on his thick head. But no, it was always a bad idea to get involved. Though there were always exceptions...

"Did you see the memo Security e-mailed today?" she asked, interrupting my thoughts of rationalizing a way for me to stick my nose in her business. "How we're not supposed to let anyone in the building who doesn't have a badge, all visitors have to be cleared first, yadda yadda yadda."

"Yeah, I saw it. I'm hoping Parker may have heard more," I said. "I'm going to quiz him when he gets back from lunch." I glanced at my watch. "Speaking of, I need to run by the cleaners before I go back. I'd better go." I shoved another huge bite in my mouth, hurriedly chewing as I grabbed my purse and tray.

"You're a total pushover, picking up his dry cleaning for him," Megan said, rolling her eyes.

I shrugged. "I don't mind. Have a good day and don't worry about Brian. Things will work out. And just remember, God loves you. He will spread his wings and give you shelter."

Megan just stared at me, eyes wide in surprise. "Uh..."

"I'm just screwing with you," I said with a wink.

"Oh my God, you are such a bitch," she said, bursting out laughing. Mission accomplished.

"Catch you later," I said.

She was still giggling and spearing another bite with her fork. I finger-waved as I dumped my tray and hurried out into the warm sunshine.

The dry cleaner wasn't far from the office, which was a good thing, because there were several suits in this batch and it got heavy quick. I was glad when I was finally able to hang them up in the closet in Parker's office. He could take them home tonight.

I called the travel desk for the firm and had them switch Hinton's ticket to New York into Parker's name as well as the hotel, then had them add me. Since I wasn't an executive, I'd be sitting in coach rather than first class like Parker, but that was okay. I was still going to New York.

Parker hadn't returned by the time that was done, which meant it was a perfect opportunity to finish the files in his office. Yeah, this skirt had been a bad idea. I had to hike it up past my knees just so I could bend. Now it was going to wrinkle.

I shook my head. Whatever. I just wanted this day to be over.

It took me several hours and it was pushing five o'clock by the time I was finally done. I'd just finished brushing myself off when the phone rang at my desk. I sighed as I hurried over to it. That was one nice thing about doing files after hours—the phone didn't ring. It had rung all afternoon and I'd been up and down enough times to count it as a workout.

"Sage, it's me," Parker said after I'd answered. "I won't be coming back to the office tonight. Take the cleaning by my place, if you would, and bring the ZNT file with you."

"Um, okay," I said, closing my eyes and rubbing a hand across my forehead. "Sure." I didn't have to do this very often, but tonight I'd really just wanted to go home and sleep.

NewYorkNewYorkNewYork.

Okay, I could suck it up for a three-day trip to New York.

"You have a key, right?" he asked.

"Yeah, I do. I'll drop off your things."

"Thank you, Sage." He disconnected.

Hmm. Another thank you. I could get used to that.

My arms were full when I left and it took a few minutes to hail a cab. "Yuck," I muttered, using my foot to shove aside some food wrappers on the floor. I gave the driver Parker's address.

I lived in a nice part of town. Parker lived in the expensive part of town. The rent for his condo cost thousands each month and I secretly envied the place. It was a gorgeous, two-bedroom with granite counters, a gas stove, and corner windows that overlooked downtown on one side and Lake Michigan on the other.

I juggled the clothes, my purse, Parker's briefcase, all while trying to unlock the door. Finally, I managed to get inside. I promptly dropped everything on his sofa, because my arms were aching. There were even indentations in my skin from the damn hangers.

"Oh, Parker! It's about time you got home! Have I got a surprise for y—" The singsong feminine voice abruptly cut off as I turned to see a woman come around the corner, clad in nothing but a thong and one of Parker's ties. She screamed, crossing her arms over her ample breasts. "Who the hell are you?"

With a sinking in my gut, I cursed Parker. He didn't have a girlfriend, no, but that didn't mean he didn't sleep around. Some women could be really persistent in trying to have a relationship with him, despite his near-brutal brush-offs. This looked like one of them.

"How did you get in here?" I asked. It wasn't as if Parker would ever give his key to one of them.

"None of your business," the blonde spluttered, her face beet red. "You didn't answer my question. Who are you?"

I raised an eyebrow. "I'm Mr. Anderson's assistant, and unless he gave you a key"—I could tell by her face he hadn't—"you're trespassing and need to go."

She tossed her long hair and straightened her spine, her brown eyes flashing. "I'm his girlfriend," she insisted. "This was a surprise for him."

"I'm sure him having a girlfriend certainly *will* be a surprise," I said, especially since he'd just told me last night that he wasn't dating anyone. I brushed past her into the bedroom. Seeing her clothes on the chair in the corner, I snatched them up. "Here's your clothes. Now, leave." I pushed them into her chest. Grabbing her arm, I started hauling her to the entry.

"He's going to fire you when I tell him what you did," she spat as I pulled open the door.

"Awesome," I said, shoving her through. "I could use a vacation." I reached for her, slipping the tie off her head quick as a wink, then slammed the door shut in her face.

I was going to have a talk with the doorman about this. Hell, maybe I should have a talk with Parker about this, not that it was really his fault. Guess he must be so good in bed he was beating them off with a stick. And no, I totally was *not* jealous. It was just…irritating, that's all.

I sniffed. Something smelled good. Had the blonde cooked dinner? No, it had probably been Deirdre, Parker's maid. She came by daily to straighten things and made dinner for him several times a week. I needed a Deirdre.

Wandering into the kitchen, I saw a covered dish on the stove. Lifting the lid, I took a whiff. Coq au vin. Yum. My stomach growled. Mashed potatoes sat in another dish. Maybe Parker wouldn't notice a little missing?

I spooned a bit of each onto a plate, eating it fast, afraid I'd get caught. Parker probably wouldn't say a word, just raise an eyebrow at me if he did catch me. My eyes drifted shut as I chewed. Deirdre was a really good cook.

After carefully washing the plate and fork, I grabbed the suits from the couch and headed into his bedroom. Now that Naked Girl was gone, I noticed she'd tried to set a "mood." Half a dozen candles burned around the room and for-real rose petals were sprinkled over the turned-down bed. Music played softly from the living room, drifting into the master bedroom. I snorted. Like a man needed any of that to want to get laid.

Opening the closet, I hung the suits, carefully removing the plastic coverings. Parker's closet was very organized, so I was sure to put them in the right order according to color and fabric weight. I hadn't known he'd been in the military, but now his compulsive closet organization made more sense.

Parker as a Marine. Okay, that was hot. I wondered if he still had his dress uniform. I'd pay a heck of a lot of money to see him in that. My imagination painted the picture in my head. Gorgeous in a suit, in a full Marine dress uniform, Parker would be...heavenly.

His bedroom smelled so much like him, it was like nirvana. Closing my eyes, I breathed deep the smell of spice and sandalwood and...Parker.

The sound of the front door opening and closing jerked me right out of my trance. I hurried to finish arranging the suits, unknotting and hanging the tie the girl had used when Parker appeared in the doorway.

"I was just finishing up," I said. He looked good today, as he did every day, no matter that he'd had about as much sleep as me last night. On him, you couldn't tell, of course.

"That's fine," he said, removing his cuff links as he headed for the armoire. "I finished earlier than—" He abruptly cut off. "Sage, why are there rose petals in my bed?"

Glancing around, I saw him holding one of the petals as though it were a dead insect. His gaze met mine and he raised an eyebrow.

"Oh yeah," I hurried to explain. "Funny story. Some girl was here, said she was your girlfriend. I . . . asked her to come back some other time." Euphemisms weren't lying.

"Girlfriend?" he asked. "I don't have a girlfriend."

My smile was thin. "That's what *I* said. Hope you don't mind me showing her out." Maybe I should've let her stay? Parker might've wanted some . . . companionship tonight. I ignored the little green imp on my shoulder at that. No sense feeling jealous over something I shouldn't want and could never have.

"No. Thank you for doing so. If it was who I think it was, then she's the last person I want to deal with tonight."

I bit my tongue to keep from asking who the girl was, instead turning my attention back to the closet. Parker continued on his way to the armoire and I heard the slight sounds of him discarding his cuff links and wristwatch.

It was oddly intimate, being in his bedroom while he did that. Though I supposed it was also kind of insulting that he didn't even notice or care that I was there. *Let's not think of that.* I heard the slide of silk that told me he was unknotting his tie. Parker . . . sort of undressing . . . in his bedroom. Yum.

I finished the closet, closed the doors, and turned to leave when the rose petals on the bed caught my eye. They'd stain the linens if they weren't picked up, so I started gathering them.

"You don't have to do that," Parker said. "I'll do it later."

"No, they'll stain," I said, setting a knee on the mattress and reaching for the ones scattered on the pillows. "If you break them at all or squash them, that red color is a total pain to get out." The minute I said it, I prayed he wouldn't ask me how I knew that.

"Sage—"

"I'm almost done," I cut him off, scrambling to grab the petals before he could stop me. There. That was all of them.

My hands full of velvety petals, I scooted back off the bed and stood, turning to find Parker right in front of me. I nearly fell backward again, but he caught my elbow, righting me.

"Oops, sorry," I said with a sheepish smile. He was looking at me oddly and I figured I had to look pretty ridiculous, crawling around his bed and now with a huge handful of rose petals. I lifted my hands slightly. "Got 'em. No stains."

"Yeah, rose petal stains on the sheets would have kept me up nights."

I blinked. Had Parker just made a joke?

"I know, right?" I deadpanned. His lips twitched.

For a moment, neither of us moved. His hand still lightly gripped my elbow as he looked down at me. His cologne had faded, but he was so close, I could still smell it combined with the scent of his skin. If someone could bottle that combination, they'd make a fortune. The fabric of his slacks brushed my bare legs below my skirt, sending a wave of goose bumps over me.

I gazed into his eyes, unblinking. Acutely aware of the very available bed at my back, I wondered what Parker would do if I sank down onto the mattress and tugged him down with me. Did he find me attractive? Would he kiss me?

Or would he push me away in shocked disgust at my forwardness? Would he be disappointed that I'd "gone there" and ruined the good working rapport that we had? There was nothing on the planet more cliché than a secretary and her boss.

Either outcome would spell the end of my job and my relationship with Parker. He didn't do relationships... and he didn't sleep with his secretary. I refused to even contemplate losing what we did have, platonic though it might be, which meant there was really only one option for me.

"So I'd better get going," I said, sidling out from between Parker and the bed.

He released me at once, although it felt as though the imprint of his hand on my skin remained.

"Yes. Thank you for bringing everything here," he said, following me as I headed for the kitchen.

I dumped the rose petals in the trash, his comment reminding me. "I'll just leave the file on your desk," I said, retrieving the thick ZNT file and heading into the second bedroom, which Parker had made into an office. I set the folder on his desk and a moment later was grabbing my purse. Nearly at the door, I glanced back and saw Parker had poured himself a scotch.

He stood with his back to me, staring out the windows at the city skyline, the crystal glass with an inch of amber liquid held at his side. As I hesitated, he tipped up the drink, emptying the contents in one swallow.

Hmm. Parker rarely drank like that. Must've been a rough day.

I felt a pang of sympathy and wished I was someone he confided in, someone he could unburden himself to, but knew I wasn't that person to him. Did he have anyone he confided in? I wasn't sure. He had guy friends, but guys had odd friendships, so I couldn't say for sure.

"Is there anything else?" I asked. All I could really do for him was to just do my job the best I could and try to anticipate anything he might need or want. I thought I was pretty good at both those things.

Parker glanced around. "No, that'll be all, Sage."

I nodded. "Okay. Have a nice weekend."

"You too."

The door closed softly behind me.

Standing on the sidewalk outside, I glanced up the street for a taxi. Nothing in sight yet. I sighed. I couldn't wait to get home and go to bed. People passed me by, but it wasn't super busy. Parker's area was nice and I didn't worry about being out here alone at night.

Glancing around as I waited, a man caught my eye. He was standing about ten feet away, dressed in a dark suit, and had just lit a cigarette. Unlike everyone else, he didn't seem to be going anywhere and just stood there, leisurely smoking. There was something about him that made me abruptly decide I wouldn't want to run into him in a dark alley. He was huge, with hands that looked like they could crush me into a fine powder. A tattoo of barbed wire crossed his knuckles. Nice.

As if he sensed my gaze on him, he shifted and looked right at me. A chill went through me and I hurriedly glanced away, gripping my purse a bit tighter. Time to go.

Lifting my arm, I stepped into the street, finally spotting a cab. I flagged it down and it pulled to a stop a short ways away. Hurrying to it, I opened the door and was just getting in when a voice said, "Mind if we share?"

I had no chance to respond as I was forcefully shoved into the backseat. I scrambled to right myself, turning to give a piece of my mind to the jackass that had confiscated my ride, but my words died on my tongue.

It was barbed-wire guy.

CHAPTER FIVE

The cab wasn't yet moving so I grabbed the handle of the door on my side, wanting to get out. He could have this cab. I'd catch another one.

"You stay." His huge palm wrapped around my upper arm and squeezed. It hurt and I winced. Now I was scared. He had an accent, but I couldn't place it. Eastern European or something—German, maybe, or Russian. I was awful with accents. Really, I could only narrow it down to "not British." He sounded nothing like Benedict Cumberbatch.

"Forget it! Let me go!"

He squeezed so hard, tears came to my eyes.

"Cooperate and this will be a short ride," he said, his voice a low growl. "Otherwise—"

"Hey, where to?" the cabbie interrupted.

"Tell him," the man ordered, but I hesitated. I didn't want this guy to know where I lived. "Tell him," he repeated, and this time he didn't sound as friendly. He jerked me, and I felt like my arm nearly came out of the socket. I gasped in pain, then blurted out my address. The car started to move and his grip eased.

"Let go of me," I said, trying unsuccessfully to tug my arm away, "or I'll tell him to drive to the nearest police station."

"I wouldn't do that if I were you," he said. He lifted his jacket, revealing a gun tucked underneath his arm in a holster. I swallowed.

"What do you want? I have money in my purse. Take it and go."

He laughed outright. "I don't want money. Just to have a conversation," he said, his accent thick. He finally let me go. He'd gripped me so hard it had cut off the circulation and now my arm tingled as the blood started flowing again. "You are Sage Reese, correct? Assistant to Parker Anderson?"

How did he know my name? And Parker's? Had he seen me come out of Parker's apartment building? I pressed my lips together and didn't answer.

"We know everything about you," he said, waving his hand. "So is not necessary for you to answer."

"Who is 'we'?"

"Mr. Anderson has inherited some very important clients. They like to keep a close eye on who handles their money," he said. "They like their business to remain very...private."

My phone started buzzing in my purse, but I ignored it. I didn't want to take my eyes off this guy, afraid of what else he might do to me.

"Listen, I don't know who you are or why you feel it's necessary to...to accost me like this, but that's not how we do business." I tried to sound firm, but my bravado was short-lived.

He shoved his face closer to mine and I jerked back, plastering myself against the door.

"It's how *we* do business," he hissed. "Remember that…
Sage." He smiled as he said my name, revealing a gold tooth.

I barely breathed, my heart pounding so loud I was sure
he could hear it. Fear made my palms sweat, and the acrid
scent of his body as he loomed over me made my skin crawl.

As suddenly as he'd gotten in my face, he pulled back.
"Pull over," he barked. The cabbie hurried to obey.

"We'll be watching. Be sure to tell your boss." He flashed
another sinister grin; then he was gone.

I gasped a breath, sucking in air. My entire body was
shaking and I struggled not to burst into tears.

"Hey, lady, you okay?" the cabbie asked, turning around
in his seat.

"Oh, *now* you're concerned!" I snapped. "Just take me
home."

He said nothing further, just stepped on the gas. Time to
add another entry to my list of Why I Hate Cabs: willfully
oblivious drivers.

I'd recovered somewhat by the time we pulled up to my
building. I handed the driver money and hurried to the door,
eager for the safety of my apartment. It wasn't until I was
ensconced inside that I allowed the mental breakdown I'd
promised myself in the taxi.

My hands trembled as I poured myself a stiff drink, bourbon straight up. My eyes were damp and I sniffed before
taking a deep swallow. Glancing down at my arm, I saw the
marks his fingers had left on my skin, which were rapidly
turning into bruises. That made my eyes water even more.

Nothing like that had ever happened to me before. No one
had ever deliberately hurt me, not physically, and it shook
me more than I'd have thought possible. I felt vulnerable and
very much alone.

A sudden pounding on my door startled me so badly that

I dropped my glass. It shattered on the wooden floor. Glancing frantically around, I realized I had no weapon, nothing to defend myself. Spotting the butcher block on the counter, I grabbed the seven-inch-long chef's knife.

The banging came again as I cautiously approached the door.

"Sage, are you in there? Sage!"

I sagged in relief. Parker. I didn't question why he was there; I was just glad he was, and I threw open the door. As soon as I saw him, I started to cry.

"What happened? Are you okay?" He was inside in the blink of an eye. I was crying too hard to talk, so I just nodded. His lips thinned as he looked at me; then he carefully took the knife from the death grip I had on it, setting it aside. Wrapping his arms around me, he shushed me. "It's all right."

I huddled against his chest, tears leaking from my eyes that I knew would stain mascara on his shirt and I'd have to argue with the dry cleaners to have them get it out, but I didn't care. His chin rested on the top of my head as he soothed me. I felt much better in his arms. Parker was tall and solidly built. Without my heels, the top of my head only reached his shoulder.

"You're shaking," he said, once my crying had devolved into sniffles. "Tell me what happened. I saw a man climb into the taxi with you. When you didn't answer your phone, I drove over here."

My phone. I'd forgotten to look and see who'd been calling me.

"He said he was with a client," I said. "Your client. And that they valued their privacy. I'm supposed to tell you that they're watching." Leaning back, I looked up at him. "What does that mean? Do you know what he was talking about?"

The look on Parker's face was grim. He produced a pocket square and wiped gently at my wet cheeks, dabbing the skin beneath my eyes. "Yeah. I do."

When he said nothing more, I added, "He had a gun."

Parker paused in his ministrations. "Did he hurt you?"

I shrugged. "Grabbed my arm. Just a few bruises." I tried to brush it off, but the quaver in my voice betrayed me.

He muttered a curse under his breath, pulling away to inspect my arm, his fingers exceedingly gentle on the abused skin. His jaw locked tight and I knew him well enough to know he was furious.

"I'll take care of it," he said, his eyes meeting mine. "They won't hurt you again."

I nodded. "Okay." My voice wasn't that strong and I took a ragged breath. I didn't know what was going on or what he planned to do, but I trusted Parker that if he said he'd take care of it, then he would.

Turning away, I crouched down on the floor and started picking up glass. Thankfully, the glass had been heavy so was just in a few big pieces rather than tiny shards. To my surprise, Parker helped, and a few minutes later it was cleaned up.

"Why don't you go change," he suggested, tossing the last of the glass into the garbage. "I'll pour you another drink."

That sounded wonderful and I didn't argue. In my bedroom, I discarded the skirt and blouse, pulling on a pair of faded denim shorts and a White Sox T-shirt I'd had for years. I sighed when I took down my up-do, running a brush through my long hair. Not professional, but I didn't care. My makeup had streaks so I washed it all off, feeling much better by the time I stepped back into my living room.

I noticed Parker had poured me another drink, and himself one, too. Glancing up, he caught sight of me. His gaze made a quick trip down my body and back up, but he didn't say anything. I didn't know what he'd expected me to change into, but it certainly wasn't going to be another skirt and heels.

"Here you go," he said, rounding the kitchen counter and handing me one of the glasses. "This will help."

I took it from him and took a drink. The bourbon burned like fire and I coughed. "What did you do with my knife?" I asked, once I could speak without sounding three-packs-a-day.

"I put it back," he said. "Let's not answer the door with knives again, shall we? Odds are you'd only end up hurting yourself."

I shrugged, heading to the couch where I sat, pulling my knees to my chest. "I didn't have anything else."

Parker followed, sitting closer than I thought he would have. "Do you own a gun?" he asked.

I looked at him askance. "Are you kidding? You know what a pain in the ass and all the crap you have to go through to own a gun in Chicago." Which was why I hadn't mentioned his having one to the cops. Parker would've gotten in big trouble having a handgun in the building.

We sat in companionable silence for a few minutes, and the bourbon no longer burned as I sipped it. I felt much better now, and was embarrassed for how I'd fallen apart earlier.

"Listen, I'm sorry about losing it," I said, keeping my eyes on the amber fluid that remained in my glass. "It's just that nothing like that's ever happened to me before, and it scared me."

"You don't have to apologize," he said.

"Yeah, but I always thought I was made of tougher stuff than that, and when it came down to it, it looks like I'm a big marshmallow." So much for channeling my inner Sarah Connor. Badass I was *not*. I upended the glass, swallowing the last of the bourbon.

Reaching over, Parker took the empty glass from me, setting it on the coffee table. "It's not your fault," he said. "You're a secretary, not a cop."

"Executive administrative assistant," I mumbled, automatically correcting him.

His lips curved upward ever so slightly as he looked at me, the corners of his eyes crinkling. His blue gaze was captivating, even at this hour. I decided I could get used to this Parker, more relaxed and approachable than he was at the office.

"My mistake," he said seriously, though his eyes twinkled.

I smiled a little, too. "Let's not have it happen again," I said, raising an eyebrow in mock admonishment.

Parker didn't reply, the smile lingering as he looked at me, and his gaze moved over my hair and all the way down to my pink-tipped toes before returning to meet my eyes. My arms were wrapped around my knees and I tightened my hold, my fingers itching to reach for him. He should really go. My defenses were way down and I was inches away from doing something I'd regret.

"Thanks for coming here," I said. "For helping."

He must have recognized the dismissal because he nodded. Tipping up his own glass, he finished off the bourbon and set it alongside mine on the table.

"I'll be going then," he said, getting to his feet. I hurried to copy him. "You'll be all right?" he asked.

"Yeah, I'm fine," I said, nervously running my fingers through my hair. His eyes followed the movement. "So, you'll take care of it? He won't...come around again?"

At the mention of the guy, Parker's face hardened and his eyes grew cold. "I'll make sure of it. But if you see anything, if something scares you, call me, okay? I don't care what time it is."

"Okay." No problem there. I had no desire to try and be the hero and deal with Mr. Gold Tooth on my own.

Parker nodded, as though satisfied I'd do as he said, then headed out the door. I watched him go, thinking how odd it seemed that, before last night, he'd never been to my apartment, and now he'd been here twice in as many days. Hurrying to the window, I saw him get into his car and drive away, and only then did it hit me that he must've been doing the exact same thing when I'd left his apartment earlier.

* * *

I slept until noon on Saturday and when I finally climbed out of bed, I felt much better than I had the night before. After brewing a cup of coffee with my Keurig, I checked my cell. I had a missed call and voice mail from a number I didn't recognize. Curious, I listened to the message.

"Sage, it's Ryker. Don't think I've forgotten about our dinner tonight. I'll pick you up at seven."

Hmm.

With everything else going on I had forgotten all about our date, and I couldn't help the shiver of excitement the low growl of his voice in my ear produced. Now I just had six hours to kill before he got here.

Rarely did a Saturday go by that I didn't hear from Parker, but it seemed he was giving me a break today. I should've been glad. Instead, I found I missed hearing his voice, even if it was just to ask me where I'd put a file or to tell me to schedule a conference call.

I changed my toe color to *Blue My Mind* and repainted my nails the pale neutral pink that was suited for the office. It's not like I could have crazy nails on my hands, but with my toes I could do whatever I wanted.

I scrutinized my closet, trying to figure out exactly what to wear tonight. If he picked me up, did that mean another motorcycle ride? If so, then a skirt or dress was probably out. It'd have to be jeans or shorts.

Ryker had said I was a "bombshell." I wanted to make him say that again, so I reached in the back of my closet, hauling out a pair of denim shorts that were so tight they looked painted on. I pulled them on over my black bikini panties, added a black bra, then dug in my closet again for a shirt.

I had a black chiffon blouse with elbow-length sleeves that was utterly see-through, but had a pocket over each breast, preserving a bit of modesty. After a moment of hesitation, I put it on, being sure to leave enough buttons undone to do justice to my cleavage. Victoria's Secret models had nothing on me, thanks to their padded, add-two-sizes pushup Wonderbra.

My hair was down and I'd put curlers in earlier that I took out, using my fingers to separate the curls into waves. A pair of black heels with straps that wrapped around my ankles, a couple of long silver necklaces, and big silver hoop earrings completed my transformation from Goody Two-shoes secretary into Saturday-night-hottie. I hoped.

I transferred my wallet, keys, and cell into a smaller, black purse with a long, silver chain strap I could wear across my body. Again, thinking of the motorcycle. At this rate, I was going to be disappointed if he didn't bring the damn thing.

I was debating the wisdom of having a drink to calm my

nerves when I heard a knock on my door. Looked like Megan had been right. He'd had no problem finding out my address, or my cell number, come to think of it.

Glancing through the peephole, I caught my breath. It was him all right.

Pulling open the door, I couldn't help the smile stretching across my face. He looked...mouthwatering.

Low-rise jeans that clung to his hips and legs, a navy T-shirt a tad on the small side that stretched to encase his chest and arms, and a black leather jacket over that. The glint of metal at his side beneath the jacket told me he had his weapon on him, which was hot. His mirrored aviators were hooked on the front of his shirt and he had the slightly scruffy jaw that said it had been over twenty-four hours since he'd shaved.

"I'm not late, am I?" he asked, his lips twisted in a half-smile. His gaze was taking me in head to toe the same way I was him.

"I think you know you're not," I replied. "Want to come in?"

I stepped back so he could come inside, taking a deep whiff of his cologne as he passed by me, so close the buttery leather of his jacket brushed my arm.

"This is a nice place," he said, glancing around.

"Thanks. Can I get you a drink?" But he shook his head.

"I'm driving, but thanks."

"Okay, well give me a second and I'll be ready to go. Is this outfit all right for where we're going?" I sat on the couch and reached for one of my heels, slipping it on and wrapping the leather strands around my ankle before fastening it. When Ryker didn't immediately reply, I glanced up at him, but his gaze was fixed on my leg. I grinned. "Ahem."

He jerked his gaze to mine and didn't look even mildly abashed at having been caught staring. Instead, he grinned.

"If not, we'll go somewhere else, because you look smokin' hot in that."

Amazing what being called "smokin' hot" did for a girl's ego.

I wasn't surprised to see the motorcycle parked outside.

"This messes up my hair, you know," I complained as Ryker strapped a helmet to my head.

"Nah," he said. A wicked grin curved his lips as he slid his sunglasses back on. "It gives you that 'just fucked' look. Pretty damn sexy, if you ask me."

My jaw dropped in shock, but his grin only widened. He slung a leg over the motorcycle and reached for me. I closed my mouth with a snap, feeling my cheeks burning as I climbed on behind him.

I'd hoped my new look tonight would make me feel on the same level as Ryker, but he could still one-up me.

He drove us to a restaurant I'd never been to before, a little Italian place that seemed to be family-run. The hostess, an older woman in her sixties, greeted him by name and pressed a kiss to each cheek.

"It's about time you show your face around here," she said, admonishing him with a smile.

"I've been busy," Ryker said. "But I'm here tonight, and look, I brought a date." Taking my hand, he tugged me forward. "This is Sage. Sage, this is Dorothea."

I held out my hand. "Nice to meet you."

Dorothea waved away my hand, instead grasping my arms and planting a kiss on my cheek.

"Any friend of Dean's is a friend of ours," she said. "Come, let me show you to your table."

It was a cozy place with little tables and booths situated in private alcoves with fake ivy tucked into the ceiling and around the wooden beams. Candles were lit on every table and the booth she showed us to was a round one. I sat, scooting around so there was room for Ryker, who discarded his jacket and slid in next to me.

"A bottle of wine?" Dorothea asked, handing us menus. "I'll bring a bottle of Chianti," she added, without waiting for Ryker to respond, "and some calamari"; then she was gone.

He turned to look at me. "Hope you like calamari," he said, grinning. "We may get to order our own meals, but I doubt it. Dorothea usually has Roberto make me something, whatever's fresh that day. It's always amazing."

I set down the menu. "Sounds good to me."

And he was right. Dorothea came back with the wine and fresh, crisply fried calamari. She returned again with two plates while three men followed in her wake, each holding a skillet with a different dish of freshly made pasta, which they scooped onto our plates. She chattered the whole time, telling us what the dishes were and then shooing the men away and refilling our glasses.

"This is the best pasta I've ever had," I said, twining long strands of angel hair around my fork.

"Thought it would be better than a salad at a cop bar," Ryker said.

I laughed. "Definitely." We'd polished off the better part of the bottle of wine and I was feeling tipsy and very relaxed. Ryker's denim-clad thigh rested against my leg, his shoulder brushing against me as he ate. I caught myself more than once staring at his hands, large with calloused palms, his fingers deftly maneuvering the pasta. My mind drifted in the direction my hopping hormones were highly in favor of.

"So, I'm pretty sure you promised me the inside scoop on you and Parker," I said, pushing the mental images away and taking another sip of wine.

"That I did," Ryker replied, taking a drink from his own

wineglass. "It's not a pretty story. You sure you want to ruin the evening so soon, talking about that asshole?"

My eyes narrowed. "I told you—" I began.

"I know, I know. He's your boss, don't talk bad about him, yadda yadda yadda," he interrupted. "Sorry. I won't do it again, okay?"

"All right," I grudgingly agreed. Parker hadn't stooped to calling Ryker names, even though he had warned me away from him.

"Parker and I go way back," Ryker said, pushing away his empty plate. He leaned back in the booth and crossed his arms over his chest, drawing my eye to his very nicely muscled biceps. "We grew up together, sort of, though we come from different backgrounds."

I remembered what Parker had told me about him and Ryker on the opposite sides of the tracks, so to speak, but didn't say anything. I wanted to know how Ryker characterized their relationship, now that I'd heard Parker's side.

"Anyway, we were buddies up through high school, even joined the Marines together. But when we came back, he stole a girl from me, and that showed me what he was really made of, when it came right down to it."

My eyes widened. Parker had said nothing about a girl.

"He stole a girl from you?" I repeated. "What do you mean?" I was pretty darn sure Parker wasn't hiding a wife somewhere.

"Her name was Natalie," he said. Ryker wasn't looking at me now, instead staring at his empty wineglass as his fingers toyed with the stem. "She was sweet, and young, and way too damn trusting."

"What happened to her?"

Now he glanced up at me, and the pain in his eyes made my breath catch.

"She died."

Wow. Ryker had been right. Talk about putting a damper on the whole evening. Nothing like discussing a tragedy to bring the mood way down.

"I'm sorry." I was at a loss as to know what else to say.

Ryker seemed to shake off his black mood, reaching to empty the rest of the wine into our glasses. "It is what it is," he said with a shrug. "And it was years ago."

While it may have been years ago, it certainly didn't seem like he was over it. I wanted to know more details about what had happened, how Parker had "stolen" Natalie from him, but thought it would be insensitive of me to ask, so I kept my mouth shut.

Dorothea came back then and I gave an internal sigh of relief. Her chatter helped break the awkward silence. She set a plate of cannoli in front of us, and despite how full I was from the pasta, I reached for one. The crispy shell melted in my mouth.

"So why did you become a cop?" I asked, washing down the creamy ricotta with the last of my wine. Nothing got the conversation ball rolling again like asking a man to talk about himself.

"The idea of putting criminals behind bars appealed to me," he said. "The neighborhood I grew up in was a rough one, and it always pissed me off how the gangs ran things and the cops just avoided getting involved. I didn't want kids to have to go through what I did just to get to school each day."

He seemed very matter-of-fact, like I should know what he was talking about, but I had no clue. My going to school had consisted of Schultz, our driver, taking me in the back of the Rolls-Royce to a private school my parents had paid out the nose for in tuition. We'd worn uniforms and our lunches were freshly made choices of things like tuna niçoise salad or roasted vegetables on ciabatta.

Ryker glanced at me and caught the blank expression on my face. His smile was rueful. "Sorry. You probably don't know what I'm talking about. Lake Forest is a long way from the south side of Chicago."

"So tell me about it then," I said, but he shook his head.

"Nah. You wanna hear it even less than I want to tell it." He cracked his practiced grin again. "Tell me what you like to do for fun, Sage."

I swallowed my disappointment. It was so obvious that he was just putting the moves on me, steering away from anything too personal. Now that I'd seen a little underneath, it was that much easier to spot when the real Ryker disappeared and the player came out.

I had a decision to make. It seemed Ryker was an expert at adding to what I was sure was a long list of conquests, and the question was, did I want to be the latest entry? While Megan had pushed me to take advantage of all the assets Ryker displayed—as well as others currently hidden— I found myself lacking enthusiasm for being another notch in his belt. I also had the suspicion that regardless of the "bombshell" and "smokin' hot" comments, Ryker wouldn't have looked at me twice without the connection to Parker.

Kind of a waste, though, I thought, my gaze again landing on Ryker's hands.

No no no. Don't go there.

"Um, I don't know," I said, remembering he'd asked me a question. "I like to shop." An understatement, though since I was paying my own bills now, the trips to Saks and Nordstrom were fewer and farther between than I'd like.

"Shop?" Ryker twitched an eyebrow in distaste. I laughed.

"I like baseball," I said.

"Cubs fan?"

I rolled my eyes. "Please. White Sox."

He grinned. "Me too. They've got a game tomorrow afternoon. Wanna go?"

The temptation was strong—I adored going to White Sox games—but I shook my head. "Thanks, but I need to pack tomorrow."

"Where are you going?"

"Parker has a meeting in New York with some new clients," I explained. "We leave Monday."

Ryker leaned forward. "Really. So what new clients?"

"Um, I'm not really supposed to discuss our clients," I hedged. "Privacy and such."

"I'm sure you could tell me a little bit without breaking any rules," he teased. "They're in New York then?"

"Um, yeah," I said, wondering at his sudden interest. "But they're Russian, I think."

Ryker's gaze sharpened. "Russian, eh? So are they with some corporation or bank?"

Now alarm bells were going off. There was no earthly reason why Ryker should want to know about some new clients of Parker's.

The man's words from last night echoed in my head. It occurred to me that maybe I should tell Ryker about it—he was a cop, after all—but I also knew he might think Parker was doing something illegal, even though he wasn't, so I kept my mouth shut.

"Have you found anything out about who killed Mr. Hinton?" I asked, changing the subject. "Or how they even got in the building?"

Ryker turned his body toward me, resting an arm behind my shoulders on the back of the booth. My pulse rate shot up at his proximity and I avidly drank in the up-close view of his chest and arms. Tearing my gaze away, I looked up to find his blue eyes glinting knowingly. Yes, Ryker was very much aware of his appeal, which should have been a turn-off, but wasn't.

"Well, I'm not supposed to talk about that," he teased. "Unless you want to exchange information, then I might be persuaded to share."

My eyes narrowed. "That's not fair."

"I never said I was fair, sweetheart."

How Ryker could get away with calling me "sweetheart," I had no idea. I should be pissed with righteous indignation at the condescending endearment. *Should* being the operative word. All I *really* wanted was to hear him say it again, only in a growly way. Minus his shirt.

"It's just a new client, that's all," I said with a shrug. "I think Mr. Hinton was going to handle the account, but now Parker's doing his job until the firm hires someone else. They're based overseas—in Moscow—and Parker's meeting with some of the head guys in New York this week."

The playboy persona was gone now, Ryker's expression serious as I told him this, and I felt a niggling of apprehension. But I hadn't divulged anything private, not really.

"Your turn," I urged him.

"The shooter got into your building by hacking the security," Ryker replied. "Very sophisticated, very hard to do, and proving impossible to trace."

Wow. That wasn't what I'd been expecting.

"Listen, Sage, I'm going to come clean with you," Ryker said. That made my ears perk up. *Come clean*? What was that supposed to mean? "I think you're the kind of girl who does the right thing. Am I right?"

"Yeah, I guess so," I said, confused now. What did this have to do with anything?

"I've been on this one case for a while," Ryker said. "The Russian mob has a strong presence here in Chicago, and we've been working on shutting them down, or at least making a dent in their organization. But they have their tentacles everywhere, and one way they keep themselves clean is by laundering their money through investment firms, just like the one where you work."

A sinking sensation in my stomach told me I knew where this was going.

"We don't have anyone on the inside who can help us," he continued, "and we can't get information without a subpoena, but to have a subpoena, you have to show cause, which we can't do. Yet. I thought maybe you might be willing to help us. This client you have, the one out of Moscow, they may very well be a front for these people."

And I was right. Ryker hadn't been interested in me at all, at least, not in the way that had me dressing like a motorcycle slut on a Saturday night. That sinking sensation became an all-out ten-pound ball of lead.

"They're awful people, Sage," Ryker said. "They're into everything bad you can imagine. From drugs, to guns, prostitution, human trafficking. You name it, they do it. And all the billions they make get funneled through banks in Europe and America, and come out squeaky clean on the other side."

"What can I do about it?" I asked with a shrug. Yeah, it sounded awful, but I was just a glorified secretary with a nice title.

Ryker's lips twisted. "You're kidding, right? You work for the top investment firm in Chicago. Your boss is the number one name in town for foreign investments."

Surprised, I said, "I thought you hated Parker."

"I do, but that doesn't blind me to the fact that he's a genius at that shit. If anyone would be able to untangle the financial web behind these people, it's him."

"Then why don't you just ask *him* to do it for you," I said. "Why bother with me?"

Ryker's face turned grim. "Because—now don't freak out—we think Parker may be involved."

My jaw was agape as I stared at him; then I got mad. I grabbed my purse. "I'm out of here." I started to slide out of the booth, but Ryker latched on to my arm, yanking me back.

"I said not to freak out," he said.

"If you think Parker's involved in something like that, then you're crazy," I retorted, trying to pull away, but he easily held me.

"Just hear me out," Ryker said, and gone was the friendly hot guy. Now he was in scary cop mode, and it intimidated me. I stilled. "How well do you know Parker? Really know him?"

"I've worked for him for—"

"I didn't ask how long you've *worked* for him," Ryker interrupted. "I asked how well you *know* him."

That shut me up, because the truth was, I didn't know Parker at all, not in the way Ryker meant. I wasn't his confidante, wasn't privy to his innermost thoughts or his private affairs. We had a very good working relationship and I could tell you all about his personal habits, work routine, what it meant if he wore a navy tie to work versus a red one, and the exact temperature he liked his coffee (180°F). But know him? I hadn't until two days ago even known he'd been in the Marines.

"I don't," I said at last, and it hurt to admit it. It hurt to stop and think of just how much time and energy I devoted to Parker and my job only to realize that at the end of the day . . . we weren't even friends. Not really.

Ryker sighed. "Listen, I know you don't want to hear this, but it's not like we make things up, Sage. We have good cause to be suspicious of Parker. And maybe he's just gotten in over his head. You can help us. You may even be able to help Parker."

That got my attention. If the cops thought Parker was involved in something bad, and I had the opportunity to help him by proving them wrong, then I really had no choice.

"What would I have to do?" I asked. "I'm not a cop."

"You don't have to be. Just be observant. Make note of names, titles, what they look like, anything they do or say that seems odd or suspicious. That's all."

"How will that help Parker?"

"If these guys are legit, then it's no problem and we can clear him," he said.

"And if they're not?"

Ryker's face was grave. "Then you want us to get involved. These people are dangerous, extremely dangerous, and you don't want anything to happen to Parker, or yourself."

I had the impression he was manipulating me, that he knew exactly how I felt about Parker, and that he was using that against me. Which was obviously a very good ploy because there was no way I was going to turn down the chance to either clear Parker's name or help get him out of the clutches of the bad guys.

"Okay, I'll do it," I said.

Ryker smiled. The satisfaction in his eyes pricked my pride, but what was I to do? He'd effectively maneuvered me.

"Can we go now?" I asked. I was so ready for this "date" to be over.

"Yeah, sure." He dug in his back pocket for his wallet and tossed some money on the table. Although we didn't have our bill, I figured he must come here often enough to know what it cost.

Dorothea pressed another round of kisses to our cheeks on our way out; then Ryker and I were standing by his motorcycle.

I really didn't want to get on the bike with him again. It wasn't like I thought this was a real date, not after what he'd just told me.

"I'm just gonna catch a cab," I said, sidling away from Ryker. I glanced down the street and saw one coming. Perfect.

"Don't tell me you're still afraid of my bike," Ryker said, grasping my elbow and tugging me back toward him. His lips were lifted in a half-smile.

I snorted. "I'm not afraid of your bike, but I'm pretty sure this date is over." I resisted the urge to quote "date" with my fingers, but only just barely.

"I thought maybe we'd grab a drink somewhere," he said.

The heat from his touch seared through the thin material of my blouse and my gaze dropped from his eyes to his mouth. I'd bet my next paycheck that Ryker knew how to kiss, like *really* knew. Too bad I wouldn't be finding out. I jerked my eyes back up to his.

"I don't like the lying, Ryker," I said flat out. "I'd rather you had just told me all of this without pretending to do the date thing. This"—I waved my hand to indicate me and him—"just makes me think that while you may be a good cop, you're also kind of a dick."

Ryker's eyes narrowed dangerously. "It's not often a woman calls me a dick after I buy her dinner," he said.

"It's not often a man uses me to get back at his arch nemesis," I retorted. Turning away, I raised my hand, signaling a taxi coming down the street.

"Wait," Ryker said, stepping in front of me. "That's not why I asked you out."

"Isn't it?" The disbelief was evident in my tone.

"No, it's not," he said.

"I don't believe you," I said. "But it doesn't matter because I don't play these games." The cab had pulled over and I stepped around Ryker, heading for it, but he snagged me around the waist. Spinning me around, I landed pressed hard against him from chest to knee, which wasn't the best thing for my resolve to ditch him.

"Hold up," he said, his blue eyes locking on mine. "You say you don't like games, but I think you're lying."

Ryker was warm, his body hard against mine. His strength was apparent from how loosely he held me, but that I wasn't getting away anytime soon. Not that I was trying too hard.

"Oh, I am, am I?" Not the cleverest response, but the most my brain could manage.

He placed his lips by my ear. "You want excitement and danger, sweetheart. You know it and I know it. Something different from the stiffs in suits you usually date. And I'm an excellent choice to make that happen."

People passed us on the sidewalk, and out of the corner of my eye I saw the cab pull away. Ryker and I were locked in position, and despite the incredible arrogance of his words, I didn't want to move. I felt the slightest brush of his lips against my skin and a shudder went through me. My hips were cradled between his thighs, my breasts pressed against the hard planes of muscle on his chest. His hands rested on my waist, their heat bleeding through to my skin.

My head was telling me Ryker was a jerk who thought way too highly of himself and presumed to know too much about me. Except...my pulse was racing and the part of me that had liked the motorcycle ride was also telling me I'd waited my whole life for a man I *didn't* want to take home to meet my parents...and that it was this man.

"Get on the bike," he ordered. "I'll take you home."

My cab was gone, so while it went against my sorely lacking judgment, I did as he said.

I endured the helmet yet again, then climbed on behind him. Traffic was light on the way to my apartment, and Ryker dropped his left hand from the handlebar to rest it on my bare thigh. His fingers hooked beneath my knee, brushing the sensitive skin behind the joint.

The touch sent a shiver through me and I reflexively gripped him tighter as I held on. His abdomen was hard beneath my palms, the rough denim of his jeans abrading the insides of my thighs. My palms were splayed flat against him. The hem of his shirt had ridden up and I felt the smallest sliver of skin against my fingers.

I closed my eyes and savored the sensations—the wind rushing past, the sound and heat of the bike's engine, the scent of spring in the air mixed with the smell of the city, the feel of Ryker touching me and me touching him. Relaxing slightly, I rested my chest against his back. In response, his palm curved more firmly to fit my thigh, and an answering heat flashed in my veins.

The ride was over too soon, with Ryker's hand going back to the handlebars to steer the bike into the parking lot of my building. I had the hated helmet off before he'd even parked, using my fingers to comb through my hair.

My pulse was hammering and my hormones were hopping up and down when I climbed off the bike. I wanted nothing more than to straddle the bike again, only this time facing Ryker rather than sitting behind him.

Another notch in his belt, I reminded myself.

"Thanks again for dinner," I said, handing him the helmet.

"I'll walk you up," he replied, swinging his leg off the bike. His tone didn't invite argument.

Ryker was a palpable presence beside me as we rode the elevator to my floor and walked to my apartment. I was hyper-aware of him, every breath he took and every brush of his arm against mine. Knowing my resolve was taking a beating, I dug my keys out and had them in my hand by the time we were at my door. Unlocking the door took just a second; then I turned to face Ryker, who'd moved much closer into my space so he loomed over me.

"I'll let you know if I find out anything," I said, tipping my head back. Though how I'd do that, I didn't know. I didn't have his number and wasn't about to go poking around the police station downtown looking for him.

Ryker's eyes had a familiar glint in them as his gaze roamed over my face—desire and lust that I felt an answering flush to underneath my skin. In desperation to avoid what almost felt inevitable, I brought up the one person who'd throw ice water on the heat between Ryker and me.

"Parker's not involved like you think he is," I said. "I'm sure of it, and if I can help prove it, I will."

As I'd expected, Parker's name had an effect, although not what I'd intended. Rather than dousing the flames in Ryker's eyes, it only seemed to fan them.

"You're loyal," he said, his voice a low rasp. "I like that. You're just loyal to the wrong guy."

Ryker's head bent, and I knew what was coming, but there was nowhere to go. He had me pinned to the door, and if I was honest with myself, I probably wouldn't have moved away even if I'd had the opportunity.

His lips met mine in a kiss that made my toes curl.

Thoughts of Parker and everything else disintegrated, Ryker overwhelming them all.

The scent of his cologne and the leather of his jacket curled around me. His hand lifted to cradle my jaw, the soft brush of his lips giving way to the warm heat of his tongue as he deepened the kiss.

He tasted like darkness and sin wrapped in the soft notes of red wine, and I was immediately addicted. I felt the door give way at my back and realized he must've turned the knob. Backing me slowly inside, his mouth never left mine. Dimly, I heard the door close.

The brush of his thumb on my cheek was like a brand. His lips gently released mine, only to trail down my neck. My eyes were shut and my breath was shallow and fast as blood pounded in my ears.

A waft of cool air hit me and I realized he had undone the buttons on my shirt, pushing the fabric off my shoulder and down my arms. It hooked on my elbows, keeping me from reaching for him, but Ryker didn't seem to mind. His mouth fastened to the sensitive skin above my breast, his tongue dipping into the cleavage enhanced by my push-up bra. The warmth of his calloused palms spanned my waist and bared abdomen, their rough texture accentuated by the smooth softness of my skin.

My panties were uncomfortably damp and thoughts of being just another notch in Ryker's belt were a long ways off. At the moment, I didn't care if I was the hundredth notch in that belt; I just wanted to be a notch. Speaking of belt...

I could reach the fastening of his jeans and couldn't resist cupping the hard length of him through the denim. Oh yeah. This would definitely be worth the morning-after regrets.

Ryker's lips moved to my shoulder and I tipped my head

to the side as he brushed my hair back. I had his belt undone, but the fly was proving more difficult, so I didn't notice that he'd gone still.

"What's this?"

Opening eyes made heavy with desire, I glanced up at him, but he was looking at my arm, a frown on his face.

I felt my face get hot. "Oh that," I said. "It's just a bruise." The imprints from that guy's fingers were clear, which was a big reason why I'd worn something with sleeves tonight. I hurriedly yanked my shirt back up, but Ryker stopped me, pulling it back down and turning me for a better look.

"It's not just a bruise," he said, and gone was the husky desire in his voice. This was business, with anger lurking just under the surface. "It's a man's handprint. Did Parker do this to you?"

And that effectively killed what little was left of the mood.

"Of course not!" I snapped, stepping out of his reach. I pulled my shirt back on, quickly buttoning it back up. "You really don't know him if you think he'd do that."

"I know you'd cover for him if he had," Ryker shot back, which really pissed me off.

"A customer assaulted me in a cab last night," I said. "Parker *helped* me." My fists were clenched in anger. "I think we're done here, like really done, Ryker. You can go."

But Ryker's eyes narrowed and he made no move to leave. "What do you mean, 'a customer assaulted' you? Which customer? It was the Russians, wasn't it." That last part wasn't a question. Somehow, he knew.

I swallowed. Shit. In my anger, I'd said something I probably shouldn't have.

"Tell me," he ordered.

"It was nothing," I lied. "Just someone concerned that

their privacy would be breached, that's all. He was very...
forceful about it."

"Did he do anything else?"

Other than scare me out of my wits and make me wish I
was Lara Croft? "No," I said. "I'm fine."

Ryker glared hard at me. "You still want to tell me Parker
doesn't know *exactly* who these people are and what they
do?"

Parker had told me himself that he knew who they were.
He'd also told me he'd take care of it. Neither statement
would uphold his innocence in Ryker's eyes, so I remained
silent.

Ryker bit out a curse, shoving a hand through his hair.
I flinched at the harshness in his voice and decided I really
didn't like being on the receiving end of his anger, which
was decidedly intimidating.

"I'd like you to go," I said again.

Without a word, he walked to the door and jerked it open.
He stepped through, then turned back to me. His blue eyes
were intent on mine as he spoke. "Be careful, Sage. If you
get in their way, they'll kill you. You can't tell me Parker's
worth that."

The door closed quietly behind him and I let out the
breath I'd been holding.

Things had just gotten way more complicated.

CHAPTER SIX

I met Parker at the airport Monday morning. All day Sunday, I'd been thinking about what Ryker had said. Was he right? Could Parker somehow be involved with these people in a way that left him vulnerable to arrest and prosecution? I couldn't imagine him doing that. I'd never, in the entire time I'd worked for him, seen him do anything illegal. Occasionally the firm might be involved with something in the gray area, but never outright against the law.

What if he'd gotten dragged in against his will? It'd be just like Parker not to say a word and to try and figure it out on his own.

Once through security, I grabbed a cup of coffee on my way to the gate, unsurprised to see Parker already there.

"Good morning," I said, taking the empty seat next to him. He glanced up from his iPad.

"Morning, Sage." He returned to his reading.

I sipped my double-tall soy latte (add whip), peering sideways out of my eye at what he was reading. Looked like a news website. I wished I had something to do, too, but the only reading material I'd brought was the latest copy of *Vogue*, which was slightly embarrassing in light of Parker reading the news. Flipping through a glossy mag looking at the pictures wouldn't exactly make me look like a brain trust. Hmm. Obviously I hadn't thought that one through.

"Did you have a good weekend?" he asked, still perusing the iPad.

"Um, yeah," I answered.

"No surprise visitors?"

"No."

"Good." He seemed satisfied at that.

"What about you?" I couldn't resist adding, "Did your... friend come back?"

Parker did glance up then and I quickly averted my gaze, taking another sip of coffee. That question had probably been out of line, but it was too late to take it back.

"No, she didn't," he replied. "I worked this weekend. What about you?"

I shrugged, noncommittal. I really didn't want to tell him about Ryker and now I was sorry I'd asked a personal question.

As if he'd read my thoughts, he asked, "Have you heard from Ryker since your... date the other night?"

Shit.

I still avoided looking at him as I answered. "Um, yeah," I mumbled. I thought about lying, but I didn't like lying to Parker, so I told the truth. "We went out Saturday evening." I plucked an imaginary bit of lint from my skirt.

Parker was silent for a moment. "I see." Disapproval laced his words. "You do realize the only reason he asked you out is because of me."

I jerked my head up, stunned and hurt that he'd say that to me. Our eyes met and his gaze was shrewd as he looked at me.

"Could you possibly be more insulting?" I hissed, keeping my voice down so I didn't make the scene I dearly wanted to make by clobbering him over the head. "In case you haven't noticed, I'm a single woman, with a decent job, good hair, who works out on a semi-regular basis." No sense stretching the truth on that last one. "It's not like I'm a troll."

Just then, a woman's voice came over the intercom, announcing first-class boarding for our flight. Parker was the first to look away in our staring contest, gathering up his things. He stood, then glanced down at me.

"Aren't you coming?"

Still pissed, I snapped, "I'm in coach."

He nodded and I expected him to leave, but he paused. Leaning down until his mouth was near my ear, he said, "Yeah. I noticed." Then he was gone.

I watched him disappear down the Jetway, my mouth agape.

With any other man, I'd say he'd been flirting with me. But it was Parker, so what did that mean? Or did it mean anything? He had just been answering my question, after all.

It didn't matter. He'd been an asshole, saying that about Ryker. I sipped my coffee, glumly staring out the window at the plane while I waited for my row to be called. Finally, it was my turn to board. I glanced at Parker seated in the first-class section as I walked by, but he was engrossed in his iPad.

Since I'd gotten my ticket so late, I had the dreaded middle seat, and when I got to my row, I wanted to groan in dismay. Seated by the window was one of the biggest guys I'd ever seen—like muscle-bound, MMA fighter, don't-mess-with-me kind of big. It amazed me that he'd been able to squeeze into the seat, but since quite a bit of him overlapped into mine, I guess I could see how he'd managed.

Stowing my carry-on in the overhead bin, I smiled at him as he glanced up when I sat down. He didn't smile back. Great.

I squeezed into the seat, digging for the seat belt. The guy's arm overlapped into my space, as did his leg. I sighed. It was only a bit over two hours for the flight to New York. Surely it wouldn't be that bad.

Just then, a woman came down the aisle with two boys in tow. The youngest could only have been three or four; the oldest looked maybe seven. The mom looked up at the rows, then sat the older boy in the empty seat next to me while she and the other kid sat across the aisle.

Joy.

It wasn't that I didn't like kids. I did. Kids were great. Just so long as I didn't have to talk to them, listen to them, or basically interact with them in any way.

I found out pretty quick that the youngest boy was named Steven and the oldest Jeffrey, because the mom was constantly saying their names, trying to get them to behave. They had a slew of electronic toys, coloring books and crayons, and various action figures that they were constantly dropping and having to squirm down to the floor to pick up.

The first few times, I tried to help, but then Jeffrey beat me to it, his foot smacking me in the face as I leaned down. The mom didn't even notice—her hands were full with Steven, the little monster—and Jeffrey didn't either. He had his hands on his toys again, though now the electronics caught his eye. No earphones meant I got to hear the beeping and repetitive music of Mario for what seemed an eternity.

When the flight attendant came by to pass out drinks, I

prayed the mom would see sense and not let the boys have them. But it was not to be. Smooshed in my seat, I watched in dismay as she set a full cup of cola on Jeffrey's tray. It lasted six minutes, until he dropped his crayons and dove to grab them, knocking the cup directly into my lap, onto my pristine white skirt.

I gasped in dismay as the ice-cold liquid seeped through the fabric. I couldn't even jump up because the guy next to me was asleep and snoring, his meaty arm blocking me in.

"Oh my goodness, I'm so sorry. Jeffrey get back up in your seat! Look what you did to that poor woman! Apologize to her! No, give me those crayons; you sit quietly in your seat. Steven, hush, you're fine. No, you cannot have more pop. Jeffrey, sit down; you're supposed to have your seat belt on. No, I don't have more batteries. Share with your brother." And so it went. Jeffrey began haranguing his mom for more cola—which I vowed to dump on the little shit's head if she gave it to him—while Steven fussed and whined.

I hit the call button and the flight attendant looked sympathetic as she brought me a pile of napkins, but there was nothing to be done. The liquid had soaked into my skirt, right through to my underwear and crotch until I knew I'd be sporting a brownish wet spot on the back of my skirt as well as the front. Frustrated tears pricked my eyes, but I blinked them back.

I really hated kids.

The flight attendant returned and handed me a drink. I glanced up, questioning. I hadn't ordered anything.

"Vodka tonic," she said quietly, glancing at Jeffrey. "Complimentary."

"Thank you," I murmured as she walked away. *It was five o'clock somewhere*, I thought as I downed the drink.

Jeffrey finally fell asleep as we were on our approach to

land, the little shit. As I deplaned, I glanced at the mom, feeling a pang of sympathy for her as she roused Jeffrey and took Steven by the hand. She looked exhausted.

My skirt was as wet as I thought it'd be, the stain nice and prominent. Lovely. If possible, I was in an even worse mood now than I had been earlier. When I saw Parker's eyebrows lift as I joined him by the baggage carousel, his gaze on my skirt, I snapped, "Don't even say it."

"What happened?" he asked, ignoring me.

"Jeffrey happened," I said. "Spilled his pop all over me. Now I look like I wet my pants and he stained my skirt." I wanted to cry, but stuck with angry. No man wanted to bother with a woman crying over a spilled pop.

Parker shrugged out of his suit jacket. "Here," he said, swinging it over my shoulders. "Put this on."

Surprised but grateful, I slid my arms into the too-long sleeves. He was right. The jacket was big enough and long enough on me to cover my soaked rear.

"I'll get the bags," he said, tugging the jacket closed around me, "if need to find a ladies' room."

I lifted my gaze to his, mine a little watery. His kindness was sweet, making a lump form in my throat. I nodded. "Thanks," I managed to say without bawling. "Mine has a hot pink luggage tag in the shape of a martini glass." A favor from a bachelorette party.

In the nearest bathroom, I went in a stall and carefully hung Parker's jacket on a hook before pulling off my cola-dampened underwear. Ick. I dropped them in the trash, then tried my best to get the stain out of my skirt, but all I was doing was making it worse. The dry cleaner might be able to get the stain out, but I couldn't, at least not while in the airport bathroom.

Pulling Parker's jacket back on, I realized the fabric was

drenched in his scent. Not stopping to ask why I was doing it, I took a quick moment to press my nose into the lapel and take a deep whiff.

When I returned to Parker, he had our bags and stood next to a uniformed driver, chatting. His gaze raked me from head to toe, a funny look coming over his face that I couldn't read.

"We're just going to the hotel," he said. "You can change there. Our clients e-mailed me with the time for dinner, so you have plenty of time."

Sounded good to me.

But my luck didn't change. When we got to the hotel and they pulled up the reservation, we found out the travel department hadn't booked me a room like I'd told them to.

"I'm sorry, but we're full tonight," the desk clerk said with an apologetic shrug. "The best I can do is get you a room for tomorrow, but tonight there's nothing available."

I rubbed my forehead, feeling a headache coming on. If I stepped outside and was immediately mugged, it wouldn't surprise me in the slightest.

"What's going on?" Parker stepped up next to me.

"They messed up the reservation," I said with a heavy sigh. "They have your room tonight, but don't have anything available for me until tomorrow. Even though I called to confirm the reservation yesterday." I gave the desk clerk a withering glare.

"There are two hotels on this block," the clerk said. "I've contacted them both, but neither has any available rooms."

"Apparently there's a convention going on," I said. "Comic books and dentists."

Parker's brows knit in question.

"Not, like, together. Separate." Though I guessed maybe dentists could like comic books, too? Whatever. It didn't

matter. My wet skirt was clinging to me and I shifted uncomfortably, mentally using all the words my mother frowned
upon to curse the hotel, the dentists, *and* the comic book
folks.

"Just make sure my room is a double," he told the clerk.
"We'll make it work until tomorrow."

"I don't mind staying nearby," I protested.

Parker looked down at me. "You'd have to go farther than
that to find a room. It's just for one night, Sage. We're adults.
We'll manage." His tone clearly said the subject was closed,
so I shut up.

"Here you go, sir," the clerk said, sliding a packet onto
the counter. Parker picked it up. "You're in room 1427. Here
are two keys and the Wi-Fi password. We'll notify you tomorrow when the second room becomes available."

"Thank you," Parker said. Taking my elbow, he led me to
the elevator while the bellman followed with the luggage.

I didn't say anything in the elevator, my nerves jangling
at the idea of sharing a room with Parker. Why in the world
had he done that? I'd be just a phone call and hasty jog
away, should he need me. Though it did cement in my mind
that he had no interest in me other than a professional one.
No boss would put themselves in this situation—not in our
lawsuit-crazy society—if there was even a hint that things
could get unprofessional, and Parker was the consummate
professional.

The room wasn't as big as I'd hoped, but was really nice.
The bellman set the luggage down and Parker tipped him before he left. I stood awkwardly by one of the beds as the door
swung shut, then hurried to shed Parker's jacket.

"Here you go," I said, handing it to him. "I'll just
change."

I bent over to where my suitcase lay on the floor, digging

through it for another skirt and blouse. My nerves were shot after the plane ride from hell, and now the prospect of sharing a hotel room with my boss made me long for another vodka tonic.

Parker cleared his throat and I glanced over my shoulder at him, but he seemed to have his gaze carefully averted. "I know it may be a bit uncomfortable, Sage," he said, "but it's only for one night. After what happened Friday, I'd rather you be here than alone in another hotel."

Ah. That made sense, though my disappointment in his explanation certainly didn't.

"Sure, yeah, thanks," I blurted, yanking out the new outfit. "I'll just be a few minutes." Clutching my clothes, I disappeared into the bathroom.

The full-length mirror showed the extent of Jeffrey-the-Terror's damage and I groaned in dismay at the stain. This was a hundred-and-fifty-dollar Michael Kors skirt! Wait a second...

I squinted, then pulled the fabric tighter across my hips.

"Oh no..."

Spinning around, I pulled it tight across my rear. Sure enough, even with the satin lining, the fabric was see-through where it was wet. No wonder Parker had loaned me his jacket. So when I'd been bending over getting clothes out of my suitcase, my underwear stashed in a trashcan at the airport...

"Oh God," I moaned, covering my burning face with my hands. No wonder he'd been so clearly looking away from my prominently displayed backside. Didn't they call that "presenting" in the animal kingdom?

"Oh God oh God oh God..."

I had to stay in the bathroom forever. No way could I go back out there and face him again after *that* little display.

"Everything okay in there?" I heard Parker say right outside the door.

"Yeah! Yes! Everything is fine!" My voice sounded strangled.

I couldn't stay in here, as much as I wanted to.

Stripping out of my clothes, I dressed in the skirt and blouse, glad I'd chosen a black skirt this time. The blouse was one of my favorites, a sleeveless wraparound in a soft bronze that brought out the gold flecks in my eyes. It hugged my figure and I thought it looked flattering on me. After what I'd just been through, I wanted to look as nice and professional as possible.

Emerging from the bathroom, I saw Parker had retreated to the desk and booted up his laptop. Grabbing my makeup bag, I touched up my powder and lip gloss and redid my hair, carefully pinning up the long strands into a twist. When I was done, I felt much better.

"Let's go grab some lunch," Parker said. "I'm starving."

I readily agreed, wanting to avoid being in the confined space of the hotel room alone with him for as long as possible. Slipping on a pair of black heeled sandals, I picked up my purse and was ready to go. Parker grabbed his suit jacket and held the door for me.

The hotel had a restaurant, so that's where we went. It was just the kind of place I liked, with lots of dark wood and leather, plush seating, thick tablecloths, and heavy silverware. The maitre d' led us to a booth.

Parker and I were both looking over the menu when the waiter came up. "Can I get you something to drink?" he asked, looking expectantly at me.

I desperately wanted a real drink, but knew Parker would frown on that. "Um, iced tea," I said.

"Sir?"

"Grey Goose martini, straight up, dirty," Parker said. I stared at him as he glanced my way. "Make that two," he added. "She'll have one, too, only not dirty."

I wasn't sure what to make of that—not just that Parker was drinking in the middle of the day, but that he knew I didn't like olive juice in my martini.

"And why are we drinking?" I asked once the waiter had left.

"I could use one," Parker said with a shrug. "After the plane ride you had, I thought you could, too."

Certainly couldn't disagree with that. I was still having trouble looking Parker in the eye without seeing my ass waving around in the air. Even as I thought it, I could feel my face warm.

"Yeah, thanks," I said, fiddling with my napkin.

As long as I'd worked for Parker, we'd never shared a meal, so my thoughts as I glanced over the menu were a little chaotic. Though I did a lot for Parker, knew probably way too much about his habits and preferences, it felt strange to be sitting across from him in this context.

I tried to shake off the feeling. It was just work. Chances were we'd eat a couple of more times before the trip was over, obviously, so I'd better get over it already.

Salad was out. Trying to stuff a too-big piece of lettuce in my mouth and walking around with a poppy seed stuck between my teeth would be how that would end up. Likewise, soup was out. After the pop fiasco, it'd just be my luck to drip something on me. Sandwiches and basically anything I'd have to eat with my hands was also out. Nibbling on fries was one thing. My big maw gaping open to take a chunk out of a dripping cheeseburger was another, though that sounded *really* good.

Which left...not a lot of options. A mushroom risotto

dish with scallops, a halibut dish with rice, a petite filet... oh wait, lobster pot pie. Perfect. I loved lobster.

Parker ordered the steak, of course. When the waiter had set down our drinks and departed, Parker lifted his in a toast.

"Cheers," he said before taking a drink.

I took a sip of my cocktail as well. Yum. Just what I needed. I let out a long, quiet sigh.

"Sorry your flight was so bad," Parker said. "Make sure you call and have Travel upgrade you for the return flight."

"Okay, thanks," I said, concealing my surprise. I would definitely take that upgrade.

A few awkward moments passed where we didn't speak, just sipped our respective drinks. I avoided his gaze, instead people-watching the other customers.

"I know it's none of my business," he carefully began, "but are you and Ryker... together? Dating?"

I stiffened. "Listen, I really don't want to talk about it, or be insulted again."

"What I said earlier, it came out wrong," Parker said. "You're a smart, attractive woman. I didn't mean you aren't worthy of the attention. It's more like he's not worthy of yours."

I stared at him, his blue eyes focused intently on me. Had he just said I was smart and attractive, then followed it up with a diss on Ryker that doubled as a compliment for me?

"Ryker uses people," Parker said, a trace of bitterness in his voice. "I'd once thought nothing could come between us. I was wrong. Don't let him use you, Sage. That's all I'm saying."

Knowing how Ryker was indeed using me to spy on Parker and our new clients, it wasn't as if I could defend him. It was on the tip of my tongue to ask about Natalie, but I kept silent. The fact that Parker was even telling me this much about Ryker and their past was a huge deal. If I pushed, he'd probably clam up again.

"It must have been hard," I said, "losing a friend that you were so close to."

Parker's gaze was steady and I wondered if I'd crossed that line again, but he answered.

"It was," he said. "You don't forget it, and I don't know if you ever really get over it. You just…move on." He tipped up his glass, emptying the rest of the martini in one swallow. I took that as my cue to change the subject.

"Who exactly are we meeting tonight?" I asked. The information Sylvia had sent me for these customers had been vague, which was unusual. They'd only wanted to communicate directly with Parker rather than me, which had been a bit insulting, honestly. But they were new clients with a lot of money, so I'd kept my mouth shut and let Parker handle it.

As I'd known he would, Parker had the information memorized. "Viktor Rowan is the man we'll be meeting," he said. "He has an interesting history. Used to be Russian FSB before he was promoted to the head of the Central Bank of Russia."

"FSB?" I asked.

"Russia's foreign security service," Parker clarified. "They've been around for a while, but absorbed a lot of former KGB as well as the functions they performed."

I swallowed. None of that sounded good.

"So if he works for their national bank, then why are we meeting with him?" I asked.

"He didn't stay there," he explained. "He went to work for Bank ZNT a few years ago. A lot of banks in Russia aren't privately owned but partially owned by the government. Bank ZNT is the largest of those. It bought a handful of smaller, private banks last year. Rowan wants to place over three billion dollars of shares on the market by next month, and that's only ten percent of the bank's equity."

The waiter returned with our food and we stopped talking for a moment as we began eating.

Wow. Three billion dollars. I couldn't even wrap my mind around that kind of money.

"It seems kind of strange," I said, after a few minutes— the lobster pot pie was really good and I didn't even want to think about how many calories I was consuming. "Why would someone who worked in foreign intelligence go into banking, of all things?"

"Russia's economy can be dicey and difficult to navigate," Parker said, slicing another bite of his steak. "The government keeps a tight grip on the banks and currency rate and are always watching to see who's buying up shares of which banks. Rowan has a degree in Economics and is worth over a hundred million dollars. I imagine he serves several functions for them in his role as head of ZNT."

"So the guy who...talked to me Friday," I said, "he works for ZNT?" He'd done more than *talk* to me, but I didn't want to dwell on that.

"Probably."

I thought about what Ryker had told me. "So, are you sure these guys are on the up-and-up?" I asked. "That they're not criminals or...mobsters or something?"

"The Russian mafia is a big part of their economy over there," Parker said. "They extort protection money from a lot of businesses and the government looks the other way. Getting involved with any Russian bank is a risk."

"Then why do it?"

He looked at me like I was a ditz. "The money, of course. These guys want to raise three billion dollars by selling shares of their bank; that's three hundred million in commission for us, twenty percent of which will be mine."

I looked back down at my pot pie, pushing bits around with my fork. That *was* a lot of money.

"Why are they coming to Chicago for this kind of deal?" I asked. "Wouldn't they go to a big firm in New York or something?"

"Are you doubting my skill?"

I glanced up at the teasing note in his voice. A smile played about Parker's lips.

"Of course not," I said, smiling a little myself. "It was just a question."

"I'd imagine they're trying to avoid scrutiny from the feds," he said. "There was a case a few years back, a Russian bank owned by the mafia laundering millions through a New York firm. Chicago is slightly less high-profile."

"Was Hinton working on this?" I asked.

Parker nodded. "He'd been putting this together for months. I'm stepping in at the last minute to close them."

The waiter reappeared and took our empty plates, leaving the bill for Parker.

"So you're sure they're legit, then?" I asked. "Even with what happened Friday?"

Parker was busy signing the check and didn't look up as he replied. "The deal book looks good to me. Investors will be made aware it's a partially government-owned bank. Those with that kind of money are fully cognizant of the risks associated with investing in Russia."

And it seemed the subject was closed. Parker hadn't specifically answered my question, but he didn't seem worried about it.

He stood, politely waiting for me to precede him out of the restaurant as I digested this. I trusted Parker, but I was anxious. "Former FSB aka former KGB" didn't sound altogether reassuring to me. While I didn't think naiveté was something Parker was prone to, I wondered if the money to be made from this deal would make him want to look the other way.

And if I were absolutely honest with myself, I was a little hurt that Parker had so quickly dismissed the way I'd been threatened Friday. It didn't make sense. He'd seemed so angry that night, but now he'd just kind of shrugged it off. I was confused, but didn't say anything.

The elevator ride back up to the hotel room was quiet, as was the walk down the hallway. When Parker reached around me to slide the key card into the slot, I had to push aside the strangeness I again felt as my thoughts went from Bank ZNT back to sharing a room with Parker.

Once inside, he discarded his jacket and sat at the desk, logging back in to his laptop and pulling folders from his briefcase. Copying him, I retrieved my laptop and booted it up. Looked like it was time to get to work, so we did.

CHAPTER SEVEN

A knock at the hotel room door startled me, and I glanced up from my laptop.

"I'll get it," Parker said, already on his way to the door.

I heard him talking and leaned over on the bed where I was sitting cross-legged with my laptop. A man stood there and I caught a glimpse of him past Parker. Shorter, with dark hair and glasses. They were talking kind of low, so I couldn't make out what they were saying. Parker stepped inside and I hurriedly sat back so it wouldn't be quite so obvious that I'd been eavesdropping.

"Who was that?" I asked as the door swung shut.

"Wrong room," he replied, heading back to the desk.

I went back to work, flipping the page on the legal pad filled with Parker's scrawl, which I was transcribing.

"Your laptop is going to overheat if you keep it on that pillow," Parker said, glancing at me.

I looked down. I'd put the pillow on my lap so I could sit

comfortably on my bed and still work on the computer without flashing Parker a crotch shot, not that he'd notice. He'd been working nonstop since we'd gotten back from lunch four hours ago.

"Well, I don't have anywhere else to sit," I said with a shrug.

Parker glanced at his watch. "I think I'm going to go work out before dinner. You can use the desk."

"Okay. What time is dinner?"

"Seven-thirty."

"Where are we going?"

"They're sending a car," he replied, unzipping his suitcase and taking out some clothes. He disappeared into the bathroom.

Sending a car, eh? Fancy.

A few minutes later, the bathroom door opened and I reflexively looked up. My jaw dropped open and I quickly snapped it shut.

Parker was gorgeous in a suit and I'd rarely seen him in anything more casual. And I'd *never* seen him in workout clothes because—holy hell—I would've remembered.

He was wearing black athletic shorts and a dark gray tank that molded itself to his chest. His arms were bare and, boy, was I ever grateful for that. Muscles that his suits had only hinted at were now on full display; his biceps and shoulders were so well defined he could have posed for a magazine shoot.

I watched with too much interest as he crouched down to tie his shoelaces. I was treated to a mouthwatering view of his back that had me wishing I could see through cotton.

"I won't be gone long," he said, glancing at me.

"Huh? Oh, yeah, sure. Okay," I blurted, jerking my gaze away from him. Lord, but I needed a date. Soon. I focused on my laptop so I wouldn't stare at Parker.

I heard the door close and let out a sigh of relief. Holy shit.

I pretended to work for a few minutes before I finally gave up. I needed a drink. Or chocolate. Probably both, but since I'd already had two drinks today (hello, empty calories), chocolate would have to do.

Grabbing my purse, I fished out a couple of dollar bills, grabbed a key card, and stepped out of the room. A quick search of the hallway turned up not a single vending machine. After checking the brochure back in the room, I saw that the vending machines were only located on one floor—the same one as the workout room.

"Well, that's just cruel," I muttered. So I had to walk by treadmills, elliptical bikes, and weight machines to get a candy bar? Nice.

But... maybe I'd catch a glimpse of Parker actually working out, which would totally be worth it.

The elevator dumped me out on the fifth floor and I padded barefoot down the carpeted hallway. Glass windows on my left showcased a huge workout room with more machines than I'd seen in some gyms. Trying to appear nonchalant as I walked by, I searched for Parker, but was disappointed. Maybe he'd gone for a run around the block or something rather than use a machine. I had no idea what he did for working out.

An alcove at the far end of the hall held two measly vending machines, which had both nearly been cleaned out. I had my choice of a Milky Way bar or Almond Joy, neither of which was peanut M&M's—my favorite—but would do in a pinch.

Punching the button for the Almond Joy, movement out of the corner of my eye caught my attention. The door to the stairwell had a small window and it looked like someone stood on the opposite side. I wondered if they'd gotten locked out somehow and took a step toward the door, only to stop.

It was Parker, and he wasn't alone.

The man who'd come by our room stood with him and they were talking. I could see their lips moving.

Instinct had me backing slowly away and slipping around the corner so I wouldn't be seen. It was beyond weird. Did Parker know that guy? If so, why had he told me that he'd gotten the wrong room? Why were they talking in a stairwell?

I didn't know what to make of it; then I heard the door open. I scooted farther inside the vending machine alcove and pressed against the wall just as Parker passed by. After waiting a few seconds, I eased around the corner again and hurried down the opposite hallway from the workout room.

It shouldn't have bothered me so much—what Parker did was his business, not mine—but it did. He didn't usually lie outright to me, and hard as I tried, I couldn't come up with a reasonable explanation.

When I got back to the room, I heaved a sigh of relief. I'd been afraid Parker would catch me and think I was spying on him, which I hadn't been. But if he didn't want me to know something, he certainly wouldn't take kindly to me finding out by accident.

I plopped onto the bed, only then just realizing I'd forgotten my candy bar in the vending machine.

Well, shit.

* * *

By the time Parker came back, I'd dressed for dinner. A few weeks ago, I hadn't been able to resist buying a new cocktail dress and I'd been dying to wear it ever since. It was a deep scarlet, which brought out a scattering of red highlights in my hair, long-sleeved with a jeweled boat neckline. Though that made it seem conservative, it was form-hugging and the hemline was well above mid-thigh, but it was the back that sealed the deal and the reason I'd bought the dress.

The entire back was cut out all the way down to my waist. Other than the bit of fabric over my shoulders from the sleeves, the only thing holding it on were two jewel-encrusted strips that ran from the collar down to my waist. They sparkled and drew the eye, making what would seem just a pretty dress jaw-droppingly stunning when I turned around.

I'd woven my hair in two loose French braids on either side of my head, then pinned it up, leaving some strands to escape and wisp around my neck. Sparkly bronze eye shadow paired with a bit of deep, matte brown and I had smoky eyes. I added dangly silver earrings and had just finished spraying my perfume when the hotel room door opened and Parker walked in.

A sheen of sweat on his skin glistened in the light and he was still breathing hard from exertion. Tossing the key card onto his bed, he glanced over at me and froze.

Oh God. I could smell him. Not in that bad construction-worker-sweat-and-dirt kind of way, but in that man-who's-pushed-himself-hard kind of way. Pheromones were a powerful thing and I took way too deep of a whiff.

"So, how was your workout?" I blurted, uncomfortable under his stare.

"Fine," he said curtly. "Is that what you're wearing?"

Surprised, I glanced down at myself. "Uh, well, yeah, I guess. Why?"

"Is it really appropriate?"

I stared at him, my eyes wide. Was Parker really taking me to task over a cocktail dress? This was new territory and I wasn't sure how to respond.

"It's New York," I offered with a shrug. "It seemed okay. Don't you like it?" I self-consciously tugged at my hem. Maybe it did show too much leg for a business dinner.

Parker swiped a hand over his face, still looking at me, while I waited for his answer. I shifted from one bare foot to the other.

"Maybe you don't have to go at all," he said at last. "I can handle it. You stay here and, I don't know, order room service or something."

My face fell. I wouldn't get to go out? In Manhattan? That seemed grossly unfair, especially after the pains I'd gone through to get ready.

"Fine," I snapped, trying to keep hold of my temper. "If you're giving me the night off, that's great, but I'm sure as heck not going to sit around the room all evening. I've been stuck in here all afternoon."

Parker's eyes narrowed and his jaw tightened, but I stood my ground. If I didn't have to work, then there was no earthly reason why I couldn't at least go to dinner somewhere by myself.

"Where would you go?" he asked.

I shrugged, irritated. "I don't know, but it's not like I can't go have dinner alone."

"Like you'd be alone for long," he muttered, making me wonder if I'd heard him right. "Fine," he said more loudly. "You can come. But can you wear something else? Like pants. Did you bring pants?"

"You're kidding, right?" Was he really telling me what to wear? "No, I didn't bring *pants*. Unless you count my yoga pants. Shall I wear those?" I raised an eyebrow, daring him to dig himself in any deeper. This was getting ridiculous.

Growling a curse, Parker stepped inside the bathroom, shutting the door entirely too hard behind him. I let out a breath. What the hell had *that* been about? For someone who was usually pretty even-tempered, Parker was in one heck of a shitty mood.

I'd hung his clothes while he'd been working out, having to take an iron to his shirt, and now the suit I'd laid out for tonight was ready and waiting for him. I slipped on a pair of black heels that added over three inches to my height and made my legs look amazing, if I did say so myself. I'd brought along a little clutch bag that I put my lipstick, key card, wallet, and phone in before sitting down to wait.

Parker's shower was quick; then I heard the sound of his electric razor. Trying not to picture him shaving, I turned the volume up on the television, halfheartedly watching the news. A few minutes later, the bathroom door opened and Parker stepped out, wearing only a towel wrapped around his lean hips.

Hot damn.

I jumped to my feet. "You know, I'll just wait downstairs, have a drink or something, I don't know. Just grab me when it's time to go." The words fell out in a rush as I tried, and failed, to keep my eyes above Parker's neck. "Your suit's hanging in the closet and the shirt's been ironed, so I'll just meet you in the bar? Okay? Okay."

Grabbing my clutch, I moved to pass him. My nails dug into the fabric of my bag so I wouldn't reach out and trail them across his chest, still slightly damp from the shower. I had my palm on the doorknob when Parker called out, "Stop!"

I froze, alarmed at the tone of his voice. What now? I

didn't dare turn back around, not with him wearing next to nothing. I had a decent amount of self-control, but Parker nearly naked would test even the most iron of wills.

"You didn't show me the back."

I jumped, startled. Parker was right behind me, his voice close to my ear. His fingers brushed the bare skin of my back so softly, I wasn't sure if I'd imagined it. I swallowed, my throat suddenly dry, and I gripped the doorknob like it was the only thing keeping me from drowning.

He smelled of cologne now, and aftershave, and just warm, clean man. My eyes slipped shut. This sharing a room thing was such a bad idea. Parker may not be attracted to me, but pushing our professional boundary like this was wreaking havoc on my side of the equation.

"If I give you my credit card, will you go buy something else to wear?" His breath was warm against my ear and this time I was sure he touched between my shoulder blades. A shiver ran down my spine that I knew he had to have felt.

My laugh sounded strangled. "I think it's a little late for that, don't you? They'll be here soon."

"It was worth a shot."

We stood like that, neither of us moving, just breathing. The blood rushed in my ears, my pulse racing. I swore I could feel the heat of his body as he stood so close behind me. I was incapable of moving because if I did, I'd turn around, and if I turned around, things would be very, very bad.

"I'd better go have that drink," I said at last, my voice embarrassingly weak.

To my...relief?...Parker stepped back and I could breathe properly again.

"Yes, you'd better. I'll be down soon."

Not trusting my voice, I nodded at the door, hoping he

saw me, then was out in the hallway. I didn't run, not in those heels, but I was clocking a pretty good speed in my rush to get as far away from Parker as I could.

I'd downed one vodka tonic and was well into my second when I caught sight of Parker in the mirror behind the bar. I sat perched on a leather stool, cooling my rather high heels while I waited. I observed Parker's reflection as he looked around the bar, searching for me.

The suit I'd chosen for him was one of my favorites, a deep charcoal European cut, his shirt a crisp white with a silk gray and white striped tie. It looked amazing with his dark hair, the thick strands brushed back in a loose wave off his forehead. He had the kind of hair that was made for a woman to run her fingers through. The jacket fit his shoulders perfectly, a single button done up to keep it closed.

I could tell when he saw me. He paused, then came striding forward. I kept watching the reflection. Parker had the kind of walk that made a woman want to be the one he was heading for and made other men get out of his way. It was nice to pretend for a moment that Parker was coming to get me for an entirely different reason than a business dinner.

That must be the vodka talking.

"Are you ready?" he asked, stopping next to my stool.

I took a bigger gulp of my drink than was ladylike and nodded. "Just have to pay," I said, crunching on a piece of ice. Also not ladylike. My mother would be giving me the stink-eye right about now. I reached for my purse, but Parker had already pulled out his wallet.

"I've got it," he said, tossing down a twenty.

I eyed the money, feeling really relaxed now. "Yeah, that's not enough."

Parker paused in slipping his wallet back inside his jacket. "How many did you have?"

I crunched more ice, holding up two fingers. Parker tossed down another twenty and I couldn't tell if he was irritated or amused. Hopefully the latter, but probably the former. Oh well.

"Let's go."

Taking my elbow, he helped me off the stool. I expected him to let go then, but he didn't. But that was okay. I didn't mind. Two vodka tonics inside of twenty minutes on an empty stomach and I was feeling pretty darn good. Not tipsy—just way better than I had felt before.

"You okay to go to dinner?" Parker asked as he led me out of the bar and into the lobby. "You're not drunk, are you?"

"I'm not *that* much of a lush," I said, offended. "Do you really think I'd embarrass you like that in a meeting like this?"

The doorman opened the door for us and we stepped out onto the sidewalk. Parker paused, glancing down at me.

"No. I don't."

I stared up at him, the breeze ruffling his hair, and had to stop myself from reaching up to smooth it.

"Mr. Anderson?"

Parker turned as a man approached, clad in a somber black suit that to my eye was expensive, though not flashy.

"Your car is this way," the man said, gesturing to a black sedan with tinted windows. Ooh. A Rolls. Very nice.

He opened the door for us and Parker waited for me to get in first. I was careful to keep my knees together, swinging my legs inside so I wouldn't flash anyone a view of the black thong I was wearing. Parker slid in next to me.

I tried to concentrate on the scenery out my window— I'd only been to New York a couple of times, both of which I'd been accompanied by my parents. I watched the throngs of people on the sidewalk, so reminiscent of Chicago and yet not, and the flashes of restaurants and stores and company headquarters streaming by reminded me I was in the heart of the City That Never Sleeps. I saw a dozen places I'd have loved to jump out and explore, including two museums.

Traffic was typical New York bumper-to-bumper, taxis honking and cutting people off as busses streamed by inches away from their side mirrors. It took almost forty minutes to get to the restaurant. By that time, my buzz had, unfortunately, worn off. Parker took my elbow again as we walked inside. We were shown to a table in a far corner of the busy place where two men and one woman already sat. Both men stood when they caught sight of us.

"Mr. Anderson," one of them said. "I am Viktor Rowan." He extended his hand, which Parker took in a firm shake. "This is Sergei Klopov, my . . . how do you put it . . . ? Ah, yes. My right-hand man." Parker shook Sergei's hand as well. "And this is Tania." He motioned to the woman, and didn't give her a title. She merely nodded, the barest hint of a smile crossing her face.

She looked younger than me, which was a bit of a surprise, considering Viktor's age. Strikingly pretty, she had deep brown eyes, long black hair, and flawless skin. Other than the nod, she didn't speak or acknowledge us.

"A pleasure to meet you," Parker said smoothly. "May I introduce my assistant, Sage Reese?" I smiled and would have held out my hand as well, but they nodded and were already sitting down. Okay, then.

Viktor was as tall as Parker, but not as wide. His face had a few pockmarks, perhaps from acne or the chicken pox. Not unattractive; he smiled at me. But his eyes . . . his eyes were a light blue and coldly calculating. Just looking at him gave me a chill down my spine.

Sergei was a big man, but it wasn't in the form of muscle.

His suit had to have been handmade to fit his girth and I guessed him to be about six feet tall and perhaps three hundred pounds. He didn't smile at me, merely nodded as he took my hand.

"Pleasure," he said, his voice like a rake through gravel and heavily accented.

Parker pulled out a chair for me and I sat down as the waiter draped a black linen napkin in my lap. Only then did I notice the three other men who sat at a table close by. Clad in the same kind of suit as our driver, they each had a wire running from under their jacket to their ear. They scanned the restaurant, their eyes continually coming back to rest on Viktor. All of them had a telltale bulge underneath their jackets.

Bodyguards.

Well, I guess if I was worth a hundred million dollars, had once worked as Russian KGB, and headed the second largest bank in Russia, I'd have bodyguards, too.

"I am pleased you could make it on such short notice," Viktor said to Parker. "My condolences on the loss of Randolph. He was a good man."

The sommelier came by, opening and pouring a bottle of wine Viktor must have ordered prior to our arrival. It was an excellent red and I sipped it carefully, appreciating the vintage. My father was something of a wine aficionado, so had taught me the difference between a good bottle of wine and a great bottle of wine. This was the latter.

"You're still in good hands," Parker said. "Our firm is committed to helping Bank ZNT raise the capital it needs and selling those shares quickly."

"Of course. We have no doubts on that front," Viktor said. "We have heard great things about you, Mr. Anderson."

"Please, call me Parker."

"Very well. And you must call me Viktor."

I took another sip of wine, eyeing them over the rim of the glass. It seemed Parker was turning the charm on full wattage, his smile engaging and friendly.

They exchanged small talk, Viktor answering Parker's inquiries into Moscow and the state of things over there, with Sergei adding comments from time to time as well. Tania and I were ignored, for the most part, which was fine with me. Tonight was a getting-to-know-you thing, everyone sizing up the other side. Tomorrow would be business.

I caught Tania staring at me several times, and it unnerved me. She seemed unabashed about doing it, scrutinizing me with an intensity that left me squirming in my chair. I tried to avoid her eyes.

The restaurant was a five-star kind of place started by a big-name chef that even I had heard of, and I was in a bit of heaven as the dinner was served. By the time dessert rolled around, I was pleasantly surprised at how cordial Sergei and Viktor were and thought Ryker was probably barking up the wrong tree on this one.

A fourth man joined the table of three bodyguards and I glanced over.

It was the man who'd hijacked my taxi Friday.

He caught my eye and winked, a smirk on his face. My gaze fell on the barbed-wire tattoo across his knuckles and a shudder went through me.

Abruptly, I lost my appetite. I set down my spoon with a clatter, leaving over half the serving of crème brûlée. My stomach churned.

Parker glanced at me, a slight question in his eyes. I looked pointedly over at barbed-wire guy. Still talking to Viktor, Parker casually glanced to his left, his body stiffening slightly when he saw the man. He looked back at me and

I could tell he wanted to know if that was the guy. I gave him a tiny nod.

Throughout our whole silent conversation, Parker hadn't stopped speaking once, and even now Viktor was chuckling at the story Parker had told. There was a pause in the conversation and I glumly toyed with the stem of my wineglass. I felt Tania's eyes on me again, but didn't look her way.

"It's a smart idea, having security, especially in this town," Parker said. "But sometimes they get a little overzealous, don't you agree?"

"My people don't," Viktor said. "They take their orders from me."

The atmosphere dropped ten degrees with that pronouncement. Parker and Viktor were locked in a staring contest.

"That's unfortunate," Parker said, and now his voice was chilly. "I work hard for my clients, but I don't take very well to someone laying a hand on my assistant, threatening her, scaring her."

Viktor smiled a bit, then waved his hand like it was nothing. "No harm intended. I wanted to ensure you understood how...personally I would take it should the wrong sort of information about our bank be leaked to the public."

"Privacy is something we take very seriously at KLP Capital," Parker replied. "I'd have told you that myself. I'll get this deal done and make you a very happy client. But let's get one thing straight." He leaned forward, resting his arms on the table. "Touch Sage again, and we're done. I will drop this deal and not look back."

A moment passed, then Viktor shrugged. "There are other investment firms."

"Not like ours," Parker said, and now his tone was cold steel. "I drop this deal and everyone will want to know why.

Given your history and the holdings of Bank ZNT, they'll know something's up. No one will broker your public offering, no matter the price, because no one wants the feds breathing down their necks. Any firm so much as touches the deal, they'll be lining themselves up for the FBI, CIA, and a whole fucking alphabet of government agencies to scrutinize every piece of paper that's ever crossed their desk. So don't threaten me. Are we clear?"

I held my breath, eyes wide, as I waited to see how Viktor would take this.

Silence reigned, the battle of wills between Parker and Viktor raging; then suddenly, Viktor laughed. Not an outright booming laugh, but a low chuckle.

"I knew you were the right man for the job, Parker," he said. "A spine of steel. I like that. I think we are going to work very well together." He glanced at me. "My apologies for Vladimir's behavior. He can be a bit rough around the edges. Former gulag, you understand."

I couldn't speak, my nerves fraught, so I just gave a jerky nod. My hands were clenched in my lap. Parker had just gone toe to toe with this guy, and while he may have won this round, I was terrified that we were way out of our depth.

Viktor returned his attention to Parker. "I'll be there tomorrow, along with the lawyers and accountants, to meet with you and go over details. I trust that's acceptable?"

Parker was all business again, the menace he'd just displayed fading under the persona of investment banker. But I'd seen the fighter in him, the man who'd been a Marine, just like that night he'd stuffed me in the closet at the office. And I liked it. I liked it a lot.

Viktor and Parker discussed time and meeting location at our hotel; then he was helping me to my feet to leave. They shook hands and Viktor again glanced at me.

"I must compliment your taste in women, Parker," he said, his gaze roving down to my thighs and back up. "I rarely find women useful for more than one thing. You, apparently, have."

Tania didn't bat an eye, but I didn't think I'd ever been more insulted in my life.

Parker grabbed my hand, tugging me away from the table, no doubt thinking I might say something stupid. Please. The guy was an asshole, but I wasn't dumb enough to antagonize him. Moments later, we were back in the car.

We didn't speak as the driver began negotiating traffic on the way back to our hotel. Parker was looking out the window, his elbow on the door and his chin resting on his hand.

"That was . . . interesting," I said, keeping my voice low.

Parker glanced at me, then gave a minute shake of his head.

I shut up.

Like Parker, I looked out my window, which is why I was so surprised to feel him suddenly take my hand.

"I don't think I've told you how beautiful you look tonight," he said. He'd moved closer to me, his body angling toward mine.

"Wh-what?" I stammered, eyes wide.

His thumb caressed the top of my hand and now he stretched his other arm along the top of the seat behind me.

"You look amazing. That dress is the stuff fantasies are made of."

I stared at Parker in openmouthed shock. His blue eyes stared right back, utterly serious. Surely I hadn't heard him correctly? Had he really said I looked beautiful?

Those thoughts abruptly cut off when he let go of my hand, moving so his palm cradled the bare knee of my crossed legs.

I looked down. This wasn't happening. Couldn't be happening. But sure enough, not only was his hand on my knee, but it was also moving steadily up my thigh.

Before I could even think of what to say, how to react, Parker leaned over me, dipped his head into the curve of my neck and shoulder, and pressed his lips to my skin.

I sucked in a breath, utterly stunned. Parker was making a pass at me...and he wasn't drunk. He'd barely sipped at his wine all evening. Not that I thought a man had to be drunk to make a pass at me, I was just saying.

Then his mouth moved, pressing light kisses to my neck, and my eyes fluttered closed. Tentatively, I tipped my head ever so slightly to the side, and I was immediately rewarded by the touch of his tongue to my skin.

Parker's hand was high on the thigh of my crossed leg, the hem of my dress leaving a lot exposed, and the heat of his palm felt like a brand. My arm lifted and I found myself gripping his shoulder. Suddenly, I didn't care *why* he was making a pass at me—I was just really, really glad that he was.

My pulse raced as Parker's lips skated up underneath my ear. God, he smelled good. He'd shaved earlier so his jaw was smooth against my neck. My hand crept up until I could slide my fingers up his nape and into his hair. The strands were soft and thick and felt better than I'd let myself imagine they would.

His arm settled on my shoulders, pulling me closer. He sucked at the pulse beneath my jaw and my nails scraped lightly against his scalp as a shiver went through me. I was breathing way too fast, my pulse racing so that I felt almost light-headed. His palm slid along the back of my thigh, nearly to my ass, and a pulse of heat throbbed between my legs.

I wanted him to kiss me, but he was still sucking on

my neck, which felt really good—too good for me to stop him. This close, Parker was overwhelming. His body covered mine, his arms around me, his hands touching me. I felt as though I were going to spontaneously combust at the heat between us. My nails dragged lightly through his hair and his palm was suddenly squeezing my thigh. I bit my lip against the moan that wanted to escape.

As suddenly as it had begun, he was moving away. I opened my eyes, then blinked. We'd stopped and the driver had gotten out and was opening the door for us. Parker was already standing, his hands going to the top button of his suit jacket to fasten it; then he was reaching back inside for me.

Nonplussed, I took his outstretched hand, sliding along the seat until I could step out. I struggled to get my bearings and automatically smoothed my dress, tugging the hem down into place.

"Did you get your purse?" Parker asked me.

I stared blankly up at him. Purse?

His lips twitched slightly; then he was leaning back into the car, pulling out the little clutch bag that I'd completely forgotten about. Oh. *That* purse. Threading his fingers through mine, he drew me next to him as we walked into the hotel.

My mind began to race. Parker had just kissed me. Well, wait, not like in the technical sense of kissing, but he'd definitely been making out with me. I was suddenly really glad I'd bought this cocktail dress. If it had been the impetus behind Parker making a move, then I'd preserve and enshrine the damn thing behind glass. *Best. Dress. Ever.*

The elevator was a bit crowded and Parker tugged me with him toward the back. I ended up standing in front of him as others got in after us and was forced to drop his hand.

What was going to happen now? Would we pick up

where we left off once we were back in the room? Did I want that? What would that do to our working relationship and my job? Had I remembered to take my birth control pill this morning?

I wasn't sure of the answers to any of those but the last one, which was yes, I had. Thank God.

The elevator door opened and people shifted to let some-one out. I moved back, brushing against Parker, which was when I realized I wasn't the only one turned on from the impromptu make-out session. I felt the hard length of him against me just as his hands settled on my hips.

That was a much-needed ego boost. I'd been so flustered when we'd gotten out of the car, whereas Parker had seemed so calm and put-together—it was a relief to know he was af-fected, too.

I melted against him, stepping close so my body touched his from my back all the way down to where his pants brushed my bare legs. If I'd had any concerns that Parker's...endowment might not live up to expectations, those were put to rest, because it felt like I would be quite pleased indeed.

He grew harder against my backside and I wanted to rub against him like a cat, but that would look weird, so I settled for pressing closer to him. His hands bit into my hips as I nestled my rear against his erection, and I hid a smile.

Oh yeah. This was going to be oh so good.

CHAPTER EIGHT

The trip down the hallway from the elevator to our room seemed interminable...and awkward. We hadn't spoken at all and I really hoped he said something soon, because I certainly didn't know what to say. Well, I knew I wanted to be screaming his name—sooner rather than later—but that was about as far as my thought processes could get.

I fished the room key from my bag as we stopped in front of the door. Parker stood behind me. I nearly dropped my clutch when I felt his knuckles trail up my exposed back to my shoulder blades, then slowly back down to my waist. My temperature shot up as my breath caught in my throat.

Oh God. If this man's mere touch on my back had this kind of effect on me, it was going to be one hell of a night. I could hardly wait.

My fingers felt like I had ten thumbs and I fumbled with the key card until Parker plucked it from my hand and inserted it into the slot. Ha! *Insert into slot.* I stifled a nerves-induced giggle at my own ridiculously bad joke.

The door opened and I nearly fell inside in my haste. Would it seem too forward to just yank my dress over my head? Or should I let him undress me? Or, frankly, at the moment I'd be happy with fully clothed, minus panties, and against the wall.

Tossing my clutch onto the table, I turned around, thinking the hell with it, I'd just strip the dress off and worry about finesse later. I'd yet to meet a man who didn't appreciate a woman wearing just heels and a thong. But Parker wasn't right behind me, as I'd expected. He was by the nightstand, inspecting the lamp.

I frowned. "What are you—"

He was suddenly right in front of me, his hand over my mouth, silencing me. My eyes widened. Was Parker into… games? Being tied up was one thing, but gagged didn't sound very appealing. But thinking again about what I'd felt against my back in the elevator…okay, sure, what the hell.

Placing his lips right at my ear, he whispered, "Shhh."

I watched in complete bemusement as Parker proceeded to search every inch of our hotel room. He pried something from the inside of the lamp, then a few minutes later, something else from underneath the desk, way in the back by the wall.

Stepping in front of me, he held open his palm. I looked down to see two small, circular devices, no bigger than a dime each. Confused, I glanced back up at him. He set a finger to his lips, then disappeared into the bathroom. I heard the toilet flush; then he came back out.

"I think I got them all," he said with a sigh. He discarded his jacket and loosened his tie while I stood in the middle of the room, wondering what the hell was going on.

"Got them all?" I repeated. "What are you talking about?"

"I showed them to you," Parker said. He had his phone out now and was typing something with one hand, so didn't look up. "Listening devices."

I didn't reply and he finally glanced at me.

"You know. Bugs," he said.

"They had…bugged us? Were listening to us?" I was trying to wrap my head around first that Parker had made out with me in the car, and that now apparently they'd bugged the hotel room. I was glad he'd destroyed the bugs, but at the moment couldn't care less if Viktor heard me screaming my orgasm right into his ear.

Parker slipped his phone back in his pocket and approached me.

"Listen, Sage, I need to apologize," he said. A sinking feeling came into my stomach at the grimness of his tone. "It was completely unprofessional to…do what I did…in the car. I knew they would be watching. They already think you and I have a personal relationship, and it occurred to me that the more they believed that, the safer you'd be. They don't want to piss me off."

"What are you saying?" I thought I knew, but hoped I was wrong. My stomach churned like I was going to be sick.

Parker's gaze was steady. "I'm saying that I appreciate your cooperation in helping ensure Viktor and Sergei believe we're involved. I apologize for not being able to warn you ahead of time."

I felt the blood leave my face as I stared in horrified disbelief at Parker. His kissing me, touching me, all of it, had been an act? He'd been pretending? The whole time? Whereas I…I had most certainly *not* been pretending.

"Oh God…," I whispered. I took a shaky step back from Parker.

I heard the buzz of his cell and he pulled it from his pocket to check the screen before glancing back at me. I knew I should do something, say something, but had no clue as to what. My boss now knew, beyond a shadow of a doubt, that I would sleep with him if he asked.

It was mortifying. Humiliating.

Parker seemed to sense that this wasn't going over very well, because he said, "Listen, why don't I give you some privacy? I'll be back soon." And just like that, I was watching him walk out.

I stood in the middle of the room, staring at the closed door. My hands were curled into fists, my nails cutting into my palms.

A wave of shame washed over me, weakening my knees. I sat heavily on the bed. My eyes stung, but I blinked back the tears that wanted to fall.

Oh my God, what must Parker think of me? He must be thinking I was a total slut was what he was thinking. I hadn't even attempted to push him away or made any move to show I wasn't totally down with sleeping with my boss.

The elevator. I cringed, remembering how I'd pressed against him. Yes, he'd had a hard-on, but he was a *guy*. That didn't mean a damn thing. They got hard-ons watching Victoria's Secret commercials, for chrissakes.

The whole night seemed like one big screwup. First with Parker having a fit about the dress, then dinner with scary Viktor, and now a cluster of epic proportion between Parker and me. Groaning, I fell back on the bed and stared up at the ceiling.

There was no help for it. I had to quit my job and leave the country. I idly wondered if my passport was up to date. Maybe I should let my dad spring for that trip to Italy he'd been tempting me with. I'd kept turning him down because I hadn't wanted to leave Parker for the three-week trip. At the moment, three weeks out of Parker's sight sounded perfect.

Knowing Parker would be back soon, I most definitely wanted to be sleeping—or at least pretending to be sleeping— by the time he returned. I hurried to change into my pajamas, brush my teeth, and take off my makeup.

Not expecting to share a room with my boss, I'd packed my usual nighttime attire—a short little chemise gown with spaghetti straps. I was thankful this one wasn't see-through, the satin an opaque black with a bit of ivory lace that trimmed my cleavage.

I turned off the lights, switched on the television, and climbed into bed, taking the one closest to the bathroom. I kept the volume turned down low, watching Jimmy on *The Tonight Show*.

I didn't want to think about what had happened earlier. I couldn't change how I'd reacted. Parker hadn't seemed mad. He'd seemed as unemotional as he usually was—merely coolly professional. Surely I could be that way, too. I just wouldn't think about how amazing it had felt to be in his arms, his mouth against my skin. Or how much I'd wanted him to strip off my clothes and make love to me.

Or how disappointed I was that he hadn't.

Tears dripped down the side of my nose and I hurriedly wiped them away. This was stupid. Really? I was going to cry about it, for goodness' sake? Yet even as I thought how ridiculous I was being, the tears kept leaking from my eyes. I heaved a sigh. I needed M&M's.

Almost thirty minutes later the door opened and Parker walked in. I closed my eyes. I was on my side, facing Parker's bed, and now I wished I'd had the foresight to turn my back to him. Too late now.

The light from the television flickered against my closed

lids, Jimmy's voice and the laughter of the audience a low murmur of sound. I'd pulled the covers up beneath my arm, though now it would've been great if I'd gotten fully beneath them to hide even more.

I felt more than heard Parker approach, then the crinkle of a wrapper as he set something down on the nightstand between our beds. Then I heard nothing. I barely breathed. Had he moved away? I couldn't tell. I didn't know how I was going to face him in the morning, much less if I had to say something to him now. I was still so embarrassed. And hurt. Yes, if I was honest with myself, I was hurt.

Oh no. I had to sniff. Water still stung behind my eyes and now, God forbid, I could feel it creeping down my nose. Shit shit shit! And, of course, the more I thought about it, the more I couldn't stand it, until finally I had to sniff. Giving up the pretense, I opened my eyes.

Parker stood right in front of me.

I couldn't help but glance up at him, to find that he was watching me, an inscrutable expression on his face.

He'd taken off his tie and undone the top two buttons on his shirt, and even as I processed this, he crouched down so he was closer to my level.

Reaching out, he gently brushed my arm with his fingers. He touched the bruises Vladimir had left and appeared to be studying them, his forehead creased in a frown. Our eyes met.

He didn't speak, but his face softened. His hand drifted from my arm to my cheek, brushing away a damp trail I hadn't been successful in holding back.

"I'm so sorry," he said, his voice barely more than a whisper.

My face heated and I couldn't look in his eyes. I lowered my lashes, shifting my shoulders in a shrug, as I didn't trust my voice to answer. What was his cryptic apology for? Making out with me? Or the effect it'd had on me when he hadn't delivered on what had seemed a done deal? He didn't elaborate and I didn't want to ask.

Parker brushed my hair back from my face, his hand slowly tangling in the long, thick strands. I lifted my gaze to his eyes, which shone like silver in the low light.

He didn't say anything else and for just this one brief moment, everything between us was stripped bare. I had nothing to hide behind—no duties or pencil skirt, no French twist or steno pad. I'd do anything for Parker, even make myself incredibly vulnerable to him in the most intimate way, and now he knew it.

I tried to see anything in his eyes, anything that might show he felt something for me. Something more than the usual gratitude and appreciation a boss had for a particularly hard worker. But it was impossible to tell.

He stood, his hand drawing slowly back, the locks of my hair slipping between his fingers, and I felt the same overwhelming disappointment that had consumed me earlier. He leaned down over me, and for a breathless moment, I thought I was wrong, that he was going to kiss me and take up where we'd left off. But he didn't.

His lips pressed against my forehead, and my eyes slipped shut; then he moved away. I watched in silence as he took off his shirt and drew his T-shirt over his head. Pressing the switch on the television, he turned it off and I heard the rustle of clothing as he finished undressing, then the slight creak of the other bed.

I didn't know how long it took him to fall asleep. I just knew I lay awake for a long time, staring at the vague outline of him in the darkness, mere feet away.

* * *

The door closing to the room woke me in the morning. I sat up, disoriented from too little sleep, and realized Parker was gone.

I flopped back down, heaving a sigh of relief. Put off facing my boss, who knew I wanted to sleep with him? Yes, please.

It had been a long night and I hadn't fallen asleep until the wee hours of the morning. My mind had been spinning, trying to think of how I was going to continue business as usual with Parker. I hadn't come up with a solution before exhaustion had overtaken me.

I was sure to hurry into the shower and get ready as quickly as possible. The armor of my usual work clothes helped me not think about last night, and I was just putting the last pin in my hair when the door opened.

Parker must have gone to work out again, because I could hear him breathing heavily and the scent of his sweat drifted to me. Nerves twisted my stomach into knots and I grabbed my purse and slipped on my heels.

"I'm going to get some coffee," I said without looking at him; then I was out the door and heading down the hallway before he'd even had a chance to say a word.

Coffee was all I was getting because the thought of eating and then spending the next eight hours locked in a conference room with Parker made me physically ill. There was a Starbucks in the lobby and habit made me get Parker's usual as well as a triple soy mocha (add whip) for me. I glanced at my watch, knowing that the meeting began at eight-thirty. When it was five after, I grudgingly returned to the room, wishing I had a shot of whiskey to put in my coffee.

Parker was finishing his tie when I walked in. He glanced at me and my eyes skittered quickly away.

"I got you some coffee," I said, setting his cup on the

desk. "I checked with the hotel. The conference room will be ready to go and I requested a coffee and pastry service to be set up." Routine was good. Routine was normal.

Parker had already packed his laptop in its case so I packed mine, then glanced around to make sure I had everything I needed and that Parker had everything *he* needed.

"Sage, I think we should talk."

My panicked gaze jerked to his. He'd finished his tie—a perfect Windsor knot, as usual—and had stepped closer.

"You're joking," I said flatly, raising an eyebrow. My embarrassment was rapidly changing into irritation. I didn't like feeling humiliated, and the very last thing I wanted to talk about was last night. "How about we just forget everything that happened? Because I know that's what I want to do." Right down to his apology in the dark and how he'd swiped the tear tracks from my cheek.

"Sage, I'm sor—"

"I swear to God if you apologize one more time, I'm walking out that door and you'll never see me again," I snapped, cutting him off. "Good Lord, I've never had a man be so sorry he kissed me in my entire life!"

Parker may have winced slightly at that. It was hard to tell.

"If you don't want to talk about it, then we won't talk about it," he said.

"Good, because I don't want to talk about it."

"Fine."

"Fine."

I could tell he was pissed, but for once I didn't care. I was pissed, too, and frankly, I thought I had more of a right to my snit than he did to his. I couldn't imagine what would've happened had the situation been reversed and I'd started coming on to him, then said, "Just kidding!"

We walked to the elevator in stiff silence and were the

only ones in the car. I kept my distance, leaving at least two feet between myself and Parker. The doors were metal, our reflections staring back at us, which was super awkward. I gazed up at the floor display, watching the numbers slowly decrease.

"Technically, it wasn't a real kiss."

I opened my mouth to unload a good piece of my mind on him, but the elevator doors slid open, revealing a handful of people waiting.

"After you," Parker said.

I gave him a look that said exactly what I thought of him arguing semantics with me, then preceded him out of the elevator and down the hall to our conference room, already packed with half a dozen suit-clad men, all waiting for Parker and Viktor. Viktor arrived ten minutes after we did.

The day flew by in a haze of work and copies, phone calls, and typing. Mid-afternoon brought the only other woman—Tania. I had no idea why she was there, but she took a seat next to me. It made me slightly uncomfortable given the staring she'd done last night, but I tried to be friendly and make the best of it. Maybe it was just some kind of cultural thing.

"I don't know about you," I said in an undertone to her, "but I'm exhausted. Is it happy hour yet?" I smiled at her, but she didn't smile back. Okay, then. I backpedaled. "I'm sorry. Just making small talk, you know." She still didn't reply, so I just heaved a mental sigh. Maybe she didn't speak English? We sat at a small table in the corner, while the men took up the long cherry conference table covered in paper, laptops, and files.

"I need your help," she said, her voice barely above a whisper. She had an accent just like Viktor and his cronies, and apparently knew English just fine.

"Excuse me?" I must have misheard her.

She glanced at the men, her eyes zeroing in on Viktor, before speaking again. "I need your help," she repeated. "Please. I can't talk here. Follow me to the bathroom." Her lips barely moved as she spoke, as though she didn't want anyone to know she was talking to me.

Before I could ask anything more about the weird turn the conversation had just taken, she suddenly jerked away from me.

"Tania, are you tiring of the business talk?"

I glanced up and saw that Viktor had approached. He rested his hand on her shoulder and squeezed. Tania was about my height, though slighter than me. I wore a six and I guessed she probably wore a two. So when he squeezed her shoulder, I could tell it hurt. She was nothing but skin and bone and she cringed under his hold.

"Of course not, Viktor," she said, her voice a low monotone.

I studiously kept my gaze averted as Viktor leaned down to whisper something in Tania's ear. Out of the corner of my eye, I saw her hands tremble slightly. After a moment, Viktor walked away.

"Are you all right?" I whispered, careful to keep working so it wouldn't look like I was talking to her.

"Yes."

"What was that about?"

But she didn't reply. I didn't push, but it was all I could think about. When she stood to leave, she gave me a significant look before walking out the door. I waited a moment, then left as well. Glancing down the hallway, I saw her enter a women's restroom and I quickly followed. She was checking that all the stalls were empty when I entered.

"Tania, what's going on?" I asked. "Why do you need my help?"

She didn't answer until she'd checked the very last stall; then she hurried to me.

"I do not have much time," she said. "He will get suspicious if I am gone too long. Here. Take this." She pulled a sealed envelope from her purse and handed it to me. "I need you to give this to someone. Will you do that for me? I have no one else to ask and he won't let me leave."

Automatically, I took the envelope, noticing it had a name and address printed on the back. I stared at her in confusion. "Why? Who?" And those were just the questions I could put into words for this bizarre encounter.

"Niki. She is my sister. She lives in Chicago. Please. Just find her. Give this to her."

I had no choice. "Of course. But, Tania—"

"Do not trust them," she said. "Just do what they say. Cross them, and they will kill you, if you are lucky. I was not." Her eyes held a sad resignation even as she warned me. With one last glance in the mirror, she exited the bathroom.

I had no idea what to do or what to think. This whole thing was getting weirder by the day. I glanced at the paper. And now I was supposed to find Tania's sister and give some mysterious envelope to her? Resolving to discuss it with Parker after the meeting, I stuffed the envelope in my purse and went back to the conference room.

Business was finally concluded around six and I could tell Parker was tired as he packed up his things, issuing instructions to me for shipping containers back to the office and for deadlines to be set on his calendar. I took notes as he talked. I never had any questions because Parker and I worked together so well, I already knew his answers without having to ask. And if there was something I needed clarification on, he usually provided it automatically.

Finally, we were ready to go. I felt more normal now with

Parker; the day of working as usual had gone a long way toward easing my nerves. I'd been Parker's assistant a heck of a lot longer than I'd been his pretend-mistress, so the role was an easy one to fall back into.

"Can I tell you something?" I asked, moving to stand beside him as he put away his laptop.

"What is it?"

"It was something weird that happened," I said. "Did you notice the girl, Tania?"

"Viktor's girlfriend?" he asked, wrapping up the electrical cord.

"Yeah, her. Well, when she came in, she didn't talk much, but when she did, she said we shouldn't cross them, that they were dangerous, and that she'd get out if she could, but he wouldn't let her."

Parker paused for a moment, then resumed fastening the laptop bag. "That seems a bit odd," he said.

My eyebrows lifted. "Ya think?" I said, my sarcasm thicker than it probably should have been, but it didn't seem Parker was taking this seriously. He glanced at me, a warning in his eyes.

He shrugged. "So? Viktor is a dangerous guy from a dangerous country. But that's not what this deal is about, and his relationship with his girlfriend is hardly our business." Hefting the leather strap over his shoulder, he turned away, but I grabbed his arm.

"It wasn't like that," I insisted. "I don't think she's here of her own free will. She acted like she was a prisoner. Tell me that isn't any of our business. She obviously needs help." I almost told him about Tania's request to find her sister, but held my tongue. Parker wasn't reacting at all like I'd expected him to.

Parker gazed at me, his expression sober. Shrugging off

the bag's strap, he set the laptop case back on the table and took a step closer to me. His hands closed on my arms, surprising me. I would have instinctively taken a step back, away from his touch, but he held me firm.

"Listen to me," he said. "I need you to do your job. I know you feel bad for this girl, but you can't get involved. *We* can't get involved."

"But—"

"You're not listening, Sage," he said more forcefully. "Forget the girl and just focus on your job. That's all I ask. No, forget that. I'm not asking, I'm telling. Do your job, Sage. Leave the rest to me."

Anger flared and my eyes narrowed. "Do my job?" I repeated. "When have I ever not done my job?"

"I'm not saying you haven't," Parker said.

"So because I tell you something scary, something I've never seen before, suddenly I'm not doing my job?" I didn't think there was anything Parker could have said that would have made me angrier.

"First, I am always doing my job," I spat, furious. "Whether it's a phone call at ten o'clock at night on a weekend or the *request* to come in early on a Monday morning. I put my job before everything else in my life. Second, I've always considered you an honorable man, someone who did the right thing, but the money involved in this deal has blinded you. I never thought I'd see the day when I lost respect for you." I took a breath. "And last but certainly not least: take your hands *off* me."

Parker and I were locked in a battle of wills and his eyes flashed blue fire, but I stood my ground. After a moment, he released me.

Turning on my heel, I walked out, so mad I thought surely steam had to be coming out of my ears. But as angry as I was, duty called, so I stopped at the front desk to arrange for the boxes left in the conference room to be shipped.

"Also, I didn't receive any messages about my room being ready," I said. "I'd really like my own room tonight."

"Of course, let me just check." After hitting some keys on the keyboard, he frowned. "Um, I'm sorry; there must be a misunderstanding. We were notified to cancel that request this morning."

"What? You're kidding!" I couldn't believe it. "I didn't do that. I need that other room. Do you have one available?"

"I'm sorry, but we don't," he said.

I buried my face in my hands. God help me, this had to be the worst trip to New York, ever.

"Miss?"

I stood up, dropped my hands, and took a deep breath. I would remain cool. I would remain calm.

"That's fine," I said. "I'll just…make do." My smile was through gritted teeth. Another night with Parker. Ugh. Last night I'd been afraid I'd jump his bones; tonight I just might smother him with a pillow.

The clerk was looking at the computer screen again. "It looks like Mr. Anderson canceled the request," he said.

And just like that, my "cool and calm" went out the flippin' window.

"I'm going to kill him," I gritted out between clenched teeth.

"Excuse me?" The clerk looked at me with eyebrows raised.

"Nothing. I'm fine. Thank you." I smiled again and the clerk gave me a weak smile back. He probably thought I was close to losing it, and he would have been correct. "Can you please have this put in my room?" I handed him my laptop case, which he readily took.

I had to get out of there. I absolutely could not face Parker right now, not when I was so angry with him. And so... disappointed in him. It hurt in my gut when I thought about it, so I pushed the thought away, switched off my phone, and headed out the door.

CHAPTER NINE

I walked until I wasn't mad anymore, which was quite a ways. By the time I really looked to see where I was, night had fallen and my stomach was complaining quite loudly that it was past dinnertime.

There were restaurants and bars everywhere and I chose one that looked slightly upscale. Heading inside, I saw I'd picked a place where a lot of people must come after work, as they all seemed to be professionals about my age or slightly older.

I made my way to the bar and snagged an empty stool. The bartender came by and I ordered a Grey Goose martini, straight up. He handed me a menu, too. I looked it over. Everything looked good...and pricey. I decided to get what I wanted and just expense it. Half the time Parker just signed whatever I put in front of him, barely glancing at it. He could sign off on my dinner, too.

The martini hit the spot and I downed it pretty quickly,

then signaled the bartender for another. I people-watched as I sipped the second drink. It was interesting, watching the interaction between the single women and men, playing the game, flirting, hooking up...

I sighed, suddenly wishing I was anywhere but in New York. I wondered what Ryker was doing, and if he'd thought about me since our date Saturday night.

A woman sat down on the stool next to me, and I glanced over. She looked to be about my age. Strikingly pretty, she had a really unusual hair color—strawberry blond—and I found myself staring slightly enviously at her long, wavy locks.

"A manhattan, please," she ordered from the bartender, "on the rocks." She caught me staring.

"Really need a drink," she said, smiling somewhat sheepishly.

"Oh, yes, I completely agree," I replied, indicating my martini. "Same here."

"Rough day?" she asked.

I nodded. "My boss is driving me batty."

She smiled. "That's as good a reason to drink as I've ever heard."

"You from around here?" I asked as the bartender set her drink in front of her. I thought I could detect a bit of an accent in her words, though it wasn't very pronounced.

She shook her head and took a long swallow before replying. "No. I'm a tourist. I swear, we've trekked the entire city today."

"We?"

"Me and my husband," she clarified. "He's outside on his cell. Said he couldn't hear a thing in here with all the noise." She took another drink just as a man stepped up behind her.

Wow.

My eyes about bugged out of my head. He was hot, in the capital-H-double-T kind of way. Inky black hair fell over intensely blue eyes framed with thick dark lashes. He had wickedly arched eyebrows, a square jaw that defined "chiseled," and shoulders wide and deep enough to make a woman weak in the knees.

"I knew I shouldn't leave you alone in a bar," he teased her, resting a hand on the small of her back.

"I'm just nervous," she said. "It's been a while since we've seen him."

"There's nothing to be nervous about," he replied. "You're overthinking it. Besides, he drove up from D.C. to have dinner with us, so it's not like we can back out now."

"I don't want to back out. I just needed a little...liquid courage." She took another big swallow of the manhattan.

"C'mon. It's just around the block," he said. Taking the glass from her, he downed the rest of the drink.

"That was mine, you know," she groused, but she was smiling.

"I'll buy you another when we get there." Leaning down, he kissed her lightly on the lips.

I sighed, watching the two of them. They seemed real sweet together, and judging by the size of the rock on her left hand and the way he was touching her as if she were made of glass, he was smitten. I wondered who they were meeting for dinner that made her nervous.

"It was nice meeting you," she said, turning to me with a smile while her husband tossed some money onto the bar to pay for her drink.

"Same here," I said.

Her husband glanced at me, a slight frown on his face, and I abruptly decided that while he was one of the best-looking men I'd ever seen, something about him made me not want to meet up with him in a dark alley. Taking her hand, he led her away just as the bartender set my dinner in front of me.

I made quick work of the filet, au gratin potatoes, and asparagus, switching to wine once I was through with my martini. Probably not a good idea to mix my liquors, but I was past caring.

I didn't know what to think about how this afternoon had gone down and what Parker had said. It hadn't occurred to me *not* to tell him about Tania. I thought that he would know what to do—Parker always knew what to do. To have him tell me that it wasn't our problem and to stay out of it and just do my job was like a slap in the face.

Millions would be made off this deal; I got that. It was a lot of money to turn your back on, but I'd never thought of Parker as someone who would compromise his principles.

Ryker was right. I didn't know Parker at all.

I was well into my second glass of wine when a man sat down next to me. Glancing over, I saw him smile at me. He was good-looking, with brown hair and brown eyes and a neatly trimmed goatee.

"Hi," he said.

"Hi yourself," I replied, the words only a little slurred.

"Alone tonight?" he asked.

I nodded. "Sometimes it's the best way."

His smile widened. "True."

I tipped my wineglass and took a drink, then saw the man signal the bartender for another round.

"No, I should stop," I said, setting down my nearly empty glass. "I've drunk too much already."

"But you haven't had a drink with me," he said with a grin. He was cute, cuter than I'd originally thought, but maybe that was the wine talking.

The bartender set down a newly filled glass that looked really tempting. I eyed it. Oh, what the hell.

"So why are we drinking alone tonight?" the guy asked as I took a swallow. "Boyfriend trouble?"

"Nope," I said. "Work trouble. Which is worse. At least I could break up with a bad boyfriend, right?"

"Right."

"But, like, with work, I'm *stuck*, ya know?" He nodded. I squinted blearily at him. "What's your name again?"

"Han," he said.

I squinted even harder. "Like *Star Wars*?"

"Yep."

"Huh." I didn't think I'd ever met someone named after *Star Wars* before. "What was I saying?" It was hard to remember, so I shrugged, taking another sip. It was really going to my head now, despite the dinner I'd eaten, but I was past the when-to-say-when stage and had hopped on the gonna-regret-this-tomorrow train.

Han was funny, and talkative, and he really liked me. Or at least he pretended to like me, which was more than I could say for Parker, who didn't even think I was a hard worker, but just a slut who'd sleep with her boss and he didn't even care about people but just money and he should know better than that because karma is a bitch and he wouldn't be able to even find his own computer if it weren't for me…

"…and it's not like I'm a pain in the ass," I complained. "I never call in sick, or take vacation days, or personal days. I'm at his beck and call twenty-four-seven—" I interrupted my own diatribe to finish off my third—fourth?—glass of wine. I had to pee. "Excuse me," I said, sliding off the stool, wobbling for a moment on my heels before my equilibrium righted itself. "I'll be right back."

The floor felt like it was shifting sand as I searched for the bathroom, the room spinning around me. I used the facilities and washed my hands, glancing in the mirror at my smeared mascara and bun that was sadly listing to the side. I started taking pins out, carelessly tossing them on the floor, then ran my fingers through the freed strands.

"Much better," I sighed. I was tired. Time to leave.

Star Wars guy—Luke, was it?—was still there when I got back and I handed my credit card to the bartender to take care of the tab.

"I gotta go," I said to him, "but thanks for the company."

"Let me help you get a cab," he said as I pocketed my card and signed the bill.

He followed me as I tottered outside, letting me hold on to his arm for balance, then whistled and flagged down a taxi. The cab pulled over and Obi-Wan opened the door for me.

"Have a good evening, Sage," he said as I settled inside. He told the name of my hotel to the driver.

I glanced back at him with a frown. "How'd you know where I was staying?"

He leaned inside and smiled, though it wasn't nearly as friendly a smile as before. "Viktor told me." Then he shut the door and the driver stepped on the gas.

A wave of cold washed over me as I struggled to think, but my mind was too fogged. I rested my head against the seat.

"Hey, lady, we're here."

I jerked awake, realizing I'd fallen asleep during the ride back to the hotel. I dug in my purse, handing over a couple of crumpled bills before climbing out of the cab.

I knew I looked like someone who was incredibly drunk but trying desperately hard to appear *not* to be.

The catnap in the taxi had helped a bit, though the lobby was spinning and tilting as I made my way painfully forward, careful with each step I took. Making a scene by falling on my ass in the lobby of a five-star hotel in Manhattan was not how I wanted New York to remember me.

At this hour, there was a bellman at the elevator and he asked me what floor. I scrunched my forehead, trying to remember. The bellman stared at me.

"Fourteen!" I said at last, proud I'd remembered. "Yes, fourteenth floor."

The hallway was long and quiet and I talked to myself as I passed the doors. "Fourteen-ten, fourteen-eleven, fourteen-twelve…wow, this hallway has great acoustics." Testing it out, I sang a few bars of one of my favorite Material Girl songs. I wasn't the best singer, but wow, tonight I sounded *awesome*.

I was finishing the second verse by the time I got to fourteen-twenty-seven. Digging through my purse, I'd just hit the chorus when the door suddenly flew open.

"Where the hell have you been?"

I stumbled back, abruptly cutting off in the middle of *didn't know how lost I was until I found you*. I lost my balance and Parker's hand shot out, grabbing hold of my arm and keeping me from falling.

"I went to dinner," I retorted. "Where do you think?" I remembered I was mad at him, but couldn't recall why. Shaking off his hand, I pushed past him into the room. I was headed for my bed when the bathroom caught my eye.

A bath sounded really good. Yeah. A relaxing bubble bath.

I detoured, my purse falling to the floor as I flipped on the light in the bathroom. Bending over the tub, I grabbed hold of the side so I wouldn't topple in, and turned the knob.

Water began pouring out of the spigot. I plugged the drain and stood.

"What are you doing?"

Glancing around, I saw Parker watching me from the doorway. He looked pissed and disheveled, the first of which was to be expected—the latter, not.

"Do you have any idea how worried I've been all fucking night?" he spat. "I've tried to call you at least a hundred times."

"Too bad," I shot back. "I took the night off."

My feet hurt. I bent a knee and tugged off a shoe, letting it fall to the floor, then did the same for the other. I wiggled my toes and sighed. Much better.

Parker made a noise of disgust and reached past me to turn off the water.

"Stop that!" I said, yanking a handful of his shirt. "I want to take a bath!"

"You're so drunk, you're liable to drown," he said. "Forget it."

"You can't tell me what to do," I said, poking him in the chest. "I mean, you can, like, during the day, but not at night, so just back off." It may have made more of an impact if I hadn't hiccupped in the middle of that.

The tub was nearly half-full now so I started unbuttoning my shirt, getting about four undone before growing impatient and tugging it over my head. The room was spinning, but I knew if I could get in the tub, I'd feel so much better.

"I'm taking a bath, like it or not, so get out." I bent to test the water temperature. Just under scalding. Perfect. I shucked my bra, then unzipped my skirt and shoved it down my legs along with my panties.

I'd put one foot into the tub when I felt hands on my

waist. I yelped in surprise. Parker was still in here. "What the hell? I told you to get out."

"Take it easy. I don't need you falling and cracking your head open."

"I do this all the time," I said as the water splashed. "It's not like I've never taken a bath before." Sinking down into the steaming tub, I leaned back against the side and let out a deep sigh, my eyes sliding shut. Oh yeah. This was what I'd needed. It wasn't as deep as my one back home, but it was good enough.

I sat like that for a while, dozing, then coming awake, then dozing again. One of the times, I opened my eyes and saw Parker still there, sitting on the closed toilet lid. He didn't speak. He just watched me.

"Shouldn't you leave?" I asked. "Just 'cuz you had your hands all over me last night doesn't give you the right to a show tonight."

"I'm afraid you'll pass out and drown," he said dryly. "And they'd probably accuse me of killing you, so no, I think I'll stay."

"Glad to know you care," I retorted. Asshole. Whatever.

I forgot Parker entirely as my eyes slipped shut again. I groped blindly for the soap, wetting it and sliding it down my arm, over my neck and breasts, and down my stomach. Everything was soapy now, my fingers sliding over my slick skin. Suddenly, I felt the soap plucked from my hand.

"Okay, that's enough. Time for bed."

I'd barely registered that before I was hauled to my feet, my eyes flying open in shock. "But I still have soap on me!" I protested.

Parker reached and grabbed a washcloth off the counter. Dipping it into the water, he pressed it roughly to my neck and squeezed. Water fell in a warm cascade over my breasts and stomach. I rubbed the soap from my skin, noticing now that Parker's eyes were glued to my chest and his forehead was dotted with sweat.

"Is it hot in here?" I asked.

His eyes jerked to mine. "Are you fucking kidding me?" he rasped. His tone held such incredulity, so uncommon for him, that I laughed, which didn't go over very well. Reaching behind him again, he grabbed a towel and wrapped it roughly around me.

"You shouldn't curse," I said, holding on to his shoulder as I stepped out of the tub. "Especially around a lady." I smothered a yawn.

"I was a Marine. Of course I curse."

"Ryker was a Marine. He curses, too," I said.

"Does he?"

"Yeah. He wanted to sleep with me."

My foot slipped on the tile and I would've fallen if Parker hadn't locked an arm around my waist. I was relaxed from the booze and the bath and sagged against him. The towel had slipped, but I was beyond caring. Scooping me up in his arms, he carried me to the bed and sat me down.

"Need my pajamas," I mumbled, but I didn't move. The pillow beckoned.

Parker bent and rummaged through my suitcase, returning with my jammies.

"Is this it?" he asked, a dubious look on his face as he held up the black nightie.

"Yep." I raised my arms, waiting for him to slip it on over my head, but he didn't. Parker just looked at me, his gaze raking down my body and back up. His throat moved as he swallowed.

"Did you let him?" he asked.

I frowned, lowering my arms. "Let who do what?"

"You said Ryker wanted to sleep with you. Did you let him?"

"Nope. Not yet. He hates you, by the way. But he's a really...um...really good ki*sssss*er." My words slurred and my eyes were too heavy to stay open. Then I felt my arms being lifted, each in turn, and the fabric of my nightgown settled into place.

Something nagged at me, but I couldn't think what it was, something bad. "Viktor," I said, frowning and trying to remember.

"Viktor? What about him?" The bed dipped as Parker sat beside me. "Sage, wake up. Tell me about Viktor. Did you see him tonight?" The urgency in his voice had me prying open my eyes.

I gave a halfhearted shake of my head. "Nope, not him. Another guy. Darth Vader."

"What?"

I waved my hand. "*Star Wars,*" I explained, but Parker just looked even more confused. I heaved an exhausted sigh, forcing my lips to move. "He bought me wine, lots of it. Then put me in a cab. But he knew the hotel and I asked him, I said, 'Hey, how do you know that?' and he said Viktor told him."

My head was too heavy and Parker's shoulder was right there. I leaned against him, his arms coming up to hold me. He smelled good.

"It scared me," I mumbled into his chest. "I don't like being scared, Parker."

His arms tightened around me, one palm moving up to cup the back of my head, his fingers sliding in the strands of my hair. He tucked me closer to him.

"Don't be afraid. No one's going to hurt you," he said. "I swear it."

But I was already asleep.

* * *

"Time to get up, Sage. We've got a flight to catch."

The words penetrated my consciousness, right along with a massive headache. I moaned, squeezing my eyes shut.

"Come on. I let you sleep in, but now you've got to get up. I don't want to miss our flight."

I blinked blearily, squinting against the massive rays of sunshine that were trying to burn my eyeballs. Parker stood above me.

"Here's some water and painkillers," he said, setting something on the bedside table. "We leave in thirty minutes." He walked away.

I sat up, blinking and wishing I'd never heard of wine, or Grey Goose. I should become a Mennonite. They didn't drink, right? Or a Mormon. No wait, Mormons didn't do caffeine either. Mennonite it was.

Scrabbling for the three pills he'd left, I swallowed them down with the water. He was shaving, using the mirror out here to do it, rather than in the bathroom. I assumed that was out of deference to me so I could get my ass in the shower and get ready to leave.

Rubbing my eyes, I realized I was in my nightgown. I didn't even remember coming back to the hotel, much less changing. Oh God, had Parker been here when I'd gotten back? I'd been drunk off my ass. Not exactly the most professional way to behave with your boss. *Nice one, Sage.* But how to find out? I didn't want to ask, which would be a dead giveaway as to how drunk I'd been.

Getting out of bed, I carefully made my way to the bathroom, recognizing that I hadn't had enough time to sleep off the booze and it was still floating through my bloodstream.

I wore nothing underneath the nightgown and my clothes from last night were nowhere to be seen.

I took a quick shower, pinning up my hair since I had no time to blow it dry. Makeup wasn't to be bothered with and I dug through my suitcase while wrapped in a towel, pulling out a skirt and blouse for today. My clothes from last night had been neatly folded and put in my suitcase, which gave me pause, but I had no time to think about it.

"Thanks for the pills," I said to Parker once I'd dressed and emerged from the bathroom. I winced. I'd tried to speak softly, but my voice sounded like a megaphone inside my head.

He was putting in his cuff links and glanced at me. If I'd thought maybe I could read something about what I'd done last night from his expression, I was disappointed.

"I need you to be functional today," he said, picking a tie and sliding it underneath his collar.

My face flushed hotly and I nodded. "Sorry about...last night," I said.

Parker looked my way again, his gaze sharp. "No need to apologize," he said carefully.

I swallowed. "Were you...ah...here...when I got back?" In other words, had I changed into my pajamas in front of him? Lord, that would be mortifying.

Parker looked steadily at me, his face unreadable. For a moment, I thought he wasn't going to answer. Finally, he said, "I was asleep."

Oh. Oh good. I breathed a sigh of relief. "I must not have woken you then," I said, fishing just a tiny bit more.

There was a knock on the door, interrupting our conversation. I hurried to open it before they could pound on it again.

"Room service," the man said. He was holding a tray that was emanating a smell. Bacon and eggs.

"Oh, God," I said, bolting into the bathroom and slamming the door. And there went the last of the wine. And the pills I'd just taken.

When I was through being sick, I brushed my teeth again and wiped my face with a cold washcloth. I felt like death warmed over and my hands shook. Glancing in the mirror, I winced. Dark circles shadowed my red-rimmed eyes and I was as white as a sheet.

There was a soft tap on the door. "Sage? Are you all right?" Parker.

"Um, yeah, I'm fine," I replied, quickly patting my face dry. I took a deep breath and prayed he'd eaten the food really fast so I didn't have to smell it again.

Opening the door, I glanced around, but the food wasn't there. "Did you eat that fast?" I asked.

He shook his head. "Wrong room. Sorry about that." Concern creased his face. "You sure you're all right?"

I nodded, glancing away from him. God, I was so embarrassed. He'd just heard me puking in the bathroom. New York hated me. I was never coming here again. "We probably need to get going," I said.

Parker hesitated, then turned away. I grabbed my suitcase, threw a few last things into it, and zipped it up. Slinging my purse and laptop over my shoulder, I started hauling it out of the room.

"Here, I'll get it," Parker said, taking the handle from me.

"Oh, um, okay." Unexpected, but I would certainly let him. Fishing in my purse, I found my oversized sunglasses and slipped them on. My throbbing head felt fractionally better.

I fell asleep on the way to the airport and Parker woke me when we got there. He was surprisingly kind, though I didn't deserve it. I was still having a hard time accepting the fact that I'd gotten rip-roaring drunk on a business trip to New York—*while* staying in the same room as my boss.

Moronic idiot didn't begin to cover it.

We didn't speak until after we were on the plane. This time I was comfortably ensconced in first class next to Parker. We were midway through the flight and he had his laptop out when the flight attendant came by.

"Coffee, please, black," he said. "And a water for her."

I still wore my sunglasses, my head resting in my hand while my elbow was braced on the armrest, but glanced at him. He was being awfully nice and considerate…and a flash of memory hit me.

Oh. My. God.

I had pranced around buck-ass naked last night. I'd stripped in front of Parker, *bathed* in front of Parker, then had draped my naked self all over him.

I gasped aloud, my dismay and horror cutting so deep, it was sure to leave a mark.

Parker's head swiveled, his eyes meeting mine, and I could tell at once that he knew I'd figured it out. Of course, my gaping mouth was probably a flashing neon sign. His jaw tightened.

"You told me you were sleeping!" Even I could tell that I'd said that a little too loud.

"Sage—"

"Oh God oh God oh God," I quietly moaned. I slid my fingers beneath my glasses, covering my face with my hands. I'd be lucky if I didn't lose my job over this. Was he even now just waiting until we got back to Chicago before telling me? The thought sent my stomach into a whole other round of churning nausea.

"Sage, listen to me—"

"Please stop. Just…don't talk to me."

To my relief, he shut up. I wanted to crawl under a rock and hide. How was I ever going to look him in the eye again? Every moment was now back in stark Technicolor clarity, the stripping, the tub, letting him put my nightgown on...

The rest of the flight was a blur, my mind a whirl of embarrassment, dread, and regret. I didn't want to get fired, and it wasn't just because I loved my job, which I did. The truth was I didn't want to not be able to see Parker anymore, which is exactly what would happen if I was canned. We had no relationship outside of work, so it wasn't like he'd call me up or text me to meet for a friendly lunch or something. It would just be...over.

Neither of us spoke as we landed and deplaned. I made my way to baggage claim, praying I'd get my suitcase quickly; then I'd grab a cab and get out of there. I knew I was being a coward, but it was all I could do right now. I'd face the music tomorrow.

Unfortunately, the universe was having a big laugh at my expense because my suitcase was one of the last off. Parker had retrieved his, but instead of leaving as I'd hoped he would, he stuck around, checking messages on his phone while I waited for my bag. When it finally hit the belt, I was there, pulling it off and yanking up the handle.

"I have a car waiting. I'll drop you at home."

Dismayed, I stared at Parker, but he was pocketing his phone and not looking at me.

"It's fine. I'll take a cab," I said. Enduring the flight had been bad enough. Adding a car ride seemed unnecessarily cruel.

This time he did look at me. "It wasn't a suggestion," he said, and there was enough steel in his voice that I knew I didn't have a choice in the matter.

I followed him out of the airport and to the waiting sedan,

the driver putting our suitcases in the trunk while Parker
waited for me to slide in the back ahead of him. My sense of
impending doom had increased with each step I'd taken until now it felt like it would choke me. Tears I couldn't hold
back clung to my lashes behind the sunglasses as I tried to
come to grips with the fact that I was about to be fired, and
that I had no one to blame but myself.

Unable to look at Parker, I stared out the window while
the driver got behind the wheel. Parker leaned forward and
gave him my address, then settled back in the seat as the car
rolled smoothly out.

I felt too small and fragile sitting next to him, my emotions at a breaking point. His knees were spread wide, in
contrast to mine, pressed tightly together as every muscle in
my body coiled in tension, waiting.

"Sage, we need to talk," he said.

I knew I couldn't tell him to stop, not this time, so I
remained silent. My hands were clenched in my lap and I
stared down at them.

"Last night was...unfortunate," he continued, "and it's
left us in a bit of an awkward situation."

Parker always did have a knack for understatement.

"You and I have always worked well together," he said,
"and I appreciate the dedication and loyalty you put into
your job."

Here it comes, I thought, bracing myself. A tear splashed
from my cheek onto my hand. I stared blindly at it. What
was I going to do? How was I going to explain to my parents
that I'd gotten fired? Though knowing them, they'd be glad
I was through being "just a secretary."

"Sage, I—" He stopped and I held my breath. Suddenly,
he leaned closer and before I could stop him, he'd snatched
away my sunglasses. I made a desperate grab for them.

"What are you doing?" I asked. "Give me those!" But he held them out of my reach.

Parker was studying my face, frowning. "Why are you crying?"

I stared at him as though he were a moron. "Because you're firing me, obviously," I said.

"Why would I fire you?"

Now I was sure he'd lost his mind. "You're kidding, right?" More tears slid down my face.

His eyes softened and he reached into his front pocket for the square of silk tucked there. I sat in bemused astonishment as he wiped my cheeks with what I knew was a hundred-dollar pocket square.

"I'm not firing you," he said gently, smoothing away the tear tracks. "So don't cry, okay?"

"What?" Surely I hadn't heard him correctly.

"Don't cry," he repeated.

"No, not that. The other," I said.

"I'm not firing you."

I blinked, confused. "You're not?"

"I'm not." He smiled a little, pressing the pocket square into my hand. "I need you too much to fire you for having a bit much to drink, and training someone new would be a total pain in the ass."

I laughed through my tears at this, sniffing and swallowing down the lump in my throat. Pressing the silk to my eyes, I dried them as best I could. The fabric smelled faintly of Parker's cologne.

"Let's just pretend last night never happened," he said. "We won't mention it again, okay?"

I nodded. That sounded good to me. "I'd appreciate that," I said. I knew I wanted to forget the fool I'd made of myself.

The rest of the ride to my apartment passed in a silence

that was only slightly less awkward. I figured it would settle back to normal once we were in the office and had assumed the roles we were accustomed to. At least, I hoped it would.

Parker insisted on helping me with my bag, walking me all the way to my door. "You don't feel well and it only takes a moment," he said.

I unlocked my apartment door and would have stepped inside, but Parker's hand on my arm stopped me.

"Let me go first, okay?" he asked, not waiting for my reply before moving in front of me.

I noticed both his hands were free as he scanned the living room, then disappeared down the hallway to my bedroom. Confused as to what the heck he was doing, I followed him.

"What are you doing?" I asked, watching as he opened my closet and glanced inside.

"Just checking," he replied.

"Checking for what?"

His gaze met mine. "Intruders. Viktor, remember? I don't trust him."

Oh yeah. What that guy had said last night. In my embarrassment over what I'd done with Parker, it had slipped my mind.

After Parker had fully checked out the apartment to his satisfaction, we stood in the foyer. I wrapped my arms around myself, unsure what to say or do, if anything.

"Take the afternoon off," Parker said, "and I'll see you in the morning."

"Okay."

He opened the door and was about to step through when I blurted out, "I'm sorry."

Parker paused.

"I mean, it was unprofessional of me and a stupid thing to

do," I said. "And I just wanted to say that I was sorry." I still held the pocket square he'd given me, clenched in my hand, as I waited for him to say something.

"There's no need to apologize," he said. "If anyone owes an apology, it's from me to you. You were worried about the girl, and I upset you, which I didn't intend."

I didn't know what to say, so I just nodded.

"Just forget it, all right?" he asked with a small smile. "I already have. See you in the morning." Then he was out the door and gone.

CHAPTER TEN

I slept the afternoon away, and when I woke around dinner-time, I felt much better. The headache was gone, thank God, and I was starving. I decided some fresh air and exercise would help blow the rest of the cobwebs from my brain, so I changed into shorts and a shirt, grabbed my purse, slung the strap across my chest, and headed outside.

There was a favorite Chinese place of mine three blocks away, so that's where I went. A half hour and a stomach full of beef and broccoli later, I felt human again. As I was digging in my purse to pay, I saw the envelope Tania had given me.

Hmm.

I knew Chicago pretty well, but had to pull out my laminated pocket map to find the address she'd written on the back of the envelope. It wasn't in that great a part of town, but it was still light outside. I figured I'd be able to catch a bus there, deliver Tania's message, and get home before it was full dark.

The bus driver looked at me a bit strangely when, forty minutes later, I was passing by him to exit the vehicle.

"Are you lost?" he asked.

I shook my head. "No. I'm visiting a friend."

He shrugged, but the skeptical look on his face didn't make me feel any better. Too late to turn back now.

The streets were darker than I thought they'd be at this hour, but a lot of the streetlamps were broken, so that was probably why. The tall brick buildings on either side of the street were showing their age and then some. I watched the taillights of the bus as it lumbered away from me, spewing gray exhaust, wondering if I'd just made a bad decision. Maybe I should catch a cab home and visit Tania's sister tomorrow?

But there were no cabs in sight, and the cars that did pass had me taking a few steps farther back onto the sidewalk. Eyes stared out at me from behind tinted windows or no windows at all. I swallowed, my palms suddenly sweaty.

I'd memorized the path to the address from my map, so I headed that direction. It was only a couple of blocks from where the bus had dropped me off. I skirted quickly by dark alleyways that gaped like empty maws as I passed, threatening to gobble me up. I could hear dogs barking a street or two over and I prayed they wouldn't come in my direction. Being chased by rabid dogs wasn't high on my To Do list. Of course, walking through parts of Chicago I'd only seen on the news wasn't either, yet here I was.

After what seemed an interminable walk, passing a few people who I avoided making eye contact with, I was finally in front of the right building. The paper said apartment 3C, so I went inside and started up the dilapidated stairs. An incandescent light flickered tiredly over the stairwell, illuminating the gloomy interior, and I could hear through the paper-thin walls—a television tuned to a game show, a baby crying, two people yelling at each other.

For a girl who'd grown up in Lake Forest, this was definitely out of my comfort zone.

Standing in front of 3C, I took a deep breath, raised my hand, and knocked. I heard nothing from inside. I tried again, knocking harder. This time, the door opened a scant inch and the sliver of a woman's face peered through the crack.

"Who are you?" she asked.

"Niki? Are you Niki?"

The woman shook her head. "Niki doesn't live here anymore."

"Oh." I didn't know what to do then. Tania hadn't said anything about her sister moving. "Do you know where she moved to?"

"Who are you?" she asked again.

"My name is Sage. Niki's sister Tania sent me to find her."

"How do you know Tania?"

"I met her in New York," I said. "Her…boyfriend…is doing a deal with mine. Do you know where Niki is?"

"They took her, a few weeks ago," she said. "Accused her of being a snitch to the police. They made an example of her."

A sense of foreboding crept over me. "What happened?" I was afraid I already knew the answer.

"They killed her."

I felt sick to my stomach. "I-I'm so sorry," I stammered, at a loss as to what to say. "Are you sure?"

She nodded. "They wanted all of us to know so we did not start getting ideas about rebelling."

I swallowed, trying to wrap my head around all this. "Rebelling against what? I don't understand."

"You need to go now," she said, trying to shut the door, but I shoved my foot in the crack. "Please tell me what's going on," I said. "Maybe I can help you."

"So they kill me, too? No thank you." She tried to force the door closed again.

"Tania trusted me," I persisted. "Is she in danger? Tell me that much at least. Please. I want to warn her."

That seemed to give her pause. I held my breath, waiting. The eye surveying me blinked once; then the door shut and I heard the rattle of a chain before it opened all the way.

"Fine," she said curtly, allowing me inside. She peered past my shoulder at the empty hallway as though to make sure we were alone, then closed and locked the door before turning to me, looking me over intently from head to foot.

Her face was strained, the lines around her mouth making her seem older than she probably was, which couldn't have been much past her early twenties. Her hair was long and dark like mine, our height about the same.

She led me to a couch that had seen better days, the cushions tired and flat. One leg was missing so a telephone book was propped underneath it to hold it up. I gingerly sat, hoping it would hold my weight. She sat next to me.

"I'm Hanna," she said. "You want to know so badly, then I will tell you. There are several of us. Not just Tania and Niki. We were born in Donetsk, in the Ukraine. It is hard there, not many jobs, especially for women. We heard of a way to come to America where we could work as maids to pay for our passage. Many came, but it was a lie. They made us prostitutes, the cartel, here in Chicago. Told us they would kill us if we did not do as they said. So... we did."

It was hard to wrap my head around. The idea of being

forced to become a prostitute or die seemed as foreign to me as the name of the city in which Hanna said they'd been born.

"Couldn't you leave?" I asked. "Run away somewhere else?"

"To where? We had no money, no food, did not speak English. We did what we had to do to survive." Her chin came up at this, defiant.

"I'm sorry," I said. "It's hard for me to understand, but I want to help you."

Hanna shook her head. "There is nothing you can do. The men who control us, all of us, they are powerful, evil men."

"Why don't you come with me?" I asked. "I can take you to a place with people who can help you. They won't find you."

A panicked look came over her face and she shook her head. "I cannot. There is no place to hide. The police—they turn a blind eye. They are like police in Russia, get paid by the mob bosses to look the other way."

"Not all of them are like that," I said, thinking of Ryker. But she just shook her head again.

"I cannot."

She seemed resolute, so I just nodded. "Okay. But take my phone number, okay? In case you change your mind. Just call me and I'll help you." I jotted my number down on a scrap of paper from my purse and gave it to her.

Hanna hesitated, gingerly taking the paper from me. "Why would you do that?"

"Because," I said. "I'd like to help you any way you'll let me."

"All right." She still looked skeptical, as though she had no intention of ever calling, but didn't want to be outwardly rude, either.

I stood to go and she did, too, walking me to the door.

"Be careful," she said as I left. "It is a dangerous neighborhood for a woman alone."

Yeah, tell me something I *didn't* know.

The envelope felt like it was burning a hole in my purse. I wondered what I should do with it. It was sealed, and though it had occurred to me to open it, I hadn't.

I quickly found that it was impossible to get a cab to stop, when I actually saw one. They passed me by like I was invisible. I had to actually call for a cab, but I was told they wouldn't be there for fifteen minutes.

Spotting a bar on the next corner, I told the cab company I'd be waiting there. Really didn't want to just stand on the street corner to wait. Somebody might get the wrong idea. The bar's lights glinted in the night, and I headed for it.

The bar was called Johnny's and I walked quickly, keeping my head down and a death grip on my purse. Now that the sun had set, more people were coming out of the shadows to loiter on the sidewalk. The streets seemed a hundred times more sinister after Hanna's story and knowing Niki was dead, her murder a "message" to the women the cartel controlled.

A car was idling in the street as a man leaned in the window to talk to the driver. I'd never seen an actual drug deal taking place before, but I was pretty sure that's what I was viewing now.

Johnny's was in no better shape than the buildings that surrounded it and I wrinkled my nose in distaste as I approached the place, my steps slowing. It was on the corner with several cars parked in front and I could see more in the lot at the back. Neon signs proclaiming the various logos of popular beers glowed in the windows.

I stood on the corner, trying to see inside but it was too

dark, and wondering if my plan to wait there was really something I wanted to do. As I watched, two men went in and I caught the sound of people talking and music before the door drifted shut.

I made up my mind. There was no way I could go in there, even just to wait for my cab. I'd be an absolute fool to do so.

I turned around, wanting to put some space between me and the seedy-looking bar, and abruptly stopped. A man stood right in front of me, flanked by two more guys.

It was obvious the man in the middle was the leader, the other two his sidekicks. He was the biggest, sported a short goatee and mustache and had massive tattooed biceps. A thin gold chain looped around his neck, and I mentally compared him to 50 Cent. A black cap sat off-center on his head and I somewhat hysterically wanted to tell him that wasn't how you wore it.

He also looked like someone who could hurt me real bad, real quick.

"Well, lookie what we have here," he sneered. "Whattsa matter, sugar? You lost?"

My stomach lodged in my throat as panic sent my heart rate skyrocketing. "N-no," I stammered, backing away from them. "I-I was just leaving."

"Not so fast," he said, following me. "We're heading in to Johnny's. I know you wanna come with us."

"No, I don't," I said, taking another step back. "But, uh, thanks for the invitation." Fight or flight took over and I turned to run, only to realize I'd been surrounded.

Four men now grouped around me and baseball cap guy, the one who'd kept me talking, grabbed hold of my elbow. I winced as he dragged me along with him toward the bar.

. "Let me go!" He ignored me. I dragged in a breath to

scream, then saw the glint of a knife blade in the hand of the man who flanked my other side—sidekick #1.

"Scream and it'll be the last noise you make," he said.

I clamped my mouth shut.

Oh, God, what was going to happen to me? Panic and adrenaline rushed through me in equal measure, my limbs trembling with the need for an outlet. Both men had an arm by now and they dragged me inside the building.

Cigarette smoke immediately clogged my lungs and made my eyes water. The room was dark, even by bar standards, and baseball-cap guy and sidekick #1 herded me toward a dark hallway in the back.

Up until then, I'd hoped there'd be some way out of this. Foolish and naive, but also not wanting to accept the inevitable, which horrified me. At the sight of that hallway, I began fighting, the kind of fighting you do when the alternative is too terrifying to consider. I screamed, I clawed, I bit. They retaliated, hitting me so hard my teeth clacked together and I saw stars, but I kept going.

We were up close now, their breath rancid in my face and I saw the glint of gold teeth in the sneer of baseball guy. The sidekick had my arms locked behind me now and I tasted my own blood. I screamed again, the sound pure rage and fury, abruptly cut off by the smash of a fist to my cheek.

Blackness crowded my vision and I sagged, the pain in my shoulders from the position of my arms the only thing keeping me conscious. Though I wished it wouldn't. It was obvious I wasn't going to get away from the men, couldn't escape the fate that awaited me. Blissful oblivion seemed preferable to full awareness. Tears stung my eyes, both from pain and hopelessness, and I could taste despair.

By now they'd dragged me into the darkened hallway. A faint light gleamed at the end—an EXIT sign glowing red over the dark outline of a door. But that wasn't where they were taking me. Baseball Cap fumbled with another door, finally shoving it open. My body was tired and hurting, every ounce of adrenaline and energy I had now gone.

"What the fuck are you doing?"

A shadowy outline of a man stood in the corridor. I blinked slowly, trying to focus, but he swam in my vision. My eye stung as blood seeped into it and I had to close my eyes.

"She was outside, man," Baseball Cap said. "Just going to have a good time with her, dump her after."

What a Romeo.

"Look at her, asshole," the new guy snapped. "She isn't from around here. Someone will come looking for her and then she's going to point the finger at you and here. We don't need that kind of attention."

"Then we'll just get rid of her."

I heard a slap and jerked my eyes open. The new guy had hit baseball cap guy, the flat of his palm a sharp sound in the dark.

"Idiot," the man said. "As if that would be better. Hand her over and you two fuckwads make yourselves scarce. If you're lucky, I won't tell Viktor about this."

Wait...had he just said Viktor?

Baseball Cap, the one who'd been using me as a punching bag, looked pissed, but scared, too, which impressed and terrified me. Who was this new guy that could tell him what to do, hit him, make him obey? What worse things were in store for me at his hands?

Glancing at Sidekick, who still had my arms pinned, Baseball Cap gave him a nod. Without any warning, I was suddenly released. My knees couldn't hold me and they buckled, dumping me on the floor. I landed in something faintly wet and I prayed it was just spilled booze.

There was the shuffle of feet as legs moved past my line of sight and then they were gone.

Fear made me pull my body up on all fours, my arms trembling at the weight of my body; then I felt an arm sliding around my waist.

"Come on, let's go," the man said.

I stiffened, my hands scrabbling fruitlessly at the arm pulling me to my feet. "Let me go," I said, the words sounding pathetically more like a sob than a demand. I finally got a good look at him, and when I did, I wished I hadn't.

It was the man Parker had been secretly talking to in New York.

"Tell Parker he owes me."

And those were the last words I heard before I blacked out.

* * *

I woke to a pain that felt worse than the roughest hangover I'd ever had. My head throbbed and my body was sore. Baseball Cap and Sidekick hadn't only hit my face, they'd thrown punches at my midsection as well, reminding me of when I punch a pillow—it leaves an indentation, which is exactly how my stomach felt. My insides hurt, and as I carefully opened my eyes, I realized my face felt swollen, too. One eye wouldn't open all the way, so it was a blurry form that I saw approaching where I lay.

I made a noise and tried to sit up, my only thought being to get away before I got hurt again.

"It's okay; it's me," the form said, and I recognized the voice. Ryker. Relieved, I fell back against the cushions of the couch I was lying on. My couch. "This will help," he said.

I felt a cold pack press gently to my cheek and swollen

eye. It felt so good that I moaned. Raising my hand, I held the pack to my face, realizing it was a bag of frozen vegetables. Peas, I thought.

"This may sting a bit," Ryker warned me. A wet cloth swiped at my other cheek, cleaning the blood I could feel had crusted there. The cut did sting, but I didn't complain. Compared to the other pains and aches, it barely registered on the meter.

I looked at him with my good eye. He wore a white T-shirt, minus his leather jacket and holster. At the moment, he wasn't looking in my eyes, just involved in cleaning up my face. How had I come to get home? Last I remembered, I'd been in the bar.

"How'd I get here?" I asked.

"I found you here," he said. "I tried calling, but you didn't answer, so I stopped by. Your door was unlocked."

"My door was unlocked? That's so dangerous." The least they could've done was lock the door on their way out.

"I think you're missing the point," he said, his voice hard. "Why the hell do you look like you've been beat up?"

I adjusted the frozen peas—when had I bought those?—and grimaced. "Because I *did* get beat up."

"Why don't you start at the beginning and tell me what happened?"

Breathing a sigh, I closed my eyes again—because that felt way better—and told him the *Reader's Digest* condensed version of Viktor, Tania, Hanna, and the men who'd wanted to "have a good time" and dump me in the alley afterward. After a brief hesitation, I added the part about the man who'd intervened and the message he'd given me for Parker.

"What do you think it means?" I asked, gingerly sitting up on the couch.

"You know what it means," Ryker said, sliding an arm behind my back to help me. He was exceedingly gentle, despite the hardness of his tone. "It means he's involved with the Russian mob and knows exactly what he's doing, even if you don't want to face that fact. I knew Niki. She was my informant. She's the one who had Parker's business card on her when she was killed."

My eyes slid shut in defeat. At this point, I couldn't really argue. Ryker was right. Somehow Parker had gotten mixed up with the wrong people, and was fully aware of who they were and what they did. And to make it worse, he'd known exactly who Tania's sister was when I'd mentioned her. Had probably even known she was already dead.

"They have to be threatening him," I said. "Parker's not a criminal. They've got a hold over him somehow."

Ryker didn't reply and I glanced up at him. My vision had cleared and he was looking at me with something close to pity.

"I don't know if I should admire your loyalty or curse your stubbornness," he said.

"And I don't know if I should kick you out or thank you for the peas," I retorted. I didn't want to fight with him about Parker. I was still reeling from my close call with certain disaster. I lowered the peas and was surprised when he reached out, the back of his knuckles grazing my cheek. I lifted my eyes and our gazes caught and held.

"You've got to listen to me," he said. "You're sacrificing yourself for a man who doesn't even appreciate you."

"That's not true—"

"Then where the fuck is he?"

My face paled at the restrained anger in his voice. I flinched away from his touch and knew I was going to fall apart. But I really didn't want him to see that and give him more ammunition against Parker.

"Just leave," I managed to get out, my voice barely above a whisper. Though I tried to stop them, tears leaked from my eyes.

Ryker muttered a curse, shoving a hand through his hair. "Christ, I'm sorry," he said. "I just—" But he cut himself off and didn't finish the sentence. Instead, he wrapped an arm around me and pulled me closer.

Sensing a truce, I leaned forward until my head rested against his shoulder. The fear that had overtaken me in Johnny's still lingered. Ryker made me feel safe, despite his hostility about Parker, and right now I had a desperate need to feel safe.

"I was so scared," I whispered. "I thought they were going to...to..." But I couldn't put it into words, because that would make it too real.

"Shh," he said, the warmth of his breath brushing my ear. "You're safe now."

"How did you know I was back in town?" I asked.

He didn't answer.

A suspicion bloomed in my head and I let out a heavy sigh. "You're watching him, aren't you." It wasn't a question.

"Like it or not, he's part of a murder investigation. And so are you. We keep tabs." His answer was matter-of-fact.

Too depressed to argue the point, I pulled away. "I want to take a shower," I said. I felt dirty, like the grime that had covered the floor of Johnny's now coated my skin.

Ryker stood to give me room to stand, but the act of getting to my feet proved to be harder than it ever had been before, and this coming from someone whose overdose on squats at the gym had made sitting on the toilet torture for nearly a week.

I about collapsed back onto the couch, but Ryker's arm was around me, steady and firm. My stomach felt like I'd done a marathon session of crunches.

"Don't be a martyr," he said. "Let me help."

I didn't argue, and with his help, we made it to the bathroom. He left me leaning against the sink while he turned on the shower and adjusted the water temperature. I watched him move, the muscles in his arms flexing. His T-shirt was white tonight and well-worn, the fabric so thin it was on the verge of being transparent.

"Any chance you need some help?" he asked, turning back to me.

"You're not trying to use this as an excuse to see me naked, are you?"

He grinned. "That would be taking advantage of the situation," he said. "So, basically . . . yeah."

His unrepentant admission made me smile. It was real tempting to say I needed help, but then that would be two men I'd bathed in front of in as many days, and that seemed a really high number for that short a period of time.

"I'll be all right," I said.

"Okay, then. I'll be outside the door. Just call out if you need anything. Like someone to wash your back. Or your front. I'm not particular."

I pushed him out the door with a huff of exasperation before easing my way slowly and painfully out of my clothes. The hot water felt amazing and I took my time. Angry bruises were already darkening my abdomen. Good thing it wasn't bikini season yet.

I wrapped myself in a towel and wiped the steam from the mirror. My cheek had a bruise that leeched under the skin toward my eye. Nice. But at least I could open my eye now. Granted, it looked like I was the victim of domestic abuse, but a huge pair of sunglasses tomorrow would help with that.

I brushed my wet hair and opened the door. Ryker was sitting on my bed waiting and he glanced up when I stepped out.

His eyes took a trip down my bare legs and back up, lingering slightly where I had the tail of the towel tucked inside my cleavage; then he cleared his throat and stood.

"Feel better?"

I nodded. "Yeah, that really helped."

"I found some pretty hefty painkillers in your kitchen cabinet," he said, getting to his feet. He held a prescription bottle still half full from when I'd badly sprained my ankle (I'd never worn those particular five-inch stilettos again). "Here," he said, dumping a pill in his palm and handing it to me. "Take this."

I glanced down at the small tablet in my hand. I really wanted to take it. But— "I can't," I said regretfully. "This'll knock me out for too long and I need to work tomorrow."

Ryker looked at me like I'd grown two heads. "Don't be an idiot," he scoffed. "You're not going to work tomorrow. You'll be lucky if you can move enough to pee tomorrow."

My toilet habits were the last thing I wanted to talk about. "I'll be fine," I said. "A good night's sleep and a few ibuprofen will do wonders." Make that a handful of ibuprofen.

"You're going in because of him, aren't you." It wasn't a question, and neither of us needed to ask who Ryker meant by "him."

Okay, my toilet habits were the *second* to last thing I wanted to talk about.

"I have a job and it's not like I do manual labor," I argued. "I sit at a desk for ninety percent of my day. I can do that with a few bumps and bruises." And maybe a shot of whiskey in my latte. "And I don't appreciate being called an idiot."

"Then don't act like one," he retorted.

Okay, helping me or not, I was getting pissed. He must have read that I was close to throwing him out, again, because he gave a sigh of resignation and scrubbed a hand across his face.

"Fine," he said. "I'm not going to argue with you, even if it is a shitty idea. But if you're dragging yourself to work, come down to the station tomorrow. You can look and see if you can identify any of the men."

"Okay," I said, glad to change the subject. "What time?"

"Whenever is convenient," he replied. "I'll come pick you up."

I thought about another confrontation between Ryker and Parker, decided I didn't want to deal with that.

"No, that's okay. I'll grab a cab."

He stood in front of me, his eyes on mine, his expression serious. When he didn't say anything, I shifted uneasily from one foot to another.

"What's wrong?" I asked when I couldn't handle the silence any longer.

But Ryker didn't reply. Instead, he leaned down and kissed me.

It was different from before. His touch was gentle, his hand cupping my cheek and jaw. I brought my arms up to rest my hands against his chest, the soft fabric of his T-shirt warm from his skin.

I didn't track how much time passed, but all too soon he was releasing me. "I'd better go," he said. "I'll see you tomorrow." He squeezed my hand.

"Okay. Thanks for coming over tonight," I said. "It would've been really awful to wake up alone after...that."

"Waking up alone is a choice," he replied. "You just let me know if you want that to change."

His lips tipped up at the corners in that wicked grin of his; then he was gone.

CHAPTER ELEVEN

I dressed carefully for work the next morning, not that I had a lot of choice in the matter. I was so sore, I could barely move. The bruises on my face and abdomen were a deep purple. I could conceal those on my stomach much more easily than those on my cheek and eye.

The button-down blouse I wore was tucked into my skirt, but I didn't add my usual belt. I didn't think I could handle the press of it against my skin, at least not for an entire day. Makeup I caked on my face, which helped, but the huge pair of aviator sunglasses I wore hid more than the concealer and powder.

Ryker's parting comment last night had me rethinking that anti-one-night-stand resolve I had going on with him. I wanted him. He was dangerous, unpredictable, and full of sharp edges. He made no promises and asked for none from me. And God help me, I wanted to dip my toe into the fire that raged between us...even if I got burned.

Although I'd prepared myself to see Parker and confront him about the man in New York who'd helped me last night, he had already been to the office and was gone by the time I arrived. He'd left a stack of work on my desk along with notes and a message that said he'd be out most of the day.

Lovely.

Not that I minded putting off the clash between him and me—I wasn't someone who enjoyed confrontation, especially with my boss.

People passing by took a little too long staring at my sunglasses, but I ignored them. It wasn't as though it mattered for my job performance if I wore sunglasses or not. I figured most people thought I was recovering from a nasty hangover, and I'd rather they think I was a drunken lush than see the bruises on my face.

"Are we hiding from the paparazzi?"

I glanced up. Megan's dry question made me smile, but that made my face hurt, so I stopped real fast.

I didn't want to lie to her, but she wasn't going to buy the hangover thing, so I slid my glasses down.

"I kinda...got mugged...last night," I explained.

The grin on her face changed to a look of horror. "Oh my God, Sage," she said, hurrying around the counter to me. "Are you all right?"

I shrugged, pushing the sunglasses back on. "They roughed me up a bit, but I'm okay."

"Did the cops catch them?"

"No, but I'm supposed to go to the police station this morning and look at pictures, maybe pick them out," I replied.

"Let's get some coffee and tell me what happened," she said.

"Okay," I readily agreed. Since Parker wasn't here, I

didn't feel guilty for stepping out of the office for a few minutes.

"Any update on Brian?" I asked as we rode down the elevator.

She sighed, following me out into the lobby as the elevator doors opened. "Well, a few of us went to happy hour the other night, and he actually came. I was hoping maybe we'd hook up after, but he left when everyone else did."

"He didn't hang around, ask you to dinner or something?"

Megan shook her head. "Nope. I managed to prolong it a little by asking him to walk me to my car, but he didn't get the hint."

"Maybe he's shy or something," I said. "Any progress with texting?"

"Nada," she said. "It's degenerated into one-word or one-sentence replies to my texts. And if I try to get him to talk about himself, he just clams up. I've never met a man who *didn't* think he was a riveting topic of conversation." She shrugged. "I guess he just isn't that into me." She looked so disheartened, I stopped to give her a hug.

"Maybe you should find someone else to obsess over," I said kindly. "He doesn't seem worth the effort." I was being nice, but I wanted to stomp up to Brian's desk and wallop him upside the head.

"I know, I know. You're probably right."

"Of course I am," I said, releasing her. "Let's get some coffee and think about other men at the firm you can obsess about who'll actually return the favor *and* who won't send you Bible verses."

She laughed, as I'd hoped she would. "That would be nice. He sent me a bizarre one the other day. I think I might've gotten dissed by Bible verse. Is that even a thing?"

"Who cares," I groused. "What an ass. Probably has a tiny dick, too."

Megan laughed again, her natural cheerful optimism asserting itself. "And who needs that shit, right? I thought Bible stuff was supposed to make you feel *better* about yourself, and he managed to do just the opposite. Asshat."

"Exactly."

I splurged with a nonfat-half-and-half-quad-venti-caramel-macchiato (add extra whip) and doubled the order for Megan, too. All too soon, we were done gossiping about the relative pros and cons of various men around the office. We hadn't hit on a replacement for Brian, but we'd had fun chatting.

After lunch—another naked hot dog that left me craving mustard—I headed down to the precinct and asked for Ryker. It wasn't Ryker who came, but another guy, maybe ten years older than Ryker and several inches shorter. He was wide, but it wasn't muscle, and the buttons of his shirt strained a bit.

"I'm Detective Malone," he said, holding out his hand, which I took. "Detective Ryker and I are partners."

His grip was firm and solid, his eyes serious, and it eased my trepidation. "Ryker asked me to come down and look through some photos to identify a man," I explained.

"He'll be back in a few minutes," Malone said. "I'll take you to a room."

I followed him to a small, windowless room with a utilitarian table and four folding chairs.

"Can I get you a cup of coffee?" he asked.

"Sure," I said.

"Cream and sugar?"

I cautiously settled into the chair with the smallest amount of graffiti and dents as I answered. "Yes, please. I'd like two packets of artificial sweetener and two sugars. And

I'd like real half-and-half, if you have it, not the powdered creamer. If you just have the powder, then...never mind." No way was I setting my purse on the floor. It looked like it hadn't been scrubbed with bleach in a decade. I set it on the table instead.

Malone hadn't replied, so I glanced up to find him staring at me, eyebrows raised.

"Never mind on the creamer...or the coffee?" he asked.

"The coffee. In that case, I'd rather have tea."

He didn't ask me how I took my tea (no sugar, but add a tablespoon of honey); he just turned and left. The heavy door swung shut behind him.

Hmm. I didn't like the odds of me getting that cup of coffee.

I took off my sunglasses and checked the state of my makeup with my compact. Still black and blue. I sighed.

The door opened and Ryker stepped inside. He wore his usual jeans and today a black T-shirt. I could see the outline of his dog tags underneath the thin cotton. His gaze moved over the bruises on my face and his jaw tightened.

"Thanks for coming," he said, all business as he sat in the chair across the table from me. He set a three-ring binder on the table and flipped it open, the pages facing me. "These are photos of known associates of Viktor Rowan and members of the Russian mob that have been seen around Chicago. Look through carefully. Let me know if you recognize any of them."

There were a lot of photos, some that were mug shots, and others that were surveillance shots taken from a greater distance and zoomed in. Some of the men pictured made a shiver crawl down my spine, the cold ruthlessness in their eyes chilling even in a photograph.

Ryker was patient while I looked, and it wasn't until I was halfway through the book that I saw him.

"That's him," I said, pointing to a photo. It was a candid photo taken without the subject's knowledge, but I recognized the face. Not a big guy, but distinctive. Enough so that I remembered him. "That's the guy that saved me."

Ryker spun the book around to take a look. He glanced up at me. "Are you sure?" he asked.

"Yeah."

"One hundred percent sure?"

I looked at the photo again, then back at him. "Yes, absolutely. Why? You asked me to pick him out."

"Because this particular man"—he pointed to the photo—"is a known assassin for the Russians."

I felt the blood drain from my face.

"Assassin? As in hired to kill people?"

"That's usually what assassins do." Ryker's response was dry.

"But…then that's proof he's threatening Parker!" I said. "He probably told Parker he'd kill him if he didn't cooperate." I was incredibly relieved. This explained everything.

"He wouldn't threaten Parker," Ryker said. "He doesn't do threats. He either kills people or doesn't kill them. They send other guys if they just want to threaten."

"You don't know that," I argued.

"Yes, I do. And even if you're right and he's threatening Parker, then why the message to you? *Tell Parker he owes me one.* That makes no sense. If he were threatening him, then he wouldn't have bothered saving you."

His logic was sound, but I didn't want to hear it. I scooped up my purse—I never had gotten my coffee—and stood to leave.

"You're wrong," I said, shaking my head. "You just… you have to be. You hate Parker and it's coloring your judgment of him."

I had my hand on the doorknob, but Ryker was up and out of his chair, his hand on top of mine as he stood behind me.

"Listen to me," he said, his voice in my ear. "Niki was killed for talking to the cops. They know you work for Parker. What if they think you're doing the same? I know you trust Parker, believe in him, but this is too dangerous to be blinded by loyalty."

I didn't reply, but then again, I was a little distracted by the light press of his body against mine. I could smell the faint musk of his cologne and I closed my eyes, forcing my head to clear.

"You don't know him like I do," I said.

"I could say the same thing."

Stalemate.

I pulled open the door and this time he didn't stop me from walking out.

My sunglasses remained in place the rest of the afternoon, but I got a lot of work done. I had to keep getting up and moving around so I didn't get too stiff. My abdomen really hurt and I couldn't wait to get home and put a heating pad on my stomach.

As if to taunt me, Parker called at ten minutes 'til five.

"Can you bring by the files from New York? They should have arrived today," he said. "Not all of them, just the financial statements from their main location up to six months ago."

"Bring them by your apartment?" I asked.

"Yes. I need to work through them tonight."

I grimaced. Going to Parker's apartment again, so soon after the disastrous New York trip, seemed like a bad idea. I preferred the routine and professionalism of the office. His apartment was too...personal.

But it was my job and he could've easily fired me yesterday, so...

"Sure. I'll bring them by."

We talked through a couple of other things before he disconnected. Going into his office, I saw where the overnight service had delivered the files from New York. Digging through them, I found what Parker wanted.

It was rush hour and it took almost an hour to get to Parker's apartment, which was frustrating, especially since the cab I'd taken smelled like someone had gotten sick in it. I wanted to hang my head out the window like a dog. Instead, I rolled the window down, though my hair took a beating. By the time I got to Parker's apartment building, it couldn't be salvaged and I had to unpin it and leave it loose.

My sunglasses made it hard to see clearly since twilight was fading into evening, but the lights of the lobby were bright enough. I didn't know what I'd say when, or if, Parker asked about the glasses. Part of me didn't want to tell him about last night. Ryker's words still echoed in my head, making me doubt what I knew to be true. Or perhaps what I *wanted* to be true.

Regardless, I was knocking on Parker's door a few minutes later. Hopefully, I could drop off the files and leave. But there was no answer. I tried again. Nothing.

"Shit," I muttered. Now I'd have to use his key. On the upside, if he wasn't here, he couldn't quiz me.

I let myself into his apartment, juggling my purse and the three-inch-thick file without dumping anything on the floor. The sunglasses were a major hindrance now, since it wasn't bright in Parker's apartment, so I tossed them onto the counter with an exasperated huff.

Something smelled good and I sniffed. Deirdre had made dinner again. Dumping my stuff onto the kitchen table, I fol-

lowed the smell to the oven, opening it to take a peek. Was
that lasagna? Oh wow—

"Sage—"

I let out a shriek, whirling in surprise to see Parker standing there. The oven slammed shut behind me, making me
jump again.

"You scared me to death!" I was breathing hard and was
angry in that way you get when someone startles you really
badly. After last night, the panic that had flooded me was
worse than anything I'd felt before, and it must've shown because Parker's eyes were wide and he held his hands up.

"It's okay," he said. "It's just me."

I nodded, trying desperately to catch my breath. Then he
frowned and moved toward me.

"What happened to you?" he asked urgently. He had a
hold of my upper arms and turned me so I faced into the
light. Taking my chin lightly in his hand, he turned my face.
I heard him suck in a sharp breath.

"Sage..." His voice was tight with anger. "Who did this
to you?"

His hair was wet, I noticed absently, which explained
why he hadn't heard my knock. He'd been in the shower.
And now was barefoot and bare-chested, wearing only a pair
of jeans. Oh geez...

"Um, yeah," I said, struggling to sound coherent. "I went
last night to find Niki, Tania's sister, and she lives in a real
nasty part of town."

"Are you kidding me?" he growled. "You went there
alone?"

I gave a jerky nod.

"You should've called me," he said. "I'd have taken you
over there."

I frowned. "First, you told me not to get involved. And

second, why would I ask you to do me a favor?" I wasn't being a smartass. It was a valid question. Our relationship—such as it was—wasn't reciprocal. I may pick up Parker's dry cleaning, but it wasn't like he did the same for me, nor should he. I was his assistant. That was all. "We aren't friends," I said matter-of-factly. "It didn't even occur to me to call you."

Parker went still for a moment, his eyes searching mine. "Maybe we should change that," he said. "If you need something, I want you to feel free to call me, ask me. We've worked together for a long time, Sage. I may not have the best way of showing it, but I'm always concerned for your welfare."

Tears stung my eyes and I hurriedly lowered my gaze so he wouldn't see. His hand felt warm and gentle brushing my cheek. It was ridiculous, how happy I was at that little speech of his. I felt like a starving woman, grateful for any scrap he'd send my way. Part of me resented the power he had over me. But the other part of me was too elated to care.

Parker did feel something for me, even if it was just friendship and an acknowledgment that he'd rather work with me than hire and train someone new.

"Um, anyway," I continued, "Niki was killed for talking to the police. Another woman named Hanna was there. She said she's being forced by the cartel to prostitute herself. Then I was attacked by some guys who I think work for Viktor."

"Attacked," he repeated slowly, and I swore his face lost some color.

I swallowed. "It…it was going to be bad, I think, but this man stopped them. And he said…he said to *tell Parker he owes me one*."

Parker stared at me. "It *was going* to be bad? You have a

black eye, for chrissakes! What else did they do? Did they—"
But then he stopped and I knew what he was thinking.

"No, they didn't," I said, answering his unvoiced question. "Knocked me around. That's all." My hand instinctively went to rest on my aching abdomen and Parker's eyes followed the movement.

The tension was rolling off him—anger, anxiety, concern. I could almost feel it. Parker mesmerized me—he always had. The intensity he brought to his job was something I'd admired from the first. Now it was directed at me, and I found I couldn't move, couldn't even look away from him.

His hands went from my arms to my waist, his gaze dropping as well. Gently moving my hand aside, he tugged on my shirt, the silken material sliding from underneath the waistband of my skirt. I could hardly breathe and cool air hit my bared skin as he lifted the fabric.

Parker went very still, and I knew he was staring at the ugly marks decorating my stomach and rib cage. A nerve pulsed in his jaw, drawing my gaze. I should probably have stepped away, but I couldn't make my feet move.

A sudden rush of longing went through me, so strong that I swayed on my feet. I instinctively shied away from examining the feeling too closely. Parker and I weren't that couple, were never going to *be* that couple, and me wanting it would only end in heartbreak.

But the wanting…it was so strong, it felt as though it was rooted in my gut, tangling its way through my chest and squeezing my heart and lungs until it hurt. And it wasn't just sexual, though saying I was attracted to Parker was an understatement of laughable proportions. It was more than that. It had been forcefully brought to my attention how much I didn't know him, and it made me sad. Sad in a place where there was no fixing it. And I wished I could. I wished so much and so hard I could be that person—the one *he* was looking for.

My thoughts were caught up in this as I watched him, my face turned up to look into his, but he was still inspecting my injuries. His fingers brushed so lightly across my skin, I thought I might have imagined it. Then he did it again and I knew I hadn't.

This time, there was no alcohol clouding my brain and I squeezed my eyes shut, savoring the feel of his skin against mine, knowing it was an ironic parody of what I really wanted, but I wasn't strong enough to push him away.

His arms slid around my waist to my back and he stepped closer. My eyes flew open as he leaned down, pressing his forehead against mine.

"I'm so sorry, Sage," he whispered, the warmth of his breath fanning gently across my cheek. He held me as though I were made of glass—fragile and delicate.

I didn't know what to say. *It's okay* was what came to mind, but it wasn't the right thing, because it *wasn't* okay. This whole thing was messed up and scary. Yes, I was scared. Russian men who forced women into prostitution— who threatened me, hurt me—were very scary. Men who were using Parker, probably threatening him, too. And the cops were only half on our side—Ryker would arrest Parker if he could—and I didn't want that.

"What's going to happen?" I asked. The question whirling in my mind, the one I was afraid to voice, was really *Am I going to die?* But I couldn't make those words come out.

"You'll be okay," he said.

And in that moment, with his forehead pressed to mine, breathing the same air, his arms strong and solid around me, I could almost believe him. Almost.

Silence enveloped us again, thick and warm like a blanketing cocoon. My senses were heightened, taking in the muffled sounds of the city and street below. Parker's scent—soap and warm, clean man. The sensation of being in his arms brought back the memory of our car ride in New York when his hands and mouth had been on me.

Maybe it was that memory and the longing I had to repeat it that made me do what I did next. Or maybe it was that I sensed things changing between us and I wanted them so badly to go one way versus the other—two scenarios and only one of which I could live with. Whatever it was that made me do it, I found myself closing the two-inch gap between us, as though I were watching myself from outside my body.

I raised my arms and rested my hands flat against his chest. His skin was smooth and warm against my palms. Lifting my chin, I slanted my face upward and pressed my lips to his.

He didn't react at all, and a jolt of terrified regret went through me. I'd done it. I'd passed the point of no return. I'd *Gone There*, made a pass (while sober) at my boss and now he'd have no choice but to fire me.

I pulled back, tears stinging my eyes. I'd ruined everything, and now I'd lose him. The tangled longing inside my chest felt like a thousand knives ripping me from the inside out.

I couldn't bear to look at him, mortification now creeping over me. Jerking my hands away from his chest as if they'd been scalded, I stumbled backward and his arms loosened.

"I'm sor—" I began, but couldn't continue, because Parker was kissing me.

He hauled me against him with one strong tug, startling a gasp from me, and then he was pressing my lips open farther to deepen the kiss.

His lips were soft, his tongue hot as it slid against mine. The kiss was urgent, overwhelming, everything I'd wanted, and I was lost in it.

My hands crept up, my arms winding around his neck, until I could bury my fingers in his hair. The long strands were damp and silky soft. I could feel the heat of his skin as it leached through the thin fabric of my blouse. He'd moved a hand up to cradle my jaw; the other still pushed against my back, holding me close. As if I needed additional encouragement to press my body against his.

Months of pent-up yearning poured from me into him, and they felt returned tenfold. All the daydreams I'd denied having about what it would be like to be kissed by Parker were a pale imitation of the real thing.

His mouth claimed mine, marking me, the hold he had on my jaw gentle but firm, keeping me in place. *As if I was going anywhere.* Please.

Then, as abruptly as it began, it stopped.

He was gone, out of my arms, and I opened my eyes in confusion, bereft at the sudden loss.

Parker was standing in front of the windows, staring out. His shoulders were rising and falling with the breaths he took and I watched as he pushed a hand roughly through his hair.

I wasn't sure what to do. What had just happened? Why had he stopped? He'd obviously enjoyed kissing me, I wasn't naive enough not to have noticed *that*, so why quit?

I took a few tentative steps toward him, staring into the windows that reflected our images. His arms were crossed over his chest and he seemed to be looking at nothing.

"Parker?" My voice was small in the expansive space, and he didn't answer.

Deciding to gamble a little more—at this point, what did

I have to lose?—I moved until I stood right behind him. The bare skin of his back presented a temptation I couldn't resist. Sliding my arms around his waist, I nestled against his back.

I pressed my lips to his skin, slowly scattering soft, open-mouthed kisses across the tight muscles in his back and shoulder blades. A shudder ran through him at the touch, which encouraged me. I rested the side of my face against him and just held on. My eyes slid shut.

"Sage."

Parker turned and stepped away. My arms dropped to my sides and I looked up at him. His eyes were crystal blue and beautiful, but they were filled with pain, and I knew before he spoke again what his words would be.

"We can't do this," he said.

I stared at him. "Why not?" I asked. "Because of work?"

"Partly," he replied. "But that's not the only reason." But he said nothing further.

I felt vulnerable—*too* vulnerable—with my shirt un-tucked and the bruises showing in stark relief on my face. Crossing my arms defensively across my chest, I said, "I think I deserve a better explanation than that."

Parker was quiet for a moment while I held my breath, waiting. "You're right. You do," he said.

I slowly let my breath out, then wondered if I'd made a mistake. Maybe what he had to say would be worse than anything I could've imagined. Then what would I do? Per-haps the outright rejection would've been easier to live with.

"You're a beautiful woman," he began.

Okay, good so far.

"And we make a great team. I couldn't ask for a better as-sistant than you."

Not exactly what I'd been hoping for, but okay.

"But I'm…not relationship material, Sage. I'm toxic to

relationships. Take you, for instance. All you do is work for me and look at what you've gone through because of that." He stepped toward me as though compelled, his eyes glued to the bruises on my cheek. Lifting his hand, I thought he was going to touch me again, but he stopped. His arm fell back to his side. "I'd be a fool to think it'd be any different with you."

I was confused. What was he talking about? *Toxic to relationships*? What did that mean?

"I don't understand," I said. "If you're not interested in me...in that way...it's fine. I can handle it. I'm a big girl. You don't have to throw me some line that's just a variation of *it's not you, it's me*."

"It's not a line," Parker insisted. "Trust me when I say I wouldn't be good for you."

"So...that's it?" I asked. "I don't get a say in it? You've had girlfriends before, Parker; it's not like you've lived the life of a monk."

His face turned hard. "Having a woman around for fucking is not the same thing as a relationship."

Well alrighty then, though at the moment with him half naked, I wouldn't have minded the former category and screw the relationship.

I was embarrassed and angry. Probably angry at being embarrassed. This was twice now I'd gone out on a limb with Parker, and damn if I'd ever do it again. Not to mention his "reason" for us not getting involved was probably the lamest I'd ever heard.

"Whatever," I said, spinning around and heading for where I'd dumped my purse. I snatched it up, then thought of something else I wanted to say. I turned, then jumped about a foot because he'd followed without me even hearing him.

"Will you stop doing that?" I snapped. "Listen, you just

remember that you said no to this"—I waved my hand to indicate the two of us—"which means you've given up touching privileges." I poked his chest for emphasis, then wished I hadn't because the muscles layered underneath his skin were hard and firm and I found my fingers lingering to touch before I jerked my hand back.

"I'm your secretary. That's all," I said.

His blue eyes stared down at me, his expression serious, and he didn't answer.

I cleared my throat and looked away. "I mean, administrative assistant." My voice sounded strange and with dawning horror, I realized I was on the verge of tears. That wouldn't do. That wouldn't do *at all*.

"I gotta go," I mumbled. I had to get out of there before my anger faded entirely and left only crushing disappointment in its wake.

"Don't go back to see Hanna," Parker said. "Stay away from that area entirely, understand?"

That made me angry all over again. Here I was trying to protect him from the cops, and he wasn't doing anything to help himself out of the situation. "I know you're working for them," I blurted, throwing caution to the wind. "I know that guy is threatening you. He's an assassin for them. Ryker told me. If you don't go to the cops, they'll arrest you for conspiring with them. They're watching you, and no one will be able to prove otherwise."

Ryker would kill me if he knew I'd just tipped off Parker like that, but I couldn't help it. Despite being rejected—twice—I was still on his side and didn't want to see him get hurt or go to prison.

Parker's eyes narrowed. "What do you mean *they're watching*?"

"The cops," I said. "Who else?"

"Ryker's told you this?"

I gave him a look that, roughly translated, said *Who else, dipshit?*

Parker looked furious. "Stay away from him, Sage," he ordered. "He has no idea what he's doing. He's putting you in danger and I won't have it."

My eyebrows flew up. "You won't have it?" I echoed in disbelief. "I'm sorry, did I miss something somewhere that entitles you to have that kind of control over my life? Not to mention that I really don't think *he's* the one putting me in danger. *You* are."

Parker's lips thinned at my angry sarcasm and he didn't reply.

"Ryker's actually told me what's going on, which is more than I can say for you," I continued berating him. "You've told me nothing. How can I help you if you won't talk to me?"

"I didn't ask for your help," he bit out, "and Ryker shouldn't be either. This isn't a game, Sage. These people are dangerous—"

"You think I don't know that?" I retorted, cutting him off. "Look at my face, Parker, and tell me I don't know they're dangerous!"

That shut him up. He looked like I'd hit him, and I regretted my outburst, but not enough to apologize for it. I was still angry and hurt.

I tried to open the door, but Parker slammed it shut again, his hand holding it closed.

"Don't leave."

I looked up at him, confused. "Why not?"

"I'm worried," he said. "You're too exposed, and if you've been talking to the cops, they'll know it."

I swallowed, the urgency in his voice making me anxious. Ryker had said something similar. What if they'd seen me go to the police station today? Would they kill me like they had Niki? But staying with Parker was out of the question.

"I'm not staying here," I said. "That's crazy. I'm leaving."

But Parker had a hold of my arms, forcing me to stay still. "You could've died, Sage," he said. "They would've raped you to within an inch of your life and left you for dead."

"Then go to the cops and end this!" I said, exasperated. "Tell them what's going on, how they're threatening you."

"I can't." His tone was implacable.

"Then I guess we're at an impasse," I said, "because if the cops want me to help them, then that's what I'll do, and you can't stop me. They killed Niki. Tania is a prisoner, and Hanna is being forced to be a prostitute. I don't want to be the kind of person who'd just ignore something like that because it's safer and more convenient for me to do so."

Parker didn't reply, so I turned and walked out the door, leaving him staring after me.

CHAPTER TWELVE

Friday was business as usual between Parker and me, or at least that's what people saw. On the inside, I died a little every time I looked at him.

You would never have known anything had passed between us the night before. He greeted me at my desk the same way he did every day, glancing through his messages before heading into his office. He called me in for various things he needed, e-mailed me documents, and inquired for updates on projects. It was as normal as it ever was.

And it was incredibly hard to take.

So when Megan popped by my desk to grab some lunch, I seized the opportunity to spill my guts to someone. I trusted Megan. She wasn't a gossip and could keep a secret, so over matching grilled chicken salads with lime-cilantro dressing (on the side—they always put too much on), I told her what had happened between Parker and me and how he'd turned me down flat.

"Aww, honey, I'm so sorry," she said, wrapping an arm around my shoulders and giving me a careful squeeze—I was still sore from the "mugging."

I shrugged, pushing some wilted lettuce with my plastic fork. "It is what it is. I just thought, you know, maybe..." But I didn't finish the thought.

"I guess I didn't realize you...liked Parker that way," Megan said.

"I've always thought he was hot," I replied. "Who doesn't? But it was kind of in a visceral way, you know? The way you think some movie star is hot or something. It's not as though he was a possibility."

Megan looked skeptical, so I elaborated. "I know it seems strange, but I like him. I like that he acts like a complete hard-ass, but can be considerate and kind, too. I like how intense he is about, well, everything. I like that he can handle billions of dollars of other people's money without blinking an eye. I like that he relies on me and needs me. And I like how well we...fit." I shrugged helplessly. It was the best way I knew to explain it. "Only now that I've thought about it in a real way, it's *all* I can think about. I feel heartbroken and we've never even gone on a single date."

She nodded sympathetically.

"So how do I go back?" I asked. "I don't want to feel this way anymore. Sad and pathetic and rejected. How do I go back to how it was before?"

"I have no idea," she said. "Men can compartmentalize that stuff so well. Women just can't, at least I've never been able to and none of my friends have ever been able to."

"But I don't want to have to find another job," I said.

"You could find another administrative assistant position

like that," Megan said, snapping her fingers. "Probably pay better, too."

"Yeah, but then I'd never see him again." Saying those words was harder than I thought it'd be.

"Maybe that would be for the best," she said. "If you feel this way and he doesn't, then what's the point of sticking around? It just makes things harder for you."

I couldn't argue with her logic, although quitting my job was something I didn't want to consider. Yet what choice did I have?

"Maybe I just need some time," I said. "I'll get over it. I mean, it *just* happened. I shouldn't make any big life-changing decisions right now."

"True," Megan agreed. "There's no time limit. You can just think on it. You don't want to quit one job without having another anyway, right?"

I grasped on to that like a lifeline. "*Exactly*. They say it's always harder to get a job when you don't currently have one. Makes you seem less desirable or something."

We both ate in silence for a moment before I pulled myself out of my lethargy and sighed. "So any news on Brian?" I asked, because *hello*, we'd been talking about my love life (or lack thereof) for a good thirty minutes.

She brightened. "No, but you know the new attorney they just hired for contracts?"

"Yeah."

"He asked me to dinner tonight."

"That's great!" I said. "He's really cute, too, isn't he?"

She nodded. "His name is Todd and he just moved here from Omaha."

"Omaha," I repeated. "So a corn-fed country boy?"

Megan grinned at me. "He did grow up on a farm. He's real polite and nice. Has manners, you know?"

"A man with manners," I mused. "They're getting harder to find. Let's hope this one treats you how you deserve to be treated and doesn't send you scathing Bible verses."

"You've got that right," she agreed with a laugh. "I think Brian was just playing with me anyway, using me to feed his ego. Half the time he wouldn't even reply to my texts. It was like trying to have a conversation with a brick wall."

"That really sucks," I said. "What a jerk." I decided Brian was one weird guy. Megan was pretty, sweet, smart, and funny. He'd have been lucky to date her, and instead he'd given her the cold shoulder. Girlfriends stuck by each other, and the next time he came by my desk to fix something on my computer, I was going to unload a good piece of my mind on him.

"Pretty much," she readily agreed, smiling even though I knew her feelings had been hurt. It just made me want to kick Brian in the nuts. If he had any.

"So what are you wearing tonight?" I asked, which brought on a whole other—much more pleasant— conversation.

I was almost late getting back from lunch but had hit my chair and had even had time to touch up the heavy-duty makeup attempting to cover the bruises on my face by the time Parker returned from his lunch with a client. He walked past me into his office without a word, which hurt but was probably better than any alternative I could come up with in- side my head.

A few minutes later, he came out carrying his briefcase. I was studiously avoiding looking up from my computer, but he stopped at my counter.

"Sage," he said, causing me to look up. "How are you feeling today?"

For a second, I just stared blankly at him. Was he really

asking how I was doing after the brush-off he'd given me last night? How was I even supposed to answer that question?

He gestured toward my face. "Your eye. How's it doing?"

Oh. That.

"Um, yeah, it's better," I said, forcing my gaze away from his. I didn't want to look at him. Didn't want to notice the deep blue of his eyes, the wave of his dark hair, or how good he looked today in the powder blue shirt with white French cuffs, deep navy suit, and perfectly knotted scarlet tie. "Thanks for asking."

I resumed typing, hoping he'd get the hint. He stood there for a moment, watching me, then said, "I'm leaving early for a meeting. You're welcome to take off, too."

That made me look up again, my eyebrows flying upward. Parker never gave me time off, not "just because." Maybe it was his version of another apology—as if a couple of hours on a Friday would help—but whatever. I'd take it.

"Yeah, I'll do that. Thanks." My voice and expression were as blank as I could make them. I didn't want him to see how much he'd hurt me. I'd rather he just think it was a one-time, in-the-moment kind of thing.

"Maybe you could, you know, go visit your parents this weekend," he continued.

I looked at him. "Go visit my parents," I repeated.

"Yes. They live in Lake Forest, right?"

Parker knew where my parents lived? How? I nodded. "Yeah."

"I'm sure they'd love to see you," he said. "I can even have my driver take you there so you don't have to ride the bus."

My mouth dropped open. "You can't be serious."

"That your parents would want to see you? I'm certain they would," he said. "As a matter of fact, I left a message for them earlier, telling them you were getting some extra time off so you could go. Take Monday, too, if you'd like. I'm sure they're looking forward to it. I even made reservations for dinner tonight for the three of you."

And I abruptly realized what he was doing. Looking around to make sure no one was close by, I leaned forward and hissed, "This is about getting me out of the way for this deal you're doing, isn't it. What a shitty thing to do, calling my *parents*, for God's sake! Tell me you didn't really do that."

Parker's face hardened. "Maybe you need to look in the mirror again," he said, his voice low. "You're a vulnerability I can't afford right now."

His frankness surprised me, draining the heat from my anger.

"The car will be here in an hour," he said. "I want you in it. No arguments. I'll see you Tuesday." He stepped away and a moment later had disappeared inside the elevator.

That just pissed me off all over again. So he wanted me conveniently out of the way until after the deal was done. Whether it was for my supposed safety or because I didn't want him to do this deal, I didn't know. Either way, him ordering me around like that—especially after last night—rubbed me all kinds of the wrong way.

No, I wasn't going to visit my parents—like I wanted to spend the weekend hiding my depression from my too-intuitive mother. Not gonna happen. But take off early on a gorgeous Friday afternoon? That I *would* do. And if I was lucky...

I pulled up the White Sox website on my computer. Yep. There was an afternoon game at three.

Logging off my computer, I grabbed my purse and hit the elevator. I had just enough time to run home, change into more appropriate clothes, and make it to the stadium.

On a whim, I called Ryker while I was waiting for the bus. We'd left things kind of shaky yesterday, but I was hoping he was around.

"I'm playing hooky from work," I said when he answered. "There's a White Sox game at three."

"I'm there," he replied.

"Okay. Meet me out front."

Just like that, my bad mood melted away. I knew Parker would find out pretty soon that I'd dissed his car—and my mother would be none too pleased that I had to cancel—but it served him right. And if I happened to let slip that I was out with Ryker when he called (because I *knew* he'd call to yell at me), well, so much the better, right? All's fair in love and war.

Being with Ryker was a relief after the emotional angst of being around Parker. He was waiting for me when I hopped off the bus, his jeans and White Sox T-shirt almost an exact duplicate of what I was wearing, only I was in cutoffs.

He grinned when he saw me, his aviator sunglasses reflecting my image when I got close enough. "Nice hat," he said, reaching out to tweak the brim of my baseball cap. "I'm glad you called. Couldn't have picked a better day for it."

And it was a gorgeous day. We bought tickets in the cheap seats, hot dogs and beers, and settled in to watch the game. I'd even put mustard on my hot dog, and it tasted fabulous.

No one sat in front of us, so I stretched my legs over the back of the seat in front of me. Might as well get some sun on my legs, too, and not just my thighs.

"It's a little hard to concentrate on the game when you do that," Ryker said, the corner of his mouth lifting in a half-smile.

"I need to start working on my tan," I explained. "Bikini season is just around the corner."

His mischievous grin was full-on now, plus dimple. "Now that's something to look forward to."

Ryker was an incurable flirt and player, and I didn't take half of what he said seriously, but boy could he pump up a girl's ego. His teasing innuendos had me laughing and blushing at the same time, and it wasn't until after the seventh inning stretch that he went somewhere I didn't like.

"So what's Parker up to today?" he asked. "Any word on the deal with ZNT?"

I finished chewing the handful of popcorn I was munching on. "He's out for the afternoon," I said curtly.

"Do you know where he went?"

I took a sip of beer (because the ball park didn't sell vodka) before answering. "Nope. Didn't ask."

"Could he be meeting with Viktor?"

"I'm not doing this," I said, turning to fix him with a glare.

"Not doing what?"

"I didn't invite you here so you could quiz me about Parker," I said.

"Since what Parker's doing has a direct impact on *you*, my asking is less about the case and more about how much danger he's putting you in."

Ryker's frank response had me staring dubiously at him. "After all the BS you've been shoveling my way today, how am I supposed to take you seriously?"

He had the audacity to look confused. "What BS?"

I waved my hand. "You know, all the compliments and teasing, telling me how great I look, et cetera. You've been laying it on thick—which I appreciate, don't get me wrong—but then how am I supposed to know when you really mean something you say?"

He didn't respond for a moment, then reached up and slid off his glasses. The blue of his eyes was as clear as the sky above us.

"Sage, I've been perfectly honest with you today. It's not BS. You're gorgeous and I like making sure you know it. This isn't a pickup line or a performance designed to get you into bed.

"If you don't want to talk about Parker," he continued, "then we won't, but that doesn't mean I'm going to stop trying to make you see sense when it comes to him."

Okay, well he'd been doing good up until the *see sense* part. I sighed inwardly. He hated Parker, distrusted him, and nothing I said was going to change that.

"Let's just enjoy the game, okay?" I asked. It was a peace offering, and it seemed Ryker recognized it as such because he smiled as he slid his sunglasses back on.

"Sounds good to me." He draped his arm over the back of my chair, his hand lightly resting on the back of my neck bared by my ponytail. It felt nice, kind of possessive, and I liked it.

A few minutes later, my cell buzzed in my pocket. I pulled it out, glanced at the screen, and grimaced. I'd known it was coming but still, a confrontation with my boss was usually something I avoided.

"Why the hell didn't you do what I said?" was his opening line the second I answered.

"You gave me the afternoon off," I replied coolly. "What I do when I'm not on the clock isn't regulated by you or anyone else at KLP Capital." Not quite true, since I'd been at Parker's beck and call for over a year, but it was past time for that to change.

"I gave you time off so you'd get out of town until it's safe for you to come back," he retorted.

There was a crack of the batter hitting a ball and the crowd cheered. Music played over the sound system.

"Are you at a fucking *baseball game*?" Parker growled in my ear.

I cringed at the anger in his voice, but kept up my bravado. "Not just a baseball game. The Sox are playing today."

"So although I tell you it's not safe, you're at a public venue, alone—"

"Who said I was alone?" I interrupted. Of course since I'd been fawning over him the other night, he'd assume I had no one else in my life. *Wrong, buddy.* "Ryker's with me."

Silence.

"Trying to get back at me, Sage?"

That stung, because it hit too close to home.

"Don't be ridiculous," I snapped. "I know it's impossible for you to comprehend that he might actually be into me, but you're wrong." I glanced at Ryker, who was listening and now had a big grin on his face. Quickly, I covered the phone's mouthpiece and spoke in a hushed whisper. "He is wrong, right?"

Ryker slid his fingers up my nape to curl around my neck. "Oh, yeah. He's very wrong."

Good to know.

I spoke into the phone again. "So have a good weekend," I said. "I plan to." I ended the call without waiting for a response. Darn close to hanging up on my boss, but I'd been pushed beyond my limits this week.

And had I just insinuated that I was going to sleep with Ryker this weekend? Kinda. Hmm.

So maybe I *had* invited Ryker just to get back at Parker, but it had been done unconsciously, so I didn't think it really counted. I was hurting from his rejection, so yeah, maybe I had wanted to prove that I wasn't a troll, and using Parker's sworn enemy to do it was probably infantile, but I couldn't help the satisfaction that came from that phone call.

Yes, I was officially fifteen years old again.

"Sorry about that," I said to Ryker, sliding my phone back into my pocket.

"Don't be sorry," he said. "Parker's a dick." No argument from me on that one, not today. "You want to use me to get to him, I've got no problem with that."

That made my cheeks heat with embarrassment, but Ryker didn't seem upset, so I gave an internal shrug and let it go.

"So tell me, how'd you get into baseball?" he asked.

I raised an eyebrow, twisting in my seat to look at him. "What? A girl can't be a baseball fan?"

He grinned. "That's not what I said. I'm asking how *you* got into baseball."

"My dad," I said, settling back to stretch my legs out again. "He loves the Sox and I grew up watching them on TV. I can't remember *not* watching baseball with him. What about you?"

"I used to play."

"Really?" It seemed incongruous, given what he'd told me about his childhood.

He laughed a bit, leaning back and bracing his elbows on the arms of his seat. "Don't look so surprised," he said. "My mom insisted I get involved in some kind of sport. Thought it'd help keep me out of trouble. So I picked baseball."

"What position did you play?"

He flashed a shit-eating grin. "Third base."

I laughed out loud. I should've known. It was so appropriate for Ryker.

"I take it you didn't play a sport in high school?" he asked.

I shook my head. "No sports, no."

"Then what? No wait, don't tell me...the debate team."

I laughed again, swatting him playfully on the arm. "Please. I wasn't smart enough to be on the debate team." Ryker caught my hand in his and threaded our fingers together, which distracted me enough to tell him the truth. "I was a cheerleader."

Now it was his turn to laugh. "No way," he said through his chuckles. "You? Not possible."

"Do I have to get up and do my 'Ready? Okay!' for you?" I asked with mock outrage. "And don't make me do the splits, because I'm telling you, I've still got it."

"I'll need proof of that," he teased, squeezing my hand.

Our eyes met behind our sunglasses and time seemed to slow in one of those moments destined to imprint on my memory. In the warm spring air, with the sunshine heating my skin, the smell of hot dogs and popcorn in the air, and the crack of the baseball, it was the most perfect moment I'd had in a really long time.

A shout broke the moment and we both looked up to see a baseball hurtling toward us. I cringed, hoping it wouldn't hit me. But Ryker's hand flashed up and the ball smacked into his palm.

A beat passed, and then we were both on our feet, cheering and laughing as he held the baseball aloft in triumph for the sparse crowd out here in the way-way outfield. Catch a homer at a White Sox game? Check.

"Damn, that hurt like a sonofabitch," he said with a laugh, shaking his hand out.

"You're not supposed to say that," I teased. "It's unmanly."

Wrapping his arms around my waist, he pulled me into him. "Oh, it is, is it?" he asked, his lips twisting in a mischievous grin. "So does that mean I don't get a kiss for saving you from injury-by-baseball?"

"I didn't know you wanted one," I said loftily, playing hard to get. "I didn't want to just *assume*—"

He cut me off with a kiss, his lips warm and soft against mine. I melted against him like cotton candy left too long in the sun. Ryker needed no more encouragement to deepen the kiss, which made the bill of his cap knock me in the forehead.

"Pretend that didn't happen," he murmured against my lips as he twisted the cap around. "I'm usually much smoother."

I smiled. "Yeah, your image is totally ruined now."

"I'm going to have to fix that," he rasped. Then he deepened the kiss and I forgot all about his hat.

After the game, Ryker took me home on his bike. I decided I could get used to this. His body was hard against mine as I held on. Illinois had no helmet laws and since we were relatively close to my apartment, we both forwent wearing one, which allowed me to lean my head against Ryker's back. His Sox T-shirt was soft against my cheek as the wind tousled my hair.

Parker was a constant presence in the back of my mind, but I was trying really hard to shove thoughts of him away. There was no earthly reason why I shouldn't enjoy Ryker's company and forget all about Parker and all that *wasn't* going to happen between us. We'd had a really fun time at the baseball game, and I liked how Ryker made me feel. I'd gone so long with a one-way admiration for Parker, it was as though I'd forgotten what it was like to have a man constantly touching me, giving me compliments, asking me about myself, and looking at me as though he was picturing me naked inside his head.

Ryker walked me up to my door, but this time I was smart enough not to unlock it. I was honest enough with myself to know I was in a vulnerable state, and sleeping with Ryker tonight would be a lot more about Parker than it would be about Ryker, and that wasn't fair to him.

"I have to work tomorrow," he said, "but I can see you on Sunday." He was close to me, his hands settling on my hips as I looked up at him. The hall light glinted off his dog tags.

His blue eyes twinkled into mine, his jaw shadowed with slightly more than a day's growth of whiskers, giving him that bad-boy look that went so well with the muscles and motorcycle.

I abruptly decided that Ryker was just what I needed to move on from Parker. There were worse things than a drop-dead gorgeous cop with an attitude matched only by the size of his ego. He may be a player and a cliché who'd lose interest the moment after we had sex, but at least I was going into it with my eyes wide open.

"What if I have plans Sunday?" I asked.

"Break them." He took my wrists and lifted my arms to wrap around his neck, then kissed me.

It was way easier not to think about Parker with Ryker's lips on mine. He tasted of beer and salt, his cologne now masked with the scent of sun and sweat from sitting outside at the ball game. And not the nasty kind of man-sweat smell, but the kind that oozes pheromones and is more potent than the most expensive cologne.

His arms wrapped tight around my waist, drawing me up onto my toes as he kissed me. He was a good kisser and my brain stopped working entirely as I sank deep into the moment. Time passed, but I didn't notice, until we finally came up for air.

Usually it took more than a man's kiss to get me going, but if we'd been inside my apartment I would've dragged Ryker to my bed without a second's hesitation. Now reality crept back in and I was glad we weren't inside. Sort of.

"I had a really nice time today," he said, his voice a husky rasp that shot straight through me. He was looking at me with a promise in his eyes that I sincerely hoped he'd keep come Sunday.

"Me too," I said.

"See you Sunday." He winked, then eased away to head down the hall, leaving me weak-kneed and propped against my door. I watched as he disappeared into the stairwell, the door slamming shut behind him.

I was lost in a misty world of daydreams about Sunday as I unlocked my door and walked into my darkened apartment. I stepped out of my flip-flops as I thought. I'd have to clean tomorrow and change the sheets on my bed. Definitely didn't want to bring Ryker back here since I hadn't had a chance to clean in a while—

I screamed.

A man was sitting on my couch in the dark, the outline of his body seen only because of the glow from outside filtering in through the slats on the blinds. A lamp flicked on, and I could breathe again.

It was Parker.

"Oh my God, you scared me," I said, leaning against the wall. My hands shook and my heart was pounding. "Why the hell would you do that?"

Parker stood and walked toward me. He still wore his suit jacket, but he'd discarded the tie and undone the top two buttons of his shirt. The look on his face had me swallowing hard and rethinking the wisdom of sassing him earlier on the phone.

He ignored me, snapping back with a question of his own. "Where's Ryker? I thought he was keeping you safe."

"He left," I shot back. "Why? Were you going to try to scare him away if he wanted to spend the night?" I loaded up on the sarcasm.

"I don't care what you do with him," he bit out. "But why the hell would you play games with me about this?"

"Play games about what?" My back was to the wall and he was all up in my business.

"Play games about your safety," he retorted. "I'm up to my neck with these people, trying to do what I have to do, and you're making things more difficult when your job is to make them easier!"

He was yelling at me, and Parker had never yelled at me. I didn't think I'd ever seen him this angry before.

"I didn't want to go visit my parents—"

"I don't give a shit!" He cut me off mid-sentence. "I told you to do something, *needed* you to do something, and you completely disobeyed me."

Tears stung my eyes at the force of his fury, and if I was honest, I was scared, too. A nerve pulsed in his jaw and his eyes were practically shooting sparks at me. His entire body vibrated with anger.

"God*damn* it, Sage!" Parker raised his hand to shove his fingers through his hair, but I didn't know that. I just saw him raise his hand and I reacted, cringing away from him and squeezing my eyes shut.

I waited, barely breathing and not even thinking. Now I was terrified and heartsick. But nothing happened. After a few moments of standing stock-still, I cautiously opened my eyes. Parker was staring at me, his expression stricken.

"Good God," he rasped. "Do you really think I'd *hit* you?"

And I promptly burst into tears.

Parker pulled me into his arms. "Sage. Sage. I'm sorry. I'm so fucking sorry."

He was trying to comfort me, but all the hurt and fear came pouring out of me, turning me into a blubbering mess, smearing mascara on the lapel of his suit. Again.

He kept talking, apologizing, his voice a hoarse, tortured whisper in my ear. I barely heard. Tears still poured down my cheeks as I tried to pull myself together.

"Please stop crying. I'm sorry. I'd never hurt you, you know that." Parker leaned back, taking my face in his hands to look in my eyes. "Tell me you know that."

He swiped at the tear tracks with his thumbs, and when I didn't answer, he pressed his lips to my cheek, kissing away my tears. First one side, then the other. "I'd never hurt you. I swear it," he murmured. "And I'd kill anyone who did."

It was overwhelming, and such a tremendous relief from how I'd felt just moments earlier, but I barely had time to process what he'd said before he lightly pressed his mouth to mine in a chaste, sweet kiss.

"Don't cry, please don't cry," he whispered against my lips.

I took a deep, shuddering breath and tentatively kissed him back. Just a tiny movement of my lips against his, but it was as though someone had thrown gasoline onto burning embers. In the next moment, we were kissing feverishly in a tangle of lips, and teeth, and tongues.

His desperation fed into me and I raked my nails through his hair, clutching him to me. His lips and tongue skated down my neck, sucking at the pulse beating a staccato rhythm underneath my skin. I sucked in air and said his name. His mouth returned to kiss the syllables from my lips.

I clutched at his shoulders, the expensive fabric of his suit crumpling in my grip. His hands moved to my arms, sliding down until he took my hands in his and stretched my arms over my head. He leaned into me, bracing my arms against the wall and holding them there.

Our fingers tangled together and his kisses gentled, teasing and seducing rather than hard and demanding. We were both breathing fast when he finally pulled away slightly.

"Tell me you know I'd never hurt you," he murmured. His nose rubbed lightly at my cheek, his lips brushing the side of my mouth.

"I know," I whispered, which was the longest speech I was capable of at the moment.

He stepped back, his hands slowly sliding down my arms to my sides, then settling on my waist. I lowered my arms to rest on his shoulders. His eyes devoured me, the hungry glint in them making an answering heat flare between my legs.

"Don't leave your apartment this weekend," he said. "Will you do that for me?"

At the moment, he could've asked me to pirouette naked on Lake Shore Drive and I'd have probably done it. I nodded.

"Good. I'll see you Monday."

He stepped away and I stared after him, nonplussed.

"Wait a second," I said, and he halted, already almost at the door. "That's it? You kiss me like that and now you're just going to leave? What the hell, Parker?"

"I told you last night. I don't do relationships."

"Well, I don't do friends—or bosses—with benefits," I retorted.

Parker walked to where I stood, encroaching on my space until I took a step back and again hit the wall. I didn't want to appear vulnerable, but there was nothing I could do.

"So you're telling me you don't like it when I kiss you," he said, lifting a hand to trail a featherlight touch down my cheek. "That you want me to stop and never touch you again?" The touch of his other hand on my hip made a shiver dance down my spine.

I swallowed. I was turned on and angry at the same time at the power he had over me. "You're using our working relationship against me," I said.

"I'm using your body against you," he corrected. "Let's make that perfectly clear." His hand skated underneath the hem of my T-shirt. I sucked in a breath as his fingers drifted over my stomach. "And if that's what it takes to make you do what I say—to keep you safe—then so be it." Leaning down, he pressed an openmouthed kiss to my neck. "It's not exactly a hardship," he murmured.

"This is wrong," I said, but the breathlessness of those words took all the impact from them.

"I really don't care so long as it keeps you out of harm's way."

I'd just reached up to hold him to me when he stepped away. A moment later, he was out the door and gone.

CHAPTER THIRTEEN

Saturday I moped. I didn't hear from Parker, which was probably a good thing. Yet it didn't feel that way. I felt depressed in the way you do when you keep waiting for the phone to ring and it stays determinedly silent. No calls. No texts. No nothing. He'd successfully sucked me back in to thinking that he and I might be a possibility. After all, he'd kissed me again, touched me again, and I was a firm believer in actions spoke louder than words.

I worried about Hanna. I wondered if anyone had bothered to tell Tania that her sister was dead, or if the police even knew that poor Niki had a sister.

I couldn't sleep and was curled up on the couch, watching a *Criminal Minds* rerun—what a gripping life I led—when my cell rang. I didn't know the number, but I did recognize the voice.

"Hanna!" I exclaimed, surprised and glad to hear from her.

"Did you mean it?" she asked abruptly. "That you would help me?" She sounded nervous.

"Absolutely," I assured her.

"I need a place to stay," she said. "I want out, but I have no place to go."

"You can stay here," I said, deciding not to ask too many questions over the phone. I gave her my address.

About thirty minutes later, I heard a knock on the door. It was her. "Come in," I said, helping her inside. I noticed that she had nothing with her but her purse. I guessed she probably hadn't wanted to take anything larger and tip off whomever might be watching that she was making a run for it.

She seemed awkward and unsure, standing in the foyer. "Are you hungry?" I asked, hoping to make her feel more at ease.

"Um, yeah. I guess."

Poking in my fridge, I took out the leftover frozen lasagna I'd picked up last night after smelling the homemade one at Parker's. It wasn't nearly as good, but it would do. I heated some up in the microwave and sat down with her at the table.

"Tomorrow I'll call a friend of mine," I said. "He'll know how to help you." Normally, I'd be thinking of Parker. Not this time. Ryker would be the one I turned to for help. Parker seemed powerless against these people and I wasn't sure if it wasn't by choice. The thought depressed me, so I shoved it away.

Hanna nodded, her attention focused on the food. She'd obviously made an effort to be real cleaned up before she'd come here. Her hair was thick and had been brushed until it shone, the deep chestnut color a mirror of my own.

"Hanna," I began, wanting to ask her a question without

scaring her. "What was Niki planning to tell the police that would make Viktor want to kill her?" To me, it seemed it would have to have been something more than just the prostitution thing, because that'd just be his word against hers, right? And there was still that small detail of her having Parker's business card.

Hanna finished her plate, daintily wiping her mouth with a napkin before replying. "Niki was good with numbers," she said. "Crazy good. She worked with Viktor on stuff related to the money. You know the phrase... cooking the books."

I sucked in a breath, my eyes wide. Okay, so *that* I could see was worth killing her for, especially if she'd been a snitch for the cops.

She eyed me. "What happened to you?" she asked, nodding toward my face.

The bruising was a lot better, but I hadn't put on a bit of makeup today. "Uh, yeah, you were right," I said. "Your neighborhood isn't very safe."

It seemed she needed no further explanation, or maybe didn't want to know the details, because she just nodded, looking grim.

It was getting late and Hanna hid a yawn behind her hand, the heavy Italian food no doubt making her sleepy. I got to my feet and cleared away her dishes.

"You can have my bed," I said, leading her back to my bedroom. "I don't mind the couch." She protested, but I wasn't having any of it. I handed her some of my pajamas to wear and left her alone to go make up the couch.

As I turned off the television and lights and lay down on the couch, I realized I was really glad Hanna was here. It felt like I was doing something. Even if it was just helping one person, it was a start. I fell asleep staring at the ceiling and wondering how I could help Tania, too.

* * *

I woke up in the middle of the night, freezing. My air conditioner had kicked on, making the living room a lot colder than I'd planned when I'd made up the couch. Getting up, I tiptoed through my bedroom where Hanna was sleeping until I reached the master bath.

Leaving off the light so as not to wake her, I opened the linen closet in the bathroom. I was feeling my way in the dark—*didn't I have a quilt in this closet somewhere?*—when I heard it.

The sound of the bedroom door creaking open.

Twisting to look out the open bathroom door, Hanna's name was on my lips, but something made me keep silent. It wasn't her. I could still see her form under the covers. I also saw two shadowy figures moving toward the bed.

My blood froze in my veins, a scream strangling in my throat. Strangers were in my apartment. Big strangers. Men who were at least six feet tall. One of them had something in his hand. The moonlight filtering through the window glinted off it.

A knife.

I couldn't think. Couldn't even breathe. I stood, cloaked in the shadows of the bathroom, staring as the men surrounded the bed. My limbs shook with fear and I thought of the men in the bar last night. Had they found me?

But they didn't turn my way. The one with the knife leaned over the bed. I couldn't see what he was doing, but I watched the lump I knew to be Hanna. She moved, sharply and abruptly, her legs straightening. I heard a strange gurgling sound, then nothing. The men turned and left as silently as they'd come.

I still couldn't move. My feet seemed cemented to the

floor, my joints locked in place. Had they really not seen me? Or was it a trick? How could it be a trick when they could so easily overpower me?

Hanna.

I forced my feet to take a step forward, then another and another, until I stood by the bed.

She was still there, a silent and huddled mass underneath the covers. There was something dark on the sheets, though, and a strange smell in the air.

My hand was shaking as I reached for the lamp on the bedside table, and I gasped when its light flooded the room.

Hanna stared at me, her eyes wide and unseeing. Blood from a deep gash in her throat soaked the sheets, the pillow underneath her dark hair, the pajamas I'd loaned her.

I wanted to scream, but I couldn't. I just stared at her. She'd been alive just minutes ago. Then men had crept in and murdered her. She'd been so close to freedom…and now it was gone.

I don't know how long I stood there, staring at her body, before I could make my brain work again. I picked up the phone by the bed and dialed. It rang several times before a man's sleep-roughened voice answered.

"Ryker. Help me."

* * *

I looked away from where the medical examiner and cops were removing Hanna's body through the foyer and out the front door. Ryker sat beside me on the couch, his arm around my waist. I clutched a glass of iced bourbon in my hands. Ryker had taken one look at me, gone into the kitchen, and returned with the drink.

"How'd they get in?" I asked.

"Picked the lock," he replied. "It's a decent lock, but not great. They were professionals."

I swallowed. "Why would they kill her? She was just a prostitute, working for them."

Ryker looked at me. "You can't possibly think they were here for her, do you?"

I stared blankly at him. "Why else would they come?"

"Sage, she looked enough like you to be your sister. She had on *your* pajamas, was in *your* apartment, asleep in *your* bed. I think it's a safe bet to say they came here for you. Not Hanna."

Shock rippled through me yet again. It hadn't occurred to me, not even for a moment, that I'd been the target. Guilt followed close on the heels of realization.

"Oh my God," I said, tears leaking from my eyes. "It's my fault they killed her." I raised a shaking hand to cover my mouth, squeezing my eyes shut. Hanna had come to me for help and had died for it. If she'd gone anywhere else tonight, she'd still be alive.

Ryker cursed. The ice clinked in the glass as he took it from my hand; then he was folding me in his arms.

"Shh. It's not your fault, Sage," he said.

"They killed her," I sobbed. "And I didn't do anything. I just let it happen. I could've helped her, but I didn't." Guilt rushed over me in thick waves.

"Shhh, calm down," Ryker said. "You couldn't have helped her. They'd have just killed you, too." His arms were tight around me, one hand cradling the back of my head.

I pulled away slightly, sniffing back more tears. The guilt I felt was now more overwhelming than the fear had been. It was crippling in a way that was the same but different from the terror that had frozen me in place.

"Let's get you out of here."

Taking my hand, he pulled me to my feet. My knees were shaking and threatened to give out, which made me glad Ryker still had a firm grip around my waist.

"Hey, Malone, I'm taking her home," he said to his partner, who was standing nearby, watching us.

"You sure she shouldn't go to the hospital?" Malone asked, skeptical.

"She's okay, just in shock. And as of yet, they don't know she's not dead."

The men shared a look I couldn't interpret; then Ryker was taking me downstairs and outside, hustling me past the ambulance at the curb to a Ford pickup that looked like it was from the sixties—not that I was an expert.

There was a chill in the air and I shivered. I was still in my pajamas—a thin pair of cotton pants and matching camisole top. Navy blue with pink lace trim. They were my favorite, but now I was cold. I wrapped my arms around my middle.

Ryker saw the gesture and pulled his jacket from the cab of the truck. "Here. Wear this," he said, swinging the leather over my shoulders. I pushed my arms into the too-long sleeves, then climbed into the cab. Ryker shut the door and rounded to the driver's side. I took a deep breath, Ryker's scent enveloping me as easily as the leather jacket had.

I tried fastening the seat belt, but my hands were shaking so badly, I couldn't. Ryker's hand closed gently over mine, removing the belt from my grip and fastening it himself.

I stared out the window as Ryker drove, willing myself not to blink, because every time I did, I saw Hanna's eyes accusing me.

There wasn't a lot of traffic at this hour so it didn't take long to arrive at our destination. We pulled up to a house, which surprised me, as I'd assumed he'd live in an apart-

ment. It was in an older neighborhood and was the kind of
row houses they'd built thousands of back in the forties and
fifties. Ryker helped me out of the pickup, but I was steadier
on my feet now. He took my hand and led me up the concrete
steps to the porch. The screen door creaked as he opened it;
then I heard the rattle of keys as he unlocked the door. A dog
barked from inside.

"Easy, McClane," Ryker said, reaching down to grab the
huge animal that lunged toward us as we stepped through the
doorway. "Sage, meet McClane."

I didn't know a lot about dogs—had never had a dog—so
the size, enthusiasm, and gaping jaws filled with sharp teeth
made my eyes widen and I stopped in my tracks.

"He's a German shepherd," Ryker said, his hand firmly
around the dog's collar. "He was going to be a police dog,
but it didn't work out."

"Why not?" I asked, my eyes glued to the dog's teeth and
lolling tongue.

"He was a little ... overly enthusiastic about tearing apart
the dummies. And he was unpredictable. Kind of has a mind
of his own."

My eyes got even wider and I took a tiny step back.

"But he's fine now," Ryker hastened to reassure me.
"He's a great dog, and well trained."

"If he's so well trained, why do you have to hold him?"
Hello, obvious.

"Just until he meets you," Ryker said. "McClane, this
is Sage. Say hello." Ryker released the collar and the dog
bounded toward me.

I squeaked, retreating until my back hit the wall, but the
dog had finally shut its gaping maw and was sniffing me.
I stood stock-still, my arms clutched to my chest, watching
McClane snuffle his way around me. It was okay, I knew

enough about dogs to know he had to smell me, but when he shoved his nose into my crotch, I balked.

"Excuse me!" I pushed his nose out of the way before I even thought twice about it.

"McClane, mind your manners," Ryker admonished.

I glanced at him. "McClane?"

Ryker looked at me as though I had two heads. "You know," he said. "From *Die Hard*."

Nope. Not a clue. The blank look on my face made him roll his eyes.

"Obviously your cinematic education is lacking," he teased with a smile.

"Obviously." I mustered a small smile in return, but it quickly faded.

"Is there anything I can do for you? Get for you?"

"Not unless you can turn back time so I could help Hanna rather than cowering while she got butchered feet from me." My words were bitter, but it was all directed at myself. I'd never thought of myself as a coward, but here was proof that I was exactly that.

Ryker wrapped a hand around my arm. "Hey," he said. When I didn't turn his way, he lifted my chin so I had no choice but to look at him. "There was nothing you could have done, Sage. I'm a cop. I know. If you had tried to save her, there'd be two dead women in that apartment instead of just one."

I wanted to believe him, but my conscience wouldn't let me. He saw the doubt in my eyes.

"How much hand-to-hand combat training have you had?" he asked.

I shrugged. "None."

"And what weapon did you have available?"

"Nothing."

"There were two of them, outweighed you by a hundred pounds each, had a knife, and you thought you could have stopped them? No way in hell."

I stared into Ryker's eyes, the blue irises intently focused on me, and saw that it was true. He wasn't lying. I couldn't have stopped Hanna's death, but that only took the edge from the guilt. It didn't erase it entirely.

I nodded. I understood the logic, though my emotions didn't.

"C'mon," he said, taking my hand.

McClane moved aside and Ryker took me through the living room. It was decorated with mismatched furniture that seemed to have been chosen more for comfort than style. A short hallway led to two bedrooms—each at opposite ends of the hall—and a bathroom situated between them. One bedroom I could see contained a desk, futon, and bookshelves, but Ryker led me to the other.

"You can stay here for as long as you want," he said.

The bedroom was uncluttered and simple, containing a queen-sized bed and a chest of drawers. I eyed the bed with some trepidation, but Ryker sensed my unease, adding, "I'll sleep on the couch."

"I don't want to inconvenience you," I said. "It'll just be for tonight, okay?"

Ryker's hand on my arm had me turning to look up at him.

"These men are trying to kill you. I'm guessing they'll know soon that they got the wrong woman. I can protect you here."

The thought that I now needed protecting startled me. I hadn't thought about it, what the men would do when they found out I was still alive—if they really were after me. Suddenly, I felt light-headed.

"Sit down before you fall down," Ryker said, taking my arm and easing me down onto the bed. "You need a drink. I'll be right back."

I sat on the bed.

It didn't take long before he was back, sitting next to me on the bed. He had another drink in hand that he pressed into mine. I took a deep swallow without even looking to see what it was and whiskey burned a path down my throat to my stomach. Ryker didn't say anything as I drank more until the glass was empty; he just took it from me and set it aside.

"I'm scared," I said, and it felt like a confession. I thought I'd been afraid before, in New York, but now it was here and it was in my home and it was in my bedroom, and I was terrified.

"I know."

Ryker reached for me and it seemed as natural as anything to let him put his arms around me and pull me onto his lap. I rested my head against his shoulder. He made no move to leave and I didn't mention it either. I didn't want to have to confess how scared I was even to be alone. It made me feel weak.

The scent of him was comforting to me, as was the warm strength of his body against mine. His palm drifted down my back and up again in a soothing gesture. I closed my eyes and before I knew it, I was asleep.

* * *

Screaming woke me. My own. My eyes flew open and I sat straight up in bed. I was drenched in sweat, my chest heaving, and my face wet with tears.

"It's okay. You're okay."

Ryker was there. He'd been lying on the floor—not the

couch—and now he sat next to me on the bed. I threw myself
into his arms and held on tight around his neck.

"It was just a nightmare," he said. "You're okay. I'm not
going anywhere. You're safe."

Gratitude and relief coursed through me and my body relaxed ever so slightly. The nightmare was still fresh in my
head. The men had been there, standing over me. One had
reached for me and blood flowed. I realized my throat was
slit and I couldn't talk, couldn't cry for help. The only sound
coming from me was a wet gurgling.

I shuddered just thinking about it, and Ryker's arms tightened around me.

I don't know how long we stayed like that, until I finally
relaxed completely and my head rested on his shoulder. He
didn't move to leave the bed and I didn't ask him to. Eventually, I fell asleep in his arms and this time, no nightmares
plagued me.

* * *

Sunday morning I was awakened by a heavy weight on my
chest and something wet on my cheek.

My eyes popped open and I screamed.

McClane barked, his doggy breath fanning right into my
face from where he was parked on top of me. Ryker sat
straight up, took one look at my face, and yelled at McClane
to get off the bed. He did. Reluctantly. And I could breathe
again.

"Holy shit," I gasped, my heart hammering.

"Sorry about that," Ryker apologized, lying back down beside me. Somehow, we'd gotten underneath the covers, and
the bed that had seemed so large last night suddenly felt half
the size with him in it. "He doesn't sleep in on Sundays."

"So I gathered."

Ryker's lips curved in a smile and his gaze wandered over me. His jaw was shadowed even more than usual and I noticed he wasn't wearing a shirt. I swallowed, wondering how bad my hair looked, not that it seemed he cared. I'd seen that look in a man's eyes before. My heart was still racing, but now for an entirely different reason.

"I'll just...go find some coffee," I said, sliding from underneath the covers. Not that I didn't really *want* to stay there with Ryker, who looked way better first thing in the morning than anyone should have a right to look, but it was really soon to sleep with him. Right? Right. And bad circumstances, and morning breath, and about a dozen other reasons that seemed to pale in significance against the sight of him half-naked in his bed.

I had no toiletries with me, so I used a finger to scrub toothpaste onto my teeth and borrowed Ryker's brush to tame my hair. After splashing some water on my face, I knew it was as good as it was going to get.

Searching through the kitchen turned up a coffeemaker and coffee grounds, and I started a pot while I heard the door close to the bathroom. McClane padded into the kitchen, his nails tapping lightly against the hardwood floor. He stared at me, tongue lolling. He was so huge, his head came to my hips.

"So what am I supposed to do with you?" I asked. "Is there a cat around for you to chase, or a small suckling pig in the fridge for your breakfast?"

McClane plopped his butt on the floor, his tail thumping. Maybe he was smiling at me? It was hard to tell with all the sharp, white teeth.

"Hey, boy, let's go outside." Ryker appeared and it seemed McClane knew what those words meant because he was up and out the open back door like a shot. Ryker closed it behind him.

"Did you find the coffee?" he asked.

I nodded. "Yeah. I put a pot on." This felt awkward, like the proverbial morning-after, but without the sex, which seemed grossly unfair. He'd showered and changed into jeans and a white tank, an unbuttoned short-sleeve shirt thrown on over that. I guessed he wore layers to conceal his holster. His dog tags were centered on his chest and the sunlight glinted off the metal.

"Tell you what," he said, "we'll have breakfast, then I'll take you back to your place for some clothes, and then we'll go do something. Get your mind off it."

"Like what?"

"Something. You've had a shitty week," he said with a shrug. "A change of scenery will do you good, trust me."

I really couldn't disagree with that, and the prospect of spending the day with Ryker made butterflies dance in my stomach, which also made me feel guilty. Hanna was still dead.

"Oh no you don't," he said. "I can see it on your face. You're still feeling guilty. Don't. It wasn't your fault."

I nodded, knowing that I could tell myself that until I was blue in the face, but it would be a while before the guilt abated.

"Can I help do something?" I asked, wanting to change the subject. "Can you cook?"

"I can cook breakfast," he said, bypassing me for the fridge. "That's probably the one meal I *can* cook."

I glanced out the back door to the patio and saw a really nice high-end grill. "And barbeque, right?"

Ryker's arms were full of eggs and a package of bacon when he turned around.

"I'm a total cliché," he said with a shrug, depositing everything on the counter. "I can cook eggs and grill a steak. That's about it." He grinned, the dimple in his cheek on full wattage. "How do you like your eggs? Scrambled or scrambled?"

I laughed. "Scrambled is good."

He nodded, but I caught him glancing at my chest before he turned away. My camisole pajamas didn't leave a lot to the imagination, not that there was anything I could do about it. But hey, I had nice boobs, and I didn't mind Ryker looking. I was doing my own share of looking, too.

His arms were absolutely maxed out. His biceps bulged, straining the cotton of the T-shirt, and even from where I stood a few feet away, I could see the outline of the veins in his arms standing out in prominent relief underneath his skin. The sign of a man who worked out hard.

I wasn't one of those women who pretended not to be impressed by a man's physique. I loved a well-built man. Ryker said he was a cliché? Well, so was I. I was definitely impressed by a strong man. Sue me.

And a man who could make me breakfast.

The eggs were perfect, as was the bacon, and Ryker chatted with me while we ate. I asked him about his job and he told me a couple of hair-raising stories about drug pushers and gangs he'd been a part of taking down. It was engrossing and I barely noticed him feeding McClane bits of bacon as he talked.

"Weren't you scared?" I asked, after he'd told me about getting cornered by some gang members who'd found out he was an undercover cop.

He shrugged. "Yeah, but it's the kind of fear that brings everything into sharp focus. Like a hit of adrenaline tinged with terror. It can help you survive."

I shook my head. I couldn't imagine living like that, but

Ryker seemed to love the rush of danger. Hmm. Probably not good for a relationship.

"I'll clean up," I offered, but he waved me away, setting the dirty dishes in the sink.

"I'll do it later," he said. "Right now, I'd rather get out of the house." I caught him looking at my chest again. "Before I take you back to bed, and it wouldn't be to sleep."

My face heated and I didn't reply. Probably because climbing back into bed with Ryker sounded like a pretty damn good way to get my mind off things.

He turned to McClane. "Okay, buddy, I'm taking the lady home. Be good. Don't eat the couch."

"Do you have a shirt I can wear over this or something?" I asked.

"That'd be a crime, but I'll allow it," he teased. "In the chest of drawers there's some T-shirts. Help yourself."

I headed back to the bedroom while he continued piling dishes in the sink. I wasn't going to complain. I hated doing dishes.

The top drawer was what I pulled out first, quickly discovering that was *not* where Ryker kept his T-shirts, though I did take a longer-than-appropriate glance at his boxer collection.

Okay, moving on.

I crouched down and pulled at the bottom drawer instead, which seemed stuck. I frowned, yanking harder, then fell back on my butt when it finally opened.

Jackpot! A pile of T-shirts.

Grabbing one, I pulled it on over my head and it came halfway down my thighs. I was just pushing the drawer back in when a corner of something glass caught my eye. Curious, I reached underneath the pile of T-shirts and pulled out a picture frame.

I held it up to see and my jaw dropped open.

It was a photo of Ryker, but he wasn't alone. A woman was with him, his arm around her shoulders and her arm around his waist. But that wasn't what was making me stare in stunned astonishment.

Parker was there, too, standing on the other side of the woman.

All three were smiling and laughing, looking into the camera. As though they were the best of friends.

The woman was pretty and young. She had short blond hair that just brushed her shoulders. Petite, she only came to shoulder-height on the men.

Natalie. It had to be.

What had happened to make things go so wrong between them? How had her death torn Parker and Ryker apart? I would have thought, from looking at the picture, that they'd have both mourned her and been there to help each other through it.

I heard a step in the hallway and hurriedly replaced the picture and shoved the drawer shut just as Ryker stepped into the room.

"Find something?" he asked.

"Sure did. Thanks." I forced a smile, my thoughts churning with the mystery that was Parker, Ryker, and Natalie.

I followed him outside and a few minutes later we were heading to my apartment in his pickup. The windows were down, and my hair teased my face as the breeze tossed it with invisible fingers. He drove with one arm draped over the wheel, his long legs stretched out in front of him.

"So did you buy this somewhere?" I asked, looking around the interior. It was an antique, yes, but very well cared for. The upholstery on the bench seat was perfect, as was the dash. Not a speck of dust anywhere.

"I bought it when I got out of the Marines," he said. "It was a piece of junk. But I fixed it up. Took me a long time. It's a hobby, fixing up old cars and trucks. I have another one I'm working on now."

"Motorcycles *and* vintage automobiles?" I asked.

He turned his smile full wattage again. "I know. Cliché."

I may have sighed a little. With his heavy boots, mirrored shades, and the dog tags dangling around his neck, Ryker had the bad-boy thing written all over him. But when he smiled, he was pure charm and boy-next-door.

Going back inside my apartment altered my mood drastically. Ryker removed the crime scene tape so I could get in, then walked with me to my bedroom.

I stopped short at the door, my horrified gaze drawn to the blood-soaked bed. I'd blocked out how much blood there'd been, but there was no hiding it in the bright sunshine streaming through the window.

Tears stung my eyes even as my stomach rolled. "Oh God," I whispered, trying to swallow down the bile in my throat, but it was no use. I made a beeline for the bathroom, making it to the toilet just as my stomach heaved up the breakfast Ryker had made me.

To my mortification, Ryker was there, handing me a damp washcloth as my stomach finally eased. I flushed the toilet, then sat on the lid. My hands were shaking as I wiped my face.

"Why don't you shower and pack up the things you'll need from the bathroom," he suggested. "I'll pack your clothes." There was an empathy in his voice that made me feel a little better about losing it like that.

I nodded, deciding a man packing my clothes was a better alternative than me being in the same room where Hanna's blood still stained the sheets. "Okay. Thanks."

I showered, blew my hair dry, and packed my makeup as quickly as I could. By the time I was done, Ryker had loaded my suitcase. I followed him out into the living room, appreciating the way he kept his body as a buffer between me and the bed as we left the scene of Hanna's death behind.

"How much did you pack?" I asked, staring at the bulging suitcase.

"Enough," he said with a shrug.

I didn't ask how long I'd be staying at his place. I just knew I needed a few days to figure out what I was going to do, if I'd stay here or move into another apartment. Part of me wanted to move out—how could I ever sleep in that bedroom again? But the other part of me loved my apartment and hated to think I'd have to move, which also seemed somehow an insult to Hanna's memory. I didn't know how to feel, so I was just grateful I'd been given some time to figure it out.

I was reaching for the front door when it suddenly burst open, startling a squeak from me. I was jerked back and shoved behind Ryker. His gun was in his hand as he faced the intruder.

But it was Parker who came through the door.

CHAPTER FOURTEEN

Parker didn't even seem to notice Ryker, just took one look at me and stopped in his tracks.

"Sage," he said, his voice a heavy rasp. "I thought you…" But he didn't continue. He was pale and dressed haphazardly in jeans and a button-down shirt that hadn't been tucked in and wasn't even buttoned all the way.

His eyes drank me in, so intent I couldn't look away.

"Whatever deal you made to protect her isn't working," Ryker said, his tone hard. It broke the spell and Parker's gaze shifted from me to him. "You've fucked something up, or they think you're going to. They thought they'd make their point by killing her."

"Fuck off," Parker growled at him. "This is none of your—"

"Wait a second," I interrupted. "You told me to stay in my apartment all weekend, and that's where they came. Right here."

Neither Parker nor Ryker said a word, but I swore the temperature dropped ten degrees.

"You told her to stay in her apartment," Ryker repeated, his voice ice cold. "How convenient."

"I wanted her to go to her parents'," Parker bit out. "She refused to go."

"So it's *her* fault that you've put her in danger?"

Parker didn't answer. Instead, he turned to me and said, "Come with me."

"Fuck that, dipshit. She's staying with me until this is over." Ryker sounded angry and looked like it wouldn't take much for him to attack Parker. Parker's fists were clenched and he was staring at Ryker as though hoping looks alone could kill. I swallowed hard.

They both looked at me, waiting for me to make a decision. I glanced first at Parker, then at Ryker. I knew which one I *wanted* to choose, and I knew which one I *should*.

"Parker, I appreciate you coming here, but Ryker's a cop. I should stay with him."

It was logical, but also maybe a little part of me was still hurting from Parker's rejection and I wanted to hurt him back. Not big of me, but it was there nonetheless.

"There you go," Ryker said, satisfaction lacing his voice. Slotting his fingers with mine, he slid on his sunglasses, grabbed the suitcase, and pushed past Parker.

Parker's eyes were on mine as I went by, and I couldn't hold his accusing gaze. All I could see inside my head was the picture of Parker, Ryker, and Natalie, and wonder whether history really did have a strange way of repeating itself.

* * *

I'd changed into shorts and a T-shirt, not having any idea what Ryker had planned to take my mind off things. I definitely needed a distraction. Choosing Ryker over Parker had me feeling a guilt that clung like a sweater charged with static electricity.

"We're going to a...fair?" I asked him, rounding the front of the pickup where he'd parked next to a line of other cars in a field-turned-parking lot.

"You sound like you've never been to one," Ryker replied, taking my hand in his.

"I haven't," I said.

Ryker stopped in his tracks and faced me. Sliding his sunglasses down a notch, he peered at me over the rims. "You can't be serious."

I shrugged. "Not really high on my family's To Do list."

"It's awesome. You're gonna love it." He resumed walking.

"I guess I'll have to take your word for it," I said.

"Fried foods, of every kind imaginable. Beer garden. Tractor pull. Pig races. Rides. Games. What's there not to like?"

"What kind of fried foods?" I'd had a funnel cake once, years ago at Disney World, and it had tasted like heaven on earth. "Do they have funnel cakes?"

Ryker grinned at me. "Darlin'," he drawled, "if a funnel cake is what you want, a funnel cake you shall have."

That made me feel good. I liked the whole country-boy thing he had going on. I'd never been to a county fair, and now it seemed I'd picked the perfect person to attend my very first one with.

The fair was teeming with all kinds of people dressed in all sorts of clothes. Denim seemed to be the preferred fabric, though the amount one actually wore varied widely. Some girls wore cutoff jean shorts that crawled so far up their rears I wondered how they could possibly sit down. These girls most often paired their outfits with cowboy boots.

After seeing the tenth or twelfth pack of girls go by dressed like this, all of them taking a good look at Ryker as they passed, I leaned over and asked, "We are in Illinois, right? Not Texas?"

He laughed. "You're definitely a city girl," he teased.

"Hey, I just didn't know there was a country-girl-hooker dress code for coming to one of these things," I retorted.

"You look pretty damn good to me," he said, tugging on my hand so I lightly bumped into his side as we walked. He didn't let up, his arm sliding behind my back and keeping me close. It was the kind of thing a man did with a woman when he had sex on the brain. I was flattered, and turned on, and was more than happy to sidle closer to him as we strolled through the crowds.

Hanna's face flashed through my mind and with an effort, I pushed it away. I couldn't change the past, and Ryker was right. If I didn't get my mind on something else for a while, my ability to cope would be even less than it already was.

Ryker smelled fantastic. I could get just a hint of his cologne over the odors wafting through the air—kettle corn, freshly mown grass, and hot dogs. The bells of the carnival games were carried on the warm breeze, as was the sound of hundreds of people talking, laughing, and generally having a good time.

True to his word, Ryker bought me a funnel cake buried under a snow-white mountain of powdered sugar. We sat at a picnic table to eat it, and I laughed as we both proceeded to get powdered sugar everywhere.

"This is messy," I complained, showing him my sugar-encrusted fingers. "Now how am I supposed to get this off?"

He didn't reply. He did something better. Taking my hand, he popped my index finger into his mouth.

I drew in a sharp breath. The warm slide of his tongue against my finger made butterflies dance in my stomach. Then he lightly sucked and I felt it much lower than my stomach.

Ryker was watching me from behind his sunglasses, but I couldn't see his eyes, just my reflection in them.

After a moment, he moved on to my middle finger, giving it the same treatment. I couldn't look away from his mouth as he held my hand, the softness of his tongue against my skin making me think things that had me pressing my thighs together to ease the sudden ache between them.

Finally, he slid my fingers from his mouth and rested my hand on his thigh.

"Better?" he asked.

In what sense? My heart was racing, my breath was coming way too fast, and my panties were damp.

The curve of his lips was knowing and said he knew exactly what he had done—was doing—to me, and that he wanted to do more. I was suddenly all for that.

"You have some more," he said. Leaning forward, his mouth settled on mine.

He tasted like sugar and spice and I decided that getting a funnel cake had been the Best Idea Ever. He was straddling the picnic bench and now slid closer to me, pulling me between his spread thighs.

The kiss was slow and languid as though we were alone, the sun warm on my hair and shoulders. His hand cradled my jaw, slipping underneath my hair to cup the back of my neck. I suddenly had the thought that I might be sweaty—it was a little warm—but then he did something different with his tongue and my concern drifted away. The man had a talented tongue.

"You and a funnel cake is dangerous territory," he murmured in my ear.

The heat of his breath and touch of his lips made a shiver run down my spine, which I knew he felt because his lips curved in a smile that could only be described as satisfied. On any other man, it would've looked incredibly arrogant, but Ryker could pull it off.

His hand was on my bare thigh, his thumb lightly brushing my skin, while my blood thundered in my ears. The slow seduction thing was working almost too well.

"I thought you promised me a tractor pull and Ferris wheel?" I asked, taking a swig of the cold beer he'd bought me. Ugh. Beer and powdered sugar did *not* mix.

"So I did," he said, getting to his feet. I stood as well, dusting powdered sugar from my shirt. "Tractor pull doesn't start until seven, so Ferris wheel first."

The air between us seemed charged with sexual tension and promise, the anticipation a prelude to what I hoped would be a night I wouldn't soon forget.

We stood in line for the Ferris wheel while the sun went down, talking and laughing as he teased me. His hands cradled my hips as he stood behind me, his chest pressed against my back. He was whispering something in my ear about where else he'd be happy to lick powdered sugar off me when I caught a woman staring at us, a disapproving frown on her face.

I cleared my throat, my face getting hot, and stepped forward to put a little space between Ryker and me. Maybe it was the bruises still on my face that she was looking at. Sunglasses hid most of the lingering marks, but those had been put away when dusk had fallen. I turned my face away, but could see out of the corner of my eye that the woman still stared at us.

It must have caught Ryker's attention, too, because he leaned down to say to me, "Don't worry about it. She's just a little uptight."

Maybe. But I didn't like getting public attention for all the wrong reasons, so I kept my distance from Ryker.

"You two look good together," the woman said, surprising me. Her eyes were a bit bloodshot and I had the feeling she'd been visiting the beer garden often today. "You are together, right?"

Awkward.

We weren't officially dating, but we were on a date, I supposed. I opened my mouth to say no, we were just having fun, when Ryker piped in with, "You bet."

"I knew it," the lady said, smiling with satisfaction. "I'm a bit psychic. I know these things."

My eyebrows flew up and I struggled to hide a grin. Psychic, eh?

"You are?" Ryker said, and I could tell by his tone that he was amused and humoring her. "Well, are you going to tell us our future then?"

She nodded. "I can see it. You'll marry her. You two were meant to be together."

Of course we were. I stopped myself from rolling my eyes, but just barely. Ryker had asked for it, so I had no sympathy for him that the lady was now predicting our future state of matrimony. He could just squirm.

"You see the future that clearly?" Ryker asked skeptically.

"I see it better if I can touch you," she said, reaching toward me. It was quick and I didn't have a chance to step back before she clutched my hand.

"I don't really—" I began, but she was already talking.

"It's not as clear now," she said, looking past us into the

distance at nothing. She frowned. "It was so clear with the two of you, but now if I just look at you, it gets fuzzy."

Yeah. I bet it did. Good Lord, how much had this woman had to drink today? I tried tugging my hand away, but she held on tight.

"There's another man," she said. "He's very close to you. You care about him a great deal."

Okay, *now* this was awkward. I certainly didn't want to talk about another man while on a date with Ryker, especially when I knew the "other man" she was talking about was Parker.

I jerked my hand out of her grip and she seemed to regain focus, her eyes meeting mine. Her face had gone pale.

"I saw heartbreak," she said. "And pain."

And this had gone from funny to irritating to downright eerie. Like I wanted to be told my future held more pain than I'd already endured, *plus* heartbreak.

"What happened to the happy-ever-after with him?" I blurted, jerking a thumb toward Ryker.

She shrugged. "I can't explain what I see. The future isn't set in stone. Different choices lead down different paths."

The Ferris wheel line moved and Ryker pulled me over to where it was our turn to get on.

"I'm really glad we didn't give her money for a fortune like that," I groused. "She's crazy."

We settled into the seat and the worker lowered the bar across our laps, then let off the brake. The compartment rocked gently as the wheel turned to empty the container behind us for new riders.

"So who's the other man?" Ryker asked. There was more than a little possessiveness in his tone.

"I'm not dating anyone else," I said, evading an actual answer, though technically a true statement.

Ryker frowned. "You and Parker haven't…" He let the sentence trail off.

I raised an eyebrow. "Are you really asking me if I've slept with my boss?" I injected a lot of self-righteous indignation into that, though I could feel my cheeks burning. What I'd done with Parker was so embarrassing, I could barely admit it to myself. No way was I telling him that Parker had turned me down flat, then proceeded to kiss me senseless just minutes after Ryker had Friday night.

"Pretty much," he said, cocking an eyebrow. "Glad to know you're not the type."

I smiled weakly back. If he only knew that my "type" was the kind of girl whose boss could get her to do just about anything, he'd probably want nothing more to do with me.

He changed the subject, thank God, and I tried to shove the weird psychic lady to the back of my mind. It was all hokum anyway. I didn't believe in psychics any more than I did ghosts or goblins.

"Let's forget about crazy drunk non-psychic lady," Ryker said, sliding his arm across my shoulders. "And get back to what we were doing before."

I smiled. "And what was that exactly?" I teased.

"You were having an awesome time with me, of course."

I laughed. I couldn't help it. Arrogant? Check. A total player? Check. Incredibly hot? Double check. But I was having more fun on this date than I'd had in a longer time than I cared to remember.

The last rays of the sun were just peeking over the horizon, the lights from the fair and carnival twinkling in the encroaching dusk. Ryker pulled me toward him and I rested against his chest, enjoying the moment as the wheel slowly turned.

After the Ferris wheel, we bought hot dogs and more

beer, then made our way to the grandstands for the apparently highly anticipated tractor pull. The stands were full of people, but we managed to squeeze in. It was a lot of noise and a lot of smoke, but after two additional beers, it seemed like fun to me, especially with the crowd so into it.

It was late when it was over and Ryker pulled me into the beer garden where a cover band was playing.

"It's late," I halfheartedly complained. "I have to work tomorrow."

"Just one dance," he prodded.

The band was covering Bon Jovi's "Livin' on a Prayer," which was an old favorite of mine, and they were pretty decent. "All right, just one dance," I agreed.

His arms wrapped around my waist and he held me close as we moved to the strains of a Journey tune. One dance turned into two, then three, and pretty soon I'd lost count. Ryker was a good dancer, taking the opportunity to slide his hands places they hadn't yet been, not that I was complaining.

The heated look in his eyes made my skin feel hot, and it was by unspoken agreement when he pulled me off the dance floor and we headed for his truck.

I was inexplicably nervous as we walked, his fingers interlaced with mine. It wasn't like I was some easily frightened virgin, but I'd never slept with a man like Ryker. He was intimidating and I was positive he'd been with more attractive, more experienced women than me. Would he be disappointed? And why did I care if he was?

I hadn't wanted to sleep with Ryker last night, but tonight I felt way different. Between the baseball game, him being there for me when Hanna was murdered, to taking me someplace fun today, he'd done more for me in three days than Parker had in the past year.

Maybe this relationship with Ryker wasn't going to be long-term, but I liked him. A lot. And he liked me, too. I believed he wanted *me*, not just sex, and that made a world of difference. But was it still too soon? I wanted it to be about us, not about me still hurting because of Parker's rejection. Should I wait? I didn't *want* to wait, but maybe it'd be for the best...

I'd worked myself up into quite a state, arguing with myself and changing my mind a dozen times, so that by the time we reached his truck my beer buzz had evaporated. Ryker reached around me to open the passenger door. I could feel the brush of his body against mine, then his hands on my waist, helping me into the cab. I settled into the seat; then he surprised me by leaning in and laying a kiss on me.

It wasn't the same slow exploration it had been earlier. This was harder, his lips moving over mine with purpose, the stroke of his tongue demanding and urgent. I lost my train of thought, the pros and cons of temptation versus guilt, the taste and feel of him overtaking everything else.

I don't know how much time passed before he eased back, leaving me longing for more. His mouth trailed along my jaw.

"Don't be nervous," he whispered against my skin.

The fact that he could tell how I was feeling should have set off alarm bells. Instead, all I could think was that if he was this attuned to me before we had sex, how much better would he be during? Maybe sleeping with Ryker wouldn't be about Parker at all, but instead all about us.

He shrugged out of his shirt, leaving him in just a white tank—the holster still holding his gun at his side—climbed in the cab, and fired up the engine. I watched him unabashedly as he drove back to his house. His sunglasses were hooked on his shirt and with one hand he pulled me toward him. I slid across the seat, forgoing the seat belt (I'm such a rebel). His hand settled on my leg, his fingers sliding between my bare thighs.

The anticipation of what was to come was giving me a whole different kind of buzz now. Here was this incredibly good-looking man, a cop no less, who appeared very attracted to me and wanted to have sex with me as soon as possible.

My fingers were practically itching to touch him, and I didn't think he'd mind, so I slid a hand underneath his tank as he drove. The warm skin of his abdomen met my fingers, the muscles there hard and lean. He sucked in his breath at my touch, which encouraged me. Stretching up, I fastened my lips to his neck and lightly sucked.

His skin tasted slightly salty and smelled like cologne mixed with the outdoors—pure man. My hand crept farther up his chest underneath his shirt as I licked and sucked his neck up to his jaw. The hand on my leg tightened and I noticed his arm wasn't lying casually on top of the steering wheel anymore. Instead, it was gripping it tightly.

The ride back to his house was quick, though I thought he might have been speeding, and then he had me out of the truck and inside fast enough to make my head spin. One word barked at McClane and the dog disappeared into another room. Then Ryker had me pinned to the wall, his mouth on mine and his hands tugging my T-shirt free from my shorts.

I was just as frantically trying to get his shirt over his head. He pulled away enough for both of us to accomplish that goal; then his arms were around me and his skin against mine. In the next moment, he'd lifted me and was carrying me to his bedroom.

His chest was warm and smooth. There was a fine sprin-

kling of hair across it and his dog tags rested against his
sternum. I stared at his biceps as I lay against him, the curve
of the muscle so defined I wanted to trace it with my fingers.

Ryker was still kissing me when he laid me on the bed.
He sat down and I straddled his thighs. It wasn't elegant;
we were both too desperate for that. His tongue slid against
mine as he deepened the kiss. I held on to his shoulders,
solid and massive underneath my palms. His lips were soft,
a contrast to his jaw, roughened with whiskers. The abrasion
against my skin wasn't unwelcome. It was masculine—a
reminder of the differences between our bodies—the hard
planes of his chest against the soft curves of mine.

I moaned as his hands curved around my rib cage, his
thumbs brushing against my nipples with delicious friction.

Ryker's mouth moved down my throat, stopping to suck
lightly underneath my jaw, and again at my collarbone. I
gasped as his hands skimmed down to my hips and his
mouth settled over one breast. His tongue flicked at the sensitive point; then he sucked and I felt it all the way to my
core.

His hands locked around my waist, pushing me onto my
back against the pillows. My thighs fell open and he settled
between them, his mouth moving to my other breast. My fingers combed through his hair, the strands soft, and my nails
scraped lightly at his scalp. I felt a shiver go through him.

The denim of his jeans was rough against my inner
thighs, but I didn't care. He alone filled my senses—the feel
of his skin against mine, the wet heat of his mouth on me,
the grip of his hands on my hips.

I felt him tugging at my shorts and I lifted slightly so he
could slide them down my legs. He sat back on his haunches,
allowing me to bend my knees enough for him to pull the
fabric off.

I reached for him but he caught my hands in his, raised them over my head, and wrapped my palms around the bars of the headboard, like I was supposed to keep them there. He was looking at me—at my body—and I saw his Adam's apple move in his throat when he swallowed. My legs rested atop his thighs, waiting for him to settle between them again, but he didn't. Unsure, I opened my mouth to say something, I didn't know what, but then he touched me and the words died on my tongue.

Ryker's palms rested on my inner thighs, skating slowly up to my hips. His hands curved, fitting my flesh to his palms, then drifted farther up my sides to my breasts. His touch was electric, making my breath hitch in my chest. His gaze lifted to mine, the blue of his eyes silvery in the darkness, and I couldn't look away.

His fingers drifted lightly over my breasts, barely brushing the nipples. I gasped at the touch, a mere shadow of what I wanted. And still he watched me.

He leaned over me, his weight resting on his knees and one hand, leaving the other free to keep touching me.

Lowering his head, his lips and tongue traced my breast, while his hand slowly moved down between my thighs. I was wet, my body aching for him, and when his fingers slid between my folds, we both groaned.

"God, Sage," he rasped. "You feel like hot, wet silk."

I hoped he wasn't waiting for a response because (a) what exactly do you say to that? *Thank you*? And (b) I was beyond the ability to form coherent sentences at this point.

He was good, really good, and sooner than I would have believed possible, I was coming, my nails digging in to his shoulders as I gasped out his name and reiterated my fervent belief in a deity. Several times.

Ryker kissed me, a long finger still moving inside me,

and my skin felt like it was on fire. I wanted him more than it seemed I'd ever wanted anything. Ripping my mouth from his, I sucked in a lungful of air, my hands going to his jeans and tugging impatiently at the zipper.

"Wait, Sage," he said, grasping my hands and stilling them. "Are you sure?" His voice was a low rasp, tight with need and desire.

"I'm sure."

Brushing my hands away, Ryker quickly rid himself of his jeans. I whimpered at the sight of him. Ryker fully clothed was a sight to see. Unclothed...he made my mouth water.

His thighs were as heavily muscled as the rest of him, and his cock...well I'd say the size and breadth of it put my dildos to shame, but then I'd have to admit owning things like that. Which I totally didn't.

This time when he leaned over me, his dog tags slid around to hang from his neck, the metal resting between my breasts. With one hand, he moved them to his back instead. It was a gesture that struck me, and I knew I'd always remember the first time he did that.

Wait...*the first time*?

I shoved that thought away since there was plenty to focus on in the present. My thighs cradled his hips as he guided himself into me.

"Tell me if I hurt you," he said, which I thought was nice. Real polite.

He took it slow, and after the first few inches, I could see why. My body took a moment to accommodate his size. I thought he was all in, but then he pushed his hips, burying himself to the hilt. For a flash of a second there was a twinge of pain, but then it was sheer bliss.

"We fit perfect," he murmured in my ear. "Just like I knew we would. Tight and dripping wet for me, sweetheart."

Ryker's mouth found mine, our tongues tangling together as he moved. I decided then and there that I would never again say size didn't matter, because boy, did it ever. His cock created a delicious friction against my clit—a tantalizingly slow withdrawal, then a deep thrust sliding back inside me. He didn't rush, and I felt the slow build of another orgasm.

I lifted my hips to meet his, my hands clutching at his ass, urging him on with my body. We were both slick with sweat when he finally gave in to my unspoken demands, moving harder and faster, until I couldn't keep up with him.

I came again, stars exploding behind my eyelids, and it was even better than before. A split second later, Ryker let out a shout, burying himself deep inside me. His body shuddered with the strength of his orgasm. I tightened my legs around him and held on, pleasurable aftershocks coursing through me like mini-earthquakes after The Big One.

Ryker's breath was hot on my neck, his weight heavy against my chest, his cock still inside me. He'd slid his arms around my back to hold me close, and I liked that. I liked that a lot.

He was breathing hard, but he kissed me. A long, slow, deep kiss that made my toes curl, which was saying something after what we'd just done.

I wondered what he'd do now, if he'd make an excuse and leave or not even bother with making an excuse, but he did neither. He pulled out of me, turning so he lay on his back, and pulled me to him. I rested my head on his shoulder, my arm across his chest. Lacing his fingers through mine, he gave a deep, satisfied sigh. I closed my eyes, a smile on my face.

CHAPTER FIFTEEN

Something was buzzing, but I was too comfortable to bother with it. After a few moments, it stopped. I sighed in my sleep, snuggling closer against Ryker. What seemed like only moments later, the buzzing began again. I frowned and made a noise, unwilling to be pulled into full wakefulness.

"Yeah. Sage's phone."

Ryker's sleep-roughened voice in my ear made my eyes fly open. I sat up, turning to see that the buzzing had been my cell and that Ryker had answered it. He lay on his side, facing me, the phone at his ear.

"Hello," he said, sounding irritated. "Anyone there?"

"Give that to me," I hissed, reaching for the phone. What if it was my mother? There wasn't enough alcohol in the world that would make Thanksgiving bearable.

"Thought it was you," Ryker said, catching my hand in his and slotting our fingers together, which was real sweet, but so *not* what I wanted right now. "How's it going, Parker?"

I felt the blood drain from my face and my eyes went wide.

"You must be looking for Sage. Hold on, she's right next to me." Ryker held the phone out. "It's your dick of a boss, sweetheart."

I snatched the phone from him, not sure which emotion I felt more of at the moment: anger or mortification. Yes, Parker had seen us leave together last night, but it was quite another thing to have it spelled out in such black-and-white that I was waking up in Ryker's bed.

"Sorry about that, sir," I said, breathless.

"You call him 'sir'?" Ryker snorted, rolling his eyes. "Don't apologize to him." He leaned over me and pressed his lips to my shoulder.

I ignored him. "What is it?"

Parker said nothing for a moment, then, "Did I catch you at a bad time?"

I flinched. His tone was ice cold and did nothing to hide how angry he was. Not that I should care after Friday...but I did.

"Um, no, sir." I squeezed my eyes shut in dismay as Ryker's mouth moved to my neck. "Did you need something?"

"Yes, I need my secretary to come to work," he retorted. "Or have you not looked at a clock this morning?"

I jerked around to where my alarm clock sat on Ryker's bedside table. I was over an hour late for work.

"Oh, God," I breathed.

"Now that sounds familiar," Ryker murmured, not at all trying to be quiet. I knew Parker had heard him because the silence on his end was deafening.

I shoved Ryker away and scrambled to get off the bed. "I'm so sorry. I-I must have overslept," I stammered, only now realizing that I hadn't thought to set my alarm for this morning. Then I remembered something. "Wait. I thought you said I had today off."

"Since you refused to leave town, I'd like you in the office today." Parker's sarcasm was edged with disdain and it cut like a razor.

"I'll be right in." I ended the call before Parker could say anything else and tossed the phone onto the table. I yanked open my suitcase, pulling out clean panties and a bra.

"After this weekend, a day off isn't a bad idea," Ryker said.

I glanced back at him. He was half-reclining, the sheet tangled around his legs, and the sight of his naked body in the morning sunshine had me pausing to memorize it. Late or not, it wasn't something any woman in her right mind would just pass up the chance to view. And the way he was looking at me made a shiver dance across my skin.

"I can't; I'm sorry," I said, and boy, was I ever. It appeared that Ryker was definitely a morning person. Or at least parts of him were. "I've got to go to work." I rushed by him on my way to the bathroom, but he caught my hand.

"Can't he go one day without you?" Ryker's scathing question was almost an accusation.

Narrowing my eyes, I jerked my hand away. "I could've died Saturday night," I said. "He wasn't faking his concern for me."

"So his 'concern' is enough to make you go running when he calls?" Ryker shot back. "He's the reason they were looking for you."

"You don't know that for sure," I said. "You're just guessing they were there for me and not Hanna. Besides, it's my job, and if they are using me to get to him, that only proves he's being coerced," I said. "Why don't you do *your* job and stop them?" Suddenly, I wanted out of there. I angrily jerked on my clothes.

"Do my job?" Now he was up out of the bed, angrily stalking toward me. I tried to ignore the fact that he was naked. "What the hell do you think I'm doing?"

I grabbed my purse in one hand and my suitcase in the other. "You mean other than screwing me to get to Parker?"

His face was so hard and cold, I took a step back.

"Now you're accusing me of fucking you because of him?" he bit out.

"Aren't you?" I shot back.

"I thought that was your job."

His sarcasm was biting and his words stung, because it was truer than I'd wanted to admit. I didn't trust Ryker's interest in me, no matter the fun we'd had yesterday or how great the sex had been. And despite my wanting us sleeping together to be about us and not Parker, it felt as though he was an invisible presence between us.

Ryker scrubbed a hand across his face in frustration. "Damn it, Sage, last night was more than just a hookup. You know that. Why are you pushing me away?"

But I couldn't answer, because if I acknowledged there might be more than an amazing one-night stand with Ryker, that meant I had to give up Parker.

That thought made my chest ache in a way that told me that losing Parker would hurt a lot longer, and a lot deeper, than I'd ever really considered.

"I have to go," I blurted, shoving past him.

"How are you going to go anywhere?" he asked, hurrying after me. "You don't have a car."

Shit! Yeah, that was a problem.

Spying his keys on the kitchen table, I snatched them up. "I'll borrow yours. I'll take good care of it. I promise."

"Wait! Sage!" Ryker grabbed my arm in a tight grip.

"Let me go!" I tried to jerk my arm away, but he held on tight.

"I'm not just letting you walk out of here," he said. "Not until you listen to me."

"I don't want to listen to you!" I was getting seriously pissed. "What do you want from me, Ryker?" I struggled against his hold, frustrated at getting nowhere.

"I want you to stay alive!"

We both heard the growling at the same time. I turned and saw McClane, his teeth bared and his ears laid flat against his head. A continuous low growl issued from his throat, but it wasn't directed at me.

He was looking at Ryker.

Ryker froze. "Easy, McClane," he said.

At his name, the dog barked twice, then growled again, louder.

I swallowed. The sight of the dog's pointy teeth made me feel light-headed. McClane barked again and took a menacing step closer.

Ryker let me go, then took a slow step back, away from me. "Easy," he said again to the dog.

Saved by the canine dropout. Huh. Who'd have thought?

I didn't waste time, heading out the door and to Ryker's truck. A moment later, I was speeding away from his house.

* * *

I didn't feel comfortable going back to my place, so I drove to the gym and used the locker room to shower and get ready for work. After that, there was no time for my coffee run and I was racing into work just...I glanced at my watch...two hours late.

After the disastrous New York trip, the rejection Thursday night and argument Friday, Hanna's murder in my own apartment—now I'd slept with Parker's arch nemesis and was late to work.

He was going to be in *such* a pissy mood.

Out of breath, I shoved my purse into the bottom drawer of my desk and plopped my butt in my chair. The phone was ringing on two lines and I grabbed one of them as I glanced into Parker's office.

"Parker Anderson's office," I answered.

Parker was standing at his paper-strewn desk, a sheaf of folders in his hand, and he was looking at me. His jaw was set tight, his lips pressed together, his whole body tense.

"I'm sorry, he's not available," I said, reading Parker's body language. No way would he want to deal with Peterson from Contracts right now. "May I take a message?"

I tore my gaze from Parker's and scrawled some words on my notepad. "Yes, sir. I'll tell him." I hung up.

By now, the other call had gone to voice mail and when I dialed in, I had fourteen messages for Parker. I was in the middle of writing the last one down when I sensed someone standing in front of me. I knew without looking that it was Parker. I swallowed hard.

The recording ended and I didn't want to hang up the phone, but there was no sense in putting it off. Very softly, I placed the handset in its cradle, took a deep breath, and raised my eyes to meet Parker's.

"I need these files consolidated and sent to Accounting," he said, handing me the stack. "And my two o'clock called to cancel. Reschedule him for tomorrow or Monday." He continued with more instructions and I jotted them down, glad he wasn't going to say anything else about this morning, but that relief was short-lived.

"Lastly," he said, and his change of tone had me glancing up. "What you do in your personal time is your business." *Oh really? Since when?* "I just ask that it not interfere with your work. Being late because you...slept in"—his tone plainly said what he believed I'd been doing this morning, and it wasn't sleeping—"is unacceptable. Am I making myself clear?"

Okay, now I was getting pissed. Yes, I'd been late, but it wasn't like I made a habit of it and he *had* given me the day off. And considering the weekend I'd had, he was way out of line.

"Yes, sir," I bit out, just this side of polite. "I won't be late again."

Our eyes were locked and after a moment, he nodded. He turned away and headed for his office. Just before he stepped inside, he turned back to me.

"Don't call me 'sir' anymore," he said. The door drifted shut behind him.

I watched him through the glass as he sat behind his desk, but he didn't look up, instead turning his attention to his computer.

Well, okay then.

It wasn't as if I called him *sir* all the time, just when the situation seemed to call for it. Like when he was in a bad mood or pissed, both of which he had been this morning.

Whatever. I didn't have time to dwell on it or any of the other confusing things that had happened between us, including the kissing, which we apparently weren't going to talk about—*fine with me*. I had work to do.

By the time lunch rolled around, I was starving, but I didn't dare take a break. Parker left for a meeting with a client at a restaurant a few blocks away, and I could practically smell the expensive entrées on his suit when he came back two hours later.

He caught me at his desk, leaving a stack of month-end reports sent from the managers who worked underneath him. I'd printed them and arranged them in the order Parker preferred. I scooted out from behind his desk as he slid into his seat.

His phone rang and I reached out to snag it as I rounded the desk. "Parker Anderson's office."

There was a pause; then a man's voice asked, "Sage? Is that you, my dear?"

I froze, my gaze flying to Parker's. I knew that voice.

Viktor, I mouthed to him. So much for him knowing I wasn't dead. Guess that particular cat was out of the bag. I hadn't even thought to not answer Parker's phone.

"Would you like to speak to Parker?" I asked stiffly.

"Yes, if you would, and may I say I'm glad to see that you're in such perfect...health."

And that put the nail in the coffin of who'd killed Hanna and why.

I handed the phone over to Parker, who looked grim, then went back to my desk. I watched through the glass until he hung up the phone; then he beckoned me back in.

"What did he want?" I asked.

"He's decided to come here himself and oversee everything, make sure the deal goes through the way he wants."

I frowned. Parker hated clients who micromanaged rather than just letting him do his job.

"Is he coming in to the office?" I asked.

He shook his head. "I'm meeting him later tonight at his hotel."

"By yourself?"

Parker glanced at me, one eyebrow raised. "Who else would I take?"

I ignored his sarcasm. "I don't trust him. Can't you take Mark or Jason?" They were a couple of senior managers who worked for Parker. But he just shook his head again.

"They've been holding down my current contracts while I've been dealing with this. I'm not going to ask them to tag along on this, too."

I was disappointed, and worried; then something occurred to me. "Wait, you're not keeping them out of it just because you'd have to give them a percentage, are you?" The question just popped out and I remembered with vivid clarity how Ryker was so certain Parker knew exactly what these people did and were capable of.

Parker looked at me. Didn't reply. His jaw was clenched and his mouth was set in a thin line.

Belatedly, I tried to backtrack. "I'm sorry, that was inappropriate—"

"My reasons for not including other members of this firm are my own," Parker interrupted, and his voice was icy steel. "You may go."

"I'm really sorry. I didn't mean—"

"I said you're dismissed."

I didn't have the guts to say anything else and I scurried out of the office, my face burning. God, it seemed I couldn't do anything right today. Tears stung my eyes and I knew what part of my problem was. I'd been trying not to think about Hanna all day, but she was there, in the back of my mind. All I could see were those bloodstained sheets.

I sank into my chair, propping my elbows on my desk and resting my head in my hands. I had to get a grip. I was going to lose my job for real if I didn't knock it off.

"Sage! Look what came for you!"

Jerking my head up, I saw a huge bouquet of red roses walking toward me. No, wait, it was Megan carrying a bouquet; I just couldn't see her because it was so big. She set it on my counter. I hurriedly swiped away the wetness underneath my eyes.

"Oh my gosh!" I jumped up to inspect the flowers just as Megan peered around to grin at me. "These are for me?"

"Uh-huh," she said. "Here's the card." She handed it to me.

I broke the seal and opened the envelope, pulling out the little card inside.

I'd tell you that I can be a total dick, but I think you already know that.

—Ryker

I smiled. I couldn't help it. This morning had gone very, very badly, but it wasn't entirely his fault. We'd both said some things that we shouldn't have.

Setting aside the card, I leaned forward, closing my eyes and burying my nose in the velvet petals of the roses. "Mmmmm. They smell wonderful," I said with a sigh.

"Glad you think so," Megan said, still grinning. "Because they were hand-delivered."

She glanced toward the elevators and I saw Ryker standing there, leaning against the wall, his arms crossed over his chest. He was watching me, a small smile playing about the corners of his mouth. When our eyes met, he straightened and headed for me. I barely noticed as Megan melted away.

Ryker had changed and shaved. He still had his jeans and leather jacket, only now he wore a different color T-shirt. This one was a dusky blue that matched his eyes and made them seem even deeper in color. I caught a whiff of his cologne as he stepped into my cube.

"Am I forgiven?" he asked, though by the twist of his lips I could tell he already knew the flowers had softened me up. He rested his hand on my hip and I had to tip my head back to look at him.

"Of course," I said, "and you deserve an apology, too. What I said—"

"Shh." He placed a finger over my lips. "This may have started because of him"—he tipped his head toward Parker's office—"but it doesn't have to stay that way. I like you, and I'm pretty damn sure you like me, too."

Leaning forward, he put his mouth by my ear. "I could smell you on my skin this morning."

My breath caught and my pulse tripled. Unthinkingly, my hands curled into fists, drawing my nails against him. He made a low noise of approval in my ear.

"Is this when I tell you about the marks you left on my back?" he said.

"Oh! I'm so sorry," I said, pulling back slightly. My face got hot.

But Ryker just grinned. "Don't be sorry," he teased. "You can scratch up my back anytime you want, sweetheart."

"Can I help you?"

Both of us turned to see Parker standing by my desk. He didn't look pleased. I quickly put some space between Ryker and me and tried to push his hand off my hip, but it wouldn't budge.

"I doubt there's anything you could do that would prove helpful to me," Ryker shot back, his smile gone.

"Sage is working," Parker said, ignoring the jibe. "We encourage visitors to consider that before . . . dropping by." His gaze dropped to where Ryker was still touching me, then lifted to meet my eyes.

"Do you always make your secretary come to work after putting her life in jeopardy?" Ryker asked. "I guess you were too busy yelling at her to ask why she was late."

"I thought it was perfectly obvious why she was late," Parker said, his voice rife with contempt as he looked Ryker up and down. His lip curled in distaste. "Though I must confess I'm surprised it took more than a few minutes."

My jaw dropped in shock. Had Parker just insulted Ryker's...sexual prowess?

"Nice. Real classy, Parker, but then you and I both know it's all an act. I know the kind of man you are underneath the expensive suits."

"At least I can afford a suit."

"Stop it, both of you," I interjected. Good Lord, they were degenerating to the level of high school girls. Soon they'd be saying *I know you are but what am I?* "Parker, can I have a minute?"

Parker's gaze was unreadable as he looked at me, but then he turned and went back into his office, so I supposed that was a *yes.*

"Thanks for the flowers," I said. "Sorry about Parker. You and he are just, um, like oil and water, I guess."

"Yeah, I'm positive that's what it is," he said, his eyes narrowing. "I'm sure it doesn't have a thing to do with you." His sarcasm was obvious and I bristled.

"What's that supposed to mean?" I asked. "It's not my fault you two go at each other every chance you get."

"Listen," he said, moving closer to me. "You may have told me that you and Parker haven't slept together, but he sure as hell acts like you have. He acts as though he owns you."

"Well, he doesn't," I said. "But he's right about me needing to work. That deal is supposed to go down tomorrow when the markets open and Viktor's in town to oversee it."

"Wait a minute," Ryker said. "He's here? In Chicago?"

I nodded. "Parker's supposed to be going to his hotel tonight, but he didn't tell me which one."

"Damn," Ryker muttered.

"Why?"

"If we knew where he was staying, maybe we could get someone in to plant some bugs," he said.

"Why would you do that?"

"To find out more about his organization. Overhear his plans, see who all's involved..."

And an idea struck me.

"What if I plant the bugs?" I asked.

Ryker frowned in confusion. "You're going with Parker tonight? That's a terrible idea. Viktor tried to kill you—"

"He already knows he didn't succeed," I interrupted, explaining how I'd answered Parker's phone. "So if I can get Parker to take me along tonight, I can plant the bugs for you." And maybe the cops would finally know that Parker was just doing his job, nothing illegal.

"I dunno..." Ryker looked skeptical.

"It's not hard, is it?" I asked.

"No, but—"

"Then I can do it. Please, Ryker."

He glanced away, rubbing the back of his neck as he considered it, and I held my breath. Viktor had tried to kill me, had killed two other women already, and was most likely threatening Parker. I wanted to help bring him down.

At last, Ryker gave a sigh of defeat. "Fine," he said. "If you can get Parker to take you along, and that's a big *if*, then I'll get a warrant and give you the bugs to plant. Just stick them somewhere people don't normally look. Underneath a desk or even a chair."

"What if I get caught?" I asked, trying to consider all contingencies, even the bad ones.

"If it doesn't look like you're going to get an opportunity to plant them, then don't," Ryker said. "Viktor's a nasty son of a bitch, but if you do get the chance, then do it. Just don't let Parker know what you're doing. It's not your responsibility to make sure Parker stays on the right side of the law."

It scared me, doing something like planting a listening device. That was something they did in the movies, and here it was now invading my real life. Yet, Tania was in trouble; her sister and her friend were dead. It seemed like I should try to do something about that, and if the cops needed someone to plant a bug, then maybe I should do it. Perhaps it would help atone for Hanna's death in God's ledger of my life—a checkmark in one column versus the X in the other.

"Okay," I agreed. I glanced at the clock. "You've got to go, though, or Parker will be pissed." I dug Ryker's keys out of my pocket and walked him to wait for an elevator.

"I'll talk to you soon," he said as the elevator dinged, and then he leaned down and kissed me.

I thought it'd be just a quick brush of his lips, but his tongue slid against mine and his hand gripped my waist. Suddenly, I wasn't in such a hurry, and I twined my arms around his neck. Ryker could really kiss and it was a few breathless moments later before he lifted his head. It confused me, making me question my earlier doubts about his feelings for me.

"Been wanting to do that for hours," he murmured. "Our morning after wasn't quite what I'd envisioned."

"Maybe next time will be better," I replied without thinking.

"If that's a promise, then you just made my fucking day." Ryker slid his sunglasses on, his lips twisting in a sultry smirk. My cheeks got hot, but I had no comeback before the elevator doors closed.

I hurried back to my desk, pushing thoughts of Ryker and amazing sex aside as I tried to figure out a way for Parker to include me tonight. Maybe I'd just have to wing it. Back in my chair, I was catching up on my work when Parker came out of his office and stood in front of my counter. I glanced up to see him moving the roses aside.

"I know I'm behind, but I should be caught up in a couple of hours," I said. "When are you leaving to meet Viktor?"

"Shortly," was his succinct reply. "But I'm not out here to talk about your work, Sage. Tell me what the hell happened. You were wanting to be with me Thursday night, and then you spent the weekend with Ryker?"

Oh, yeah. That.

I started typing again. "I don't want to talk about it," I said. As far as I was concerned, nothing more needed to be said, though he made me sound like a real slut and I wasn't too crazy about that.

But he didn't go away. Instead, he rounded the counter until he stood right next to my chair, facing me, and leaned back against my desk. "Are you trying to get back at me for not sleeping with you?"

My fingers froze over the keyboard. I looked up at him in shock. "Did you just ask me that?"

Parker's gaze was unrelenting. "It's a valid question. I turned you down; you know Ryker and I don't get along. It's the perfect revenge."

I gritted my teeth, ignoring how his words hit a little too close to home. But he was also wrong. "I wouldn't have slept with Ryker if I didn't feel something for him," I bit out. "Not everything in my life revolves around you."

Something flashed across Parker's face—a wince maybe—and was gone.

"Fair enough," he said evenly.

"Can we just get back to normal?" I asked. "Last week was...an aberration. You told me you don't want to train a new assistant, and I don't want to lose my job, so we're in agreement, right?"

He reached out and tucked a stray lock of hair behind my ear. "Right."

Okay, that was new. The barest touch of his fingers against my skin had sent a shiver through me. I wanted to say something—tell him to stop doing that—but I couldn't make myself. He'd said no to anything more, so if the occasional innocuous touch was all I would get, I'd take it.

I took a deep breath, suddenly having an idea of how to go along with him tonight. "You told me you wanted to be friends," I said, remembering what he'd said in his apartment Thursday night. "So I have a favor to ask."

"Name it."

"I'd like to come with you tonight," I said, "to the meeting. I'd like to be the one to tell Tania about Niki and Hanna. She deserves to know."

"I don't think that's a good idea," he said flatly, pushing himself to his feet and rounding the counter.

I jumped to my feet and followed him. "Please," I said, catching hold of his sleeve. He stopped, turning to look at me. "You weren't there. Hanna was just feet from me. I did nothing and they—" My throat closed up and I couldn't continue. I stared up at Parker, blurred by the tears in my eyes, and prayed he'd understand.

"Shh, don't cry," Parker said, wrapping his arms around me. "You shouldn't have had to see that. Shouldn't have been anywhere near something like that."

I tried not to be disappointed when he pulled away, his hands moving to clasp my arms.

"Fine, you can come," he said, "but try to stay under the radar. If Viktor is trying to target you, I'd rather he went for me instead."

"I'll stay out of the way, I swear." I held my breath and gazed hopefully up at him.

He heaved a sigh of resignation. "I hope I don't regret this," he muttered under his breath.

Yeah, me too.

CHAPTER SIXTEEN

I texted Ryker while standing in front of the mirror in the ladies' room and got a reply back almost immediately saying he was on his way to the office with the bugs and I should meet him around the corner. Twenty minutes later, I was pushing a little plastic bag inside my purse while Ryker gave me instructions.

"Remember, they need to be somewhere open, but hidden, which is why underneath a table works so well. They'll stick to any surface, so no worries there. And above all"—he placed his hands on my waist and drew me toward him until our bodies touched—"don't do it if you are in any danger of getting caught. These men are dangerous."

I nodded. "Okay. I won't."

He kissed me, then said, "Call me when you get home, okay? I'll be waiting."

That made me feel warm and fuzzy inside. It had been a long time since a gorgeous, sex-on-two-legs man told me he'd be waiting for my phone call. I could totally get used to that.

I hurried back inside, mindful that Parker had said he wanted to head over around seven and it was pushing that now. My stomach gave a horrendous growl. All I'd consumed today was coffee, which seemed a pretty bad idea, but I just hadn't had a chance to stop and eat.

Parker was waiting for me and glanced up from where he was putting files into his briefcase when I stepped to my desk. In moments, he was standing by my counter.

"Ready?" he asked, not really waiting for an answer as he headed for the elevator. I scrambled to keep up with him.

We were the only two inside the elevator and neither of us spoke. The doors were a burnished bronze material that reflected our images, only slightly distorted.

You wouldn't have been able to tell he'd been working all day, other than the faint shadow of whiskers on his jaw. I always loved seeing that, but I tried not to stare.

It seemed awkward now, the silence heavy between us, and it made me sad. Could we really be friends, *just* friends, after everything that had happened between us? It seemed I had no choice but to either give it a shot, or lose him entirely. My decision was a no-brainer.

No food, lack of sleep, and too much stress was giving me a pounding headache and I let out a tired sigh. Closing my eyes, I rubbed my forehead.

"You all right?" Parker asked.

I glanced up at him. "Yeah. I'm fine," I lied.

His gaze was steady as he studied me, and I gave him a weak smile, which he didn't return. Okay then.

The elevator dinged and I looked away, preceding him out into the parking garage. It felt less surreal now to slide into the passenger seat of the car with him. I guess once you've taken a bath in front of a man, there's not a lot left to be uncomfortable about.

"You had dinner, right?" Parker asked, pulling out into the street. My eyes caught on his hand as he handled the gearshift.

"Um, no," I said. "I didn't really have time."

He glanced quizzically at me. "Then where did you go?"

It wasn't like I could tell him I'd met Ryker in the alley to get listening devices the cops wanted me to plant. I rubbed my forehead again, the headache throbbing.

"Had to run an errand," I mumbled, hoping he'd drop it.

"Then we'll make this quick with Viktor and get you home."

Making it quick with Viktor sounded awesome.

More silence. Then, "So I guess you're...seeing...Ryker now?" A nice way to put it.

That headache was getting worse by the second.

"Um, yeah, maybe, I guess..." Wow. That sounded so bad. If I said I *wasn't* seeing him, that pretty much meant I was a one-night-stand kind of girl, right?

Parker didn't reply for a moment. "I hope it doesn't end badly for you," he said at last.

I stiffened. "We just met last week," I said. "It's not like we're engaged."

He glanced my way and our eyes met. "You just met him last week and yet he's already gotten you into bed," he said bluntly.

My eyes narrowed. "Are you slut-shaming me?"

"No, of course not," he denied, backtracking.

"Because it sounds like you are."

"I'm not—"

"Talk about the pot and kettle," I sputtered, indignant and embarrassed. "That's so politically incorrect, I can't even—"

"That's not what I'm saying," he interrupted, his voice very loud in the car, which shut me up. "I'm surprised," he continued more quietly, "because I thought you were look-ing for something... more."

I frowned. "Okay, first, you're saying that because I've had sex with Ryker, that our relationship is therefore shal-low and destined to be short. Second, you're presuming to know what I want in a relationship, and third, since when have you begun analyzing my love life?" All of which I thought were very valid points. "Also, that does sound pretty damn judgey to me."

Parker's lips twitched at my tone, which should have ir-ritated me, but didn't because I was too relieved to get a response from him other than the cold shoulder he'd dished out all day.

Our conversation was cut short by Parker pulling up to the hotel. A valet hurried to open my door while another scurried around to his. A few moments later, I was following a step behind Parker as we entered the lobby.

I wasn't surprised to see that Viktor was in one of the best hotels in Chicago, and Parker must've known where we were going because he headed straight for the elevator.

As we were walking down the empty hallway of the twenty-first floor, our steps muffled by the thick carpet, Parker spoke.

"Remember," he said, "keep a low profile. Don't draw at-tention to yourself."

"Okay." Though Parker seemed to think it mattered, I doubted that it would. Viktor had already threatened Parker with me and knew I was alive and well. It probably wasn't going to be a surprise that I was accompanying him tonight.

We stopped in front of a room and Parker knocked. A mo-ment later, the door opened.

Tania stood there, her expression impassive as she motioned us in. Her eyes flicked over me, then back to Parker.

"Viktor will just be a few minutes," she said.

"That's fine," Parker replied.

"Can I get you a drink?"

"Scotch on the rocks."

Tania turned and went to pour his drink from where a small bar area had been set up in the spacious suite. She didn't ask if I wanted anything, but that was fine. My stomach was in knots from what I had to tell her and alcohol would've been a bad idea.

She handed Parker his drink and he took a sip, heading to where there was a large dining room table in the main living area. I watched as he set his briefcase down and began taking papers from it.

Turning to Tania, I spoke in an undertone. "Is there somewhere we can talk? Can we go to your room for a few minutes?"

She glanced at me. "This *is* my room," she said flatly. "I have to stay with Viktor. I'm not allowed my own space."

Tania wore an elegant, fitted black dress that ended just above her knee. The neckline was a deep V and the sleeves were made from sheer chiffon. With her black hair and ivory skin, she looked beautiful—so long as you didn't look at her eyes, which were dull and devoid of emotion. It hurt to look in them.

"I need to tell you about your sister," I said. "I can make up an excuse, say I need your help or something, and we can leave."

Her face had brightened at the mention of her sister, which made me feel awful, but I didn't just want to blurt it out to her. After a moment's hesitation, she nodded.

"Okay."

Just then, the door to the bedroom opened and Viktor stepped out. He glanced our way, his eyes seemingly, unerringly, drawn to Tania, then headed over to Parker.

"I have a feeling you and I have a lot more in common than I thought," Viktor said.

Parker's face was blank as he rifled through some papers. "How is that?" he asked.

"I see the lovely Sage is at your side this evening. It seems you require her presence as much as I require Tania's."

Parker glanced up at him. "I don't *require* anything," he said.

Viktor's smile was thin and cold. "Of course."

Knowing I was going to draw Parker's wrath—which couldn't be helped—I grabbed a sheaf of papers from the leather satchel I carried and took several steps forward until they both looked over at me.

"Um, I forgot to make copies of this," I said, holding up the papers. "Tania's going to show me where the business center is. We'll be right back."

Viktor reached for his cell phone. "I'll call Jon to go with you."

"I think we can make copies without help," I said curtly. The last thing we needed was one of Viktor's henchmen babysitting us. Turning, I headed for the door, taking Tania's arm along the way and herding her along with me.

I breathed more easily once we were out in the hallway.

"The business center is on the fifth floor," she said, heading toward the elevator. She waited until we were inside and the doors had slid shut before she spoke again. "Did you find my sister?"

Her eyes were hopeful as she looked at me and I had to take a deep breath before I said what I'd come to say. There was no easy way to break the news, so I went for the blunt truth.

"I'm so sorry, but your sister...she was murdered."

Tania didn't do anything for a moment, just stared at me, until I wondered if she'd understood what I said. Then she suddenly turned and punched the button for the floor we'd just left.

"Wait," I said, "I think we probably need a few more minutes before we go back." No way could she have processed that information. She had to be in shock.

"I'm going to kill him," she ground out from between clenched teeth.

Okay, that was alarming. "What do you mean, you're 'going to kill him'?" I asked.

"Viktor. He was behind it. I know he was. He deserves to die and I'm going to kill him."

The elevator was nearly at the previous floor now, and I was starting to panic.

"Tania, you can't do that. Not just that you don't kill people, but literally you *can't*. He's twice your size! You'll be the one who ends up hurt."

The doors slid open as I tried to reason with her, but she ignored me. She stepped out into the hallway, her strides long and filled with purpose. I latched on to her arm and yanked her to a stop, my grip as tight as I could hold her.

"You cannot just go in there and attack Viktor," I said urgently. "But if you think he was behind it, we can go to the police and tell them."

"The police can't help," she said, trying to pull away from me. Tears sparked in her eyes, but didn't fall.

"They can," I insisted. "We just need to give them something they can use. They already know he's a criminal; they just need something concrete." I hesitated, then decided to tell her. "They gave me two bugs to plant in your suite tonight so they can listen in. You can help me do that."

At that, she finally stopped struggling against my hold on her.

"Really?" she asked.

I nodded. "I just need Viktor to be distracted for a few minutes so I can plant them."

"And the police will be listening? They'll arrest him?"

I didn't think Tania knew a lot about our justice system, but we didn't have time to go into details now about evidence and probable cause and warrants, so I just said, "Yes."

She studied me, and the tears spilled over. "Why did he kill her?" she asked. "What happened?"

Her voice broke and my heart went out to her. I wrapped her in a hug. "I'm so sorry," I said. "I don't know why. What I do know was that she was helping the police, and you should know, if *you* help the police, you could be in danger as well," I warned her. "I don't want that." I had enough guilt on my conscience. I didn't need something to happen to Tania as well.

"It doesn't matter," she said. "My sister is dead. I'll do whatever I have to do to bring her killer to justice."

The door to the suite suddenly opened and one of the bodyguards from New York came out.

"Viktor is looking for you," he said to Tania, and the words may have seemed innocuous, but they were laced with warning.

"I'm coming," she said. Straightening her shoulders, she preceded me into the room.

The hair on the back of my neck stood up as I passed the man, and it took all I had to turn my back to him.

Parker and Viktor were still going over files, but I noticed Viktor looked up when Tania walked in and his body relaxed.

I tried to figure out how I was going to plant the bugs. I

needed to plant one out here and probably the other in the bedroom. But how to get in there? Then inspiration struck.

"I'm not feeling very well," I announced to the room at large. "I-I think I might be sick." I clutched at my stomach and rushed into the bedroom, flinging the door closed behind me.

There. *That* should deter anyone from following. Nothing kept people away quite like the prospect of being witness to someone vomiting.

Reaching in my purse, I dug for the plastic baggie and pulled out a bug. My hands were shaking I was so nervous. Hurrying to the bed, I inspected the lamp on the table. Surely there was a place I could stick it on there...

I was just lifting it to check the bottom when the door suddenly opened. I nearly dropped the lamp before I realized it was Parker.

He saw me standing there, jaw agape and lamp in hand, and immediately closed the door behind him.

"What in the hell are you doing?" he hissed.

I had no idea what to say. I hadn't considered getting caught, much less by Parker. "I-I..." My stammering only made his lips press together in a tight line and he was next to me in three strides. I was still holding the bug and he took it from my fingers, studying it, and realizing what it was. If possible, he looked even angrier.

"Are you fucking kidding me?" he growled. He snatched the lamp from me and replaced it on the table. "Do you have any more?" he asked.

He was furious and I didn't dream of lying to him. I nodded.

"Give them to me."

Digging again, I handed him the baggie. He put it and the other bug into his pocket.

"Go flush the toilet and run the water," he ordered. I scurried to do his bidding. After a moment, he was next to me in the bathroom. I stood in front of the sink, the water going full blast, and our eyes met in the mirror. He reached forward and shut off the faucet.

"We're going to walk out of here and we'll say you're ill, that we have to leave," he said. "Don't say a word, understand?"

I was cowed into obedience, his anger frightening me. I nodded again.

"Great. Now, look sick."

Taking my hand, Parker led me out of the bedroom. I didn't have to try very hard to look sick. I'd royally screwed up. Not only had I gotten caught, but also Ryker believed Parker was in on it. He was going to know for sure that Parker was aware of the authorities' suspicion.

"I'm sorry, Viktor, but I'm afraid we need to continue this in the morning at my office," Parker said, his voice calm and a far cry from the icy way he'd spoken to me. "Sage is ill and I should get her home."

Viktor glanced from Parker to me, then back. "Of course," he said easily. "I will see you then."

"Thank you."

Viktor motioned to Tania, who gathered Parker's things and fastened his briefcase before bringing it to him. A moment later, his bodyguard held the door for us, scrutinizing us on the way out.

Parker had my hand in a vise grip and led me to the elevator. We didn't speak until we were in his car and driving away from the hotel.

"Now tell me what the hell you were doing in there," he said.

I swallowed. "I-I can't."

He'd been driving down the street at a pretty good clip.

At this, he suddenly swung the car onto a side street and whipped into a parking lot, where he slammed the transmission into Park. He turned toward me.

"Ryker gave those to you, didn't he," he accused.

I didn't answer, but it didn't appear I had to. Parker might not know my deepest secrets, but he knew me well enough to know that he'd guessed correctly.

He snarled a vicious curse that had me wincing. Digging in his pocket, he rolled down his window and tossed the baggie and bugs out into the street.

"Do you have any idea what Viktor would have done to you if he'd caught you planting those?" He nearly yelled it at me and I cringed away from him. "I swear to God, I'm going to fucking kill him."

Parker slammed the car back into Drive and took off. Alarmed, I watched and hung on for dear life as he tore through the streets.

"What are you doing? Where are we going?"

But Parker didn't answer me. His jaw was clenched tight, his hands gripping the steering wheel as he drove with single-minded purpose.

I recognized Ryker's house when we squealed to a stop in front of it.

"Parker, no, wait!"

But he was already out of the car, not even turning off the engine or shutting his door. I stumbled in my haste to follow him, terrified of what he was going to do.

"Parker!"

He was beating on the front door and I was still ten feet away when it swung open. Ryker stood there, looking surprised.

"You son of a bitch," Parker snarled, before smashing his fist into Ryker's face.

CHAPTER SEVENTEEN

Ryker came back at Parker full-force and before long they were on the ground, fighting.

"Stop it!" I cried, cringing as I became every cliché there was for a girl watching two men in a fistfight. But I couldn't intervene. As hard as they were hitting each other, I'd break something if I got between them. So I stood by, helpless to do anything.

I thought McClane would go crazy at Ryker being attacked, but it appeared he really did have a mind of his own. He sat on the porch watching, his tongue hanging out and his ears perked forward as though it was entertaining to him.

They both seemed to be getting in some pretty good blows, and I winced at the sound of knuckles on bone. God, men were stupid. What was this going to solve? And I didn't even know why Parker had gotten so angry. Had he thought the police weren't going to be watching men they knew to be part of the Russian mob?

Back on their feet, Parker swung and connected a vicious right-hook to Ryker's jaw. He went down. It seemed to disorient him, because although he managed to get onto all fours, he didn't stand. Seeing my chance, I rushed over and crouched down beside him.

"Ryker, are you all right?" I asked anxiously.

Blood dripped from his mouth and oozed from a cut above his eye. He glanced at me. "Fine," he rasped, getting painfully to his feet.

I stepped between them. "Enough," I said. "That's enough."

Parker was breathing hard and looked no better than Ryker. His suit was dirty and torn, and there was blood on his face and knuckles. He swiped his sleeve at the blood underneath his nose, his eyes fixed on Ryker. The dry cleaner was so going to hate me.

"You want somebody to plant fucking bugs for you, then find somebody else," he spat. "You put Sage in danger. Not that I expect you give a shit."

"Fuck you," Ryker retorted. "If it wasn't for you, those assholes wouldn't even know about her."

"What if she'd gotten caught tonight, Ryker? She'd be dead."

"And it'd be *your* fault. Again," Ryker shot back. "Another dead woman to add to your tally. How many have there been since Natalie?"

I sucked in my breath at Ryker's vicious jeer, but Parker didn't attack him as I'd expected he would.

"I think you're forgetting exactly why she killed herself," Parker bit out. "It wasn't just me."

Whoa, wait a sec—newsflash. Natalie had committed suicide? Because of them?

Ho-ly shit.

"Tell yourself what you want," Ryker sneered. "Whatever you have to do so you can sleep at night."

"Just stay the fuck away from Sage. Don't pull her into your cop bullshit."

Hey, now. "I wanted to do this," I interjected. "Ryker didn't make me. It was my idea."

"And you think it was just coincidence that the man who let you put yourself in grave danger just happened to have been in your bed the night before?" Parker asked me, his tone rife with condescension.

Ouch. "So you're saying that if I screw a guy, I'll do whatever he tells me to do?" I retorted, anger and embarrassment getting the better of my good sense. "That can't possibly be true, because I take orders from *you* constantly."

Parker's jaw clenched as we faced off. "I'm saying that Ryker is a manipulator."

"And you think I'm easily manipulated?"

"Aren't you?" he shot back.

I sucked in a sharp breath, feeling as though he'd slapped me. Was that how he saw me? As someone he could easily manipulate? But...he had, hadn't he? Friday night he'd kissed me and touched me—something he knew I wanted from him—and he'd told me what to do...and I'd done it.

Parker seemed to realize he'd screwed up because he muttered a curse, shoving a hand through his hair.

"Sage, I didn't mean—"

"Save it," I snapped, cutting him off. I turned to walk away, but he grabbed my arm.

"Listen to me—"

"Don't touch me," I snarled, ripping my arm out of his grip. "Just go, okay? I don't want to talk to you or see you right now."

"Let me take you home," he said, his tone contrite, but

I knew better. He didn't want to leave me here with Ryker because then it would seem like he'd "lost" and Ryker had "won." What-the-fuck-ever.

"I don't need you to take me home," I said. "Just go."

He stared at me for a long moment; then Ryker spoke. "You heard her. Go," he said. "Or do I need to arrest you for trespassing? Just give me a reason."

Parker's gaze flicked to Ryker, his expression turning hard and cold. He turned away without another word and we watched as he got back in his car and tore off down the street.

Well.

Tears pricked my eyes as I stared down the street. I tried to process what had just happened, all that Parker had said about what were apparently his *real* thoughts about me. I felt Ryker's hand envelop mine.

"Come inside," he said, lightly tugging.

Wordlessly, I followed him into the house.

He went to the freezer and took out an ice pack, laying it against his jaw, then sat down at the kitchen table with a grimace of pain.

I sat across from him. There was a box of pizza on the table and I lifted the lid. It was still lukewarm and I was ravenous, so I took a piece. I chewed glumly as we sat in silence.

"I take it you didn't get the bugs planted," Ryker said at last.

I looked at him. "Ya think?" My sarcasm was thick. "Parker walked in on me, saw what I was doing, then got incredibly pissed off. He threw the bugs out the window on the way here."

"Something that will count against him when this all goes down," Ryker said.

I bristled. "I don't think it's because he's working for

them," I said. "He was mad that I was putting myself into a dangerous situation."

"Still defending him? Even after what he said?"

Ryker's gaze was shrewd and I opened my mouth to deny it, then abruptly shut it. He was right. I was still defending Parker, like it was an instinctual thing.

I sighed. I was exhausted.

"Viktor's secretary was there," I said, deciding to change the subject. I didn't want to talk about Parker anymore. "Tania. She's Niki's sister. I told her about Niki and she swears Viktor was involved. She wants to help the police."

Ryker mulled this over. "If she's someone Viktor trusts, then we can definitely use her."

"The cops need to protect her, not *use* her. She's been used enough." I took another huge bite of pizza. It had mushrooms and normally I didn't eat fungus, but I was too hungry to care.

"We'll make sure she's protected," he assured me. "Can you get in touch with her? Help us set up a meeting?"

I thought about it, then nodded. "Viktor and Parker had to postpone the rest of their meeting tonight. They'll get together again in the morning before the markets open. I should see her then."

"Okay. Tell her we can protect her, but she has to bring something of value to the meeting. Something we can use that proves she's in a good position to help us."

"That seems rather mercenary," I said.

"It's not me," Ryker said. "It's just how things work. If we're going to develop an asset, they have to be in a position that's going to be useful to us and the DA."

I finished the slice, still in thought. "Do you think I'm easily manipulated?" I asked, Parker's words still echoing inside my head.

"No," Ryker replied. "You're trusting, which isn't the same thing."

I wanted to believe him, but maybe Parker was right. It hadn't taken anything more than Ryker insinuating I could protect Parker for me to jump on the bandwagon with whatever he'd wanted me to do, including planting those bugs. It depressed me.

Ryker set aside the ice pack, reached across the table, and took my hand. I glanced up at him.

"Don't listen to Parker," he said. "He's an expert at making people doubt themselves. He can crawl inside your head and make you do things you wouldn't normally do."

I hesitated, then asked the question that had been flitting through my mind, just waiting for me to give voice to it. "Is that what he did to Natalie?"

As I'd expected, the mention of her caused Ryker to stiffen and draw back, but I tightened my grip on his hand.

"Tell me," I implored. "I know it's got to be hard, but I need to know." I needed to know if the man I'd been so loyal to all these years, the man I'd grown to respect and admire, was a fraud. "What happened between you two and Natalie?"

Ryker scrubbed a hand across his face and sighed. I waited. Finally, he spoke.

"Parker and I were in the Marines together," he said. "I don't know if you know that, but when we got back, there weren't a lot of jobs available. There are places that help returning soldiers find work, and I went to one. Parker...he was fine. Went back to school and finished his degree, then had a job ready and waiting for him.

"There was a woman who volunteered at the center where I went. It was Natalie. She was sweet, kind. Her husband had been a pilot."

"Had been?" I asked.

"He'd been shot down and was MIA, presumed dead. She was sad and tragic and beautiful. I think I fell in love with her immediately. But she wasn't ready for a relationship, so we just hung out, got to know one another. Of course, I introduced her to my best friend, which was the worst mistake I ever made."

I was caught up in his story, watching him tell it with eyes gazing far away in the distance, as though reliving it. "What happened?"

Ryker glanced at me. "They hit it off," he said. "Parker moved in behind my back, though he lied to me about it. I told him I was in love with her, but he didn't care.

"They spent a lot of time together and one night I caught them. Parker and I got into a fight and Natalie started crying, saying she didn't want to come between us."

He stopped there and I waited, hoping he'd finish the story.

Taking a deep breath, he said, "She found another way out. She took her own life that night. Drove her car into the river and drowned."

It was an awful, horrible story, and my heart went out to him. "I'm sorry," I said, at a loss as to anything else I could possibly say.

Ryker's lips twisted into a humorless smile. "It is what it is," he said with a shrug. "It's in the past."

Acting on impulse, I got up from my chair, rounding the table and settling myself sideways on Ryker's lap. He seemed a little surprised, but his arms went around my waist while mine circled his neck to squeeze him.

"I'm really, really sorry," I whispered. I couldn't imagine losing someone under those circumstances, them committing suicide. It was awful and tragic.

Ryker's grip tightened around me and we stayed like that

for a long moment. I had the feeling he'd probably never really allowed himself to be vulnerable, not with his background and most certainly not with the job he did. But right now in the quiet of his kitchen with only the refrigerator humming and only me to see, I could feel his body curving in to mine.

Finally, he drew back and I sat up, too. Reaching out, he tucked my hair behind my ear.

"You're pretty incredible, you know that?" he asked with a soft smile. "You've had a lot of bad shit happen to you lately, and yet here you are, consoling me about a girlfriend who's been dead for years."

His compliment embarrassed me, and I didn't know what to say. My cheeks must've turned red because he chuckled softly, his knuckles brushing the warm skin.

"Love the blush," he teased. "Please tell me you're staying tonight and that I don't have to take you home."

"You don't mind an impromptu sleepover?" I asked.

"Not if you're naked."

* * *

Morning came too soon, but it was greatly enhanced by a shared shower with Ryker. I wasn't sure I'd gotten all the conditioner out of my hair, but I was positive my breasts were as clean as they'd ever been, courtesy of Ryker.

He dropped me off at my apartment—bed replaced and crime scene remnants all gone, thank goodness. I couldn't have handled seeing Hanna's blood again. But I'd given the number of the credit card my dad had given me to a special company Ryker had told me about, and they'd taken care of everything. The card had a two-hundred-thousand-dollar limit and the bill went straight to Dad.

Soon after, the sun came up and I was dressed and waiting for the bus well before my usual time. I thought the driver looked shocked to see me on time for a change.

I settled in to my seat, smoothing the lines of my favorite dress. Cornflower blue, it reminded me of summer. Though there was a slight chill in the air, I'd worn the short-sleeved dress anyway. It was formfitting and ended right above the knee. A thin, silver belt wrapped around my waist and I'd worn silver earrings and a necklace, too. I'd even pulled out my silver heels, despite them not being quite appropriate for work.

It's amazing how much better you feel about life thrown into utter disarray if you add to it a great pair of sparkly platform sandals.

There was a spring in my step as I went into Starbucks for my usual order. I had to look on the positive side of things. I was dating a gorgeous man, a *cop* no less, who didn't appear averse to having a serious relationship *and* who was without a doubt the best sex I'd ever had.

Of course, the *negatives* from this week were pretty hard to ignore. My boss—the man I'd been unswervingly loyal to for years, who I thought was incredibly smart and successful—had kissed me senseless, then turned me down, then implied I was a pushover.

It wasn't so much that he thought I was a pushover that made me so angry. It was the fact that I'd been loyal to him because of who he was, not because he'd manipulated me into doing so. It was as though he wanted to steal my sense of honor and satisfaction from doing my job well, boiling it down to just a sexual thing between us, and it pissed me off.

I resolved to keep doing my job as well as I'd ever done it, even after and *especially* since Parker thought I was slavishly following his demands. He could be as much of an asshole as he wanted to be. I'd still do my job, because screw him.

That thought kept my chin up and my spine straight as I walked into work. I set Parker's breakfast and coffee on his desk as usual, then went to mine. No sooner had I sat down and logged into my computer than I looked up to see Viktor standing in front of my counter.

I abruptly sat back in surprise, more than a little trepidation filling me.

He leaned on his arms, bending over the counter toward me.

"How are you this morning, Sage?"

The way he said it sent a shiver of fear down my spine. I knew who he was and exactly what he was capable of, and all of it scared me.

"I'm fine, thank you," I said, trying to sound normal.

"You know," he said, "I have…had…a friend who lived here in Chicago. Her name was Hanna. She's recently been the victim of a nasty break-in. I heard they slit her throat from ear to ear. Can you imagine?"

Bile rose in my throat and if I'd had any doubt as to Viktor's involvement in Hanna's murder, I didn't any longer.

I shook my head. "That's awful. But I'm sure the cops will catch who did it."

"Doubtful," he said.

I didn't respond to that. Looking behind him, I didn't see Tania. I wanted to talk with her, tell her what Ryker said. "Is Tania with you this morning?"

He shrugged. "She's no longer with me, I'm afraid. I found out she'd taken something from me—something quite important. I don't take kindly to those who betray me."

I stared at him, hoping he didn't mean what I thought he meant about Tania.

"It'd be a shame if I found out you or anyone else here had also betrayed me," he continued, and gone was even a pretense at friendliness. This was a threat, and I was ashamed to realize it scared me. A lot.

"People who talk to the police about things they think they know have a tendency to end up dead," he continued. "So be careful who you trust, Sage. It just might kill you. And that includes your boss."

Our gazes were locked on each other and my mouth was utterly dry. There was no mistaking his meaning. Somehow he'd found out that I'd been to see the cops and not only was he threatening me, but he was also threatening Parker.

"Viktor, good morning."

Parker had approached from behind him and now Viktor turned, the menace on his face melting away into a warm smile.

"Thought we'd get a head start today," Viktor said. "You don't mind, I'm sure."

Parker's smile was forced. "Of course not. Let's head into my office."

Viktor preceded him and Parker briefly glanced at me as he walked by. Something on my face must've clued him in because he stopped.

"Are you all right?"

I forced myself to smile, though my face thought it might crack. "Yeah," I said, my voice too quiet. "I'm fine."

His gaze was steady. "Tell me."

My smile faltered a bit and I forced it back, tipping my lips upward, just in case Viktor was watching. "It's nothing. I'm fine."

Parker's lips thinned, but I kept smiling. I didn't know what was going on, who the good guys were, and who the bad guys were. Should I tell Parker what Viktor had said?

Would Viktor make good on his threat to Parker if I went to the cops? And most importantly of all, what had Tania taken from Viktor?

The wisest course of action at the moment seemed to be to remain silent, so that's what I did. Several long moments passed. Parker was just watching me and waiting. Both of us knew he could break me; he just had to wait it out.

I was saved by the ringing of my cell phone. Tearing my gaze from Parker's, I dug the phone from the depths of my purse.

Ryker was calling.

"Um, I'd better take this," I said to Parker.

His lips thinned, but he walked away into his office. The glass door swung shut behind him and I saw Viktor had already seated himself in front of the desk.

"Where are you?" were the first words out of Ryker's mouth.

"I'm at work," I said. "Why?"

"Because they just called to tell me they pulled Niki's sister out of Lake Michigan this morning."

Tania. My eyes slipped closed.

"Okay. Thanks for letting me know," I said.

"Don't go anywhere," Ryker said. "I'll come by and get you, put you into protective custody."

"You can't do that," I said. "Parker needs me to finish this deal. The markets open in a few hours. I can't just leave." God knows what Viktor would do to Parker if the cops suddenly dragged me out of here.

"Sage, listen to me—"

"I gotta go," I interrupted him, spying Parker heading my way again. "Call you later."

"Can you begin accessing these accounts?" Parker said, handing me a list of account numbers, each one not less than twenty-four digits long. "I'll need them all consolidated and ready to access their shares for putting on the market when the bell hits."

I nodded. "Yeah. I'll get started right away." I took the paper from him and our eyes met. This was it. He was going to do the deal and there was no going back once it was done. The bad guys would have their money, giving further legitimacy to their cartel that was nothing more than mafia criminals in suits.

Parker looked at me, a question in his eyes, and neither of us moved. After a moment, I gave a minute nod of my head, a silent understanding passing between us. Yes, I would do this, regardless that I thought he was doing the wrong thing. I wasn't going to desert him, not now, not ever.

Parker got the message loud and clear, our communication with business as faultless as ever, and his body relaxed slightly.

"Okay, then," he said quietly. "Let's do this."

I watched him go back in his office and flash a smile at Viktor. I couldn't hear what they were saying, but it didn't matter. I had work to do.

Grabbing my purse, I tossed my cell phone inside, then saw something and stopped.

It was the envelope Tania had given me to hand over to Niki.

I'd never opened it, and with the attack on me and the murder of Hanna, I'd completely forgotten about it. Glancing around to make sure no one was watching—though who would care if I was opening an envelope at my desk? Hello, this *was* a business and I kinda did that all the time—I pulled it out and set it on my desk.

The paper was crumpled slightly from being in my purse so I flattened it out, then slit it open with my letter opener.

Only a single sheet of paper was inside. I unfolded it, then frowned at what was on it.

Account numbers. A whole list of them. Just like the ones Parker had just given me. Taking the two sheets, I set them side by side, skimming through the accounts. I found matching ones, then another set, then another. After a couple of minutes, I realized that all the accounts on the sheet Parker had given me were also on the sheet from Tania.

What did it mean?

I didn't know and didn't have time to try and figure it out. These accounts were worth Tania dying over, but I didn't understand why.

Shoving Tania's paper inside a drawer, I went to work, pulling up and consolidating all the accounts so all Parker would have to do was enter his passcode, then the trade amounts and buyers.

It was a good hour later and I was only halfway through the list when Viktor and Parker emerged from his office.

"...see you this evening to celebrate," Viktor was saying to Parker. He glanced at me. "And be sure to bring Sage with you."

"I'll do that," Parker replied with a smile, walking Viktor to the elevator. I couldn't hear any more of what they were saying and kept working until Parker appeared at my desk, minus Viktor.

"How's it going?" he asked.

"Fine," I replied, not looking up. "This'll be ready in time. I'll send the screen to your laptop when I'm through."

He didn't say anything, but remained standing there. I could feel his eyes on me, so I glanced up.

"Thank you," he said.

The words were spoken so sincerely and with such emphasis, I could only nod in response; then he walked away.

It took another forty-five minutes to get things ready for this large of a sell, but Parker and I worked perfectly together. I sent the screen and data to his laptop, then went into his office to confirm the transactions as they were made on my iPad. By noon, it was done.

"Three hundred million dollars later," Parker said with a sigh, leaning back in his chair.

"That's a lot of money," I said. "What will you do with your share of the fee?"

Parker just shrugged and glanced at his watch. "I'm going to grab lunch. I'll be back this afternoon."

"Do we really have to go to dinner with him tonight?" I asked, but Parker shook his head.

"No. Don't worry about it. I'm sure he'll be busy with other things by then."

It was an odd thing to say, but I was so relieved not to have to go to dinner, I didn't question it.

The rest of the day passed as usual, though I thought about Tania and those accounts, wondering what it all meant. Parker came back from lunch and we didn't talk much. Usually, after a big day like that, we'd celebrate. But not today.

I was in a bad mood when I went home and halfway there I realized I'd never called Ryker back. Pulling out my cell, I dialed as I stepped off the bus. It rang several times, then went to voice mail.

"I'm sorry about this morning," I said, "but I guess I'm safe now. Parker...did the deal. The shares were sold and the money transferred to ZNT in Moscow. Three hundred million. I'm sorry I couldn't help you get these guys..."

I was approaching my building now and someone stood

near the entrance. I squinted, trying to see who it was, but couldn't tell. Some man. Maybe it was a neighbor who'd forgotten their key.

"Anyway, when you get this, give me a call—"

The man turned toward me and I froze in my tracks.

It was the guy from New York, the one Ryker had said was an assassin. And he was coming straight for me.

CHAPTER EIGHTEEN

I didn't do anything for a few precious seconds; then I did the only thing I could think of. I turned and ran.

"Oh my God, he's here!" I said into my phone.

The silver sandals weren't made for running and I stopped to toe them off, glancing behind me to see that the guy was crossing the street at a jog, dodging traffic. I started running again, frantically looking for someplace safe, but where was there to go? Apartment buildings had codes and locks—I couldn't just walk in one.

I looked behind me again and saw he was gaining.

My heart was beating so hard, it felt as though it would leap from my chest. Ice-cold adrenaline made my limbs feel weird and unsteady. I looked in the street, searching for cars. Surely someone would stop for me if I ran into the street, right? But this was Chicago. I didn't know if anyone would stop to help a stranger.

But what choice did I have?

Running several feet into the avenue, I waved frantically at cars.

"Stop! Please stop! Help me!"

But my shouts went unheeded, one car swerving around me and another angrily honking their horn.

I looked around. The assassin was closing in, now only yards away.

Desperation made me turn back to the cars just to see one screech to a halt in front of me. Relief turned to horror as the back door flew open and Viktor stepped out.

"Just the woman I was looking for," he said.

I took a step back, but he grabbed my arm, pried the phone from my fingers, and shoved me into the backseat of the car.

Scrambling across the seat, my hand was on the latch of the opposite door when Viktor grabbed a handful of my hair and yanked me back.

I cried out in pain and heard the slam of the car door; then we were speeding down the street.

"Hold still," he said, and I heard the rack of a slide on an automatic. A man in the front passenger seat was pointing a gun at me while another man drove. The gun was very steady in his grip, despite the speed of the car. I held still.

Viktor grabbed my arms and twisted them behind my back. He wrapped a plastic zip tie around my wrists, which he drew painfully tight. Then he leaned down and did the same thing to my ankles.

"I presume you have your boss on speed dial," he mused, sitting back up and scrolling through my phone. He pushed the button, ending the call with Ryker's voice mail, then hit another button and put the call on speaker.

"What do you want?" I asked.

"Shut up."

The cold distance in the way he said that made me even more terrified. I knew Viktor saw women as utterly disposable. Look what he'd done to Tania and he'd professed to "needing" her. Why he'd come after me was a complete mystery, not that I cared much at the moment. I just wanted to escape.

The phone rang twice; then I heard Parker say my name.

"Sage, are you all right?"

"She is at the moment but I can promise you that won't be the case for long," Viktor said. "I know what you did, Mr. Anderson, and if you don't find a way to *un*do it, Sage will pay very dearly indeed."

Done? What had he done?

"I don't know what you're talking about, Viktor," Parker said. "We did the deal just how you wanted."

Viktor's hand lashed out, slapping me hard. I yelped at the pain, tears springing to my eyes. And my bruises had been just about gone, too.

"For every lie, I'll hurt her," Viktor said, his voice as calm as though he were ordering dinner in a fancy restaurant. "Your choice whether or not Sage survives the next few minutes."

"Tell me what you want, Viktor," Parker said, his voice icy but edged with panic. "There's no need to hurt the woman. We're both businessmen."

"You're not. You're a spy and you've exposed my accounts to your government."

"That's not true—"

Another loud slap that cut Parker off mid-sentence echoed in the car. I couldn't help another cry of pain, my jaw and cheek burning.

"I'll do what you want, Viktor, just stop!" Parker's anxious voice emanated from the phone.

"Delete those trades and move those accounts back under the corporations that hedged them," Viktor said.

"I need time to do that," Parker said.

"You don't have time," Viktor replied. "At least, not if you want Sage to remain alive. I imagine it's hard to swim with your arms and legs bound."

Oh God.

"All right! Okay, I'll do it," Parker shouted.

"That's better, but let's make sure you have some incentive."

Viktor reached toward the front and the guy holding the gun passed him something plastic. By the time I realized it was a plastic bag, it was too late. He grabbed my head and pulled the bag over my head. I tried twisting my head away, but he pulled the bag tight around my neck, cutting into my throat.

"Do you want to know what I'm doing while you're fixing my accounts?" Viktor asked. "I have a plastic bag over her head, Mr. Anderson. She'll run out of air very quickly. It takes approximately six minutes, thereabouts, for a person to be brain dead from lack of oxygen. Add another couple of minutes just to be on the safe side. Shall we use her as a timer for you?"

"Sage!"

"My associate is waiting for confirmation, Mr. Anderson," Viktor said calmly, glancing in the front seat. "I suggest you move quickly. Sage is turning a bit blue, though it's hard to tell through the plastic."

I squirmed harder, trying to get away, but my strength was no match for his and the plastic pulled tight over my nose and mouth. I couldn't see, everything was blurred, and I ceased being able to make out the conversation between Viktor and Parker.

I fought it, the zip ties cutting into my wrists as I tried in vain to free my arms. Panic made me suck in more air, but there was none to be had, just the slippery plastic in my mouth. I was crying and trying to breathe and I realized... I was going to die, and my death would be horrible. Terror clawed at me and I was in pain, in a car with a sociopath who planned on dropping my body in Lake Michigan.

My lungs were starved for air and blackness edged my vision. I couldn't fight anymore, my limbs going slack even as my mind was still in a panic, urging my body to move. But it was useless.

A resounding crash sent the car hurtling sideways. My body slammed against the passenger door, causing Viktor to lose his grip on the bag and air leaked in. I took a breath. Not enough with the plastic still sticking to my tear- and sweat-soaked face, but it helped.

Gunshots sounded, but I couldn't tell anything that was going on. My door was yanked open and I nearly fell out of the car, which would've really hurt since I couldn't cushion my fall. But someone grabbed me, hauling me up into their arms.

I heard voices, shouting, as I was carried to another vehicle and put in it, the man who'd caught me climbing in after me.

"I've got her!"

"They're coming!"

"Go! Go!"

A squeal of tires and more gunshots, then we were flying down the road. The bag was ripped off my face and I sucked in a lungful of oxygen, the sweet chill of fresh air against my face causing a flood of relief.

"Sage, oh my God, Sage..."

Shocked at the sound of his voice, I turned to see Parker

sitting next to me. His hands were busy pushing my hair back from where strands were stuck to my face and in my mouth.

I couldn't talk—I was still breathing too hard for that—but it didn't seem to matter. He quickly pulled a switchblade from his pocket and cut the ties from my wrists and ankles. The hard plastic had bit into my skin, leaving bloody abrasions behind, but I didn't care. I was just relieved to be alive.

Once I was free, I flung myself at Parker, wrapping my arms so tight around his neck, I was sure I was close to strangling him. But if I was, he didn't seem to mind. His arms were just as tight around me as I scrambled onto his lap, anxious to be as close to him as humanly possible.

"Sage, Sage, Sage," he whispered, repeating my name over and over.

I was crying, sobbing uncontrollably. I'd been so close to dying, just minutes away, and that wasn't something you just walked away from.

"I think we're in the clear," someone said from the front seat.

Parker was smoothing my hair as he held me. I didn't care where we were going or what we were doing, just so long as he held on to me.

"Does she need medical care?" the voice asked from the front.

"Sage." Parker's voice was soft in my ear.

My tears had abated, but I still trembled in the aftermath of my ordeal. His collar where I'd pressed my face was damp and I could smell the scent of his skin. It was familiar and comforting to me—I felt safe.

"Baby, look at me."

Parker's hand was exceedingly gentle on my chin, turning

my face up to his. My eyes were closed, but I heard him suck in a sharp breath.

"Tell me if you're hurt anywhere," he said. "Please tell me."

I pried open my burning eyes and looked at him, gave a minute shake of my head.

"I think she's okay," Parker said, loud enough for the guy in front to hear.

I glanced over my shoulder and caught sight of the man in the front passenger seat. He was looking at me and my body went rigid with fear. It was the assassin.

"Sage, shh, it's okay," Parker soothed. "He's on our side. I promise."

My nails were digging into Parker's chest, my eyes still glued on the man.

"Trust me," Parker said, prying one of my hands from where it clutched his shirt. He laid my palm flat against his cheek. I cautiously turned back to see him watching me. When our eyes met, he pressed his lips into my palm.

The car pulled to a stop. I didn't ask where we were or what we were doing. My mind had stopped processing anything. I felt numb. My only thought was that I had to cling to Parker, that I'd be safe with him.

I didn't speak as he helped me out of the car. He turned to the men in front.

"Men are watching?" he asked.

The assassin answered. "Yeah. No one's going to get through. Not tonight."

Parker nodded and took a step back. That was when I noticed the front end was all dented up. Then the car drove away and we walked into the lobby, the concrete rough against my bare feet, and I recognized his apartment building. His arm was around me, supporting my weight as I leaned on him, my head against his chest. The doorman didn't ask any questions, just hurried to get the elevator for us.

A couple of minutes later, Parker was unlocking his door and leading me into his apartment. Tossing his keys on the counter, he took my hand and led me into his bedroom.

"Lie down," he said, easing me onto the bed.

I didn't argue.

He disappeared into the bathroom and I heard the water running. The pillow under my head smelled like him.

When he returned, he had a washcloth and a first aid kit. He didn't speak as he pressed the warm cloth to my face, his touch on my bruised cheek exceedingly gentle. After he'd washed away the tear tracks and blood that had seeped from my mouth, he left and wet the cloth again. This time he carefully cleaned the wounds around my wrists and ankles, then began rubbing antibiotic cream into the marks.

My brain was processing things again, the numbness evaporating as the minutes ticked by. When Parker was finishing with my ankles, I opened my mouth and asked, "How did you find me?"

"I was with Sasha," he said, "at your apartment, waiting for you."

"Who's Sasha?"

"The guy that was in the front," he replied. "The one who scared you."

"Of course he scared me. He's an assassin for Viktor."

Parker looked up from my leg at that. "Not really. He's actually a CIA agent."

My eyes widened. "What?"

"The CIA contacted me after Hinton was killed. They'd been following Bank ZNT and Viktor, knew what they were trying to do. They wanted me to help."

I was confused. "Wait...the CIA wanted your help? Why

would they need your help? They're the CIA, for God's sake."

"Yes, but the accounts held by ZNT were beyond their reach. The public sale of shares gave them an avenue where they could freeze all the US-held assets of ZNT, which totaled over fifty billion dollars."

I stared at him. "So you were doing this...working for the CIA...the entire time?"

He nodded, putting my ankle down and reaching for my wrist. Squeezing more ointment out, he began slowly rubbing it in.

"Why didn't you tell me?"

"No one could know. Plus, I was under the apparently mistaken belief that not telling you would keep you safe," he answered. "If they knew I was working for the CIA, they'd have killed me and anyone else associated with me." He looked up then and our gazes collided. "What I didn't count on was Viktor seeing how much I care about you, and him using that against me."

I didn't know what to say to that. Parker had been transparent about keeping me safe, but those words—*how much I care about you*—seemed laden with meaning that was more than his instinctual protectiveness. I didn't want to dare hope that he meant more. He'd disappointed me twice already. I couldn't handle a third time. Not tonight.

Finishing with one wrist, he laid it down and picked up my other, beginning the process again.

"I can do that," I said, suddenly self-conscious about him taking care of me in such an intimate way. I tried to tug my arm away, but he tightened his hold.

"Let me," he said. "I want to. Or need to, I should say."

Silence reigned for a few moments as he worked assiduously on my wounds.

"Why were you at my apartment?" I asked.

"I had a gut feeling he might go after you," he said. "Sasha was keeping a lookout. I was going to talk to you inside, away from prying eyes and ears. I didn't realize you knew Sasha's undercover identity and would run when you saw him." His face hardened. "I'm guessing Ryker told you that."

Ryker.

"I need to call him," I said, sitting up. "Viktor hung up on his voice mail when he grabbed me. He's probably worried."

"Relax," Parker said, gently pushing me back down onto the bed. "Let's take care of you first; then we'll worry about Ryker." Getting up, he went to the closet, returning with a faded T-shirt with the word "Marines" emblazoned across the front.

"I don't have any women's clothing," he said, "but you can wear this if you'd like to change."

"Yeah, thanks." I took the shirt, then looked expectantly at him. He'd seen me naked before, but it was different now, and not just because I was sober.

"Oh. Sorry," he said after a moment, seemingly just realizing why I was waiting. "I'll just give you some privacy."

He turned and left the bedroom, pulling the door shut behind him.

I was glad to get rid of the dress, and after a brief hesitation, shucked my bra, too. I wanted to be comfortable and curl up in Parker's bed, under his sheets, and go to sleep.

Grabbing my phone, I dialed Ryker, but it went to voice mail immediately.

"Hey," I said. "It's Sage. I'm so sorry for the voice mail earlier. Something...bad...happened." An understatement. "But I'm fine now, so just call me, I guess, when you get this, okay? Bye."

Going into the bathroom, I found a brush and ran it through my hair. My face had seen better days. Viktor had split my lip and there was a cut on my swollen cheekbone. Nice.

I heard a noise and frowned, putting down the brush. Coming out of the bathroom, I heard voices shouting.

Panic flooded me and I wanted to hide, but Parker was out there...alone.

But I had no weapon, nothing to help him with. I glanced frantically around the bedroom, but before I could decide what to do, the door was suddenly flung open.

I screamed.

CHAPTER NINETEEN

My scream was abruptly cut off when I saw Ryker standing there, gun in hand.

"Holy shit!" I exploded. "I thought you were...you were..." But I couldn't finish the sentence, too overwhelmed by the relief that had so quickly followed the sheer terror.

Ryker was by me in an instant, his arms around me. "God, Sage, I thought you were dead," he rasped, his voice in my ear.

I couldn't talk yet, not past the huge lump in my throat, so I just nodded.

"It's okay now. We've got him."

That got my tongue going pretty darn quick. "What do you mean you've *got him*?" I asked, taking a step back.

"Parker," Ryker clarified. "We can't charge him with conspiracy or racketeering, but we still have Niki with his business card. An arrest on suspicion of murder will have to do."

"Murder!" I exclaimed. "Are you out of your mind? He didn't kill Niki."

Ryker's face was hard. "You're still defending him? You were nearly killed tonight! Street surveillance video shows you being shoved into a car that was later involved in an accident. Two men killed, shot to death."

"Ryker, we're heading downtown to book him." The voice came from Parker's living room.

I shoved past Ryker and saw Parker, handcuffed and flanked by two uniformed cops. Our eyes met and I saw his gaze flick downward over the T-shirt I wore. His lips twisted in a tiny, satisfied smile; then it was gone.

"Ryker, you can't do this!" I implored, but he ignored me.

"Did you read him his rights?"

I rushed to Parker. "What's going to happen?" I asked him, eyeing the cops.

"Don't worry. Stay here. It'll be all right," he assured me.

I hated seeing him that way, with his arms cuffed behind his back, but he didn't seem fazed. He just watched me.

"Go on ahead. I'll follow in a few minutes," Ryker told the cops.

I watched in dismay as the two men led Parker out the door; then I turned on Ryker.

"You know he didn't do it," I spat. "This is just you being vindictive."

"No, this is just me doing my job," he retorted. "Isn't that what you wanted me to do?"

"But Parker's been working for the CIA all this time!" I said. I knew Parker had said no one was to know, but he'd just been *arrested* for *murder*. I wasn't sure the rules still applied.

Ryker stared at me like I'd just grown two heads. "He told you that?"

"Yes!"

"And you believed him?"

I covered my face in my hands, but he was right. How was I supposed to convince him? He hadn't been there to see the two CIA guys and Parker rescue me. They'd shot those men.

"You know what," Ryker said. I looked up at him. "You're here with him, in his apartment, wearing his clothes." He gestured to the T-shirt I wore. "No matter what he does, you think he's innocent. So maybe you should just stay here."

I had a feeling he wasn't just talking about tonight. "Wait, Ryker, don't—"

"Don't what?" he interrupted. "This isn't something you can straddle the fence on, sweetheart. It's either him or me."

I stared at him, my mouth hanging open. "You're not serious? I work for Parker! It's my *job*."

"Call it whatever the fuck you want," Ryker retorted. "But don't call me until you've made a choice."

He was gone before I could even think what to say to that.

I didn't know what to do, who I could call that would help Parker. All I could do was sit and wait. Parker had said it would be okay, that he'd be back, and that I should stay here. So that's what I did.

Going back into the bedroom, I pulled down the sheets and climbed into bed. Sitting up, I pulled my knees to my chest, hugging them.

The clock ticked the minutes and hours slowly by. After two hours, I started nodding off, but then I'd jerk awake and glance at the clock. Worry ate at me, exhaustion close on its heels.

A soft touch on my cheek startled me awake. I'd fallen asleep again. I jerked upright.

"Shh, it's all right."

Parker was sitting beside me on the bed.

I threw my arms around his neck. "Thank God!" I hugged him long and hard and he hugged me back. Finally, I pulled away. "What happened?"

"The CIA came through for me," he said. "I was in a holding cell for a while, then interrogation, where of course I said nothing. Then a little while ago clearance came through for me to be released and the charges dropped."

"I'm so relieved," I said. "I was so worried..."

"Did you doubt me?" he teased. "Shame on you."

I huffed a small laugh, surprised he could be in a good mood after all that had happened today.

"You seem awfully chipper for being arrested," I said.

"Why shouldn't I be?" he asked. "I did my job, helped the government seize billions of dollars that would've gone into criminals' pockets, outwitted the cops, and saved the girl. Life's pretty fucking perfect right about now."

Okay, call me weird, but I really liked hearing Parker curse. For such a straight-laced kind of guy, hearing him spout the F-word was all kinds of hot.

"Saved the girl?" I said. "Any reason why you listed that last?"

"The best is always last," he replied, his lips twisting in a half-smile.

I liked that. I liked that a lot.

He stood. "I'm going to shower the station-house smell off me. You'll stay with me tonight." It wasn't a question and I didn't argue. After all that had happened, I felt a strong need to be close to him tonight. Our lives had nearly been torn apart today—mine almost snuffed out—and the after-effects of that lingered.

I lay back down and Parker's hand smoothed my hair

back from my face. I watched him go into the bathroom and heard the water start. I promised myself I'd stay awake for when he returned, but the last thing I remember was pressing my face into his pillow, inhaling deeply, and smiling.

* * *

I opened my eyes. It was dark and I was in an unfamiliar room. It took a moment; then I remembered.

I was in Parker's apartment. Parker's bedroom. Parker's bed.

With Parker.

I felt his body at my back, one arm slung over my waist. His breathing was deep and even.

I lay there in the darkness, listening to him breathe and soaking in the feel of the moment. It was something that would never come again and I wanted to enjoy it, remember the sound of the clock ticking in the corner and his breaths as he slept. I wanted to memorize the scent of him surrounding me—so like what he smelled like in the office, but deeper here at home in his bed. And I never wanted to forget how it felt to be spooned next to him, a position I wouldn't think a bachelor like Parker would be overly fond of.

There was an ache in my gut that I knew was dangerous. Here in the silent hours in the deepest part of the night, I could be honest with myself. I was in love with Parker. Probably had been for quite some time now, though I'd refused to acknowledge it. But it was there all the same. Undeniable.

And there was nothing that could come of it.

Parker had been clear on the possibility of a relationship between us—there wouldn't be one, whether I worked for him or not.

I'm toxic to relationships.

His words made more sense now that I knew more of the story with Natalie. I wasn't foolish enough to think tonight had changed that, no matter how sweetly he'd taken care of me or how he'd wanted me to stay the night. But being there, waiting for the morning light to brighten the room and Parker to withdraw again as I was certain he would...I couldn't do it. My heart would shatter into a million pieces and I wouldn't be able to hide that from him.

The decision for what to do next sat in my mind for several long minutes, waiting. I didn't want to make it. Didn't want to do what I knew I had to. Habit and the routine of reserving a part of my heart for Parker fought with logic and sense. Continuing to allow my unreciprocated love for Parker control my life wasn't going to get me anything I wanted. Whereas Ryker...

He cared about me and I cared about him. Our relationship was new, but maybe he and I could have a future together. Granted, it was uncertain and I didn't know where it would lead, but I knew it would be doomed already if I stayed here tonight. I'd be a fool to throw away what Ryker and I might have for a man forever beyond my reach.

The decision was clear-cut, and only the absolute certainty that I'd hurt worse and would lose Ryker entirely if I didn't do this forced me from Parker's side.

I eased out of the bed, careful not to disturb or wake him. Reluctantly taking off the T-shirt, I pulled my dress over my head and tugged it into place. I couldn't find my bra in the dark and with my eyes watering from tears, so I left it.

Tiptoeing out of Parker's bedroom, I took one last glance at him, still asleep in the bed. No doubt it would be the last time I saw that particular sight.

The doorman downstairs let me borrow his phone, since

I had nothing with me. No purse, no shoes, and no phone. I dialed a number from memory.

"Ryker, it's me," I said. "Can you come take me home?" I hesitated. "Please? I-I've made my choice."

I stood in the lobby for the ten minutes it took Ryker to get there, trying not to think at all. I was tired, so tired, and all I wanted was to lie down. I felt jittery from exhaustion and nerves that were shot, but I thought I was holding it together pretty well...until I climbed into Ryker's truck and laid eyes on him.

It was as though the tense ball of trepidation inside my chest evaporated. The expression on his face as he looked at me said more than words ever could about how he felt, and it was a huge relief. I'd been afraid that it might have been too late, that he wouldn't want me anymore.

I managed a watery smile, tears stinging my eyes as I climbed into the truck.

"Shh, it's okay," he said, easily reading me. He pulled me over by his side and wrapped an arm around me. I cuddled into his chest and felt his lips press against my forehead as he drove.

By the time we'd reached his house, I was dozing against him. Ryker turned off the engine, then pulled me into his arms to carry me inside. The slam of the truck door woke me fully.

"You can put me down," I murmured sleepily, rubbing a hand across my eyes. "I can walk."

"Just hold on to me," his voice rasped softly in my ear. "I've got you."

So I did.

Sage Reese is caught between bad-boy detective Ryker and sexy power player Parker. But when a brutal mobster wants to use her for the men's mistakes, Sage must play to win—even if it means getting dirty...

Please see the next page for a preview of

Playing Dirty

PLAYING DIRTY

PROLOGUE

Parker watched as Ryker's truck rolled to a stop in front of the building. Sage emerged from the entry, scurrying across the sidewalk barefoot before climbing into the passenger seat. The truck pulled away from the curb, lost to sight in moments down the avenue.

He'd heard the door close when she'd gone, leaving him alone in his bed without so much as a word of farewell.

Not that he could blame her.

She'd nearly died tonight. Had been moments away. Viktor hadn't cared if he killed her or not. He'd put a fucking plastic bag over her head and slowly suffocated her.

Parker's hands balled into fists just remembering how she'd looked when he'd pulled her out of that car. Deathly pale, her mouth bleeding from where Viktor had hit her, mascara smeared by the tears soaking her cheeks...

Sage deserved better. Far better. But Parker needed her in his life... in his job. No matter how tempting it was to want to slip into a more personal relationship with her, he knew he couldn't. Relationships never lasted, and just when you thought you'd found the forever kind of love—it would end. And when it was over…she'd be gone. Permanently.

Better to let her go with Ryker, a man who'd wanted a wife and kids—a family—for as long as Parker had known him. Maybe it had been because he'd been raised by a single mom, but Ryker had talked of nothing else but wanting to fall in love and get married. Why he wasn't married already, Parker had no idea.

Maybe he'd marry Sage.

That thought was like a kick in the gut.

Unable to stand the bedroom anymore and unwilling to climb beneath sheets still warm from Sage's body, Parker walked into the living room. A faint glow from a dim light under the kitchen cabinets filtered in through the space, providing enough illumination for him to pour a healthy shot of scotch.

Memories assailed him as he stood in the silent apartment, staring blindly out the window. Memories of Sage and the day they'd first met.

"How many applicants do we have?" he asked the HR rep in charge of helping him find a new secretary.

She set a half-dozen files on his desk. "These were the ones I thought were the most qualified."

He glanced through the stack, flipping one open at random, then frowned. "An art history degree qualifies someone to be a secretary?"

"Executive administrative assistant," she corrected him. "And that's the least qualified candidate, but she had a solid 3.8 GPA and her application was very well done. I thought an interview couldn't hurt.

I can cancel it, if you'd rather. She's scheduled last so—"

"No, it's fine," Parker interrupted, tossing aside the files. "Just send them in when they get here." Surely one of them would work out. And could start immediately. He was drowning under the pile of work and the incessant phone calls.

"Yes, sir." She left the office, but Parker barely noticed, already plowing through his inbox, currently cluttered with over two hundred unread emails.

The first applicant was Joanne, a no-nonsense woman who'd spent the last twenty years as assistant to some Wall Street hedge fund manager. He'd retired and she'd moved to Chicago to be closer to her grandchildren. Parker was bored before she'd even gotten to the name of the third one.

The second applicant chewed gum. In an interview. Nope.

The third wore a blouse two sizes too small and a skirt so short he had to look away when she crossed her legs or it would go all Basic Instinct on him. She had a predatory look in her eye and Parker would swear she eyed his crotch when he stood to shake her hand.

The fourth and fifth were both bland possibilities, neither one standing out as particularly ambitious or enthusiastic. Parker wouldn't want to stereotype—that would be politically incorrect—but if he did, he'd say they both seemed like women biding their time in a temporary job until they married and quit to pop out babies.

By the time the last one—the art history major—was due, Parker had had about enough. This interview shit was putting him even further behind. Accounting had just delivered a stack of billables he was supposed to check, he had a meeting in less than thirty minutes that he hadn't had enough time to prepare for, and he was starving because he'd had to work through lunch. Irritated didn't begin to describe his current mood.

A tentative knock sounded on the glass door and he didn't even glance up as he called out a "Come in." He heard the door open and he shifted a stack of folders. That Carlson file had to be around here somewhere...

"Just have a seat," he said. "I'll be with you in a mo—" Glancing up, his words abruptly cut off.

The woman who'd entered his office was dropdead gorgeous. Not pretty. No, way more than that—curvy and sexy, with legs up to there and thick, chestnut hair down to there. Her body looked like it had been made for sex, lovingly encased in a peach dress that hugged every delicious curve. The neckline was demure, scooped and only hinting at what lay beneath. The hemline teased, hitting right above her knees. The skin of her legs was so perfect, Parker couldn't tell if she was wearing nylons or not. But then he caught sight of her shoes, bronze sandals that wrapped around her ankle on top of a three-inch heel.

And her toes were painted the exact shade of her dress.

"Hi, I'm Sage Reese."

The voice was throaty and smooth like twenty-year-old scotch, and made Parker jerk his gaze up to her face. She was smiling, a warm, open smile that showed *perfect white teeth. Her eyes were the same shade of mahogany as her hair, framed in lush, dark lashes.*

She was holding her hand out expectantly and Parker jumped to his feet, thrusting his hand toward her and knocking over the entire stack of accounting files in the process.

Shit.

"Oh no!" she exclaimed. "That was totally my fault." She dropped down and started picking up the scattered files, treating Parker to first, a view down her cleavage, then of the fabric of her dress stretched tight across her hips and ass as she bobbed up and down.

"Don't worry about it," he said hurriedly. "Just leave it." This time he grabbed her wrist when she placed a file back on his desk. Her bones felt fragile beneath soft skin and he quickly let go. He gestured to one of the two chairs in front of his desk. "Have a seat."

Her smile wasn't quite as wide now, but she sat down. Parker fished through the disaster on his desk looking for her file while the silence grew long and awkward. He felt incompetent and unprepared, her appearance throwing him off, which was ridiculous. It wasn't as though he'd never been with a beautiful woman before.

The phrase "been with" provoked all the wrong kind of images for a work setting and he cleared his throat, banishing those thoughts as he finally laid hands on her file and flipped it open.

"Why don't you tell me a little about yourself, Sage?" he asked, trying to recover what was left of a first impression. She probably thought he was a disorganized, unprofessional klutz.

"*Um, sure. Well, I graduated magna cum laude from the University of Chicago with a degree in art history. I interned at the Art Institute of Chicago—*"

"*And why didn't they hire you?*" he interrupted, glancing up from the pages.

Her cheeks flushed. "*I don't know,*" she said. "*I don't think there was an open position.*"

He'd embarrassed her, and he could have kicked himself for the tactless question. It wasn't like they would've told her a reason for not hiring her even if they'd had a job available.

"*Do you have any experience with investment banking?*" he asked, hurrying to change the subject. Her eyes were focused on him, deep and fathomless, and he had to look away. He flipped through her application and resume, barely seeing the words.

"*Um, no.*"

"*Any experience with the stock market? Hedge funds? Economics? Finance?*" She shook her head after each one, her cheeks growing redder with each word. "*Ever been a secreta—administrative assistant—before?*"

"*No.*" Her voice was quiet and even the small smile she'd had earlier was nowhere in sight now.

Parker felt like a schmuck now, but what the hell was he supposed to do? It was an interview, not a date.

"*Are you from Chicago?*" he asked, wanting to hear something from her other than a no.

"*Lake Forest,*" she replied, naming one of the wealthiest suburbs of Chicago.

"*Sisters? Brothers?*" Boyfriend? Husband? He knew he couldn't ask the last two, but wished he could. He hadn't spied a ring earlier, but nowadays, that didn't necessarily mean anything.

"Only child."

Daddy's little princess. He could see it on her as clearly as if she'd had it bedazzled on the dress she wore. Which begged the question, why was she interviewing for a job like this when surely she could live with her parents until something in her field opened up?

"I know what you're thinking," she said.

He doubted it.

"You're thinking why would I apply for a job I have absolutely no qualifications for," she continued.

Okay, maybe she did know what he was thinking.

Tossing the file onto the desk, Parker sat back in his chair and waited.

"I'm smart," she said. "I'm a hard worker, and a quick learner."

"You have zero business experience at all," Parker said bluntly. "Can you at least type?"

"Yes, I can type," she said, sounding affronted.

"You're an art history major," he said flatly. "It was a valid question."

The corners of her lips lifted slightly in an almost smile. It entranced him. Then he found he was staring at her mouth and jerked his gaze away.

She swallowed, her next words seeming to take an effort to get out. "I need this job. I have bills to pay. Please, Mr. Anderson. Give me a chance. I won't disappoint you."

Considering her background, it was odd that she'd need a job quite that badly. Had her parents fallen on hard times? Maybe they'd disowned her? He felt a pang of sympathy at the thought—uncharacteristic for him—and he frowned, which was the wrong thing to do because her face immediately fell as she misinterpreted his response.

She shot to her feet. "I'm sorry for wasting your time," she blurted. "I'll just go." She looked near tears, which was the proverbial final straw. He mentally cursed his weakness for tears on a pretty girl.

"Wait," he called, halting her on her way out the door. She turned back. "This job won't be easy and you'll probably be working more than forty hours a week," he cautioned, wondering if he was out of his mind. Not only was she inexperienced, but he also didn't know if he could trust himself around her. And he refused to be the cliché boss screwing his secretary.

Administrative assistant.

Fuck.

"I can do that," she said, hope lighting up in her eyes.

"If you don't cut it, then you'll be let go," he warned.

"I understand."

Coming out from behind his desk, Parker approached her, noting the subtle scent of her perfume as he drew closer. Holding out his hand, he said, "When can you start?"

Her smile was blinding as she placed her hand in his, and Parker knew he'd made a huge mistake the minute their skin touched. He'd just consigned himself to God only knew how much torture. If he hadn't hired her, he could've asked her out, taken her to dinner… then to bed. All of which was utterly out of the question now.

"Thank you so much, sir," she enthused. "I won't let you down. I promise."

Parker's expression was grim, he knew, so he mustered a faint smile. "See you tomorrow morning, Sage. Seven-thirty."

She'd nodded, still smiling, then turned and left. Her scent had lingered in the air of his office. He'd scrubbed a hand over his face in frustrated resignation. He'd made his bed. Now he had to lie in it. If he had any luck at all, she'd hate the job and quit.

But she hadn't hated the job. She'd taken to being his assistant like she'd been born to it, their communication clicking immediately into place. Somehow, she'd understood him, the job, and what he needed almost without trying. In a frighteningly short amount of time, she'd become indispensable to him.

And he'd liked her. Besides being so attracted to her it made concentrating difficult sometimes when she was in his office—like when she was crawling around on the floor in her skirt and bare feet, emptying box after box of documents—he enjoyed her personality. Funny, a bit quirky, almost always lighthearted and positive, she was his own personal breath of fresh air in the stale business environment that sometimes felt suffocating.

In the end he was glad he'd hired her, even though it ruled out anything physical between them, because it meant their relationship could continue. Because if he hadn't hired her and had dated her instead, he had no doubt it would have been short-lived. He didn't do relationships. Not even with Sage. *Especially* not with Sage.

Watching her date other men had been hard, and if someone were to ask him if he'd deliberately sabotaged those short-lived relationships, he'd deny it. But deep down, he knew that jealousy had played a factor in how often he called her when he knew she was out with another man. Was it fair to either of them? No. Yet he hadn't been able to stop himself.

And now she'd chosen to go from his bed to Ryker's. Jealousy was too pale of a word to describe how that made him feel, but if the last couple of weeks had shown him anything, it was that he needed to let it go. He'd flat-out turned her down, which had been the hardest thing he'd ever done. To *know*, definitively and not just guessing, that Sage wanted him had been a heady thing. The feel of her in his arms, the press of her lips against his...the sight of her naked in that bathtub, her soap-slickened hands touching her breasts, her stomach—

Parker tossed back the rest of the scotch in one swallow, forcing the images from his mind. He had to stop obsessing, and stop sabotaging her. It wasn't fair to Sage, and it was just his own fucking bad luck that he had to figure this out now, when she was with Ryker, than before when she'd been dating what's-his-name. The guy she'd said had been bad in bed.

His lips twisted at that. She'd been so adorably embarrassed when she'd blurted that out, he'd had a hard time not laughing outright, until he'd realized that she'd only know that because she'd slept with him. Then the green monster had dug into his gut and he'd been viciously glad to have interrupted her date the night before.

But not anymore. Enough. It was done. Parker would exercise self-control and ignore the jealousy, because otherwise he'd never let Sage find someone, and she deserved to be happy.

Even if it was with Ryker.

Fall in Love with Forever Romance

POWER PLAY
by Tiffany Snow

High-powered businessman Parker Andersen wears expensive suits like a second skin and drives a BMW. Detective Dean Ryker's uniform is leather jackets and jeans...and his ride of choice is a Harley. Sage Reese finds herself caught between two men: the one she's always wanted—and the one who makes *her* feel wanted like never before...

RIDE STEADY
by Kristen Ashley

Once upon a time, Carissa Teodoro believed in happy endings. But now she's a struggling single mom and stranded by a flat tire, until a vaguely familiar knight rides to her rescue on a ton of horsepower...Fans of Lori Foster will love the newest novel in Kristen Ashley's *New York Times* bestselling Chaos series!

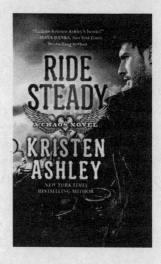

Fall in Love with Forever Romance

SUMMER AT THE SHORE
by V. K. Sykes

Morgan Merrifield sacrificed her teaching career to try to save her family's bed-and-breakfast and care for her younger sister. So she can't let herself get distracted by rugged ex–Special Forces soldier Ryan Butler. But her longtime crush soon flares into real desire—and with one irresistible kiss, she's swept away.

LAST CHANCE HERO
by Hope Ramsay

Sabina knows a lot about playing it safe. But having Ross Gardiner in town brings back the memory of one carefree summer night when she threw caution to the wind—and almost destroyed her family. Now that they are both older and wiser, will the spark still be there, even though they've both been burned?

Fall in Love with Forever Romance

A PROMISE OF FOREVER
by Marilyn Pappano

In the *New York Times* bestselling tradition of Robyn Carr comes the next book in Marilyn Pappano's Tallgrass series. When Sergeant First Class Avi Grant finally returns from Afghanistan, she rushes to comfort the widow of her commanding officer—and ends up in the arms of her handsome son, Ben Noble.